The Importance of Being Emma

Juliet Archer

W F HOWES LTD

This large print edition published in 2012 by
W F Howes Ltd
Unit 4, Rearsby Business Park, Gaddesby Lane,
Rearsby, Leicester LE7 4YH

1 3 5 7 9 10 8 6 4 2

First published in the United Kingdom in 2008
by Choc Lit Limited

A CIP catalogue record for this book is available
from the British Library

ISBN 978 1 40749 635 1

Typeset by Palimpsest Book Production Limited,
Falkirk, Stirlingshire
Printed and bound in Great Britain
by MPG Books Ltd, Bodmin, Cornwall

MIX
Paper from
responsible sources
FSC
www.fsc.org   FSC® C018575

To the heroes in my life,
especially Gordon, Bill, Tim and Mark.

FOREWORD

by Will Darcy

Naturally, nowhere else in England compares to Pemberley. But Ashridge, an estate in Hertfordshire that once belonged to the Duke of Bridgewater, is almost my second home.

Like Pemberley, it has an elegance of architecture and setting that helps me to think and talk more elegantly – or so I tell myself. Very appropriate, since it's a world-renowned business school. And I'll never forget my first visit there some years ago – not so much for the teaching, although the Leadership course I attended was exemplary, but for a conversation about a painting.

You see, I love art – whether expressed through words, music, or brush strokes on canvas. And Ashridge has a little gem by famous eighteenth-century portrait painter Sir Joshua Reynolds, entitled 'A child asleep'. When I first saw it, I had no intention of having any children myself; where in the world was there a woman who would make me want that sort of commitment?

I now realise how much I had to learn.

Back then, however, there was only one child that this painting brought to mind: my sister Georgie. I was in my teens when she was born, and could remember her vividly – so happy and biddable. In that respect, she'd hardly changed . . .

Behind me, a man's voice interrupted my thoughts. 'Good God, that's just like Emma!'

I turned to him, eyebrows raised but my mood mellow. 'Your daughter?'

He shook his head. 'More of a little sister, although not so little now.'

'We must be secretly related then, because this is the spitting image of *my* little sister when she was a baby.'

The man – Mark Knightley, according to his name badge – gave a good-natured laugh. Instinctively, I decided that he could be a good friend – and I always trust my instincts.

'They're adorable at that age, aren't they?' he said.

'Especially when they're asleep,' I added dryly.

He laughed again, then frowned. 'But they're not adorable for long. The last time I called Emma my little sister, she ran away. She isn't actually my sister, I just think of her like that.' I detected a slight flush under his tan, as if something was troubling him. He went on, 'We used to get along brilliantly until – well, I found out recently that she had a teenage crush on me. Very embarrassing.'

'The crush – or finding out about it?'

'Both.' He cleared his throat. 'But she's a sensible

girl, I'm sure we'll soon be back to normal.' A pause. 'Not that I've seen her much since it happened – and, anyway, I'm about to move to India.'

Little did I know that Georgie, fifteen years old at the time, was harbouring a teenage crush of her own – one that would have far-reaching effects. While the little incident between Mark and Emma had caused a rift that he only discovered years later.

This is their story . . .

APÉRITIF

EMMA

'You could take me, Mark.'

'You, Mouse? To a posh ball like that?'

'Yes.' I tucked my hand in his as we crossed Donwell Abbey's vast entrance hall, our footsteps drumming on the ancient stone flags. 'Batty said the other day I looked a lot older than fourteen.'

A basic requirement, of course, for the girl lucky enough to partner Mark Knightley: twenty-five, tall, dark and handsome, and known among my older sister's crowd as the Sex God.

He laughed. 'Mary Bates says whatever she thinks you want to hear. Don't be in a hurry to grow up, it's not that great.'

And he gently disengaged his hand to open the oak front door. Outside, soft summer rain stained the garden paths and muffled the sounds of men and machinery from nearby fields.

'But you'll take me?' I went on. 'I'll get my braces removed, or maybe I'll just smile enigmatically all evening, and I've seen the perfect dress in Kingston.'

1

He frowned and looked me straight in the eye. 'I can't, it would be like taking my little sister.'

I stared up at him. 'But I'm not your sister.'

'You are, in a way. Your sister's married to my brother.'

'That's not the same thing at all.'

'I still think of you as my little sister.'

My eyes filled with tears. I turned away so that he couldn't see, but it was too late. When he pulled me round to face him, I fixed my gaze on the floor.

'Mouse?' He paused, then I heard his sharp intake of breath. 'Oh God . . . You can't possibly . . . You haven't got a crush on me, have you?'

I said nothing, but my cheeks burned.

'Shit! You have.'

I pushed past him and ran through the rain, towards the bridle path and home. His voice trailed after me, encumbered by a rare note of entreaty.

'Mouse . . . Emma . . . Wait! Come back.'

But I didn't. Not until a week or so later, when it was all over – both the ball, which he apparently enjoyed in the company of a giggly blonde, and the crush. No crush could survive such a rejection. The bluntness of a big brother, dismissively served. With a double helping of disbelief.

In any case, it was only a short-lived, typically teenage crush. My deeper, longer-lasting passion was for someone else. A man just as handsome, clever and rich as Mark Knightley but far more elusive.

A true romantic hero, surrounded by almost myth-like mystery and spin.

Flynn Churchill.

Just his name set my pulses racing. Whenever I heard it, my heart fluttered in some sort of Pavlovian response. Whenever I said it aloud, in the privacy of my room, I punctuated it with a yearning sigh.

You see, although people talked about it each year as something inevitable, like Christmas, Flynn had never set foot in his father's home town of Highbury. But nobody minded. His progress was still followed with unfailing enthusiasm, his arrival was always contemplated with breathless anticipation.

And from the age of ten I knew that I, Emma Woodhouse, was destined to become Mrs Emma Churchill. It was meant to be. Our lives were inextricably linked.

I never discussed these thoughts with anyone, of course. Especially Mark Knightley. He'd just laugh at me.

I could wait.

Some day my prince would come.

CHAPTER 1

GENTLEMAN'S RELISH

EMMA

Good, the boardroom was deserted. When I was a child, it filled me with awe; dark panelling, solid mahogany furniture, large leather-bound minute books and forbidding photographs of former Highbury Foods Board members, their names usually ending in Woodhouse. Now, although there were no obvious signs of change, it all looked the worse for wear; the photographs faded, the furniture scuffed.

I closed the door and selected a seat at the long table with care. I'd have more privacy here than in my own office, but I still wanted advance warning of anyone approaching.

I flicked through the magazine I'd brought with me and found what I was looking for on page thirty:

Change is in the air at Highbury Foods, one of the nation's most traditional small companies, in the glamorous form of new

4

Marketing Director Emma Woodhouse. But has this enthusiastic novice bitten off more than she can chew?

Emma has everything going for her. She's stunning, highly intelligent and wealthy beyond the wildest dreams of mere mortals, thanks to some shrewd property investment by her great-grandfather. She has one of the most sought-after addresses in England: Highbury. Not the old Arsenal football ground, but a picturesque and prestigious village in Surrey, where her family is well known for its charitable giving, courtesy of the Woodhouse Benevolent Trust. And, for someone whose life reeks of privilege and plenty, Emma seems refreshingly grateful for her good fortune.

Now, at only twenty-three, she has decided that the family business is in need of her talents. Her father Henry has run Highbury Foods along very conservative lines for two decades, following faithfully in the footsteps of previous generations. In fact, the company has had the same game plan for the last 52 years: supplying a range of non-perishable delicacies to upmarket homes and hotels via mail order. It has yet to discover the advantages of selling over the Internet and, until now, did not even see the need for a Marketing Director.

5

But Emma wants to drag the company into the 21st century and has set herself only twelve months to achieve this.

We say it's mission impossible. Even with an MBA from Stanford, USA. But Ms Woodhouse says, 'Watch this space.'

I threw the magazine down. They'd got it completely wrong; it was Harvard, not Stanford. Hadn't that cretin of a journalist listened – or had he been too busy ogling my legs? He'd certainly chosen a photo that showed not much else; the angle suggested I'd ordered the photograper to grovel at my feet.

If I had, I couldn't remember it.

I didn't read on. It was the usual witless blurb they published in those glossy magazines that came with a couple of forests' worth of Sunday papers. I should have guessed as much from the saucy headline, 'Gentleman's Relish', a reference to the highly seasoned anchovy paste that was one of our most established and successful products.

But this was my first press interview and I'd hoped for something better. I hadn't even expected to see it in print until next weekend, so I was taken aback when Batty, our Company Secretary, handed it to me this morning with a squeal of excitement. Knowing her, she'd already have shown it to the other directors, just when I wanted to make a good impression. This fatuous nonsense portrayed me as having all the subtlety of an Exocet missile.

The September sun warmed my back. I turned my head and gazed at its low rays slanting in through the long dusty windows. I could see the factory, a jumble of squat brick buildings, and, in the distance, the tall copper beech hedge that hid my home from view. Mark Knightley had once observed that it was actually the other way round; the hedge was designed to hide the grim reality of work from the pampered occupants of Hartfield Hall.

Meaning me.

He was wrong, of course. I'd been fascinated by Highbury Foods for as long as I could remember. I came here during school holidays, University vacations, even occasional weekends when only the maintenance team was in. I studied production methods, analysed sales trends and talked to employees – about themselves, as well as their jobs. Our company culture was like that; relationships mattered more than results. And it worked. We turned a nice profit most years while still employing people who were long past their sell-by date, like Batty . . .

Lost in thought, I wasn't aware of footsteps outside in the corridor until it was almost too late. The door creaked open and I heard a familiar twittering sound. Talk of the devil: Batty, in full flow. I dived for cover under the table.

'This is where the Board will be meeting, dear

– no, don't go in now, I'll show you after we've had a cuppa. That's your main job this morning, to take the minutes at the . . . I'll be sitting beside you, in case you need any help. Henry – that's the Managing Director – speaks awfully quietly at times, such a martyr to his chest. You'll be PA to him and his daughter – lovely family, so caring. And I should know, I started work here under Henry's father more years ago than I like to . . . I must say, dear, that was a glowing reference from your last temping job at Abbey Mill Haulage, Robert Martin couldn't praise you highly enough and he's never one to . . . This way to my office, dear, then I'll tell you all about . . .' At last, Batty and her unfortunate victim moved out of earshot, leaving the door ajar.

With a sigh of relief, I crawled from my hiding place and brushed myself down. I was in no hurry to see Batty again and have her fawning about the magazine article. She might surprise me, of course, and ask exactly how I proposed to drag Highbury Foods into this century; but somehow I doubted it.

Modernising the company was a challenge I'd prepared for over the past five years. I'd focused on the academic side, starting with a BSc at the London School of Economics and following it immediately with my MBA. Wherever possible, I'd made Highbury Foods the subject of my essays and assignments, usually scoring top marks for perception and ingenuity.

Now that I had a formal position with the power – and the budget – to make a difference, I could put my plans into action. And I would start at today's Board meeting . . .

Once again a noise interrupted my thoughts. This time it was the buzz of a wasp, high up on the window, sluggishly searching for a way out. I frowned. If Dad saw it, he would postpone the meeting. Convinced he was allergic to any sort of sting or bite, he kept an EpiPen on him at all times although, to my knowledge, he never used it.

I placed a chair next to the window, rolled up the magazine – it might do nothing for my CV, but it made a great wasp zapper – kicked off my Dior shoes and used the chair to climb onto the sill. My stockinged feet slithered on the wood and I had to grip the sash with my free hand to steady myself.

Eyeball to eyeball with the wasp, I drew back my other arm, took aim and –

'Mouse! What on earth are you up to?'

Only one person called me Mouse.

The magazine fell to the floor. For a moment there was silence, except for the wasp buzzing nonchalantly, unaware it had escaped certain death.

I took a deep breath and turned round, forcing a smile. 'Mark. Great to see you after all these years.'

Strange being at Highbury Foods. Strange being back in England, full stop. If only temporarily, to take over the reins of Donwell Organics while Father indulged my stepmother in another of her whims, this time a specially extended round-the-world cruise. Several months of binge eating and drinking, constantly in each other's company; no doubt to be followed by an equally long period at a health farm and/or psychiatric unit, to repair the damage.

I could understand Father wanting to leave Donwell in a safe pair of hands; what I couldn't understand was why the hands had to be mine or my younger brother John's. But Father refused point-blank to consider an external interim appointment. And John, who was also our Finance Director, opted out before I could. So I had to come over from India, where I'd spent the last eight years setting up and running our regional operation in Mumbai.

To add to the culture shock, I'd taken on some of Father's other duties. Occasional speaker at local Chamber of Commerce events; chief judge at the Autumn Flower and Produce Show, a perilous responsibility which I hastily delegated to John; chairman of the Woodhouse Benevolent Trust; and, last but by no means least, non-executive director at Highbury Foods, only two miles down the road from Donwell but light years away in terms of how it was run.

That's how I came to be invited to their Board meeting, a commitment I could have done without on this particular morning. I'd landed at Gatwick barely four hours earlier, after a delayed flight, and I needed to put in a few phone calls to India before business there closed for the day.

On my way to Henry's office, I noticed that the boardroom door was open. I glanced in, assuming it was his PA, Kate Taylor, doing what she liked to call her 'last-minute' preparation – a full hour before the start of the meeting. Then I remembered. Kate Taylor was no more; as of two days ago, she was Mrs Kate Weston. And, although she was coming back to live in the village after her honeymoon, I'd heard she had no intention of returning to Highbury Foods.

My eyes widened as I took in the view from the doorway. Long legs silhouetted against the window, lines and curves in perfect proportion. Short beige skirt stretched taut across more curves – nicely rounded, a pert promise of pleasure. Matching jacket with side vents, no doubt designed to draw the male eye to the symmetry below.

Then, as the vision brandished a rolled-up magazine, I saw her face in profile. It couldn't be, surely . . .

It was.

'Mouse! What on earth are you up to?'

She jumped, dropped the magazine and, after a pause, turned round.

'Mark. Great to see you after all these years.'

There was a distinct lack of enthusiasm in her voice. I put down my briefcase and held out my arms.

'I think I deserve a warmer welcome than that.'

She hesitated, then climbed carefully down from the sill and slipped into four-inch heels; this meant that, when I gave her the usual bear hug, there was less of a height difference than I remembered. I rested my cheek against her dark brown hair and smiled to myself. Underneath all that gloss, I knew she'd still be the same maddening little Mouse.

But she'd certainly overdone the gloss. I leaned back slightly and inspected her face. The hazel eyes flashed and the full red lips tightened, as if she could read my mind.

Undeterred, I gave it to her straight. 'Too much make-up, you don't need any at all. Most women would die for your skin, and that stuff round your eyes makes you look like a panda.'

The panda glared at me. 'Bloody cheek. How would you feel if I criticised your appearance?'

'Go ahead. You can hardly accuse me of wearing too much make-up.'

'While you've been away I've grown up, believe it or not.'

'Apparently. Although it didn't look like it when you were dancing about on the window sill. Put me out of my misery, Mouse, what were you doing?'

She moved abruptly away. 'There was a wasp. And I'd prefer it if you didn't call me Mouse.'

'You're right, it's not appropriate here. Whenever I'm at Highbury Foods, I'll forget I know anyone called Mouse.'

Her voice was edgy. 'I'd prefer you to stop calling me that, period.'

This was something of a turnaround, since I'd called her Mouse for at least fifteen years. It started when she accidentally introduced herself to someone as Emma Woodmouse. I teased her about it, called her Mouse for short and it stuck. Back then it suited her perfectly: such a small, scrawny thing, with big bright eyes. But now . . .

Maybe she'd outgrown it. She certainly didn't look like a mouse any longer; and she'd never behaved much like one.

I grinned. 'OK, Emma. Where's the wasp?'

'Up there, on the middle window. I need to get rid of it before Dad comes.'

'Naturally.'

Henry Woodhouse was the biggest hypochondriac I'd ever known. He was so obsessed with his 'fragile' state of health that he'd become a walking medical dictionary. He was so risk-averse that he was practically a recluse, hardly venturing beyond his home and his company, just a mile apart. Whenever I visited Hartfield, I half expected to be given a clean suit and mask or, at the very least, an antiseptic foot bath and hand wash. Accordingly, he prized the use of conventional pesticides, fertilisers and irradiation to safeguard his company's products from contamination, almost as much as I valued organic methods to produce mine. In spite of such precautions, he never ate anything labelled 'Highbury Foods'; he said his digestion was far too delicate.

Nevertheless, he was a long-standing friend of my family and, well, I respected his views and liked him enormously.

'I'll sort it,' I went on. 'India's given me plenty of practice in dealing with insects, the humane way of course.' Crossing to the window, I picked up the magazine, stood on the chair, pulled down the sash and gently manoeuvred the wasp outside, before securing the catch.

As I stepped down from the chair, I unrolled the magazine. What an intriguing headline. And that photo – legs a mile long, inviting smile, eyes looking deep into mine as if we were . . .

I gave a disparaging laugh. 'So fame hasn't gone to your head – yet. You obviously weren't planning to keep this for your scrapbook.'

She folded her arms. 'No, I wasn't, it's a pack of lies. I thought they'd at least get their facts right.'

'You've got a lot to learn. Give the press an inch and they'll take a mile.' I looked again at the legs in the photo. 'Shall I dispose of this for you?'

'Give it back to Batty, she brought it in for me. So helpful, as always.'

'Still going strong, is she?' I said, slipping the

magazine into my briefcase. 'Poor Henry, he's only got you and her to cosset him now that Kate's gone.'

This was evidently more comfortable ground; she unfolded her arms and managed a pale imitation of the smile in the photo.

'That's a sore point. Dad thinks Kate'll come back, he says she doesn't really want to set up an antique wine business with her new husband. That's why he refused to find a permanent replacement, but fortunately Batty's got a temp in. I'm hoping he'll soon forget all about Kate and then we can advertise her job.'

'From what I remember, she'll be a hard act to follow.'

'Definitely, she kept this place running like clockwork. And she's been such a good friend. If she hadn't been willing to move into Hartfield to keep an eye on Dad, I'd never have gone to Harvard.'

'Ah yes, you went there straight after University.' I paused. 'You know, there's a lot more value in an MBA if you've worked for a few years first.'

Her eyes narrowed. 'You're entitled to your opinion, I suppose.' Then she sighed. 'Anyway, there's Kate married at last – and it's all down to me.'

'What do you mean?' I said.

'I've discovered I'm an expert at matchmaking. When Tom Weston came back here four years ago, I knew he'd be perfect for Kate. And it didn't take

15

much to arrange, even though people said he'd never settle down at his age.'

'So you controlled their every move?'

She nodded, oblivious to my sarcasm. 'Mind you, there were one or two hiccups. For one thing, I would have preferred it if they'd lived together before they got married. Then Tom could have moved into Hartfield with Kate while I was away, which means Dad would have got used to a man about the house.'

'Oh? Why would he want to do that?'

She gave an impish grin. 'In case I meet the man of my dreams. I couldn't possibly leave Dad on his own, so he – whoever *he* is – would have to live at Hartfield.'

'Lucky man,' I said drily. 'And why didn't Tom move in with Kate as ordered – sorry, suggested?'

'Because he'd set his mind on them living together at Randalls and nowhere else. At the time, Randalls wasn't even on the market and, when he did manage to buy the place, it needed a lot of work. Remember, Mrs Sanderson lived there for centuries and never spent anything on it.'

'How annoying for you, to be outmanoeuvred so easily.' I raised one eyebrow. 'Presumably their wedding turned out as you planned?'

'Oh, it was lovely. I know it's a cliché, but Kate looked radiant. And I thought Tom might look old enough to be her father, but he didn't.'

I frowned. 'Don't be ridiculous. He's only fifty or so and Kate must be at least thirty-five.'

'She's thirty-eight, he's forty-nine. Quite an age difference.'

I thought of my girlfriend back in India – she was twenty-six, I was going to be thirty-five in a few weeks – and decided to change the subject.

'Did Flynn Churchill make it to the wedding?' I was referring to Tom's son, who'd achieved cult status in Highbury over the years. All the more incomprehensible since nobody had ever met him, except his doting father.

Emma's face clouded. 'No, he didn't. Kate and Tom were very upset.'

'I'm not surprised.'

'He *was* coming, right up to the last minute, then something cropped up.'

'That man wouldn't turn up to his own funeral if he had the choice.' I added, casually, 'What about me, was I missed?'

'Probably, since you're still meant to be one of the most eligible bachelors in Surrey. And you know what they say, even these days – one wedding leads to another. I'm sure some of the women only accepted the invitation in the hope of seeing you reduced to a romance-sodden wreck at the sight of confetti.'

'Thank God I couldn't get home until today, then.'

She gave me a sidelong glance. 'Still seeing Tamara what's-her-name?'

'Yes.'

'Isn't it about time you got married?'

'Why?'

'Because you've been together for five years.' Her lips tightened. 'What's the point if it's not leading anywhere?'

'We each have certain needs and our arrangement suits us both very well.'

'So it's just for sex?' she said, rather bluntly I thought.

'No, it's not. We help each other out when we need a partner, either for a particular function or simply to scare other people off.' I grimaced. 'If I'd been coming to Kate and Tom's wedding, I'd definitely have brought Tamara.'

She moved towards the door. 'Sounds positively dreary and, you're right, not a good basis for marriage. Anyway, thanks for getting rid of the wasp. Were you on your way to see Dad?'

I didn't answer immediately. She was wrong, what Tamara and I had was anything but dreary. Predictable, yes; and convenient. But that was its appeal; although I had to agree, it was hardly the basis for marriage. Actually, it was better, I had all the advantages of marriage with none of its emotional warfare or financial complications.

'I'm meeting him at nine thirty,' I said curtly.

'I'll come with you. He asked me along for nine thirty as well.'

'How is he, by the way?'

'Same as always. Whatever he may say, he's got no major health problems. But he's sixty-one and sometimes I wonder how much longer he should go on working. I don't mean he's incapable, more that he can't seem to move with the times. Business is done so differently these days.'

I waited until we were walking along the corridor to Henry's office, then said, 'In some ways. But the essentials don't change, you still need things like integrity, and ethical principles, and sound common sense.'

I winced as she burst out laughing.

'Mark Knightley, they should stuff you and put you in a museum!'

EMMA

Dad sipped his fennel tea and eyed us over the rim of his cup. 'My stomach's terrible, I'm sure it's because Kate's not here. And, do you know, I had to boil the kettle myself? The new PA's nowhere to be found.'

I gave him a reassuring smile. 'She's in with Mary, and I told you not to have that second helping of porridge this morning.'

'You look remarkably well, Henry,' Mark said.

Dad shook his head as he placed the cup down on its saucer. 'Ah, Mark, sometimes I just have to battle on regardless. And this is one of those times. Emma's first day as Marketing Director, the first Board meeting for both of you, my first Monday without Kate . . .' His voice trailed off and I guessed there were too many firsts around for comfort.

'We'll manage,' I said, reaching across the desk and patting his arm.

'I'll never be able to get used to – whatever her name is.'

'Now, Dad, come along, Kate's been on leave in the past and you've coped wonderfully. Just imagine she's on an extended holiday.'

'So wise for her age, isn't she, Mark?' He gave Mark no chance to agree or, more likely, disagree but continued, 'I'm worried about you, darling, you're taking on a lot of responsibility. Kate's not here to help, and Mary's not the woman she was . . . . Neither am I, for that matter . . . the *man* I was, I should say.' He took refuge in another sip of tea.

'Meaning?' I prompted, as a nasty, Knightley-shaped suspicion formed in my mind.

Dad turned to Mark. 'Meaning that, if it's not too much to ask, I'd like to hire you as a sort of mentor to Emma for the next six months.'

Mark Knightley as my mentor? Bloody hell, more like my tormentor.

'I don't need—' I began, just as Mark said, 'I'd be delighted.'

Dad looked at him approvingly. 'You know the food industry inside out and you've got such a successful track record, especially on the marketing side.'

I tried again. 'But we need to be forward-thinking and innovative—'

Mark cut in. 'Are you suggesting I'm neither?'

I forced a smile. 'I know you're very know-ledgeable and experienced in the more traditional markets, but that's not what Highbury Foods needs right now. And, who knows, I might be looking to compete with Donwell Organics in some way. You couldn't possibly mentor me in those circumstances.'

He laughed. 'From my outdated knowledge and experience, I'd say any sort of attempt to enter the organic food market at the moment would be commercial suicide.' Then he was serious again. 'But I take your point. You'll simply have to trust me to tell you if I ever feel there's a conflict of interest.'

I didn't retaliate, even though I wanted to. Let him win the first battle; his complacency might cost him the war.

'So I'll leave it to you two to decide how best to arrange the mentoring,' Dad said. 'Now let's just go over the agenda for the Board meeting—'

There was a knock at the door and Batty peered in.

'Henry, I thought you'd like to meet your new PA, she's from Temp Tation, Pam Goddard's agency, you know. Although poor Pam's talking of changing the name, she gets the most peculiar calls sometimes, very distressing. There was one young man who—' She broke off just as her conversation threatened to get interesting. 'Oh Mark, how lovely to have you back in Highbury! I won't interrupt you, we can do this later.'

Dad sighed. 'It's all right, bring her in, you can introduce her to Emma and Mark at the same time.'

As Batty pushed the door open and stood aside, I remembered the fragment of conversation I'd overheard earlier. All I knew about this person was that she'd temped at Abbey Mill Haulage; but it was quite possible I'd met her before. Highbury was such a small place, with people rarely moving away, and we often asked our existing employees to recommend friends or relatives for jobs. So I looked carefully at the young girl who tottered into the room on impossibly high heels, wondering if I'd recognise her.

I didn't – and, in an odd way, I did. On the one hand, she was a complete stranger; on the other, I felt I'd known her for years. With her long wavy blonde hair, spiky black eyelashes and rosebud mouth, she was the spitting image of Lisa, my adorable Annette Himstedt doll that I'd had since I was nine.

Except I'd never have dressed Lisa in such a loud check suit.

'Hiya, I'm Harriet Smith,' the girl squeaked.

And I'd have to do something about that accent, Pseudo Posh meets Estuary English.

Dad got slowly to his feet. 'Good morning, Harriet, I'm Henry Woodhouse. No doubt Mary's been telling you what an old ogre I am.'

Harriet stared at him, obviously unsure how to

respond, while Batty tittered, 'Oh Henry, you and your little jokes.'

Dad went on, 'This is my daughter, Emma Woodhouse.'

Harriet took my outstretched hand and managed a shy smile. 'Hiya, Miss Henhouse. Shit – I mean, sorry . . .'

I laughed and tried to put her at ease. 'Just call me Emma, Harriet.'

'Hiya, Emma-Harriet.'

My eyes widened. To my right, Mark seemed to be having a coughing fit.

Dad looked at him anxiously. 'And this is Mark Knightley, our friend and non-executive director. Mark, that's a nasty-sounding cough, would you like to chew on a garlic clove? I always keep some handy, with my troublesome throat.'

'Thank you, Henry, but I seem to have recovered. Delighted to meet you, please call me Mark, Harriet.' Mark shook her hand and gave her one of his most dazzling smiles.

The poor girl went crimson. As she opened her mouth to speak, I intervened before she came out with 'Hiya, Mark-Harriet'.

'It must be confusing being bombarded with so many new names. I'm sure Mary will make you a seating plan for the Board meeting, then you'll know who's saying what.'

Batty's face lit up. 'Such a good idea, Emma, as always, I don't know how you . . . Harriet dear, come with me and we'll get started.'

They went out and I smiled to myself. More through luck than skill, Batty had found me the perfect PA. First, Harriet's nervousness wasn't a problem. It was even understandable, since Highbury Foods was a big step up from a half-baked outfit like Abbey Mill Haulage; and I much preferred nervousness to brash self-confidence. Second, she was crying out for my help. A complete makeover was needed and I had plenty of spare time now that my academic studies were at an end. Finally, she had neither the intellect nor the experience to challenge my ideas – or so it seemed. I made a mental note to reserve judgement; anyone would act like a halfwit after a long dose of Batty.

As if he could read my mind, Mark said, 'Let's hope Harriet's up to the job.'

'Poor Kate, why did she get married?' Dad spread out his hands in despair.

Mark was incredulous. 'Poor Kate? More like clever Kate. She's just halved her workload – only Tom to run round after, instead of you two.'

I noticed a teasing glint in his eye and decided to rise to the bait. 'Especially when one of us is such a pain.'

'You took the words right out of my mouth,' he said, with a grin.

Dad gave a wan smile. 'I know I can be a bit of a nuisance at times—'

'Oh Dad, we didn't mean you!' I darted behind the desk to give him a swift kiss on the cheek.

'Mark thinks I'm the pain, not you. But it doesn't bother me, we always say whatever we like to each other, then forget all about it.'

Dad shook his head in bewilderment.

'If that was true, I'd be wasting my time – and Henry's money – mentoring you for the next six months,' Mark said, a note of irritation in his voice. 'Anyway, I'm probably underestimating Kate, I expect she's already got Tom running round after *her*. And I bet she's enjoying every single minute.'

Then it hit me. Kate's life had taken a new direction and she was no longer at my beck and call. I made a big show of arranging the pens on Dad's desk.

Mark broke the silence. 'Now, Henry, where's that agenda you mentioned?'

MARK

With the mentoring in mind, Henry had suggested I share Emma's office whenever I was at Highbury Foods. I sat there now, pretending to re-read the Board papers but secretly watching her as she scowled at her PC.

I still couldn't get over how much she'd changed physically. The only photos I'd seen of her were the slapdash efforts of my sister-in-law Izzy, whose camera lens was always focused on her kids. More often than not Emma was just a blurred face, or hardly visible under a pile of chubby little arms and legs.

So, no more Mouse. It was the end of an era.

But the dawn of a new one, neatly summed up by that headline, 'Gentleman's Relish'. Ironic, of course; when I'd first caught sight of her earlier today, my thoughts had been anything but gentlemanly . . .

I closed my file with a snap. Time for the Board meeting.

EMMA

I couldn't resist checking Batty's seating plan from across the boardroom table. At one end of a long rectangle she had 'HLW – Henry Woodhouse, Managing Director'; at the other, 'MGK – Mark Knightley, Non-Executive Director'. I knew what the G stood for, of course. The Knightleys believed in recycling the same solid old-fashioned names, as if promoting themselves as fine specimens of English manhood; the father was George James and the two sons were Mark George and John James.

My parents had been more imaginative; my sister and I were named Isabella Maria, Izzy for short, and Emma Carlotta. That was all down to Sophia, our Italian mother, who died in a car crash when I was three and Izzy was twelve. She'd apparently been a breath of fresh air in Highbury – outspoken and headstrong, but charming with it. It made me wonder how she'd coped with Dad, although Mark once told me that he used to be full of energy.

On Batty's plan, I was at right angles to Mark: 'ECW – Emma Woodhouse, Marketing Director'. Next to me was 'PTW – Penny Worthington, HR Director', then 'JM – Jon Marshall, Operations Director' and 'TSW – Terry White, Sales Director'. Opposite was Batty herself, 'MEB – Mary Bates, Company Secretary', then Harriet and finally 'PE – Philip Elton, Finance Director'.

Finance, yawn, was my least favourite MBA subject and Philip himself was new to the company. I'd only met him once before, briefly, whereas I'd known the others for years. One of my priorities was to make them forget I was Henry's little girl and accept me as an equal.

Fortified by a cup of nettle leaf tea, Dad opened the meeting and welcomed the new faces. We went through apologies (none), minutes of the last meeting (approved) and then to the substance of the meeting, the directors' reports.

Everything was fine until my turn came. I'd persuaded Dad to give me a slot on the agenda, as I wanted to share my marketing plans with the Board and get some early buy-in. I'd prepared a presentation on my PC, then found there was no projector, so everyone had a paper copy of my slides instead.

I started with a brief review of our markets and competitive position. I listed the emerging trends in consumer demographics and buying behaviours and other factors, such as some pending EU food legislation which would adversely affect one of our longest-running lines.

'Any questions at this stage?' I asked.

Everyone was silent. Dad had his head in his hands, as if the picture I'd painted was all too much for him. Then Mark, who'd been scribbling notes throughout my presentation, leaned forward. I tensed; somehow I knew a lecture was on its way.

'Your analysis is too limited,' he said. 'You need to look at competition in a broader sense. For example, what are the trends in eating out as opposed to staying in and cooking with Highbury Foods products? And your focus is all UK, you should be selling world-wide. Expat communities would be an ideal target market for your traditional English product lines.'

'Such as Gentleman's Relish,' Terry said, with a wicked grin. 'Now where did I see that mentioned in the press recently?'

I closed my eyes for a moment and debated which of the two to castrate first, metaphorically speaking. I decided to ignore Terry and deal with Mark.

'I assumed the trends in eating out would reflect disposable income and therefore be linked to inflation and the other general economic outlook forecasts.' I selected a page and held it up. 'Those figures were on slide five, as you can see.'

Mark frowned. 'That's OK at this level. But

when you get down to the detailed planning, you need to look at something like the Mintel reports. Remember when I did my MBA at Ashridge? As an Alumni member, I can access all sorts of business information at no cost. Just let me know when you're ready and I'll take you there for the day.'

'How kind,' I said, feeling about ten years old. 'Shall we move on?'

I squared my shoulders and prepared for battle. I was about to step on people's toes big time, including Dad's. 'Corporate image. What's our strapline?'

'Purveyor of traditional foods for the discerning palate,' came the chorus from everyone except Mark and Harriet.

'Rather a mouthful, isn't it? And can anyone under sixty relate to it?'

Dad blanched. 'You're not going to change it, are you?'

'Not yet. But I would like to commission some research into corporate image, among other things, for our main product range.' I paused. 'Betty's Best.'

There was a sharp intake of breath around the table.

'Betty's Best?' Batty whispered, as though uttering something sacred.

'Named after my grandmother,' Dad said to Harriet, who was looking baffled. 'Our very first product, fifty-two years ago, was Betty's Best

Seville Marmalade. Since then, the range has expanded to almost sixty products and is still going strong.'

I lifted my chin. 'But, as we heard earlier, not as strong as it should be. Philip, remind us of the sales and profit figures for Betty's Best division.'

'Certainly, Emma.' Philip gave me a knowing look and shuffled his papers. 'Sales two percent down in the last quarter, mainly in the South-East, and operating profit down five percent, due to some aggressive discounting by key distributors.'

Dad sighed. 'Yes, Mark picked up on that and Terry agreed to negotiate more favourable terms.'

'But it's getting more and more difficult to hold the price, Henry,' Terry said in a whingeing tone. 'Betty's Best seems to have lost some of its appeal, or maybe its loyal customers are dying off.'

I couldn't help a little smile of triumph. 'Exactly. Now I'm not saying we get rid of this range, far from it. It's still our main cash cow, in spite of the heavy discounting. What I want is a new range brought in to appeal to a customer segment that we're currently neglecting. If you turn to page twelve in the presentation . . .'

I'd mocked up a picture showing a very attractive, smartly dressed, young-to-middle-aged blonde at a well-equipped kitchen table, a far cry from homely old Betty and her rolling pin. And underneath I'd used Word Art for the name of the new product range. Except – oh, shit.

Philip's face lit up. 'Victoria's Secret? Isn't that—'

I felt myself go red. 'A US lingerie company? Yes. This is meant to say Victoria's Secret Recipes, but the last word has gone missing somehow.'

To my left, Mark said quietly, 'It's a basic – read through your material before you present it.'

I took a deep breath. Keep calm, retain presence. 'The name's not important, it was just to convey the sort of positioning I'm after. The smart woman of today, single or married, it doesn't matter, juggling a job and/or family with frequent entertaining. She needs a helping hand in the kitchen but wants to give the impression she's made everything herself. I want to re-market Betty's Best to give her products that need the minimum of preparation, with recipes for sophisticated ways of using them. Her guests will think she's done it all herself. That's Victoria's Secret. Or something,' I added, making a mental note to find an alternative to Victoria as soon as possible.

Philip beamed at me. 'Marvellous, Emma.'

'I can certainly identify with Victoria's situation,' Penny said. 'I think it's a great idea.'

Terry chuckled. 'Maybe that US company would be interested in a joint marketing campaign. Victoria, in her kitchen, with our products and dressed in their lingerie. Could appeal to another untapped market, men aged anywhere between twenty and seventy.'

31

Dad looked horrified. 'Men buying our products, whatever next?'

I glared at Terry. 'Actually, the Victoria I have in mind is above cheap gimmicks. She's cool and efficient and the envy of her friends in everything she does.' I looked around the table. 'I'm sure you can all think of a real-life Victoria.'

There was silence.

Then Harriet spoke for the first time. 'Victoria Beckham?'

Jon burst out laughing. 'No way. Does she even know she's got a kitchen?'

I ignored him and smiled at Harriet, who was pink with embarrassment. 'You've got the right idea, but I'd prefer someone who's not a celebrity. Someone with beauty, class and brains that women in the real world can aspire to be.'

Philip said, 'Well, gentlemen, I'm sure we need look no further than this room—'

Mark interrupted him impatiently. 'Basically, you're looking to revamp Betty's Best products for a younger customer segment?'

'Correct,' I said. I couldn't fault his concise summary.

'Have you done any research to justify this?'

'Of course. Only desk research so far, but I'd like to do some primary research with focus groups. That'll mean spending some money, concept boards with photos and so on. If the Board approves, I'll put together a proposal and some costings for our next meeting.'

'Seems a sensible approach,' Dad said. 'Who's in favour?'

Philip and Penny raised their hands instantly, followed by Batty and Terry. Jon hesitated, then nodded.

Dad looked down the table. 'What about you, Mark?'

'I have some reservations, Henry, but nothing major. And I'm sure that, between us, you and I can keep Emma on the right track.'

I stared at the papers in front of me. He made me sound like a wayward teenager.

'That's settled, then.' Dad sounded relieved. 'Harriet, add Emma's proposal to the agenda for our next meeting. We've got no other business to discuss, so let's finish there. Jon, I'd like a word with you before you disappear off to the factory. And would anyone like to try some nettle leaf tea? It's highly recommended for eliminating waste.'

Pity it couldn't eliminate Mark Knightley. From this boardroom or, better still, from my life. How could Dad ask him to mentor me? It would be like turning the clock back to Mouse. He'd always been one for criticising me and bossing me around; I'd accepted it then, even looked up to him. And there'd always been Kate to restore the balance; in her eyes, I could do no wrong.

But now the last thing I needed was The Tormentor telling me how to do my job. I'd have to make my plans without consulting him, and take action before he noticed.

As I moved towards the door, Philip rushed to open it. I gave him a warm smile, remembering his encouragement and support during the meeting, unlike some I could mention.

He leaned forward and murmured, 'I was really impressed by the way you defended Harriet against that idiot Marshall. Of course, I was about to say something myself, but you beat me to it. I suppose you can guess who my real-life inspiration is for your divine Victoria?'

Just then, I heard a shriek. It was Harriet, knocking over the milk jug as she reached for the last biscuit. Batty dashed out of the room to fetch a cloth, while Harriet blushed and giggled. She looked the opposite of cool efficiency, yet there was something about her . . .

'There she is,' I said softly. 'My divine Victoria, as you call her. Just give her some decent clothes and there's my mock-up brought to life.'

Behind me, Philip let out a long sigh. 'Beauty, class *and* brains.'

So that was it, he'd fallen for Harriet! Beauty she certainly had. Class I could give her. Brains? He was taking a flyer there, but I put it down to the delusions of a man already in love.

I turned to him with a mischievous grin. 'You were going to tell me about your real-life Victoria.'

He went bright red. 'I'm sure you can guess who

she is, it must be obvious to someone as intelligent as you.'

'I have a pretty good idea,' I said with a laugh. 'Anyway, I'd better go and start my research proposal. It's good to know you're onside, I may need some help with the costings.'

His eyes gleamed. 'I've got a standard cost-benefit analysis spreadsheet we could use, quite complicated, but I'm more than happy to go through it with you. How about this afternoon?'

I knew he just wanted an excuse to come and see Harriet. 'OK, we can at least have an initial chat so that I know what sort of detail you'll need. Ask Harriet to check my diary.'

I smiled as I left them together in the boardroom; it looked as though my next matchmaking project was underway.

Mark was in my office, looking out of the window. I couldn't see his face, but his hands were behind his back and he was fidgeting with his watch, always a sign he was worried.

No wonder; Izzy had told me all about Tamara and his carefree expat lifestyle in India. Now he was stuck on his own for six months in Highbury, where the old biddy mafia tracked your every move and the highlight of the social calendar was Batty's Charity Bridge Drive.

I touched his sleeve. 'Mark.'

He spun round and gave me a long, serious look. 'Mouse. I mean Emma. Sorry, I was miles away.'

35

'Listen, why don't you come for dinner tomorrow night? We can catch up properly and you can terrify Dad with tales of Delhi belly. Shall we say seven o'clock? It'll be just like old times.'

He hesitated and for a moment I thought he was going to refuse.

Then he said simply, 'Sounds great.'

CHAPTER 2

SELECTION OF CHOICE MEATS

MARK

'It'll be just like old times.'

'Sounds great.'

I should have added, 'Except everything's changed.'

I wasn't against change as much as Henry, but I did like to keep things in their separate compartments. Of course, some things were the same as before. Henry. Mary. Highbury Foods, at least until Emma started whipping it into God knows what shape.

But *she'd* changed. She'd climbed out of her old compartment, the slightly grubby one labelled 'Mouse', filled with silly jokes and endless games of Monopoly, into a totally inappropriate one. The one labelled 'Sex', dark with desire and velvet-padded to stifle sounds of pleasure. The one I usually kept locked when not in use.

Now I wished I hadn't agreed so readily to Henry's request to mentor her. Never mind; I'd simply open up a new compartment, 'Masochism'. I was sure I could handle it.

Then, as I rifled through my briefcase for my non-executive director contract, I found her photo.

I don't know why I didn't hand the magazine back to Mary and have done with it. Maybe I thought the article might come in handy for the mentoring. But why didn't I file it with my Highbury Foods papers? Instead, I found myself tearing it out, taking it home and looking at it far more than was good for me.

The next day Father and I went to Donwell Organics for a detailed handover. I knew standing in as Managing Director would be a sharp contrast to my role in India. Out there I had a free rein, because Father believed in empowerment rather than a more traditional command and control approach; here, it was more a case of maintaining the status quo until his return.

We'd reckoned without my stepmother Saffron, however; she was like her name – brightly coloured, horribly expensive and best in small doses. Her first phone call came at five past nine and I was privileged to hear every word, despite Father holding his mobile close to his ear. She was afraid four days wouldn't be enough for her to do the packing, so could he take a few hours off to help? Father declined as gracefully as he could and we got about ten minutes' work done before she rang again. She'd been thinking (always a worrying sign) – was it really necessary to put Tao (her shih-tzu) into kennels? Couldn't I look after him, with help from Mrs Burn who'd still be coming to cook and clean most days? Father told her it was out of the question. I was coming from a culture where people fed their dogs curried leftovers; far safer for Tao to live on sirloin steak at the Glen Beagles Hotel for Discerning Dogs. At this point, he switched off his mobile and suggested we went out for a coffee.

'Thanks, that was a lucky escape,' I said, as we drove off in his Mercedes.

'More than you'll ever know. I had to dog sit when Saffron had her last facelift, I spent the whole time running Tao around. Grooming salon, vet's surgery, social engagements with its little furry friends, it was like having another woman in the house.' He grimaced. 'For God's sake, Mark, be careful who you marry. Not that I've any regrets,' he added quickly, 'although I couldn't have chosen anyone less like your mother.'

'No,' I said, thinking of the tall, dignified woman who had died of a heart attack eight and a half years ago. Saffron had appeared on the scene almost immediately, when my father was in no state to resist, and his wallet had suffered the consequences ever since.

The coffee turned into a working lunch that lasted all afternoon. By the time evening came, I decided I would walk to Hartfield for some exercise. As I made my way along the bridle path, dusk was falling, cool and damp, a refreshing change from the intense heat of India.

Emma answered the door in faded jeans and a T-shirt, her face bare of make-up. At first glance she looked more like Mouse, thank God.

I handed her a bottle of Château Cheval Blanc. 'I'm assuming Henry still drinks claret – for medicinal purposes only, of course.'

'Of course,' she said, with a giggle, 'and this one's still his favourite, thank you. Let me take your jacket, you won't need it. Dad wanted a fire in case you felt cold and the room's so hot I've had to change my clothes.'

I looked again; her T-shirt was low-cut, her jeans tight-fitting. I followed her across the hall, my gaze riveted to the easy swing of her hips.

At the entrance to the dining room, I paused. It was just as I remembered – large, square and elegantly furnished with Italian pieces from Sophia's childhood home and vibrant oil paintings of her beloved Tuscany. The curtains were already drawn, the lamps lit, one end of the long rectangular table set for three. Then, as I went in, a wall of heat hit me from what appeared to be a small inferno in the grate. There were three assorted armchairs round it, with a bookcase, CD player and card table nearby; all the signs of a man reluctant to move from his own fireside, literally.

Henry was hibernating in the largest chair, a rug tucked round his knees. He stirred at my approach and smiled sleepily. 'Come and sit here, Mark, you must be chilled through just walking from the car. I did the same earlier and now my arthritis is playing up terribly.'

Emma and I sat down on either side of him and immediately edged our chairs further from the fire.

'Actually,' I said, 'I didn't bring the car, I walked.'

His jaw dropped. 'At this time of year? Your clothes will be wet through, you'll catch your death. Darling, pop upstairs and bring Mark one of my flannelette shirts and those baggy fawn cords, they *might* fit him. If not—'

I laughed. 'Henry, I'm fine, I enjoyed the fresh air and my clothes are perfectly dry. Look at my shoes, not a speck of mud on them.'

'But how will you get home? Darling, order a taxi for Mark, shall we say about ten o'clock?'

'That's kind of you, Henry, but I'll walk back. Along the road, of course, the bridle path will be pitch black.'

Emma, who had stayed seated despite Henry's instructions, said briskly, 'I'll give you a lift.'

I shuddered. 'No thanks, I've heard all about your driving from John.'

Henry gave me a reproachful look. 'Emma's a wonderful driver, your brother doesn't know what he's talking about—'

Emma hastily held up the claret. 'Look what Mark's brought you, Dad.'

'Thank you, so thoughtful.' He beamed at me, then turned to Emma. 'Shall we drink it tonight, or have you already opened something?'

'I have, but I'm sure we can manage more than one bottle. After all, it's a celebration, our first meal together in years.'

'Not for lack of trying on my part,' I said. 'But whenever I was back in England, you were away.'

Her smile didn't quite reach her eyes. 'Pure coincidence, nothing personal. And now I can't avoid you even if I wanted to, because you're mentoring me. Oh joy.'

'Just like old times, Big Brother looking over your shoulder.'

She got up rather abruptly and walked towards the door with the wine.

'You must notice a big difference in Emma since you last saw her,' Henry said, gazing after her.

I watched her stop by a glass-fronted cabinet, put the wine down and start to re-arrange the figurines inside.

'Yes.' I paused. 'And no.'

'What do you mean?'

'She's changed physically, filled out here and there, acquired a bit of sophistication. But when I look at her I see the same old Emma, and I suppose I always will.'

Across the room, Emma slammed the cabinet door shut, snatched up the wine and hurried out; leaving me to reflect that, when necessary, I could be a bloody good liar.

'Filled out here and there . . . acquired a bit of sophistication . . . but still the same old Emma'?

I kicked open the kitchen door. It was going to be an uphill battle to get him to treat me like an adult. At least he'd stopped short of calling me his little sister. If he had, I swear I would have inserted the Château Cheval bloody Blanc somewhere about his person, without an anaesthetic.

Mark Knightley had a reputation for being fair and honest, but always diplomatic. Except when it came to me. It was as if he judged me by different standards from everyone else, the lowest being perfection and the highest something beyond sainthood.

Several deep breaths later, I returned to the dining room with the decanted wine and three glasses.

As I sat down, Mark gave me one of his calculating looks. 'I was about to come and see if you needed a hand.'

'I think I can manage to open a bottle of wine, not much call for mentoring there. Dad, would you like a little of this before dinner?'

'I shouldn't, but I will.' He watched me like a hawk as I poured him an eggcupful. 'That's far too much for me, darling. Never mind, as you said, it's a celebration.' He raised his glass. 'Your health!'

'And especially yours, Henry,' Mark said,

gravely. He turned to me. 'Here's to our new relationship. I mean, of course, the mentoring.'

I forced a smile. 'Cheers.'

Dad sipped his wine. 'I hope you change your mind about going back to India, Mark. Dreadful-sounding place, you're lucky to have got out alive. I trust you're going to have a full medical check-up, in case you've picked up any nasty diseases?'

'I'm fit as a fiddle, Henry. India's like anywhere, do as the locals do and you won't go far wrong.'

'But you are going back?' I said, trying to keep the eagerness out of my voice.

'That's the plan. Unless, after a life of leisure for six months, Father decides to retire and asks me to take over permanently. But I can't see that happening.'

Dad shook his head. 'Neither can I. George is like me, wants to keep his hand in. Of course, Emma will take over from me one day, but not until she's got a lot more experience.'

'How have your first couple of days gone, Emma?' Mark asked.

'Fine,' I said, refilling Dad's glass despite his feeble protests. 'Harriet's settling in nicely. And I think I've found my next matchmaking assignment.'

'Please, darling, not again.' Dad put his hand on my arm. 'Whenever you make a prediction about people, it comes true. Look at poor Kate.'

I laughed. 'I know. My first attempt at matchmaking was a complete success.'

'Success?' Mark leaned forward in his chair and gave me a disapproving look. 'Rubbish. Success implies a plan, and some effort. Knowing you, you made a lucky guess then sat back and did nothing.'

This from the expert, the man whose idea of a fulfilling relationship was dragging each other along to functions! 'Everyone knows that guesses need skill as much as luck,' I said through clenched teeth. 'And no, I didn't have a plan exactly, but I didn't sit back and do nothing either, the truth's somewhere in between.' I smiled as I recalled how easy it had been. 'I got things rolling as soon as Tom came out of the Merchant Navy and settled back in Highbury. I invited him and Kate to dinner, with a few other people as well, so that it wasn't too obvious, then made sure he gave her a lift home. After that, it was just a matter of prodding them along. When I was in the States I couldn't do much, of course, but by then it was cut and dried.'

'You should have left well alone, people are quite capable of choosing their partners without any help from you.' Another disapproving look.

Dad pounced on Mark's last few words. 'That's just like Emma, always helping others, never thinking of herself. But matchmaking's such a risky business! Giving romantic notions to a man and a woman who've probably never thought of each other that way before – it's no wonder so many couples break up. Save yourself the trouble, darling, you'll only be disappointed.'

'You worry too much, Dad,' I said gently. 'And I hope you're not suggesting that Kate and Tom will break up, because actually they're better suited than most couples. Just look at Izzy and John—' I stopped, remembering who I was with.

'Maybe Kate and Tom seem better suited because they're much older – and wiser – than Izzy and John,' Mark said drily.

Dad frowned. 'I can't agree with you there, Isabella's so sensible and a marvellous wife and mother, although John can be rather—'

'Anyway,' I put in, getting up to check that I'd finished setting the table, 'it's too late, my next assignment's well underway.'

Mark drained his glass. 'The time to really worry, Henry, is when Emma starts matchmaking for herself.'

'I'd rather die,' I said, with a dismissive laugh. 'As far as I'm concerned men can stay on Mars, or wherever it is they come from, at least for the moment.'

'So do enlighten us, who's your next victim?'

Victim? He made me sound like a black widow spider. I straightened the place mats and braced myself for criticism. 'Philip Elton.'

'Elton? You must be joking.'

'I am not, he's the ideal candidate.' I ticked off the reasons on my fingers. 'He's in his prime, can't be any older than thirty . . . Handsome, not my type of course . . . Good career prospects, I mean with another company, he's already got as far as

46

he can at Highbury Foods . . . And he's just bought a house, he says he spends every weekend in Ikea. That's a Swedish furniture chain, in case you don't know. I remember doing a case study on them for my MBA, although I've never been in any of their shops. Poor Philip, he seems to have everything, but have you noticed how lonely he looks? He's got such big mournful brown eyes, just like Dr Perry's labrador when he thinks you've come to the surgery to take him for a walk.' I smiled as I re-folded the napkins. 'Yes, when I find the right woman for him, I guarantee she'll be sharing his little Ikea show home in a matter of weeks, or even days.'

Dad looked at me in utter dismay. 'But there's no need to go that far, if it's company he wants then Mark or I could help. You'll be seeing some of your old friends while you're here, won't you, Mark?'

'I'm not sure Philip'll fit in with my crowd,' Mark said, 'but I don't mind having the odd drink with him.'

Dad's eyes lit up. 'I'll find out if he plays bridge. You know, we still play every Thursday, Mark. That's myself, Frank Clarke, Mary and her mother. But Frank had a triple heart bypass last year and some weeks he doesn't feel up to going out, so I could invite Philip instead. Or would you be interested?'

'No thank you, I'm very rusty.'

'Pity, it's an excellent way of passing the time, especially now the nights are drawing in.'

I scowled as I moved the decanter to the table. Cosy drinks with Mark and games of geriatric bridge were certainly not on my agenda for Philip.

Dad went on, 'And we could always give a party, just a little one, so that Philip gets to know people better.'

'Maybe,' I said, knowing that Dad's idea of a party would be vastly different from any normal person's. 'As long as you let *me* choose the food and drink.'

Mark smiled patronisingly as I took his empty glass. 'By all means choose Philip's food, Emma, but not his women. Believe me, you'd be completely out of your depth.'

I said nothing, although I thought plenty. We'd see which one of us was proved right, Mr Know-it-all Knightley.

MARK

As we sat down to eat, I decided that in one respect Emma hadn't changed; she was still maddeningly pig-headed. She seemed determined to ignore my advice and learn the hard way about Philip Elton. I'd sized him up as soon as I met him, a dangerous combination of limited ability and unlimited ambition.

'Not my type,' she'd said. Thank God for that. I wondered what her type was . . .

Her voice intruded on my thoughts. 'I've assumed you still like lasagne?'

I nodded, pleased that she'd remembered. There

were various salads and warm ciabatta to accompany it; for Emma and me, at any rate. Henry restricted himself to a tiny portion of what looked like regurgitated baby food.

Emma kept the conversation flowing, mainly with questions about India. I explained the nature of our operation there and how I personally selected growers to supply many of our leading product lines: tea and spices, obviously, but also rice, fruit, cashew nuts and even coffee. I described my fascination with a country where you'd be gazing at breathtaking natural beauty one minute and turning away from sordid man-made poverty the next. Predictably, Henry was interested in public hygiene, while Emma wanted to know how the growers complied with the UK's organic food standards.

I realised how much I'd missed Hartfield. Dinners like this had been a regular event at one time; initially for everyone in the two families then, once John married Izzy, just for Henry, Emma and me. The quality of the food varied occasionally, if Emma went through an experimental phase; the quality of the company, never – except when she had that teenage crush on me. But she'd soon got over that.

I looked at my watch and saw with surprise that it was after ten o'clock. 'I'd best be off. It's been such a relaxing evening that walking back to Donwell Abbey has lost its appeal. Are you still offering me a lift, Emma?'

'Of course. I've not had much wine, let's hope you've had enough to be able to tolerate my driving.'

I laughed; I'd always loved her wicked sense of humour. Good to know that hadn't changed. It made me want to reach out and hug her.

I would have done, before; but not now.

EMMA

The usual passenger in my silver BMW 325 convertible was Dad. He liked to have the seat in its most forward position so that he could fiddle constantly with the air conditioning controls; funny how he could never seem to find the right setting until I pulled into our parking space at Highbury Foods . . .

I waited while Mark moved the seat back and got comfortable. Then, just as we set off, it started to rain. I flicked the windscreen wipers on and didn't speak until I'd negotiated the twists and turns in our long driveway.

'Thanks for tonight,' I said at last. 'Dad really enjoyed it. Why not come again next week?'

Silence. I glanced across; he was sound asleep.

The journey to Donwell Abbey took only five minutes by car. Although I hadn't been there much in the last few years, I would have found my way blindfold. Down Wheel Lane, left onto the Kingston road, left again after a mile or so and there we were, approaching the house under a dripping canopy of horse chestnut trees. I drew up as quietly as I could on the gravel drive, just in case George and Saffron were already in bed, and gently shook Mark's sleeve.

No response. I sighed and switched off the engine. 'Mark, wake up.'

He stirred and turned towards me. His eyes were still closed; his face, caught in the glare of the security lighting, looked younger, off guard, more vulnerable. I heard the rain pattering on the car hood and felt cocooned from reality, safe and dry. But somehow not safe. And my mouth too dry.

I swallowed. 'Mark, you're home.'

His eyes opened and focused immediately on my mouth. For a split second, I thought he was going to kiss me. Not the brotherly peck he'd occasionally condescended to in the past, but a tongue-down-the-throat job.

I gave a nervous laugh and the moment passed, unexplored. 'I thought I was going to have to slap your face to wake you up.'

'Did I do anything to make you want to slap my face?' There was something unfamiliar in his voice, almost like . . . fear.

'No more than usual,' I said, staring at him.

He stared back. 'Lovely evening, thank you. Sorry I dozed off just now, must be the jet lag. Why don't you come in and—'

'No!' I turned on the ignition. 'I'd better go, you know how Dad worries.'

'Goodnight, then.' He got out of the car, bent

51

his head against the rain and dashed to the front door. I revved the engine, swung the car round in a careless arc and drove off with a lot less consideration for the Knightleys than when I'd arrived.

All the way home I thought about that look on his face when he woke up. It was weird. No, not weird, ridiculous.

Mark Knightley wouldn't want to kiss me like that.

Ever.

MARK

I was shattered, but I didn't go straight to bed. Instead I went to the family room, now seldom used, and switched on the PC. I waited impatiently while the machine wheezed into life, then logged into my personal email account.

Nothing from Tamara, but that was no surprise. We weren't ones to correspond cosily over the Internet, or chat on the phone. As Tamara said, we communicated best between the sheets.

Tonight, though, I wanted desperately to be in touch.

Tam,
Missing you.
Any chance of you coming here before October?
Love M.

I sent the email and waited a few minutes, hoping she was online; but there was no reply.

Then I glanced down at the top drawer of the desk beside me. It was slightly open, revealing a glimpse of thigh, that photo of Emma. I closed my eyes and allowed my thoughts to drift.

Soft skin against my lips, the heat of her, the taste . . .

I rammed the drawer shut and headed upstairs for a shower. A cold one, to numb my mind – and everything else.

EMMA

During that first week, I found out everything I needed to know about Harriet Smith. My first impressions were accurate. Clothes-wise, she was a walking disaster, lots of fake leather and cheap gold jewellery. And as soon as she forgot to talk properly, her speech became unintelligible. 'Me farva's got a tan ass' apparently meant 'my father lives in a town house'; 'that geezer's roofless' was not a reference to a homeless person, but her term for a man without compassion.

I had to face facts. Harriet was a chav, a phenomenon I'd heard about but never actually experienced. The nearest I'd come to it was trailer trash in the States. Giving her a touch of class would be more of a challenge than I'd anticipated; but, in my book, nothing was impossible.

Her curriculum vitae was uninspiring. She'd

been born and bred in Basildon, Essex, where her parents and younger brothers still lived. At sixteen she'd left school, done the basic secretarial qualifications and worked ever since. I wasn't yet sure if it was her typing skills that guaranteed her constant employment, or simply her looks. Now twenty-two, she was renting an old house on the far side of Highbury, with three girls of a similar age.

When she told me that her father had been a professional and now earned his living as a book-keeper, I felt a sudden surge of interest, visualising Philip's spellbound face as Mr Smith held forth on the latest Statement of Standard Accounting Practice. Unfortunately, I'd misheard. Her father was a book*maker*; and he'd previously been a professional *footballer* with a team called Saffend United, before being injured in an off-pitch incident involving large amounts of alcohol.

And she had the most deplorable taste in men. One morning, I asked to see her temping contract. As we sat down to go through Batty's Temp Tation file, the first thing I saw was a letter from Abbey Mill Haulage. It began like a reference, but ended on a surprising note.

To whom it may concern:
Harriet Smith worked at Abbey Mill Haulage from 6th June to 26th August inclusive, assisting our senior secretary Mrs Wagstaff. She was polite and punctual.

Harriet brightened up the office every day.
I'll miss her terribly.
Robert Martin
Managing Director.

We used Abbey Mill Haulage for most of our transportation and I knew Martin by sight. A large, lumbering man, rather like a carthorse, he reminded me of an intellectually challenged quarterback I'd dated briefly in the States. I tried not to let this prejudice me, just as I refused to be influenced by Harriet hovering excitedly at my shoulder, waiting for my reaction.

I gave a short laugh. '"Brightened up the office . . . miss her terribly" . . . Most unprofessional, you should never say anything personal in a reference, you could be sued.'

Harriet's face fell. 'He said it was only the troof.'

'*Truth*, Harriet. It's quite over the top, for someone like him.'

'D'you know Rob Martin?' she said eagerly.

'I've seen him around,' I said. 'Tradesmen are always touting for Highbury Foods' business.'

'He says he's going to expand Abbey Mill now his farva's retired.'

'*Father*. How old is Robert?'

'He was twenty-eight on 8th June, and my birthday was 23rd June, Rob says there's only fifteen days' difference. Or is it sixteen? Anyway, Rob says we're both Gemini, I thought I was Cancer, but he says I'm definitely Gemini like him.'

'Let's hope he doesn't use astrology to run his company,' I said drily. 'Is he married, or living with anyone?'

She blushed. 'No, he's still living at home, his mum says he's ready to settle down, but she doesn't know who's good enough for him.'

'In other words, she can't wait to get rid of him. How did you meet her?'

'She works at Abbey Mill, only two days a week since Rob's dad retired. And she doesn't want to get rid of Rob, she says she couldn't have a better son.'

'Really, Harriet, every other sentence is "Rob says" or "Rob's mum says". Do you fancy him or something?'

Another blush. 'I didn't at first, Trace says he's a bit of an ug.'

'A what?'

'Ugly geezer. But we get on really well. And on my last day he took me to The Ploughman after work. You know, that pub in Little Bassington that's just been done up.'

'I don't know actually, I never go to pubs.'

'You're joking, aren't you? Anyway, we've been out twice since then and I fancy him rotten now.'

This was the last thing I wanted to hear. 'But Harriet, with your looks you could do so much better. You just need a classier image and that's why—'

'Hello, ladies.' With perfect timing, Philip poked his head round the door.

'Come in, Philip.' I gave him a dazzling smile, then continued, 'And that's why you're going to be the face of Harriet's Secret Recipes.'

'Me?' she squealed. 'What about Victoria?'

'Harriet sounds just as upmarket as Victoria. And I want to get away from any association with that US lingerie company, I still can't understand how I had their name in my presentation.' My lips tightened as I recalled the humiliation of the Board meeting.

Philip placed a hand on my arm. 'Don't be too hard on yourself, it was probably subliminal, I bet you've got drawers full of the stuff at home.'

I gave him a frosty look. I didn't mind him speculating about Harriet's choice of underwear, but there was no need for him to do the same for me.

He went red and hurriedly removed his hand. 'Sorry, didn't mean to embarrass you. I came to see if you needed a hand with the photo shoot, you did say you were doing it yourself to save the expense of hiring an agency.' He grinned sheepishly. 'You certainly know the way to a Finance Director's heart.'

I thawed a little. Here was another flimsy pretext for his daily pilgrimage to Harriet's desk. I had to give the man top marks for effort.

'How kind, maybe you could help with editing and printing the photos.' And I bet one or two find their way onto your bedroom wall, I added to myself.

'Delighted to, I've got some very good software

on my computer at home. Why don't you come over one evening and we'll work on it together?' His gaze flickered rather uncertainly across to Harriet and I guessed he was afraid she might refuse.

'I'm sure that can be arranged,' I said. 'We'll be taking the photos in the kitchen at Hartfield, but Harriet and I could come over to your place straight after.'

He looked a little put out. Perhaps he'd hoped to have the photos taken at his house; Harriet draped over his Ikea worktops, a symbol of future domestic bliss. Shame I couldn't indulge his little fantasy, but the kitchens of my target audience were more likely to be at the Bulthaup end of the range.

I gave him a reassuring smile. 'Don't worry, I'm sure it'll all work out to everyone's satisfaction. Was there anything else?'

The doggy expression came into his eyes. 'Yes, I'd like to go over the Marketing budget with you, we're nearly at the end of the financial year and things are a bit tight, but I'm sure we can find some extra funding for an important project like Harriet's Secret Recipes. How about later this week?'

'Fine, just check my diary with Harriet.' I escaped to my room, leaving the door open so that I could hear them. It sounded as though things were progressing nicely; he was droning on about something and she was giggling.

After a few minutes, Harriet came in. 'Amazing, Philip lives in Little Bassington and we both think The Ploughman's much better since it's been done out, it was minging before.'

'So when's he taking you there?'

'Philip, taking *me*? Get real.' She looked at me as if I had two heads.

'But you were discussing the pub, he might have been going to ask you out.'

'No, he was fixing up that meeting with you—'

'Tell me about that later.' I leaned across my desk towards her and made my tone as persuasive as possible. 'You see, Harriet, as I was saying before Philip came in, I think you can do far better than Robert Martin. He's working class, poorly educated, and you said yourself he's downright ugly. Just compare him to some of the men you've met at Highbury Foods.'

She cocked her head on one side. 'You're right, I really like Rob, but even I can see that he's different from someone like Mark.'

'Mark?'

'Yeah, Trace would say he's well shaggable.'

Nine years ago I would have agreed with Trace's opinion, although not her way of expressing it. Now, with practised ease, I sidestepped memories of my teenage crush and merely said, 'I was thinking more of Terry, or Philip. They dress smartly, talk intelligently, behave impeccably. So does Mark, except—'

I was going to say 'he's out of your league', when

she cut in with, 'Yeah, but Terry's so old, forty-five at least.' She pulled a face.

'Well then, what about Philip? He's young, handsome, attentive – look how often he's in here, offering to assist a pair of helpless little females.' I lowered my voice to a yearning whisper. 'And there's a sort of gentleness about him that women find very appealing. He's not overbearing, like Mark.'

Her face lit up. 'Oh, Mark isn't like that with *me*. On my first day, he came to find me after the Board meeting and he looked at me with those sexy blue eyes, same colour as mine, spooky!' She smiled dreamily. 'He said he hoped I'd enjoy working here and Mary was the ideal person to help me settle in. Isn't that a nice thing for someone like him to say?'

'If you think that's nice, just listen to this. After the very same Board meeting, when Jon Marshall was so rude about your Victoria Beckham suggestion, Philip told me he would have rushed to your defence if I hadn't got there first.' I shook my head knowingly. 'You have no idea how much that man fancies you. The other day, when I said how lovely your hair looked – remember you tied it back, as I told you? – he went into ecstasies, I couldn't shut him up for about ten minutes.'

'Did he really?' She paused. 'Are you going out with anyone?'

I laughed. 'No, thank God. My last boyfriend

became a real pain in the butt so I've given men up for the time being.'

'Don't you fancy anyone?'

'No.' I hesitated. 'At least, no one round here. So, when's my meeting with Philip?'

'Thursday lunchtime, at The Ploughman. That's why we were talking about it, he thought it would be—'

'The Ploughman? You must've got the wrong end of the stick, Harriet, you're the only person he wants to take to The Ploughman. We'll have the meeting here, then you can sit in as well. And tell him not to worry about lunch, I'll order some sandwiches.'

MARK

With Father and Saffron off on their cruise and Tao in kennels, I had Donwell Abbey to myself. Mrs Burn came in most weekdays, but our paths rarely crossed. And it looked as though my solitude would continue for several weeks; Tamara emailed me to say she couldn't come any earlier than the date we'd already arranged, 19th October, my birthday.

I felt I owed it to Henry to kick off the mentoring as soon as possible. It proved easier said than done; whenever I phoned to speak to Emma I was told, usually by a giggling Harriet, that she was in a meeting.

Three days after my first call, she rang me back.

61

'Sorry I haven't been in touch until now, I'm having a busy week.'

'Glad to hear it, we'll have lots to discuss at our first mentoring meeting.'

'Can't wait. Things should calm down in a fortnight or so, what about week commencing—'

'If you're so busy at work,' I put in, sensing stalling tactics, 'why don't I come over to Hartfield this weekend? Your father's very keen for us to get started.'

There was a pause. Then she said coolly, 'If you must. Saturday afternoon, about four?'

'Perfect. I'm meeting Steve Chapman – my mate from school, remember? – at six thirty, so our meeting will have to finish by six, but that should give us enough time. No need to bring anything from the office, it'll just be an informal chat.'

At twenty to four on Saturday afternoon, I set off for Hartfield along the bridle path. Small white clouds scudded across an azure sky, the air was crisp and invigorating and the leaves were starting to turn. I was in no mood to appreciate the beauty of an English autumn, however. As I walked, I rehearsed how the meeting would go. I would be business-like, objective, professional. In short, I would pretend I was dealing with anyone except Emma Woodhouse.

I reached Hartfield at four o'clock prompt. An elderly and unfamiliar Vauxhall Nova was parked on the drive, but I was absorbed in my thoughts and didn't pay much attention.

Emma came to the front door, in a green V-necked jumper that brought out the colour of her eyes. 'Hi there, would you believe I've got some unexpected visitors.' She grinned like a Cheshire cat. 'I'll get rid of them as quickly as I can, then we can get on with the mentoring. I know you need to get away by six.'

To my surprise, I found Harriet in the drawing room. Apparently she was the model for Emma's marketing campaign and had dropped by to find a suitable outfit. Kate was there too, just returned from honeymoon. Somehow I knew that neither visit was unexpected; everything had been planned with military precision.

'Harriet and I'll be upstairs looking at clothes,' Emma said airily. 'I'm sure you two have plenty of catching up to do, help yourselves to tea.'

As they went out of the room, I turned to Kate with a smile.

'Do you mind if I make a quick phone call?'

'Not at all.'

I sat down and called Steve to put our meeting back an hour. It was just a local pub crawl with some of our crowd; it didn't really matter if I was delayed, as long as I knew where to find them later in the evening.

When I'd finished, Kate handed me a cup of tea. 'It's great to see you.'

'And you. I don't need to ask if you've had a good honeymoon, it's obvious. Congratulations, by the way. I'm sure you and Tom will be very happy.'

63

'We should be, we've had four whole years to get to know each other.'

Her words made me think. How well did I know Tamara? In theory we'd had the time, but maybe not the inclination.

I changed the subject. 'What do you think about Emma's latest fixation? By that I mean Harriet.'

'It's good for her to see someone her own age, she's lost touch with most of her old friends from round here.'

This namby-pamby reply was only to be expected from Kate Weston; in her eyes, Emma was perfect. And since Emma went through a pretence of consulting Kate before doing exactly as she liked, they were always in complete harmony.

'Sorry, I have to disagree with you, as usual where Emma's concerned. I don't think it's good for her, it's a very unequal relationship. She's treating Harriet like some sort of giant doll – for God's sake, she's even dressing her up as we speak!' I glared at Kate, but she just smiled and carried on drinking her tea. I took a gulp of mine, then added, 'The trouble with Emma is that she thinks she's got nothing to learn.'

Kate laughed. 'Actually, Emma's learnt an awful lot over the last few years. About economics and business administration, for a start. And men.'

I nearly choked on my next mouthful of tea. 'Men? She knows as much about men as I do about leg waxing. Know what? She needs a man who won't let her wind him round her little finger, that might waken her ideas up a bit.'

'She doesn't seem to go for men like that. Have you ever met any of her boyfriends?'

'No,' I said shortly. 'I get the occasional update from John and Izzy, I seem to remember she's had two serious relationships to date and isn't seeing anyone at the moment.'

'That's right, and both those boys were much keener than she was. She met Piers in her first year at LSE, he was heartbroken when she went to the States. Then for most of her time at Harvard she lived with Scott and he even followed her back here. But she wasn't that interested. Just as well, I didn't rate either of them as good enough. Neither did Tom, he thinks the world of her of course, she's like a daughter to him.' Another little smile.

I put my cup carefully down on its saucer. 'Got plans in that direction, have you?'

She went pink. 'You mean Emma and Flynn? Not plans exactly, Tom and I just think they'll hit it off extremely well. They were due to meet at our wedding of course, then Stella wangled Flynn a TV chat show appearance and he had to drop everything and stay in Australia.'

'I see.'

And I did; the man I believed Churchill to be would always choose fame over family. He'd never yet been to England to see his father and it wasn't for lack of funds. When his mother died giving

65

birth to him, her sister Stella, a Sydney-based property tycoon with more money than sense, adopted him and brought him up. Tom was obliged to go along with this arrangement; he had never married Flynn's mother and his career in the Merchant Navy wasn't conducive to childrearing. He visited Flynn whenever Stella allowed, which wasn't often, and kept in contact by phone and email; which meant he'd been able to give detailed and regular updates about his son to everyone in Highbury for the last twenty odd years. I'd always suspected these glowing accounts were wildly exaggerated, but I seemed to be in the minority.

Kate seemed to think I needed convincing. 'He's quite a celebrity over there, you know. Has his own TV series, Flynn's Cook-in.'

'I didn't realise cooking was one of his many talents.'

'Neither did I, but apparently he's amazing at it. And anyway, being a TV chef is as much about personality as skill, isn't it? Each week he has to turn up unexpectedly at someone's house, with the TV crew obviously, and make a three-course meal out of whatever they've got in their kitchen. Can you imagine what it takes to do that?' She paused to sip her tea.

'Sheer balls or crass stupidity,' I thought. 'If not both.'

She went on, 'And it's been such a huge success that he's hoping he can repeat the same formula over here. He was due to have a meeting about it at the BBC last week. He's talking of re-arranging it for next month, but Tom and I daren't get our hopes up.'

As I had little interest in Flynn Churchill, and even less patience with his cavalier attitude towards his father, I steered the conversation back to Emma.

'But you know Emma and her obsessions. When something – or someone – new comes along, she'll drop Harriet like a hot brick. Except it'll be problematic, because the poor girl works for her.'

'I think you're being a bit harsh.'

'Really?' I raised one eyebrow. 'Remember when she was thirteen, she was going to read all the classics? She made a list, and a work of art it was too, I got it framed for her as a joke. How many did she read?'

'She started three, but—'

'—didn't finish any of them,' I put in. 'She just won't stick at anything that requires discipline. And what about that bloody piano? She pestered Henry for lessons until he gave in, then never practised from one week to the next.'

'All right, I give up,' Kate said, laughing. 'But, according to Emma, Harriet isn't very clever, so maybe she won't notice if she's dropped.'

'Whereas Emma's too clever for her own good,' I said, with a frown. 'She's been running rings round Henry and Izzy ever since Sophia died. She's an expert at making everyone do what she wants, usually without them even realising it.'

'Except for you, you never used to let her get away with anything.'

'Someone needed to keep her under control. But I've been away a long time . . .' I gave a rueful smile. 'Henry obviously still has faith in me, he's asked me to mentor her. That's why I'm here, it's our first meeting.'

Kate eyed me over the rim of her teacup. 'You might have a battle on your hands, she's not a little girl any more.'

'I had noticed.'

'Every time I see her, I think she looks more stunning than last time.'

'She's certainly prettier than she used to be,' I said, getting up and walking to the French windows.

'Pretty?' Kate sounded outraged. 'I'd call someone like Harriet pretty, but Emma's absolutely gorgeous, she could easily have been a model.'

'Too curvy,' I said, staring out at the garden.

'Nonsense, look at Sophie Dahl. And Emma's one of those lucky women who don't need make-up, such a beautiful complexion, Tom says she'd make a fortune promoting vitamin tablets.' She paused. 'You must see a huge change in her after eight years, surely?'

Henry had asked me the same question; this time, Emma wasn't around to hear my answer. I watched a robin hop onto the edge of the bird bath, its vivid red breast a reminder that winter was on its way; and when winter was over, I'd be going back to India.

I took a deep breath and let down my guard. 'I do see a big change, I hardly recognised her at first. As you say, she's gorgeous. And she doesn't seem to realise how attractive she is. She's never been vain, at least not about her looks—'

I jerked round as the door burst open and Emma came in, looking extremely pleased with herself. 'Harriet's had to go, but we've had a great time.'

Kate stood up and turned to me. 'Told you it would do her good,' she said, under her breath.

Emma's face fell. 'No need for you to go too, Kate. Mark and I want to hear all about Tenerife.'

'Mark and you need to have your meeting, I'll tell you about Tenerife tomorrow when you and Henry come for lunch. Don't worry, I'll see myself out.'

And then it was just Emma and I, at last.

She picked up the tea tray. 'I'll make some fresh, won't be a moment.'

'I'll come with you, we can start the meeting in the kitchen.' I was determined not to let her out of my sight in case she invented more delays.

I sat at the kitchen table while she made the tea. I told her the ground rules for mentoring; when and where we'd meet, what information I'd expect her to provide, and so on. I explained that a mentor would help her deal with the longer term, with strategic business goals and career objectives, whereas her line manager, Henry, was there for day-to-day performance issues.

As I spoke the words I'd rehearsed, I watched her. The swing of her hair when she turned to refill the milk jug. The little frown when she prised the lid off the tea caddy. The curve of her breasts when she reached up to a shelf for more sugar. And those slender fingers caressing the handle of the kettle as it came to the boil, then directing its flow expertly into the silver teapot.

How could she make such a simple everyday task look so sexy?

'By the way,' she said, as she brought the tea tray over, hips swaying in time to the throb of my pulse, 'I read something interesting the other day about organic farming in India.'

'Checking up on me?' I said.

She avoided my gaze and set out the cups and saucers. 'Actually, it does give me a bit of an issue with your so-called successful track record. I hadn't realised that organic methods were causing such massive environmental problems in India.'

I frowned. 'What on earth do you mean?'

She sat down and poured the milk into the cups. 'All the irrigation water that's needed to produce organic foods and manure and animal fodder. It has to be pumped from deep underground, so it's draining reserves without replacing them. Rather irresponsible, wouldn't you say?'

'Not if—'

She ignored me and pressed on, filling the cups with tea as she spoke. 'Apparently it takes two thousand litres of water a year to grow the fodder to yield just one litre of milk. That's not just unsustainable, it's unethical!' She looked across at me, her eyes bright with triumph.

I took one of the cups and helped myself to sugar. 'Is this an attempt to discredit me and persuade Henry to abandon the mentoring?'

'Of course not, I just thought it was interesting. Although, now you come to mention it, I'm sure Dad would have something to say.'

'I'm sure he would, if those statistics were true of Donwell Organics' growers. But they're not, and maybe you should have checked your facts first.'

I took a sip of tea and watched the gleam in her eyes fade.

'You see, Emma,' I said, half amused, half exasperated, 'I have a very good Indian friend called Vivek, a retired civil servant and a great reader. He discovered that a form of irrigation known as rainwater harvesting was used in India until the early nineteenth century and decided that this practice needed to be revived. Donwell buys all of his village's organic produce, so he came to me to explain what he planned to do and ask for some financial assistance.'

I paused to drink my tea while she stared down at the table, her face like thunder.

'With our backing,' I continued, 'Vivek redesigned his village's drainage system to slow the passage of the monsoon rain long enough for it to collect in specially dug ponds. The water percolates into the soil and refills underground reserves. This means wells can find water at seven metres instead of thirty metres previously. It's a truly sustainable system. So, yes, in general terms organic farming is causing India a major environmental problem. But Donwell is repairing whatever damage it's responsible for, we're funding initiatives like Vivek's right across the country. Sorry to disappoint you, but we're not being unethical.'

She made a show of looking at her watch. 'Thanks for the lecture, didn't you say you had to be somewhere at six?'

As she reached over for my half-empty cup, I seized her hand. Our eyes locked. That jumper really did bring out the green in her irises . . .

'No rush,' I said softly. 'I've put off seeing Steve until seven thirty, I thought it only fair since you couldn't have known that Harriet and Kate would turn up so *unexpectedly* this afternoon.'

She looked startled, then she laughed. 'God, I'd forgotten how bloody devious you can be.'

I grinned back at her. 'Takes one to know one.'

Her hand stirred in mine and, as if responding to some deep dark instinct, I ran my thumb over her smooth warm skin. It was more the gesture of a lover than an old friend. She didn't even flinch, as if to her it was nothing remarkable.

I abruptly let go of her hand and took a long drink of lukewarm tea. Then I pictured a little girl with plaits and braces and no boobs and spent the next hour discussing her personal goals, business strategy and marketing plans. It felt odd talking about such things with her, but of course she'd always been a precocious child.

I'd cracked it. All it involved was doing two things in parallel: making my mouth say 'Emma' and my eyes see 'Mouse'.

CHAPTER 3

KÖTTBULLAR
(SWEDISH MEATBALLS)

EMMA

After several delays, including Harriet catching a nasty cold, the day of the photo shoot arrived. It seemed that half of Highbury was planning to attend.

First, Philip wanted to be involved, from the crack of dawn if need be. I managed to put him off until lunch time, when Harriet would be dressed, made up and ready to be admired. I arranged that the three of us would go to his house after I'd taken the photos, to do all the editing and printing. My plan was then to leave the two of them together and let nature take its course.

Next, Dad decided he'd better be on hand, to give us the benefit of his food hygiene expertise. Even though Harriet wouldn't actually be cooking and the photos were for market research purposes only, he felt duty bound to comply with health and safety requirements.

Then Mark phoned to say he'd like to come for some input to my mentoring. When I asked him what input he could possibly get from a photo shoot, he told me he'd learn a lot from watching me with Harriet and Philip; or, if I preferred business jargon, 'observing me interact with my subordinates and peers'.

The day was looking more stressful by the minute.

Finally, to my relief, Kate volunteered to help with the lunch. Whereas Harriet and I would have made do with a couple of sandwiches while we worked, I now had six to feed. And we covered a whole culinary continuum: from Dad, with his poor appetite and fastidious tastes, to Mark, who could eat not just a horse but an entire stable.

Harriet and I had the house to ourselves for most of the morning. After we'd set out a buffet in the dining room, she prepared the kitchen, under my instruction, while I set up my high-spec digital camera and tripod. That took far longer than expected, because I hadn't used them since my brief interest in photography a couple of years back. Then I dressed Harriet in the outfit I'd chosen, a grey suit with a pink polo-necked jumper underneath. I tied her hair back – just as Philip liked it, I reminded her – and toned down her make-up.

At half past eleven, the doorbell rang. When I opened the front door, I found myself grappling with an enormous bouquet of red roses, orange gerbera and golden lilies.

'For Highbury Foods' new star,' said a smarmy

voice. Philip, evidently hoping to impress Harriet with flower power – but mistaking me for her.

I thrust the bouquet back at him. 'How lovely! Now don't be shy, go and give them to Harriet yourself.'

He seemed about to object; but I marched him straight to the kitchen, where Harriet was painting her nails, and announced his arrival with a flourish.

'Ta-da, special delivery for Miss Harriet Smith.'

Her eyes were like saucers. 'Th-these are for *me*?'

'Looks like it,' Philip said, rather tersely, and I guessed he was a little in awe of Harriet's new image.

I'd hardly put the bouquet in water when the doorbell rang again. It was Kate, with two foil-wrapped parcels.

'This one's a quiche, fresh out of the oven, and the other's some of our wedding cake.' She grimaced. 'I'm afraid Henry won't touch either with a barge pole, but I know you'll have catered for him separately.'

As if on cue, Dad came in and informed me that he'd just seen Mark's car coming up the drive. I took a deep breath, added the finishing touches to the buffet and called everyone through to the dining room.

I wanted Harriet to eat quickly, so that I could get the photo shoot underway; the others could eat at a more leisurely pace, watching us at work in the kitchen if they wished. But Harriet wandered slowly round the room, staring at the furniture and paintings in stunned silence. Then she stopped right beside Philip, who was droning on to Mark about something, and beckoned me over excitedly. It seemed too good a matchmaking opportunity to miss; I curbed my impatience and went across to her.

She was studying a group of black-and-white photos in heavy silver frames. 'These kids are so cute, who are they?' She giggled. 'That man's got a funny look on his face, as if he's constipated. The woman's a bit like you, isn't she?'

It worked beautifully. Philip broke off in mid-sentence and gave us his undivided attention.

'That's my sister Izzy, her husband John – he's Mark's brother – and their children,' I said. 'I took these photos at their house the January before last. Not quite up to a professional's standard, I know, too much clutter in the background. And the children were misbehaving, that's why Izzy looks sort of distracted. Although I'm rather proud of this photo, because it's her to a T.'

Mark laughed. 'Not quite. I've never seen her sitting as still as that, she's normally up and down like a yo-yo.'

I couldn't help smiling. 'Mark's got this theory that Izzy is totally at the beck and call of her kids. But he's wrong. I've seen her be very assertive with them, especially in front of John.'

'I'm sure you have, she's totally inconsistent as well as everything else,' Mark said. 'My other theory is that she secretly loves being bossed about by precocious children. Perhaps it reminds her of when she lived at Hartfield.'

'Is that a nasty little dig at me?' I put on an injured expression.

'Not at all, I was just stating a vague possibility, you're reading far too much into it as usual.' He sipped his orange juice and watched me over the rim of the glass, a wicked gleam in his eye. And I remembered that this was why I'd once adored him; he was the only one who could outwit me with words.

I lifted my chin. 'You were asking about the children, Harriet. These are the three eldest. That's Harry on the left, his real name's Henry, after Dad, he was eight when this photo was taken. That's James, who was five, and Bella, three. James is half turning away because he was about to rush off and be sick. We found out afterwards that he'd eaten a whole packet of chocolate biscuits. Really rich ones, Izzy had bought them specially for her NCT meeting.'

'Ah, the National Childbirth Trust,' Philip said. 'A wonderful organisation, or so my sister tells me. I've no experience of it myself *yet*, but who knows in the future?'

Mark gave a sardonic smile. 'Izzy certainly seems to have signed up as a lifetime member.'

I nodded. 'Five children already and maybe more to come. Anyway, on to the next photo, her youngest son Mark when he was a year old. He's good as gold, never says a cross word, unlike his uncle here. This is my favourite photo of them all – his hair's standing up in those adorable little tufts, I could just kiss him to bits.'

'Apparently my hair used to be like that,' Mark said, as if to wind me up.

Philip was not to be outdone. 'Mine goes like that even now, if I don't slick it down with gel.' He glanced across at the mirror above the fireplace and preened himself.

This impromptu mating ritual was completely lost on Harriet. She frowned and started counting on her fingers. 'That's one, two, three nephews and one niece – only four children. Didn't you just say your sister had five?'

'Yes, but Emily hadn't been born when I took these, she's only nine months old now.' I indicated the last photo. 'And finally John, the man you thought looked constipated. I must admit, he does have rather a pained expression.'

'He was probably irritated at having his precious time wasted by someone who thought she could teach David Bailey a thing or two,' Mark said.

I ignored him and went on, 'Izzy hates this photo, every time she sees it she says I've turned her gorgeous husband into Nicolas Cage with a hangover. I think she wanted him to come across as a doting father, which he is, but it's nothing to do with my technique, he always looks grumpy. Anyway, today there are no couples involved so I can take my photos just as I like.'

Philip smirked. 'That's right, Emma, no couples involved, at least not *yet*.'

'And what could you possibly mean by that, Philip?' I gave him a teasing look, then put my arm firmly through Harriet's; now would be a good time to leave him dangling. 'Excuse us, please. The sooner Harriet and I eat, the sooner we can take the photos and be on our way to your place.'

Philip didn't reply, but I noticed him staring soulfully after us. That was all the answer I needed.

MARK

Elton's gaze was fixed on Emma and Harriet as they walked away.

'Poetry in motion,' he said, under his breath.

I couldn't resist asking, 'Which one, Emma or Harriet?'

He flushed, as though annoyed that I'd over-heard. 'Both of them, naturally.'

'But they're so different.'

'Yes, just as a man can like different types of poetry, surely.'

'In my experience, a man who's inspired by Byron doesn't care much for Betjeman and vice versa.'

He stalked off, saying over his shoulder, 'I haven't the slightest idea what you're on about.'

I remained where I was, content to watch everyone else, listen to snatches of conversation and speculate on hidden agendas.

Henry was trying to convert Harriet to an invalid diet, his plaintive voice laced with persuasion. 'I've eaten one boiled egg, but I'm afraid I couldn't manage the second . . . Emma does them exactly right, not too soft-boiled of course, in case of listeria . . . You must be feeling very nervous, Harriet, this would be perfect for your digestion . . .'

Harriet giggled and fluttered her eyelashes and generally seemed to enjoy being the centre of attention. She looked frequently in my direction, going bright red whenever I smiled at her.

Elton spoke to nobody except Emma and Harriet. I couldn't decide which one he was after; I certainly didn't think it was both, as he'd suggested. If it was Emma – well, I couldn't blame him. And, as he was one of those men who truly believed he was God's gift to women, it wouldn't enter his head that she didn't fancy him. If it was Harriet, then I had to question my judgement; I'd marked him down as more of a social climber. At any rate, when he wasn't chatting them up, he was either shovelling food into his mouth at a rate of knots or grooming himself surreptitiously in the mirror.

Kate was calmly ensuring that everyone had enough to eat and that Henry didn't get too fractious. This was usually Emma's role, but she was too busy with Harriet: on the one hand protecting her from Henry's ridiculous notions about food, on the other encouraging her to hang on Elton's every word.

It was Emma I watched most; every elegant turn of her body in her figure-hugging red jumper and black trousers; every graceful flick of her hand as she tucked a stray tendril of glossy hair behind her ear. Her eyes sparkled as she constantly checked what everyone was doing – apart from me, it seemed; and her full, well-shaped lips were never still as she talked, smiled, ate and drank . . .

Then Henry gave a loud moan of disgust. 'I hope that's not some of your wedding cake, Kate, we'll all be ill. I haven't allowed dried fruit in this house for six years.'

Emma used her normal diversion tactics. 'Dad, I need you in the kitchen, to make sure I've got the right coloured chopping boards for the fruit and vegetables.' As she propelled him towards the door, I heard her say coaxingly, 'Don't make a fuss about the cake, remember Mark couldn't get to the wedding so he'll be wanting to try it. And I bet he's eaten far worse things out in India.'

She returned a few moments later for Harriet and then a second time, to ask us to fill up our plates and come through to watch the photo shoot. The lights were full on, the camera was ready on its tripod and Harriet was standing rigidly behind the kitchen table. In front of her was a dazzling array of kitchen equipment and food, both fresh and tinned.

Henry frowned. 'What about gloves, darling?

Shouldn't Harriet be wearing some of those disposable plastic ones?'

'No, Dad, I don't think so.'

'And where's her cap and apron?'

'No one under sixty wears an apron any more, unless it's a rude one. And there's no need for a cap if she's got her hair tied back.' She gave him one of her winning smiles, then turned to the rest of us. 'Just to explain, I've thought up some scenarios to help Harriet get into character. In the first one she's preparing for a very important date, her new boyfriend and his parents are coming to dinner and everything has to be perfect. Are you visualising the new boyfriend, Harriet? He's a young, up-and-coming guy, director of an SME—'

Harriet looked blank. 'Annessemmee? That's a designer label, innit?'

'SME stands for Small or Medium-sized Enterprise,' Elton said grandly. 'Like Highbury Foods.'

Emma seemed to be trying not to laugh. 'Exactly like Highbury Foods, Philip. Now, Harriet, you want to cook something impressive, yet foolproof. Don't look so terrified, it's just pretend, remember you ooze self-confidence from every pore. That's better. You reach for something from the Harriet's Secret Recipes range . . . Just hold up that tin to your right, it's Betty's Best Creamed Rice Pudding, but no one will be any the wiser. And smile – brilliant!'

She bent over the tripod in a very provocative pose, to which she seemed totally oblivious, and started snapping away. I switched my gaze to Harriet. She still looked tense and there was something odd about the whole scene . . .

'Hang on,' I said, 'there's a picture of a tree directly behind you, Harriet, and it looks as though it's growing out of your head – which I'm sure isn't the sophisticated image Emma has in mind. I suggest you move slightly to the left.'

My intervention did two things, as I'd intended. It made Harriet giggle, which meant she looked more relaxed and in character; and it reminded Emma that she needed to focus less on matchmaking and more on the task in hand.

Whether she paid the slightest attention remained to be seen.

EMMA

At half past three, with the photo shoot over, Harriet and I followed Philip to his house. There'd been some confusion over the transport arrangements; naturally, Harriet and Philip had brought their own cars to Hartfield and each of them offered me a lift to Little Bassington. However, I was determined to take my own car so that I could get away when it suited me and leave Harriet and Philip together for the evening. I persuaded Harriet to leave her old Nova at Hartfield and travel with Philip (I lingered on his name with great emphasis) or me.

The simpleton chose me.

Little Bassington must have been quite a pleasant village at one time. Unfortunately, it had been 'enhanced' by the addition of what I could only describe, in the style of Prince Charles, as carbuncles: pustules of tasteless modern architecture deforming the original rows of picturesque cottages that lined the high street. Philip guided us into one of these carbuncles, a small, newly built estate termed, rather optimistically I felt, Paradise View. From the outside, his house was a repellent neo-Georgian mock-Tudor monstrosity. Inside, words failed me; but they certainly didn't fail Harriet.

She looked round the poky lounge and gabbled some sort of foreign language. 'Oh, you've got a Klippan, so have we, isn't that amazing? And some Gubbos, or are they Klappstas? And over there, don't tell me, that's a Lack.'

Philip grinned. 'Correct, with a Dunker next to it.'

They both burst out laughing.

'I don't get the joke,' I said, with a tight little smile.

Philip was immediately contrite. 'Sorry, Emma, you've obviously never shopped at Ikea, they give their furniture the weirdest names. They're Scandinavian,' he added, as if that explained everything.

'My little brother has a Fartfull,' Harriet said, almost in hysterics.

I rolled my eyes. 'Really?'

'Yes, it's a child's desk—'

'And it means speedy in Swedish or Norwegian or something,' Philip put in.

'How interesting. Now, where's your PC, Philip?'

Harriet and Philip exchanged knowing looks. Then she said, 'On something called a Jerker, I'll bet!'

'I beg your pardon?' I tried not to let my irritation show; at least they were bonding nicely.

'A computer table,' Philip said, hastily. 'It's upstairs, I've turned one of my spare bedrooms into a study. Come on, girls.'

He led us up a narrow staircase to a little room with hardly enough space for the computer table (I couldn't bring myself to call it by its Ikea name), a chair and a couple of bookcases. The idea of it being described as a spare bedroom was ridiculous, unless the guest was small enough to sleep on nothing bigger than a two-by-four-foot shelf. Philip suggested I sat in the chair while he and Harriet watched over my shoulder. This arrangement suited me perfectly until I lost my way in his photo editing software. At this point he started leaning over me and breathing heavily into my ear. I firmly suggested we swapped places.

During the photo shoot, I'd been convinced that hardly any editing would be required. Now I could see all sorts of problems – strange objects visible in the background, peculiar mannerisms from Harriet and the dreaded red eye. Thanks to Philip's expert editing, however, we managed to salvage enough photos for my purposes: to circulate them as part of my proposal at the next Board meeting in late October and, subject to the directors' approval, use them in some focus group research.

Afterwards, Philip went into the kitchen to make a pot of tea while Harriet and I sat in the lounge. I was past caring whether I was sitting on a Klippan or a Klappsta; all I knew was that it had been a long, tiring day and there was something bothering me.

I spoke my thoughts out loud. 'We need a marketing strapline to go with the photos. It's a good idea to have one from the start, even if we change it as a result of the research.'

Harriet stifled a yawn.

'I'm after something inspiring that the target audience can identify with,' I went on. 'I can't think what, though.'

Just then, Philip came in carrying a bright blue tray.

Harriet pointed at it and shrieked, 'Blimp! Have you got any Groggy as well?'

I groaned inwardly; the Ikea name game was really getting on my nerves. 'Philip,' I said hurriedly, 'any suggestions for our strapline? You know the sort of thing – "let Harriet's Secret

Recipes save your day!" Obviously, that's not very inspiring, but I'm sure you get the picture.'

Philip handed each of us a mug of tea and settled himself on what passed for a sofa. 'What you're alluding to with this new range is freedom for a certain type of woman, someone who feels constrained by the demands of life today. As you so eloquently said at that first Board meeting, she's juggling work and family and entertaining – and wanting to do it all perfectly. She needs to be released from her inhibitions, given the means to explore her adventurous side.'

That last bit sounded like some sort of sexual fantasy; I wondered whether to go straight home and leave him and Harriet to it. But I couldn't resist prompting him further. 'I think you may have something there, go on.'

He looked straight at me, his eyes glittering. 'You see, Emma, the woman I'm thinking about is trapped by routine, burdened by responsibility, repressed by other people's expectations. What she craves is – emancipation. Or rather – ema-ncipation!' For some reason, he paused after the first two syllables and gave a mysterious smile.

I frowned. 'Emancipation . . . Emancipation . . . No, not snappy enough.'

He leaned forward and said in a husky voice, 'How about "Get ema-ncipated in the kitchen . . . with Harriet's Secret Recipes"?'

I laughed. 'D'you know, that's not bad at all, it'll definitely do until I find something better, which may not happen before the focus groups. So thank you, Philip.' I picked up my handbag and got to my feet. 'Well, I must be going, just need my camera, wherever that is.'

Harriet stood up too. 'It's upstairs, I'll get it for you.'

She dashed out of the room. I went to follow her, but Philip blocked my path. His face was flushed and he was almost panting. 'Emma, I'm only too happy to help Marketing out in any way I can, any way *at all*. And that strapline' – he grinned, unpleasantly – 'I'm sure it won't take someone as clever as you very long to work out that it contains the name of my ideal woman—'

'It's glaringly obvious,' I put in, with a pitying look, 'even Harriet—' I stopped as she came back into the room with my camera. 'Thank you, Harriet, why don't you stay and help Philip print those extra hard copies we discussed?'

Philip stepped away from me with a scowl. 'Unfortunately, I have to go out now. And anyway, you need to take Harriet back to Hartfield to get her car.'

'And the flowers,' Harriet added. 'I might have to borrow a vase thingy from you, Emma, there's nothing like that at my house.'

I sighed. I felt like knocking their heads together, but on the other hand I was delighted at the way matters were progressing. 'Come along then, Harriet. Thank you so much, Philip, see you tomorrow.'

'I hope so, Emma. 'Bye, Harriet.'

As I drove off, I checked the mirror and saw him standing at his front door, gazing wistfully after us.

'A very long but successful day,' I said. 'We've got our photos taken and printed off and we've even got a strapline. "Get emancipated in the kitchen . . . with Harriet's Secret Recipes." It's growing on me.' I paused. 'While you were out of the room, Philip told me it contains the name of his ideal woman. He had the nerve to say it wouldn't take me long to work it out. I mean, Harriet's Secret Recipes – duh!'

Harriet said slowly, 'But don't you remember? When *he* said it, he made "emancipated" sound so-o-o like "Emma-ncipated". So couldn't he mean you?'

I burst out laughing. 'Oh, Harriet, really! You'll be saying next that he brought that huge bunch of flowers to give to *me*. You're far too modest for your own good, you know.'

She giggled. 'Oh, you're right, silly me, I wish I was clever like you, Emma.' She hesitated, then went on, 'By the way, did I tell you I'm going out with Rob tonight? So I couldn't have stayed at Philip's anyway.'

It was an effort, but I said nothing. I made up my mind, though, to move things up a gear on the matchmaking front. Philip was obviously interested; I just had to get any notions about Robert Martin out of Harriet's head and suggest to her

90

that, in my humble opinion, Philip was far superior.

Harriet didn't need to be clever; she had me to do all the brain work for her.

MARK

After Hartfield, I went to Abbey Mill Haulage to discuss the latest food transportation directive with Rob Martin. We sat drinking tea in his office, putting the European Union to rights and regretting that it was run by politicians rather than sensible people like us.

I liked Rob a lot. His bulk – he was built like the proverbial brick shithouse – and stern, craggy features put people off, but to me he was just a gentle giant.

When I mentioned I'd been at the photo shoot, his face lit up. 'Harriet's telling me all about it tonight. We're going on our third date and I'm really looking forward to it.' He gave me an anxious look. 'How did she get on today?'

'She did as well as could be expected, given the limitations of the photographer.'

'That was Emma, wasn't it? She's been very friendly to Harriet, even invited her to Hartfield the other week. Surprised me, that did. Emma's so posh, I wouldn't have thought she'd bother with Harriet outside work. I hope it doesn't give her the wrong idea, you know, that she could be like Emma Woodhouse.'

91

'No one could be like Emma Woodhouse,' I said drily. I almost added, 'She has the attention span of a gnat, so when she loses interest in Harriet, make sure you're there to pick up the pieces.'

But I didn't. Experience told me that the most innocent of remarks had a tendency to come back and bite you, even years later.

EMMA

It was certainly Harriet's week for flowers. A couple of days after the photo shoot, she received another bouquet, this time at Highbury Foods. Marie from Reception brought it up to my office.

At first I thought it might be from Philip again. But it was inferior to his in every way: size, style, quality of wrapping paper and the flowers themselves. Harriet buried her face in them, breathing in their non-existent scent.

I couldn't help staring. 'Good grief, I've never seen blue carnations before.'

She looked up and grinned. 'I bet it's because I support Saffend United.'

'This came with them, Darren's waiting downstairs for the answer.' Marie held out a rather grubby-looking white envelope.

I resisted a strong temptation to snatch it out of her hand. 'Darren?'

'Darren Griffiths, he's a driver with Abbey Mill Haulage.'

I knew immediately who'd sent the flowers.

Harriet placed the bouquet carefully on her desk, opened the envelope and read the note inside, over and over again. Then she lifted shining eyes to mine. 'They're from Rob.'

As if I hadn't worked that one out! I moved swiftly into action. 'Marie, perhaps you could go and see if Darren wants a coffee or something, while Harriet thinks about her answer. We'll call you when it's ready.'

As soon as Marie had gone, I said casually to Harriet, 'Any particular reason for the flowers?'

'You can read his note if you like, it's so-o-o sweet.'

The note was on cheap paper and the handwriting rather immature, but I could tell he'd given it a lot of thought; there wasn't a single spelling mistake or crossing out.

Dear Harriet,
I've been thinking a lot about Tuesday night, especially when we went back to your place. If only the girls hadn't come home early and if only you weren't sharing your room with Sharon's friend until she moves into her own house . . . Anyway, these flowers are to say 'I love you'. They reminded me of your fantastic eyes as well as Southend United.

Also, Alison told me this morning that she and Tony can't go to Amsterdam this weekend after all. Like the kind big sister she is, she's offering me and you their places on the trip. Please, please say yes. You know what it means – two whole days to relax in each other's company (oh, and with ten other people from the pub quiz team!) and two nights in a nice hotel room together, say no more.

I could have asked you about this over the phone but I didn't want you to feel pressured. Just let me know as soon as possible if you can come.
Love, Rob.

Harriet bobbed up and down on her chair. 'Don't you think it's a good letter, Emma?'

'Ye-e-es, I do,' I said slowly. 'Surprisingly good, someone must have helped him write it. I've never really spoken to the man, but I wouldn't have thought him capable of this. On the other hand, there *are* men who can hardly string two words together, but express themselves quite nicely on paper.' I handed the note back to her.

'What do you think I should do?' I was pleased to hear a hint of doubt in her voice.

I picked up the proposal she'd been typing for me. 'Do? Oh, Harriet, you ask the strangest questions. Let him know as soon as possible, as he says.'

'But what shall I say? And shall I do it over the phone?'

'I would write, since Darren's loitering around

downstairs anyway. And be absolutely clear, give him no room to misunderstand you. You know, "really honoured . . . sorry to disappoint . . . no future in the relationship". That sort of thing.' I went quickly through into my room.

She came after me and stood at the door round-eyed. 'You mean – say *no*?'

'What else? I thought you were just asking me the best way to say it.'

She chewed her lip.

'So you were going to say yes?' I hoped I sounded suitably incredulous.

'I – I don't know. What would you do if you were me?'

'Harriet, I can't tell you whether you should have a dirty weekend in Amsterdam or not, that's entirely up to you.'

'I didn't know he was so keen, you know, love and all that.' Harriet unfolded the note and gazed vacantly at it. I waited for her to speak, but she didn't.

After a few moments, I said briskly, 'What I *can* say, from my considerable experience of men, is that if I don't feel I can say yes to something immediately, then it's just not meant to be. But I don't want to influence you, Harriet, it wouldn't be fair.'

'Yeah, I know, it's up to me. And I really like him.'

'I really like lots of people, but I wouldn't sleep with the vast majority of them.'

She reflected on this. 'It's a big decision, innit, to go away with someone for the weekend? I mean, we got a bit carried away on Tuesday night but we were interrupted. And maybe that was a sign, you know? Maybe it wasn't meant to be. It's not as if I fancied him right from the start, is it? I think maybe it's safer to say no?'

'I can't possibly give you advice. If you can honestly say Robert Martin appeals to you more than anyone else . . .' I shrugged, then went on, in a more animated tone, 'But isn't it weird getting bouquets from two different men in the same week? I thought Philip's was very elegant, but then red roses are my particular favourite. I once studied the Victorian meanings of flowers and, of course, red roses signify sincere and passionate love.'

'What about blue carnations?'

'Harriet, blue is not a natural colour for a carnation, so they can't have any meaning at all. Come along, you need to reply to this note, can't keep Darren waiting for ever.'

She stared out of the window, twisting the note over and over in her hands until it resembled a corkscrew. I waited again for her to speak, but this time I was more hopeful.

Then she sighed. 'I know you won't give me advice, but I think I've made up my mind. I think – I think I'll say no. To everything – going out with him as well as the weekend in Amsterdam.' She looked imploringly at me. 'Am I doing the right thing?'

I went up to her and hugged her. 'Of course you are. I didn't dare say this while you were still making up your mind, but I've been quite depressed about your relationship with Robert Martin. He and I – well, we obviously have such different values, and values are what make people and organisations tick. I was starting to think you weren't suited to being at Highbury Foods after all.' I paused. 'As you know, we don't want a temp for ever, we were going to advertise the permanent post soon. But why waste money advertising? You've just put yourself in the frame for the job. Harriet Smith, PA to the Marketing Director and the Managing Director, imagine that!'

She jumped up and skipped round my room, a broad smile on her face. 'Ooh, I'd love to work here all the time, temping's so-o-o hard, all that new stuff to learn every time I go anywhere.'

'I'll have to see what Dad thinks, but there shouldn't be a problem.' I pulled out a chair for her at my table. 'Now sit here and reply to that note. Here's a pen and some paper – Conqueror Vellum, of course, only the best for Highbury Foods.' I sat down at my PC to check my email.

After a few minutes, I noticed that she'd un-screwed the note and was staring at it. I coughed to attract her attention. 'Shall I ask Darren to bring a tent and camp overnight? It looks as though it'll take you that long to answer a few lines.'

She looked up; to my horror, her eyes were full of tears. 'This is really, really hard,' she whispered. 'I don't want to hurt his feelings. And what will his mum say?'

'It's always difficult to tell someone the truth, especially if they've got an inflated opinion of themselves.'

'But he's not like that at all, he's very shy. That's why it's so hard to know what to say.'

So I did the letter for her. At least, I dictated, she wrote; which was how it should be, since she was my PA.

Of course, I didn't make it too obvious that I was telling her what to say. I made suggestions, trotted out little phrases that I told her could be very effective in these situations. When we'd finished and sealed the letter inside a matching envelope, I summoned Marie to give it to Darren. I wasn't going to let Harriet take it, in case she had second thoughts.

She went back to her desk and I got down to some work. Half an hour later, I went into her room and found her toying miserably with the unopened post.

I stood in front of her and waited until she looked up.

'Harriet, we have a crisis,' I said, in hushed tones. 'I'm sure Philip printed off ten sets of photos but I can only find nine. I wonder what he's done with the other set . . . Do you know what I think? I think he's kept it at home.'

She went bright red.

'I can see those photos now,' I continued, 'stuck on the wall in the study, above his Jerker.'

She giggled.

I put on a Philip-like voice. 'Oh Harriet, let's make secret recipes together in my kitchen at Paradise View. Don't be the face of Highbury Foods, my darling, be the icon of Ikea!'

She burst out laughing.

Everything on the matchmaking front was going exactly to plan.

MARK

When I phoned Rob with the information I'd promised him after our last meeting, he sounded even more brusque than usual.

'What's the matter?' I said. 'I know this proposed EU legislation is aggravating, but it's hardly the end of the world.'

'It's nothing to do with the bloody EU,' he said.

'Oh?'

There was a lengthy pause so I tried again. 'Want to talk about it?'

'Not particularly.'

'I'm free for a pint or two this evening, if you change your mind.'

He did change his mind. He rang me ten minutes later, apologising for his bad mood, and we arranged to meet in The Hare and Hounds at six thirty.

When I arrived at six twenty-five, he was already sitting there nursing a pint. I bought my own and joined him. It didn't take long for him to come to the point; he wasn't one for small talk.

'It's Harriet. Remember I was afraid she might turn like Emma Woodhouse? Well, it's happened. When I saw her on Tuesday night, she was all over me. Now she doesn't want anything to do with me.'

'What exactly has she said?'

'Here, read this.' From the breast pocket of his jacket he took a crumpled sheet of paper and handed it to me. It was covered in a childish scrawl, a sharp contrast to the stiff formality of the words themselves.

Dear Robert,
Thank you for your kind note and the flowers.

I am really honoured to be invited on a weekend to Amsterdam with you, but I do not feel able to accept. There are various reasons for this, but the primary one is that I do not think there is any future in our relationship.

I am sorry to disappoint you and hope we can remain on friendly terms.
Yours sincerely,
Harriet.

I knew one thing for certain; the letter may have been written by Harriet Smith, but the words were someone else's.

'Give me the background to this,' was all I said.

It turned out he'd meant to send Harriet flowers after their date on Tuesday, but various work problems had delayed him. Then today his eldest sister had offered him two places on a trip to Amsterdam this weekend, as she and her boyfriend couldn't go. Galvanised into action, Rob had rushed out, bought some flowers and told one of his drivers to deliver them to Harriet with a note and wait for an answer. He'd been confident of a positive response; they'd have slept together on Tuesday night, for God's sake, if her room-mate hadn't come back early.

He'd been totally unprepared for her reply. He'd tried her mobile but it was switched off, so he planned to go round to her house this evening and ask her to tell him to his face that there was 'no future in their relationship'.

It all made me very uneasy; I was sure it was Emma who'd had a hand in the letter, but I didn't say so. I merely suggested that he would only make things worse by seeing Harriet in his present state of mind and that, if she was turning into an Emma clone, the damage would not be repaired overnight. I added that, in my experience, a man who appeared to cool off often had the woman throwing herself at his feet. My advice was to leave her alone and wait.

He bought us both another pint and seemed to want to drop the subject. We talked about other things, mainly the local rugby scene. However, as we left the pub, he thanked me for listening and said he would take my advice and give Harriet some space.

On my way home, I could think of nothing but his rejection. I found myself stopping at Hartfield, determined to speak to Emma and discover just how much she'd been involved. When she answered the door, I ignored her invitation to come in and stayed outside in the cold.

She must have seen my grim expression in the glare of the security lighting; her eyes widened and her hand flew to her mouth.

'Oh God – something awful's happened – it's one of the children, isn't it?'

'Nothing like that,' I said abruptly. 'I've just been trying to cheer up Rob Martin.'

She said nothing, but she smiled; a little gloating smile that told me all I wanted to know.

I stared at her. 'You were there, weren't you, when Harriet got his note and sent back that idiotic reply?'

Her smile broadened. 'Funny, isn't it? A man can never understand why a woman says no, he thinks she'll fall into bed with him – and in this case go all the way to Amsterdam to do it – just because he asks her.'

'What a load of crap! I'm not like that for a start, and I'm positive Rob isn't. He had every reason to think there was "a future in their relationship", as you so coyly phrased it in that letter.'

'You think I had something to do with her letter?'

I took a step forward, almost into the house, forcing her to retreat a little. My voice was low and menacing. 'Didn't you?'

She laughed. 'What if I did? I may have done them both a favour, he's just not good enough for her.'

'Not good enough for her? Are you blind or stupid or what? He runs his own company, she's a temp . . . He's financially independent, although he chooses to live with his parents, while she can afford only a clapped-out old car and a room in someone else's house . . . He's well respected throughout Surrey, she's a nonentity . . . He's a capable and educated man, mainly self-educated which is even more to be admired, whereas I suspect she's bordering on simple. Yes, she's pretty and compliant, but that's about all. Not good enough for her? Bollocks, she should be grateful he's lowering himself to her level.'

Her eyes flashed. 'Lowering himself? An ugly, coarse, jumped-up lorry driver wanting a relationship with a beautiful girl like Harriet? You think he's all she should aspire to, when she's got the potential to – to—'

'To what? Marry Prince bloody William?' It was my turn to laugh.

'Stranger things have happened,' she said loftily. 'But she isn't setting her sights *that* high.'

'And just where are *you* setting her sights? If it's Philip Elton, then, as I've already told you, you're wasting your time. His choice of woman will be like his choice of career – safe and lucrative. Even if he does fancy Harriet, he'll just use her for a quick shag, nothing more. He may talk like a romantic fool, but he'll act like the calculating bastard he really is.'

She glared at me in silence for several seconds; when at last she spoke, her voice was soft and calm. 'Look, I don't know why you're getting so wound up. I haven't any specific man in mind for Harriet at the moment. I'm just relieved she's seen the light about Robert Martin and I'm glad I could be of help.' Her tone hardened. 'But I don't agree with your description of her, it's unflattering and unrealistic. She's actually the type of woman that would suit most men down to the ground. How did you put it? Pretty and compliant. In other words, good to look at and take to bed, but no threat to the male ego. You know, if you and Tamara ever broke up, you could do worse than go out with Harriet yourself.' She smiled sweetly and went to shut the door in my face.

I wedged it open with my foot and grabbed hold of the door knocker to steady myself. I was breathing hard and fast, as if I'd just run a marathon.

'I'm telling you, you should have left well alone. You're trying to make her into something she's not and never will be. For God's sake, Emma, sometimes I wonder if you've even got the sense you were born with!'

Her lip curled. 'I'm afraid we'll just have to agree to differ on this one. I'm sure your friend Robert will get over it sooner than you think.'

Something snapped inside me. 'You don't seem to realise that you're pissing about with a man's heart – do you know what the fuck one is?'

There was an insolent glint in her eye. 'A man – or a heart?'

'Both!' I turned on my heel and stormed off.

Behind me, the front door slammed. I got into the car, leaned my arms on the steering wheel and rested my head on them, briefly. Then I straightened up, started the engine and drove home.

EMMA

I lay in bed, drained but unable to sleep, thinking about what Mark had said. I'd only ever heard him swear like that when he was almost beside himself with rage. Until tonight, however, I'd never been the target for one of his rare outbursts.

I knew I had nothing to reproach myself for. But I felt so miserable. Sort of incomplete. A jigsaw with one piece missing, the Mark-shaped one that didn't quite fit, yet somehow belonged.

We'd had our falling-out moments, of course.

Particularly when he'd discovered my teenage crush on him, all those years ago.

I'd dealt with that then and I'd deal with this now.

CHAPTER 4

GOOSEBERRY FOOL

MARK

Early on the morning of my birthday, I woke to the phone ringing next to my bed. I groped for the receiver and grunted into it.

Saffron's voice almost burst my eardrums. 'Happy birthday, darling!'

Before I had time to bellow something back at her, Father came on the line. 'Many happy returns, Mark, did you get our card and cheque?'

'Yes thanks, they arrived yesterday I think. What time is it where you are?'

'God knows. Some time in the afternoon, we're in Singapore, remember? Just come back from Haw Par Villa, a sort of theme park. Didn't think I'd enjoy it, but it was fascinating. We're off out again in a few minutes. Is Tamara there?'

I rolled onto my back and grinned. 'No, she's coming later today.'

'So you're all alone.'

'Apart from a couple of hookers I picked up last night.'

'I know you're joking.' He paused. 'You are, aren't you?'

'What do you think?'

He said gently, 'I think the sooner Tamara's with you, the better. It's not natural for a man to be on his own.'

'I'm going into the office, I'll hardly be on my own there.'

'You know what I mean. By the way, have we got the new Parkinson contract agreed yet?'

This led to a brief discussion about the need to keep particularly close to our biggest customer, who was being courted even more than usual by our competitors; then he was off on his next outing, Saffron nagging in the background.

It made running Donwell Organics seem like a picnic.

I lay in bed a little longer, thinking. Not about the Parkinson contract, I'm ashamed to say, but about the list of instructions I needed to give Mrs Burn in preparation for Tamara's arrival; such as 'Lay fire in drawing room' and 'Put bottle of Krug on ice'.

At least the phone call meant I got to the office earlier than usual. Since I was leaving shortly after lunch to pick up Tamara from the airport, then taking the rest of the day off, I needed to get a head start.

It felt like I'd only just got going when Cherry, my PA, rang through.

'Ready for coffee?' she asked.

'Not yet, it's only—' I glanced incredulously at my watch. 'Five past eleven? Yes, coffee please, then can you get hold of Mitch and ask him to come up here before one o'clock.' David Mitchell was our Sales Director and in charge of the Parkinson account. 'Oh, and could you check that Tamara's plane's on time? The details are in my diary.'

'Fine. And you've got a visitor.'

'There's no one scheduled—'

'It's Emma Woodhouse, she says it'll only take a few minutes.'

'Oh. All right, but . . .' The words died in my throat.

'I'll bring coffee for two, then, shall I?'

'OK'.

I'd hardly put down the phone when the door opened and there stood Emma in a too-short skirt, holding a large round tin emblazoned with 'Fortnum & Mason'. We hadn't seen each other – hadn't even spoken – since our quarrel over a week earlier. And yet I'd lost count of the times I'd almost phoned her, almost called in at Hartfield . . .

I forced a smile. ''Morning.'

She took a few steps into the room and hesitated. I got up and shut the door. As I passed behind her, she spun round and thrust the tin at me.

'Happy birthday. And Mark,' – sharp intake of breath – 'let's call a truce and make up.'

I took the tin from her and placed it on the desk. 'Make up?' I said, cautiously.

'You know, for the whole Robert Martin thing. How I wish I'd never even heard of that stupid man! But what I hate most of all is this – this bad feeling between us. I've been so unhappy, I thought you'd never speak to me again.'

I don't know which came first, my arms opening in welcome or her eager step forward. Did it matter? She was there, burying her face in my chest, gripping the belt at the back of my trousers. My hands, as if guided by an unseen force, came to rest firmly on the curve of her suede-clad hips. My eyes closed; but whether in pain or pleasure, I had no idea.

After a while, I became aware that she was crying – or rather trying not to. I opened my eyes, held her slightly away from me and raised one hand to cup her chin and tilt her face towards mine. Slowly, reluctantly, she obeyed and I watched, fascinated, as a teardrop quivered on her lower lid – and fell. Without thinking, I pressed my lips against her cheek to catch it and tasted a fleeting moment of intimacy.

Not physical intimacy. That was all too familiar, although not with her.

Something else. A closeness forged by shared memories, tempered by deep – affection.

My hand dropped back to her hip and I let out a long breath. 'Just making the hurt better, same as when you were little,' I said in a hearty voice. Too hearty, perhaps.

She stifled a sob, then frowned. 'I don't remember it ever being like that.'

'Really? It should be me who doesn't remember things. Thirty-five today, can't you see all the grey hairs that have appeared overnight?' To my relief, her frown became a smile. 'Look,' I went on, 'the Rob and Harriet incident's over. Let's forget about it. Especially now you've come to apologise.'

I felt her stiffen in my arms, saw her eyes flash. 'I haven't – I've come to let you apologise to me!'

'What on earth have I—?' I stopped and let out another steadying breath. 'As you said at the time, we'll just have to agree to differ.'

'I still don't think there was any harm done, not on Harriet's side anyway.' She gave a dismissive shrug. 'I don't know about *him*, of course, but I can't imagine he's too upset.'

After spending several evenings with Rob Martin in The Hare and Hounds, I knew exactly how upset he was; but I was also determined to avoid any more arguments with Emma. So I pulled a clean handkerchief from my pocket and handed it to her.

'Here, dry your eyes.' I walked over to the desk. 'Now, what's in this tin you've brought? Don't tell me – Henry's sent me a supply of garlic cloves to see me through the winter.'

'Oh, Mark.' She made a funny sound, a cross between a laugh and a hiccup, then dabbed distractedly at her cheek with the handkerchief. 'Sorry to disappoint you, Dad's present is in the blue envelope there. He's so worried about the effect India must have had on your, er, system that he was going to get you a voucher for colonic irrigation. But I persuaded him to go for Gentlemen's Tonic instead, much more relaxing.'

'Gentlemen's Tonic?' I said, doubtfully. It reminded me of Gentleman's Relish and that photo . . .

'It's a posh male grooming place in Mayfair, you'll love it. I've got you one of their vouchers as well.'

There were two envelopes taped to the tin. I opened the blue one first and found a card and voucher from Henry. Then I opened the silver one; same voucher and a card with a corny joke about getting old. It was signed 'Love, Mouse', followed by three kisses.

I immediately thought, 'One down, two to go.' Then, 'But that first kiss hardly counts, it was more like first aid.'

I cleared my throat. 'You told me Mouse was gone for ever.'

She blushed and looked down at the floor. 'She popped back, just for your birthday.'

The door opened and Cherry appeared with the coffee tray, which she placed on the little table at the other end of the room. When she'd gone, I prised the lid carefully off the tin.

Emma watched me nervously. 'I made you a coffee and walnut cake, your favourite. At least, it used to be your favourite.'

'It still is. Thank you, let's have some now.'

We sat in the armchairs either side of the table. She poured the coffee while I cut two generous slices of cake with a plastic ruler, the most suitable implement I could lay my hands on, and used sheets of printer paper as plates.

She giggled. 'Not quite in keeping with the image of a high-powered business executive, is it?'

'Your image or mine?'

'Both. D'you know, as there's no one watching, I might even lick my fingers.'

I was watching, but obviously I was just part of the furniture. And I didn't watch her for long. There was only so much a sex-starved man could stand.

'That was delicious,' I said, when we'd finished eating. 'Another slice?'

'No thanks, this skirt is tight enough as it is.' She patted her stomach, the merest hint of a curve beneath smooth silver-grey suede. 'Oh, I nearly forgot, Kate's having people round for dinner this Saturday and she'd like you and Tamara to come. Seven for seven thirty. She's asked her usual crowd – Izzy, John, Dad, me, Batty and her mother. And she's also invited Harriet and, er, Philip.' A pause, then a well-judged change of subject. 'Is Tamara here yet?'

'No, I'm going to pick her up from Gatwick this afternoon.'

'I've never met her.'

'I know.'

She scooped up a few crumbs from her lap and dropped them into a nearby waste paper bin. 'Izzy says she's not interested in anyone but herself. And presumably you.'

I frowned. 'Izzy thinks that anyone who doesn't instantly adore her kids is bizarre. Tamara did *not* appreciate having chocolate smeared in her hair by Bella last time she was over, she'd just spent a small fortune at the hairdresser's.'

'I can understand that, I suppose. Anyway, I'm dying to see her.'

'So am I. And I've only got another four hours to wait, thank God, it's been six weeks since—' I broke off. I'd never discussed my sex life with anyone and I certainly wasn't about to start now. Maybe Father was right after all; it wasn't natural for a man to be on his own.

I got to my feet, crossed the room and busied myself with the in-tray on my desk. Out of the corner of my eye, I noticed Emma walking over to me.

Her voice was cool. 'I'm sure you've got lots to do, so I'll be off now. Hope your birthday celebrations with Tamara don't wear you out.'

I turned and looked down at her sulky face.

'Look, I really appreciate you coming to see me this morning. And thank you for that delicious cake, and the vouchers, so thoughtful. Tell Henry I'll thank him in the next day or so.'

'No rush, he's not going anywhere. And it sounds like you'll be very busy once Tamara's here.'

'Emma, you're giving me the feeling I still owe you an apology – this time for something else, although I don't know what.'

She said nothing, just scowled at me.

I sighed, placed my hands on her shoulders and did a really stupid thing; I bent my head and kissed her.

Not properly of course, just brushing her lips – so full, so soft – with mine. I'd done it occasionally when she was younger, without a second thought. But this time it was different. This time, my casual platonic kiss was charged with the knowledge that, at any moment, I could deepen it. The knowledge that I wanted to deepen it, whatever the consequences.

But my mouth disobeyed my thoughts and the kiss ended safely.

I let go of her shoulders with a relieved smile. 'Friends?'

She stared at me in silence for several seconds. Then she said quietly, 'Mark, I can't imagine *not* being friends with you.'

And she went out of the room without a backward glance, leaving me to mull over that last remark. Did she mean that she couldn't envisage us ever being enemies? Or that she couldn't picture us as more than friends – as lovers, in other words?

Another disturbing thought came to mind: of the three kisses on her card, we were now two down.

One to go.

EMMA

I had it all planned out.

I'd give Mark a chance to calm down after our quarrel and let him make the first move. If he hadn't apologised by his birthday, I would take him a peace offering and see if that did the trick.

But there was no apology; in fact, he was waiting for *me* to say sorry to *him*!

Maybe, as he suggested, we should forget we'd ever quarrelled. But I couldn't forget those kisses, however brief and insignificant. Insignificant? To him, perhaps. Not to me. I knew they were a sign of friendship, nothing deeper; but his friendship mattered more than almost anything else in my life. Funny, I'd only realised that over the past week or so, when I was afraid it might have gone for good.

So – I didn't want him as my mentor but I needed him as my friend. And I'd expect any long-term partner of mine to understand that.

116

I just hoped Mark would expect the same of Tamara.

MARK

I drove home from the airport in record time. Tamara felt chilled, so I went straight to the drawing room to light the fire while she had a shower and unpacked. By the time she came downstairs, in just a bathrobe, the room was warming nicely but the Krug was still ice cold.

It was only late afternoon and the evening stretched out ahead of us. We sat on the sofa, drank champagne and chatted for a while about the people and places we had in common.

It didn't take long.

In the silence that followed, I studied her. Black hair, dark eyes, white skin – despite living in India for years. Everything about Tamara was either black or white. No shades of grey; or woodmouse brown, come to that . . .

'Like what you see?' she said, with a provocative pout.

'What do you think?' I leaned forward, cupped her face and kissed her hard, over and over again. Blotting out memories of other lips, other kisses. Feeling, with relief, the familiar heat of physical response.

She brought me expertly to heel, coolly detaching herself from my embrace. I watched as she slipped off her bathrobe and spread it out on the rug in front of the fire. Burnished by the glow of the flames, her body beckoned.

'Come here, Mark. Show me just how much you've missed me.'

And that's exactly what I did.

EMMA

On Saturday afternoon Izzy, John and their tribe came to Hartfield. From upstairs, I saw their Volkswagen people carrier arrive and rushed to the front door, just in time for the children to hurl themselves at me.

I laughed. 'What a noise, I thought the monkeys must have escaped from Chessington Zoo. Now, Grandpa's asleep and you know how cross he gets if he wakes too soon. Go and hide *quietly* in the garden and I'll come and find you.'

The children stampeded off; over by the car, Izzy froze in the act of unfastening Emily from her safety seat.

'But it's almost dark,' she said. 'What if they trip and hurt themselves?'

John appeared from the driver's side. 'Nonsense, it's light enough and they need to use up some of their energy. Anyway, they know that garden like the back of their hand. Hi there, Emma.' He made a quick detour to kiss my cheek on his way to unload the luggage.

Izzy gave a heavy, long-suffering sigh and muttered to herself; I diplomatically bent down to fasten my outdoor shoes. When I straightened up, I found Emily watching me from her mother's arms, her lovely little face still flushed with sleep. Izzy carried her the short distance from car to house and began to download her worries.

'John has no idea about the dangers that lurk in gardens. And I wish he'd parked nearer the house, Emily's probably caught a chill being out in the cold air after that warm car, it only takes a few seconds.' A pause while we kissed, then an anxious look. 'Who's babysitting? John wouldn't let me ring you to find out. I hope it's not that girl with the motorbike, she promised Harry he could sit on it next time she saw him, I'll be ill all evening just thinking about it.'

'I've asked Sarah Perry,' I said, letting Emily tug at my hair.

'The *doctor's* daughter, excellent, I hope she'll contact her father if she's got any concerns, any at all, I'll check she's got his mobile number. How's Dad? Is that aloe vera cream I sent him doing any good?'

'Oh, I shouldn't think so,' I said, 'but it'll do him good to discuss it at great length with you. Now I'd better go and find the kids before they fall into that pit the gardeners dug the other day.'

Her face was a picture. I extracted my hair from Emily's chubby grasp and set off after the children.

'Only joking!' I called over my shoulder. 'And John, if you're taking those bags upstairs, I've put everyone in the usual bedrooms.'

It took all of the next two hours to get Izzy ready to go out, not so much physically as mentally. She grilled me about the babysitter's IQ, fretted that James was sickening for something and generally convinced herself that she'd return from an evening of self-indulgence to find all her children hospitalised. She'd just resigned herself to abandoning them, when I happened to mention that Harriet had been off work with a sore throat and wasn't able to go to Kate's dinner. I might as well have announced the arrival in Highbury of the Black Death.

Izzy took a hasty step away from me. 'Harriet's your PA, she'll have infected you before she went off sick.'

'I'm fine, actually, I never seem to get colds or sore throats.'

'Keep right away from the children and go and gargle with TCP, just in case.'

I glared at her. 'I'm wearing Clive Christian No. 1, no way am I smothering one of the most expensive perfumes in the world with the smell of TCP!'

It was very frustrating that Harriet was unwell. I'd had it all organised: Philip lived on Harriet's side of Highbury, so I'd asked him to pick her up on his way to Randalls and, of course, take her home at the end of the evening. It would be the perfect opportunity for him to make a move. Yesterday, however, I had to tell him that the poor girl was ill. He made sympathetic noises but, when I asked him if I should give Kate his apologies too, he looked at me as though I had two heads. Then I remembered my theory that he was lonely and would no doubt enjoy the company, even if Harriet wasn't there.

So, with Izzy, Harriet and Philip all causing me grief in their different ways, I wasn't in the best of moods on Saturday evening. And it got worse. I dressed in a hurry, then kept wondering if my long dark brown skirt was too tight and my gold strappy top too revealing. All the way to Randalls, Dad and Izzy vied with each other as to who would enjoy the evening least. Finally, although we weren't late, we found Kate and Tom's drive already occupied by a little blue two-seater sports car, which I recognised as Philip's, and a sleek black Mercedes – George Knightley's car, which Mark was using while he was away. John had to park the Volkswagen on the main road, which irritated him no end and consequently made Dad and Izzy more nervous than ever.

Looks-wise, John was a typical Knightley – tall, dark and handsome – but he lacked the easy manner of Mark and his father. I didn't mind that; I knew him well enough to see his reserve for what it was, the character of an introvert. No, what I minded was his behaviour towards Izzy and Dad; he often took Izzy for granted and lost his patience far too quickly with Dad, with the result that they never seemed to relax when he was around. In contrast, Mark brought out the best in them, but dealt firmly with their eccentric little ways.

When it came to me, however, John and Mark were the same. They both treated me like a kid sister, to be fed a wholesome diet of what they called constructive criticism; a diet that didn't seem as if it would ever vary.

Tom was at the door to welcome us and take our coats, waiting with good humour while I helped Dad remove his many layers of outer clothing. I was very fond of Tom. He brought energy and enthusiasm to everything he did; and I'd never heard him say a cross word about anyone, a remarkable achievement in four years of insular village life.

'By the way,' he said to me as we went into the large open-plan living room, 'I had an email from Flynn this morning and you'll be thrilled to know he's—'

At that moment, a squeal from the far corner diverted his attention. Batty, in some sort of fluster as usual.

'Oh, Mother's spectacles! Thank you, Mark, wherever did you find them?' I didn't hear his reply, but it made her titter. 'Goodness, she must have dropped them when she . . .' Her voice rose to a crescendo. 'Mother, here are your specs – no, they're your spare pair, you're wearing your other ones . . . No, it's not George, it's his son Mark,

George is away on a . . . Yes, it was George's car we came in, but Mark was driving it, so kind of him to give us a lift.'

Mark and Tamara had their backs to me. In her high heels she was the same height as him, too tall to need protection from those broad shoulders of his. Her hair hung down to her non-existent hips in a heavy black curtain and, as I watched, he lifted one hand and gently twisted the glossy ends through his fingers. A sensual, intimate gesture; I looked quickly away.

Tom seemed to have completely forgotten the thrilling contents of Flynn's email. 'Come and meet Tamara.' He waved Izzy and John on ahead, then shepherded Dad and me across the room after them.

As Tamara greeted Izzy and John with a polite kiss, I stayed back and studied her face. Impossibly white skin, blood-red lips, dark almond-shaped eyes accentuated with dramatic make-up. A very attractive face, I had to admit; but marred by a 'What the hell am I doing here?' expression, which she made no effort to disguise. And she reminded me of someone, particularly in that slinky black low-cut dress; I just couldn't think who.

Mark introduced us. 'Tamara, this is Henry Woodhouse, Izzy's father. And her sister, Emma.'

The shrewd dark eyes merely glanced at Dad, but sized me up from top to toe. 'Delighted.' She sounded anything but.

'I'm just as delighted,' I said, with a bright smile.

Dad took Tamara's arm. 'Come nearer the fire, my dear, you must be finding England very cold after India.'

She kept her eyes on me. 'Mark.' It could have been a question but she made it a command, as if he was a dog at obedience class.

I noticed him flush slightly. 'I'll join you in a minute, darling, I just need a word with Emma.'

She shrugged and allowed Dad to lead her over to the fireplace. I wondered what had kept Mark by her side for five whole years, apart from her obvious physical appeal; my first impressions were of a woman with no social finesse whatsoever.

I turned to Mark. 'What did you want a word about?'

'Nothing, I just thought Tamara needed to mingle.'

I almost laughed out loud. Watching her with Dad, who seemed to be struggling to make conversation, the word 'mingle' seemed utterly incongruous; she was like a panther toying with its prey. Then I realised who she reminded me of and, this time, I did laugh out loud.

Mark raised one eyebrow. 'What's the joke?'

'You – you don't want to know.'

'Trust me, I do. I need some light relief, I have a feeling this evening's going to be a hard slog.'

I took a deep breath. 'It's just – I didn't know you were bringing Morticia.'

He burst out laughing. 'Oh, Emma!' As Tamara glanced in our direction, he pretended to have a coughing fit, which immediately had Dad looking across as well. When he'd recovered, he grinned at me. 'I remember you being obsessed with the Addams Family at one time. You used to recite what seemed like every show, word for word, it drove us all round the bend.'

'And to think I was desperate to be like Morticia when I grew up.' I let out a long, nostalgic sigh.

'Thank God you're not,' he said sharply.

I was about to ask what he meant when Philip came up to us. He gave Mark a curt nod, then handed me a glass of wine and smiled complacently.

'A little bird told me you prefer white before the meal, Emma. I'm so glad you're here, I was terrified you'd caught what poor Harriet's got.'

Mark excused himself to join Dad and Tamara, while I smiled back at Philip, pleased he couldn't stop himself from mentioning Harriet.

'Poor thing, she's suffering in more ways than one. Dad sent her a couple of his remedies, slippery elm bark tea and his all-time favourite, raw garlic cloves. When she phoned me to ask how often she should take them, I told her to stick to Lemsip! But the worst thing is that she's on her own – all the girls in her house have gone away for the weekend. I don't suppose you could call in tomorrow and check on her? I've got my hands full with my sister and family.'

He looked horrified. 'No, I couldn't, I might catch what she's got. And it's your presentation to the Board on Monday, I don't want to miss that. Plus we need to discuss your budget some time next week, in *considerable* depth.'

For a moment, I was disappointed. Then I decided he was just being sensible; and, to be fair, his commitment to his job was exemplary.

I suddenly realised he'd asked me a question. 'Sorry, what did you say?'

He laughed. 'Don't worry, Emma, I'm finding our conversation equally distracting. I merely asked who looks after *you* when you're ill? I don't suppose Henry's up to it and I couldn't bear to think there's no one taking care of you.'

I stared at him in alarm. I told myself that he was probably thinking of Harriet and feeling frustrated that he couldn't risk going to see her. However, just in case, I resolved to circulate a bit more.

'Fortunately, I never get ill,' I said coolly. 'That reminds me, I'd better go and see how Mrs Bates is. She had a nasty attack of shingles a while ago.'

I hurried off to spend the next ten minutes shouting pleasantries at Old Mother Bates about her state of health. All the time I had the feeling that I was being watched. It was weird, though. Whenever I looked round at Philip, I sensed he'd just that second averted his eyes from meeting mine. And whenever I looked in the other direction, I sensed Mark had just done the same. Or had they been gazing at each other – and I was simply in the way?

Even one of Kate's superb meals didn't improve my mood.

Perhaps it was being opposite Mark and Tamara. She picked at her food and hardly spoke a word. Mark occasionally tried to jolly her out of it, without any noticeable success; she was determined not to enjoy herself.

Or maybe it was seeing Philip enjoying himself far too much. After that first comment about 'poor Harriet', it was as though he never spared her another thought. Again, I justified his behaviour to myself; a sociable man who lived alone had to make the most of these occasions, didn't he?

While Kate served the main course of beef bourguignonne, Tom returned to an earlier subject. 'We've had exciting news today from Flynn – that's my son, he's a TV chef in Australia,' he added, for the benefit of Philip and Tamara. He paused, then said impressively, 'He's coming to Highbury!'

This announcement provoked mixed reactions around the table: gasps of delight from Batty, Dad and Izzy, polite interest from Philip, indifference from Tamara – and from Old Mother Bates, who at least had the excuse that she was hard of hearing. Mark and John exchanged knowing looks.

Tom went on, 'He hasn't given me a date yet, but he's actually in England as we speak. Out of the blue, he got an invitation to cook at The Mulberry Tree, that's a Michelin-starred restaurant over in the West Country apparently. He'll be there for another week or so, then he's coming straight here.'

I glanced at the large photo that had the place of honour on the sideboard; a man's face in close-up – dark red curly hair, crinkly green eyes and a devilish grin. Flynn Churchill, drop-dead gorgeous and, at twenty-eight years old, still un-attached. Tom often joked that he'd not met the right woman – yet.

I allowed myself a little smile of anticipation.

'Of course, his aunt Stella's not best pleased he's come to England,' Kate said. 'But Flynn's got his career to think of, he's meeting with the BBC while he's over here. And I'm sure he'll bring Stella round, in time.'

'I'm sure he will, since she's got a few million to dispose of,' John put in. 'And who could blame him . . . Any more of this amazing beef stuff?'

As Kate dished out second helpings, the conver-sation turned to other matters and Flynn was forgotten. Not by me, however; my thoughts were full of him. To think that, after all these years, he was only a few hours' drive away . . . I paid little attention to what the others were saying, just nodded and smiled and laughed in what I hoped were the right places.

Then, over dessert, the mention of my bête noire, Jane Fairfax, brought me up short.

Saint Jane of Highbury, as I called her, was around the same age as me; but that was all we had in common. Unfortunately, it didn't stop everyone thinking we should be the best of friends and, as children, we were forced to play together whenever she came to stay with Batty, her aunt. Even worse, Jane always seemed to have mastered a new skill, like playing the piano or crocheting coasters. How could I be friends with the girl who outshone me at everything?

Not surprisingly, it was Batty who brought her name into the conversation. 'Lovely gooseberry fool, Kate, a real taste of summer. That's when we last saw dear Jane – my niece, for those of you who don't know, such a lovely girl. Oh, that reminds me, she phoned just before we came out. A tiny favour,' – coy giggle – 'I was going to ask you on Monday, Henry, but it's the Board meeting and there may be other things on your . . . Remember Jane's work placement, in Weymouth, as part of her degree? Well,' – conspiratorial whisper – 'it's ended rather suddenly, she won't say why, but there are nine months left to go and I just wondered . . . ?' She stopped and looked expectantly at Dad.

I guessed what was coming and nearly choked on my gooseberry fool; which, given its perfect consistency, would have been quite an achievement.

Dad seemed perplexed. 'You wondered what, Mary?'

Kate came to Batty's rescue. 'Mary's hoping you can give Jane a work placement, so that she can meet her course requirements.'

'Not that Jane wanted me to ask, you know,' Batty twittered, 'but I offered to, as soon as she . . . And it's rather urgent, although the friends she's lodging with, the Campbells, would love her to stay on with them.'

Dad's face brightened. 'Of course we can find work for Jane. What's she studying? I'm sure you've told me, Mary, but my memory's not what it was.'

'Business Studies, quite a broad course, even some Finance.' Batty simpered at Philip, while I heaved a sigh of relief. Then, 'But her special subject for this year is' – demure look in my direction – 'Marketing.'

I nearly choked again, this time on my wine. Across the table, Mark grinned at me. He knew my opinion of 'dear Jane' and, needless to say, disagreed with it completely.

After that, there was no time for pleasant daydreams about Flynn; I spent the rest of the evening thinking up arguments to keep Saint Jane as far away from Marketing as possible.

Even though it was a Saturday, everyone seemed keen to go home at a respectable hour, no doubt for quite different reasons. Dad, Batty and Old Mother Bates to embark on their various bedtime rituals; Izzy to check on the children; John to watch Match of the Day; Mark and Tamara to make up for lost time in the bedroom; I didn't like to speculate what a lonely bachelor like Philip got up to last thing at night; as for me, I was just longing to curl up with a book.

There was a change of plan, however, when Mark went to start the Mercedes and nothing happened. He tried a few more times, then got out of the car and lifted up the bonnet.

'Father told me the battery plays up sometimes, I'll have a quick look.'

'Not in that new Versace jacket, darling,' Tamara drawled. 'Leave the car alone and call a taxi.' It was the longest speech I'd heard her make all evening.

'No need,' John said. 'I can give you four a lift, the Volkswagen holds seven. Hang on, there are eight of us—'

Philip cut in, his tone unusually assertive. 'I'll take Emma.'

I hesitated, then decided I was the most obvious person. Izzy and Tamara didn't know him and the others would struggle to get in and out of his low sports car or, in Mark's case, to sit comfortably. And maybe I could have a little chat about Harriet on the way home.

'Thank you, Philip,' I said, giving him a dazzling smile.

He grinned back. 'Fantastic, I'll just clear the front seat, won't be long.'

While he rummaged around in his car, Mark said in an undertone, 'Emma, are you sure about this?'

Typical 'Mark knows best' attitude, as if I'd just

accepted a lift from Jack the Ripper. I glared at him. 'Absolutely.'

He said nothing more, but then John took me to one side and muttered, 'I can always come back for you, if you'd rather not go with Elton. He's been eyeing you up all evening, obviously got the hots for you. Mind, you certainly egged him on during dinner, you laughed like a drain at all his crap jokes.'

This was getting silly. 'I laughed at everyone's crap jokes, including yours,' I said haughtily. 'And I'm not a simpleton, don't you think I'd know if Philip fancied me? Believe me, he's not the slightest bit interested.'

John shrugged. 'In that case, I'll leave you to it.'

As Philip opened the car door for me with a flourish, I reflected that people – especially men – would never cease to amaze me. There was John Knightley, a very able Finance Director but hardly what I'd call intuitive, meeting Philip for the first time and thinking he could read him like a balance sheet!

Soon Philip and I were speeding off towards Hartfield. He glanced across at me frequently and grinned, but made no attempt to talk.

I found the silence unnerving. 'Lovely meal, wasn't it?' I said at last. 'Kate's a very – oh Philip, I thought you knew we had to go left there, you've missed it.'

A lay-by came into view; he swerved into it and brought the car to an abrupt halt.

'Yes, best to turn round,' I went on, 'otherwise it's quite a detour – oh no, the engine's cut out.'

He flung off his seat belt and loosened his shirt collar. For a moment, I thought the fan belt must have broken and he was about to substitute his tie.

But I was mistaken. About everything.

It all happened so quickly. He let out a peculiar sort of groan and lunged at me – grabbed my arms – clamped his mouth to mine. Somehow, I twisted out of his clumsy embrace and shrank back against the passenger window, gasping, unable to speak.

In the moonlight, his eyes glittered. 'I know, Emma, you take my breath away too . . . No point wasting time, let's go to my place.' He leered at me as his hand scraped along my thigh. 'My Ikea bed's not called a *Ram*berg for nothing.'

'Get – off – me.' I slapped his hand away.

He smirked. 'Come on, stop acting the prude, you've been leading me on for weeks. When you bent over your tripod and wiggled those hips at me during the photo shoot, I thought I'd died and gone to heaven.'

I stared at him. 'Don't be so bloody ridiculous! You fancy Harriet, not me.'

He gave an unpleasant laugh. 'Harriet? You're mad, what would someone like me see in Harriet? Oh, I'm sure she'd be good for a quick shag, but why would I bother with her when you're giving me all the encouragement I need?'

'Encouragement?' I said, hotly. 'You're the one that's mad, I've never given you *any* encouragement, except where Harriet's concerned.'

'You mean pretending those flowers I gave you were for her? I thought that was all part of your little game.' His lip curled. 'Most of the time you understood me perfectly, I bloody well know you did.'

'Oh yes? Like when?'

'The Board meeting, when I said that you had beauty, class and brains and that you were my real-life inspiration for Victoria's Secret Recipes.'

'But you never actually said who you were talking about, so I—'

He interrupted me, grim-faced. 'And when we were looking at those photos of your sister's family, and you said there were no couples involved in the photo shoot, and I said not yet – you behaved as if you knew I meant you and me. And *then*, when I told you that my idea for the strapline had the name of my ideal woman in it, you said it was glaringly obvious to you!'

'It was,' I said, coldly. 'Harriet's Secret Recipes.'

'For fuck's sake, only Harriet would think it was something *that* obvious. I meant "Emmancipated" – the way I said it was a big enough clue, surely!'

I sat in silence, twisting my hands in my lap. What a fool I'd been, what a blind, self-opinionated fool. And now here I was, alone in a deserted place with a man I knew very little about – and even less than I thought I did – whose advances I'd just rejected. What if things got – out of control?

I took a deep breath. 'Look, Philip, I'm not interested in you and I'm really sorry if you got the impression I was. Please take me home – now, before the others find out I'm not back.'

There was a nerve-racking pause. Then he yanked his seat belt on, bullied the engine into life and reversed the car, at speed, all the way back to the turning he'd supposedly missed. Once again, he drove fast and in silence; but this time he kept his eyes on the road and I made no attempt at conversation. I was trembling, both with relief that he was taking me home and with fear that we wouldn't get there in one piece. Only when he stopped the car outside Hartfield, in a squeal of brakes, did I relax.

I forced myself to look at him. 'Let's be sensible about this, Philip. We've both made a mistake, but I hope we can still work together in a profes-sional way. I won't breathe a word about this to anyone and I'll make sure Harriet sees you as nothing more than a work colleague from now on.'

'Great,' he said, glowering at the windscreen.

Getting out of the car in my long tight skirt was tricky. Needless to say, the attentive Philip who'd helped me into it was nowhere to be seen; I'd barely shut the passenger door when he drove off, tyres screeching. I stayed outside for a few minutes, taking big gulps of the fresh night air, fighting back tears, cursing my stupidity.

I'd completely misjudged Philip Elton. When it came to women, he wanted the 'safe and lucrative' option – exactly as Know-it-all Knightley had predicted.

CHAPTER 5

STUFFING

MARK

Since Sunday morning was dry and sunny, and the autumn colours at their best, I decided I'd walk to Randalls to have a look at the car.

Tamara opted for a lie-in, especially when she heard where I was going. She'd been less than impressed by the Westons' dinner party, dismissing Mary, Mrs Bates and Henry as 'a bunch of old women, especially Henry', Tom, Kate, John and Izzy as 'too boring for words', Philip as 'a waste of space' and Emma as 'quite the surprise package'. When I probed a little further into this last comment, she said she'd imagined Emma to be more like her nickname and refused to say more.

As I strode along the bridleway, I realised how good it felt to be on my own. With Tamara's frequent demands, the last few days had been a bit of a strain . . .

Ahead of me, a twig snapped. A small boy came hurtling along the path and skidded into my legs. My nephew, Mark.

'Up!' he said, with the supreme confidence of a three-year-old.

I grinned down at him. 'Hello to you, too. Who are you out with on such a beautiful morning?'

He pointed to a woman in red trousers some distance behind him; as she approached, I saw that it was Emma, with Emily in the backpack. Her trousers were tight-fitting, leaving little to the imagination. A bit like that skirt she'd worn to the Westons' . . .

'Up!' Mark said again. 'Please.'

I switched my thoughts firmly away from last night. 'OK then, one – two – three.' I swung him onto my shoulders and he clapped his hands in delight.

'Aunty Emma, look, I'm the king of the castle!'

'And who's the dirty rascal?' she said, as she reached us.

'Uncle Mark.'

We all laughed; except Emily, who surveyed me gravely with her big hazel eyes, so like her aunt's.

Mark whispered in my ear, 'Are you coming to Grandpa's to see us?'

'No, I'm going to see my poorly car. I could call in on my way home, though.'

'We'll turn back now and walk as far as Hartfield with you,' Emma said.

We set off side by side, falling easily into step with each other.

'Izzy and I are taking the children to visit the Bateses as soon as they get back from the nine o'clock service,' she went on. 'But John and Dad will be in, if you decide to drop by. Or you could bring Tamara for lunch, we're having roast pork and all the trimmings, there's plenty to spare. You never know, she might enjoy it.'

'Thank you, but I've booked a table at The Hare and Hounds.'

'You could always cancel it.'

'Best to leave the arrangements as they are, if you don't mind.'

We walked in silence for a while, Mark crooning to himself and Emily tugging at Emma's hair. Despite the slightly awkward conversation about lunch, I felt at peace with the world. And I had a strange, random thought: to anyone that didn't know us, we would seem the perfect family, out for a Sunday morning stroll, happy as can be.

Or maybe not. When I glanced across at Emma, she was frowning and biting her lip. I had a silly urge to take her in my arms, but I didn't; bit tricky with a child on my back.

Instead I asked, keeping my tone casual, 'Did you get home all right last night?'

'Obviously, why wouldn't I?'

Her blush and the defensive note in her voice were a dead giveaway. So Elton had tried it on, the little shit.

I cleared my throat and went for a less direct approach. 'You know, Emily, there's no need for your aunt to overreact like that, I just had a feeling something embarrassing might have happened. Of course, it can't have, because she prides herself on being able to read people like a book—'

'I got a new book,' Mark put in. ''Bout Mog.'

Emma sighed. 'Yes, and guess how many times we've read it, Uncle Mark? At least ten, and that was just before breakfast. But don't let me interrupt your lecture to Emily, I bet she's finding it riveting.'

I was pleased to see that my tactics were working; she was already looking more relaxed. 'As I was saying, Emily, your aunt thinks people can be judged by their covers, like books. I'm afraid she still has a lot to learn.'

Emma gave a rueful smile. 'You see, Emily, Uncle Mark's lived so long in the big bad world that he thinks he knows everything. But he has a point, I do *occasionally* make the wrong call. So, when you grow up, make sure you're twice as clever and only half as conceited as your aunt and you'll be fine. Isn't that right, Uncle Mark?'

I reached across, tickled Emily under her chubby little chin and watched her rosy cheeks dimple. 'For once, little one, your aunt's talking sense,' I said softly, 'and I can't argue with her.'

Then Mark yelled, 'There's Grandpa's gate!'

He was right; we'd arrived at the arched wrought iron gate that led into the Hartfield garden. I lifted him down and he ran towards it, whooping loudly.

Emma turned to me. 'See you tomorrow, then.'

I grinned. 'That's right, your big presentation. I'm looking forward to it.'

'So was I, until last night . . . Still, that's a problem of my own making and I'll just have to sort it.'

And, with a defiant lift of her chin, she followed little Mark through the gate.

EMMA

To all intents and purposes, this would be a repeat of the last Board meeting: same place, same people, probably even sitting in the same seats. Only Philip and I knew that something had changed. It seemed that he couldn't hide his animosity, however. As soon as I entered the room, he turned his back on me and continued talking to Terry. Even when Terry nodded and smiled in my direction, Philip refused to acknowledge me.

Harriet had struggled into work, looking washed out and smelling strongly of garlic. We'd prepared the boardroom together and I'd set up my laptop and the new projector I'd ordered immediately after the last meeting. Harriet had also put printouts of my slides, together with a selection of photos from the photo shoot, into smart information packs to accompany my PC presentation.

As I flicked through my copy one last time, I

spotted that she'd spelt 'Highbury' as 'Highbary' on one of the slides.

'Slide ten,' – I waved the page in front of her – 'just change the "a" to a "u" on the disk version, please, and reprint it for the packs, then bring everything along to the boardroom.'

And I'd left her to get on with it, otherwise I would have been late. After my little mishap at the last Board meeting and Mark's reprimand about checking my work thoroughly, I was determined today would go perfectly. Or as perfectly as it could, given the bruised ego of the Finance Director.

At last Harriet came in and Dad started the meeting. I contributed very little to the discussions around the directors' reports and kept especially quiet during Philip's. Then it was my turn. I switched on the projector, took the disk from Harriet and inserted it into my laptop. The information packs would keep until the end; I didn't want any distractions from my pitch.

It started off well. The first nine slides were a summary of my research proposal for repositioning Betty's Best as Harriet's Secret Recipes. I stressed the requirement for some early primary research, using a concept board approach with focus groups of customers and non-customers. I explained that I wanted to do as much as possible in-house rather than use agencies, to minimise cost. I mentioned the need for an initial strapline, but didn't refer to Philip's suggestion. Finally,

I circulated a sample concept board, featuring a scenario of Harriet planning an informal lunch for her girlfriends, and showed how it would be used in the focus groups.

There were murmurs of approval round the table, with one exception.

Philip gave me a nasty look before turning to Dad. 'As I've already said, Henry, we're going to have to cut back on expenditure and this proposal's the sort of amateurish initiative that we may have to drop completely.'

'I take your point,' Dad said mildly, 'but at the moment Emma's well within the outline budget you agreed with her. If we have to cut back, there may be more obvious savings to be made in other areas.' His tone became sharp. 'And the word "amateurish" seems rather harsh. Mark, do you think we need some professional agency input here?'

'Not vital at this stage, and certainly not if you want to keep within such a modest research budget.' Mark paused and fixed his gaze on Philip. 'I think Emma's practical, low-cost approach is ideal for the circumstances and I'm surprised the Finance Director isn't being more supportive.'

Philip flushed and looked down at his papers. I decided to wrap up my presentation as quickly as possible.

'OK, I just wanted to talk briefly about Christmas.' I held up my hand as Jon started muttering about his production schedule. 'Not this year's, which I know we planned months ago, but next year's. This is a simple idea that our competitors are already doing and it doesn't involve any major production changes.' I clicked onto slide ten. 'Introducing—'

I broke off in dismay. Harriet had certainly changed the 'a' to a 'u'; trouble was, she'd done it in the wrong word. Instead of 'The Highbury Hamper', the slide read 'The Highbary Humper'.

My cheeks burned. I closed my eyes, but I couldn't shut out the howls of laughter from Jon and Terry, or Philip's angry exclamations. Of course, he'd think this was a dig at his behaviour on Saturday night, even a deliberate attempt to expose him . . .

I opened my eyes and looked straight at Mark. His expression was blank, but I knew he was disappointed in me.

'It was a last-minute change,' I said in a small voice. 'I know I should have checked it, but I didn't.'

Harriet added, with a loud sniff, 'It's my fault really, I was in too much of a rush.'

'What's a humper?' Batty asked brightly.

Silence. Then Dad swallowed and said, 'I believe the expression "to hump" means to, um, have sexual intercourse.'

Philip puffed himself up like a bullfrog. 'You see, Henry, I know she's your daughter but this is what I mean by amateurish, she's lowering the tone of the Board meeting. And I can assure you there's no such person as the Highbury Humper, it's all in her overactive imagination!'

I stared at him, unable to believe my ears. This was totally unprofessional, a personal attack. And how could I defend myself without revealing what was behind it?

'I'm sure there are as many humpers in Highbury as anywhere else,' Mark said drily. 'Anyway, this was obviously meant to say "The Highbury Hamper". A typo, that's all. Easily done, Harriet, especially when you're not feeling well. It sounds like a great idea, Emma – why don't you tell us what you had in mind?'

I gave him a wan smile and moved on to the next slide, a list of the products I envisaged for the hamper, followed by the seasonal distribution channels I'd researched in addition to our usual outlets. I dealt with Jon's questions and provided additional facts and figures to Mark and Terry, all with a confidence I certainly didn't feel.

Because I was already visualising the damage a resentful Philip could do to my credibility at Highbury Foods. And there was only one person I could turn to for help: The Tormentor.

MARK

After the Board meeting, I went to find Emma. She wasn't in her room, however, or with Henry;

145

so I returned to Donwell Organics where it seemed everyone had been storing up their problems for me.

I left the office promptly at five, to make sure the house would be warm when Tamara returned from her shopping trip in London. As I finished lighting the fire in the drawing room, the doorbell rang. I knew it wasn't Tamara; she had a key and, anyway, she'd only just phoned to say she was at the station, waiting for a taxi to Donwell.

It was Emma, still in her work clothes, the same beige suit she'd had on when I found her in the boardroom that September morning – the first time I saw her as Emma, not Mouse . . .

'Er, come in,' I said. 'Tamara's not here, but she'll be back any moment.' I was warning myself as much as telling her.

'I'm not staying.' She paused. 'I wouldn't have come, except I couldn't get you on your mobile—'

'The battery's flat, I've just put it on charge.'

'Oh. Anyway, I'm here because – look, I need a mentoring meeting as soon as possible.'

'Any particular reason?' As if I didn't already know the answer.

She was finding the hall floor fascinating. 'Yes. It's – it's Philip. You saw how horrible he was to me today, and how badly I handled it, and—'

'If the problem's what I think it is, that he made a pass at you on Saturday night and you rejected

146

him, then yes, that's a tricky situation. But I'm not sure it's within my mentoring brief.' In fact, I'd bloody well make sure it wasn't.

'The – the details of Saturday night aren't within your brief, but how I get on with him as a work colleague is, surely?' She lifted pleading eyes to mine.

I said nothing.

She went on, 'I wouldn't ask if I wasn't desperate. Highbury Foods is my job for life, as it were. Philip can move on – but I can't. And we still need to discuss your observations from the photo shoot, they're probably more relevant than ever.'

I gave an exasperated sigh. 'I know, but can't it wait for a week or so?'

'Until Tamara's gone?' Her voice was edgy.

'No – actually, yes.'

'On that basis, you mustn't have got much work done in India.'

I flushed. 'This is entirely different. We haven't seen each other for six weeks and she's only here for ten days. We're determined to make the most of it.'

Her lips tightened. 'I'll bet. So, when you can spare a moment from making the most of it, give me a ring and we'll fix up a meeting for next week.'

I knew I'd let her down, but I also knew I couldn't face a mentoring meeting right now, especially if its focus was another man's infatuation with her.

'Next week's fine,' I said gently. 'By then, you know, the Philip thing may have started to resolve itself, whereas today he was probably still a bit raw from Saturday night.' I couldn't resist adding, 'I did warn you about getting a lift home with him. And before, about him not being interested in Harriet.'

'Yes, you were right all along, while I was about as perceptive as that bloody doorpost. I can't believe how stupid I've been!'

To my horror, her eyes filled with tears. I couldn't understand why she was getting so emotional, unless . . .

I cleared my throat. 'Emma, what did he – what happened exactly?'

She looked away. 'It – it was more what might have happened. We were on a quiet road, and he was so surprised when I wouldn't . . . And then humiliated and – and angry. I didn't think he'd push his luck, but you're never completely sure about someone, are you?' She let out a long, shuddering breath. 'Oh Mark, I was so relieved when he took me back to Hartfield.'

How right it felt to draw her close. Stroke her hair. Be there for her . . .

The front door swung open and Tamara came in, laden with Harrods bags. When she saw us, she shut the door with a vicious kick.

I let Emma go and smiled at Tamara. 'That's good timing, darling, I'm just about to warm something up for dinner.'

148

'So I see,' she said, with a venomous look at Emma.

'We've been discussing our next mentoring session—' I began.

'I'd better go,' Emma cut in, drying her eyes with the back of her hand. 'Dad'll be getting anxious, I said I'd only be away twenty minutes.'

Tamara arched one perfectly plucked eyebrow. 'Just a quickie, was it?'

I glared at her, then turned to Emma. 'I'll ring you tomorrow, when I've checked my diary.'

'Thanks,' she said quietly. ''Bye, then. 'Bye, Tamara.'

'Goodbye, Mouse,' Tamara said, with a sneer. 'I can call you that, can't I? Or is it only Mark who's allowed to use your little pet name?'

Emma blushed. 'No, feel free.'

She avoided my eye and almost ran out of the house. I made to go after her, but checked myself. Tamara stood watching me, her face taut with anger. Then a car door slammed, shattering the silence, and we heard Emma start the engine and drive off.

Immediately, Tamara threw her bags down on the floor and stormed into the family room. I followed, determined to clear the air. She switched on the PC and waited for it to boot up, scowling and drumming her long red fingernails on the desk.

I folded my arms and leaned against the door. 'What was all that about?'

149

'You tell me.'

'How can I, when I don't know what you're getting at?'

'I walk in on you and her, and your hands are all over her, and you're doing that thing with her hair that you always do to me when you're feeling horny – and you say you don't know what I'm getting at?' She gave a scornful laugh.

Were my hands all over her? Was I doing that thing with her hair? I felt the blood drain from my face. 'You're reading too much into this. She was upset about a problem at work and I was giving her a hug, nothing more.' I went towards the desk. 'There was absolutely no need to embarrass her like that.'

'She wouldn't have been embarrassed if she had nothing to hide.'

'Don't be so ridiculous! She thinks of me as an old friend, that's all.'

'Maybe it's you who has something to hide, then.'

'What the hell does that mean?'

She slid open the drawer beside her, took out a page torn from a magazine and held it up, just out of reach, as if to taunt me.

'Found this when I was looking for some printer paper this morning. Recognise it?'

'Of course I do. So?'

'So why's it here?'

I heard myself blustering, 'For God's sake, I'm mentoring her. That photo tells me a lot about her public image, something she clearly needs to work on.'

'And your mentoring file is – where?'

I paused. 'In the office.'

'Ah. But you keep this charming photo at home. Presumably it's normally at your bedside, nicely to hand, but not required while I'm here.'

'If you're insinuating what I think you are, then you're—'

'And the way you were eyeing her up on Saturday night, was that in the name of mentoring too?'

'I wasn't eyeing her up.' Was I?

'Every time I looked at you, you were staring at her.'

I shrugged. 'If I was looking at her more than usual, it was because I thought Elton was eyeing her up.'

'Funny, you didn't look at *him* very much, which makes it a bit difficult to know what he's doing, doesn't it? You see, Mark, I'm putting two and two together. Ever since I arrived, you've been – different. As if your mind's on something, or someone, else. And now I know who.'

I took a deep breath. 'Let's go into the drawing room and discuss this in comfort.'

In one fluid movement, she pressed herself against me, her voice a husky whisper. 'Mmmm, that depends, darling. If it's in front of the fire, with no clothes on – you know I'm up for that sort of discussion. Talking's such a waste of your gorgeous mouth, I always say.'

I shook her off, took a step back. 'No, for once let's talk properly. About us. About whether there's any future in our relationship.'

Shit, wasn't that the phrase Emma had used in that heartless little note to Rob?

Her eyes narrowed. 'You're serious, aren't you?' After a brief pause she said, 'Well, I'm not spending the whole night discussing all that crap and going round in effing circles. I can find out what I need to know right now. I'm going to ask you a question and I expect an honest answer, OK?'

'OK,' I said, warily.

She hesitated. Then, 'Can you picture me living here, at Donwell Abbey, with you, in the years ahead?'

Relief flooded through me. The question I'd feared hadn't been about her at all . . . But I needed to consider my answer carefully; I owed her that, at least. So I thought about the past few days and how it had felt to be here with her on my own. Whenever she'd stayed previously, Father and Saffron had been around, filling the silences, fuelling our sense of togetherness.

But this time there'd been no distractions, no disguise. Away from the heady expat social life of India, I realised we had very little in common. Five years of wild partying, exotic holidays, good sex – and not much else.

And yet I couldn't bring myself to say the word 'no'; such a stark epitaph. Instead, I gave a barely perceptible shake of my head.

She smiled, but her eyes were empty. 'I thought as much.' She squared her shoulders. 'I'm going upstairs to start packing. Once that stupid PC's up and running, I'll look up the next available flight. Don't try and change my mind, you'll be wasting your time. We've already wasted five years, haven't we?'

'Don't say that, it hasn't been—'

'And here's your precious photo.'

Before I could stop her, she tore the photo of Emma into little pieces and threw them at me. We both watched in silence as they fluttered to the floor; then she stalked out of the room.

I crouched down and picked up the pieces, one by one, cradling them in my hand. The last piece was her face, a face that I could picture only too well living here, with me, in the years ahead.

I crushed the pieces in my fist and walked slowly into the drawing room. The fire was well ablaze and I stood in front of it, comforted by its warmth and light; yet, at the same time, disturbed by recent memories . . .

Who had I really been making love to, here on the rug – and upstairs, in my bed?

It was all so obvious. I'd spent the last few days in some sort of denial; even the normally thick-skinned Tamara had detected that. Denial of our crumbling relationship. Denial of my growing fascination with someone else; someone who thought of me as at best a friend, at worst a boring old fart.

I unclenched my fingers and let the pieces fall into the hungry flames.

EMMA

These days Dad was far less receptive to discussing work matters at home, which I took as yet another sign that he was ready for retirement. So I saved the subject of Saint Jane for our weekly one-to-one on the morning after the Board meeting.

I came straight to the point. 'Giving Jane a work placement in Marketing will cause me big problems. First, I'll have to spend time I can't afford, bringing her up to speed with my ideas for the research project. Second, she won't have anything like the thorough grounding in marketing theory I got at Harvard, so she'll only be able to do basic stuff. And last but not least, Harriet can barely cope with the work you and I give her, let alone any extra. I'm having second thoughts about taking her on permanently.'

Dad nodded gloomily. 'Yes, she's a lovely girl, but – oh, if only Kate would come back!'

I ignored this and went on, 'And I don't see why we need to help Jane anyway. She got herself into this mess, she can get herself out of it.'

'Now, darling, Mary's asked me a favour and I can't refuse, she's one of my oldest friends *and* my bridge partner.' He winced and clutched at his stomach. 'Must make some more peppermint tea, such a nuisance having to do it myself, but I'm still suffering repercussions from Saturday night.'

'Aren't we all?' I said, under my breath. I certainly was with Philip; and I suspected Mark was with Tamara – you could have cut the atmosphere between them last night with a knife. I went on, in a louder tone, 'If you hadn't sent Harriet home yesterday and told her to stay there until she was better, she'd be here to make your tea. In the meantime, the work's piling up, and that's even before you've hired Jane Fairfax.' I paused to let this sink in. 'If Harriet's not back tomorrow, we'll have to find another temp for a few days to get up to date – a cost we can easily avoid.'

He sighed. 'I suppose she could come back, but we'd all need to wear breathing masks, like the ones John used when he sanded those doors down in their last house—'

'Dad, please! If she comes back this week, I'll keep her with me, I won't let her anywhere near you.' I bit my lip; that meant I'd have plenty of opportunity to tell her about Philip.

As if he could read my mind, Dad said, 'And now Philip's going away just when he's meant to be working on next year's budgets.'

This was news to me, especially as I'd found a

snotty email from him in my inbox this morning, hassling me for some figures by tomorrow.

'Where's he going?' I asked, hoping for Outer Mongolia on a one-way ticket.

'To Bristol, on a training course. He claims he told me about it ages ago, activity-based costing or some such nonsense. He's back in the office on Friday, but he'll probably be so caught up in newfangled ideas that he won't be able to concentrate on his priorities.'

Unlike Dad, I was relieved; the less Philip and I – and Philip and Harriet – had to do with each other at the moment, the better.

Then a wonderful thought occurred to me. 'You know, if Jane *has* to come here, she could work in Finance rather than Marketing. Philip's been saying he needs an assistant and it could make all the difference to him getting the budgets out promptly.'

His eyes lit up. 'Good idea, darling, I'll give Mary a call and see what she thinks.' He dialled Batty's extension. 'Quick question, Mary – oh? All right then.' He replaced the receiver. 'She says I must be psychic, she was about to pop along and see me about something extremely urgent.'

He'd hardly finished speaking when Batty burst in, panting.

'Ah, you're here as well, Emma. Good, that saves me a journey.'

Instead of hovering at the door as she usually did, she settled herself on a chair; I knew then that the 'something extremely urgent' was nothing more than a juicy piece of gossip.

She lowered her voice, although there was no one else around. 'Have either of you heard from Mark recently?'

'Why do you ask?' I said, wondering what she could possibly know about him that I didn't.

'Well, Mother had to go to the doctor's this morning, and I couldn't take her because I had Pam Goddard coming in for a little review meeting about . . . So I got Jack Thomas along, you know, from Aardvark Taxis, he's related to Doreen Davies in our Purchasing department, such a nice . . . Anyway, he said he had a call last night from Donwell Abbey and – guess what?'

'They wanted a taxi?' Dad said, tentatively.

She tittered. 'Oh, yes, that goes without saying. *But* . . . the taxi was just for Tamara *and* she had all her luggage with her *and* he had to take her to Gatwick. She must have gone back to India, that's almost a week early.'

'A business crisis perhaps,' Dad said. 'I can't remember what she said she did, but it sounded very important.'

Her eyes gleamed. 'That's what I thought, but Jack said she swore at Mark when he tried to help with the bags. Must be a lovers' tiff, mustn't it?'

I recalled Tamara's reaction when she'd found me at Donwell. At the time, I'd dismissed it as

157

natural malevolence combined with a hard day's shopping. Now I wondered if her crazy suspicions had come between her and Mark.

I merely said, 'I'm aware that they had a little problem, but of course I would never dream of discussing it with Mark.'

Her face fell. 'Wouldn't you? Oh, well . . . Now, Henry, what did you want to ask me?'

'Jane's work placement.' He paused. 'Would a role in Finance meet her requirements?'

She gasped. 'Goodness, I'm afraid that wouldn't do at all. Much as I like Philip, I couldn't bear to think of dear Jane closeted with him day in, day out. You never know what might happen, he's got such a shifty . . . No, it has to be Marketing if you don't mind, Henry. That's what Jane's specialising in after all, did I tell you she got top marks in her . . . ? And I know she and Emma will love working together, they've always got on so well.'

'That's settled, then,' Dad said, with a helpless look at me.

I got abruptly to my feet. 'If you'll both excuse me, I've got lots to do.'

I made it all the way back to my office before I gave vent to my frustration. 'That old bat knows exactly which buttons to push with Dad! And as for dear bloody Jane—' I grabbed my car keys. It would do me good to get out of this place for half an hour – and with any luck I could kill two birds with one stone.

Five minutes later I was at Donwell Organics, making sure the Mercedes was in its usual parking space; so far, so good. I breezed into Reception and announced that I had an appointment with Mark. The girl rang Cherry and I could tell from her nervous glances in my direction that there was a problem.

'Shall I speak to Cherry?' I said coolly. The girl handed me the receiver with obvious relief.

'Hi, it's Emma, didn't Mark mention our mentoring meeting? . . . Yes, we only arranged it last night, he must have forgotten to let you know . . . No, don't do that, I'll surprise him.'

I entered his office without a sound. He was standing looking out of the window, hands clasped behind his back, fiddling with his watch.

'Hello there,' I said.

He whirled round, his eyes wide and his face pale despite his tan, as if he'd seen a ghost.

'Sorry if I gave you a fright,' I went on, 'I just had to come and find out if it's true.'

His voice was a hoarse whisper. 'If what's true?'

'That you and Tamara have split up.'

He flinched, then turned away. 'God, I'd forgotten what this place is like, how there's no sodding privacy. Don't tell me, this morning you somehow bumped into the taxi driver . . . Probably at Highbury Foods, when he was dropping off his wife's cousin's mother-in-law who just happens to be one of your employees . . . He couldn't help mentioning that he took Tamara to the airport late last night and of course you both jumped to the conclusion that we'd split up.' He gave a sardonic laugh. 'One other thing, have you broadcast it to the whole village yet, or are you seeing if there's a perfectly innocent explanation first?'

Poor Mark, he was obviously devastated by the break-up. I crossed the room, put my arms round his waist and hugged him.

'Tell me about it,' I said. 'After all, that's what friends are for.'

For a split second he let me hold him, just as I'd let him hold me last night. Then he said brusquely, 'Thanks, but no thanks', and shook me off, gently but firmly. He sat down at his desk and started leafing through a neat pile of post, evidently unimportant until now.

I followed him and perched on the edge of the desk. 'So have you split up?'

'Yes.'

'I'm sorry.'

He yanked a mind-numbingly thick document from the pile and turned the pages absently. 'Actually, it's been in the offing for some time.'

'Really?' I paused in surprise, then went on, 'It can still hurt, though. I remember when I finished with Piers, and then Scott, I was ever so upset – even though it was absolutely the right thing to do. And I hadn't been with them for anything like as long as you've been with Tamara.' I added wistfully, 'D'you know, it's been over two months since I even kissed a man, let alone—'

'For God's sake!' He put his head in his hands. After a few seconds, he looked up at me and frowned. 'Sorry, don't think I can cope with hearing about your sex life right now. Or anyone else's, for that matter.'

'No, I'm the one who should apologise, it was very insensitive of me. But, in case you're wondering, Saturday night doesn't count because I didn't kiss Philip back.' I pulled a face. 'Which sort of brings me to our mentoring meeting, you were going to ring me today with a date. Now that you've, um, got more time on your hands, how about this week?'

He sighed and looked at his PC screen. 'My diary's full, meetings from this afternoon onwards, I'm afraid.'

I gave him an encouraging smile. 'If office hours are no good, what about after work?'

'I've already booked something up for the next two evenings, made some phone calls first thing this morning. And Thursday's our Board meeting, that always involves dinner.'

'Friday?'

He hesitated. Then, 'I'm at Ashridge. Alumni dinner, with a speaker.'

I leaned forward. 'Anyone of interest?'

'No one mainstream, you won't have heard of him.' He busied himself with the post again, apparently engrossed by something on an Inland Revenue letterhead.

'Have you, er, got a spare ticket?'

Another sigh. 'If you mean, was Tamara coming with me – then, yes, she was.'

'So why don't I come instead?' I said eagerly. 'You wanted to take me there to look at market research reports, remember? We could have our mentoring meeting at the same time.'

'I don't think so.'

'Please, Mark.' I reached across the desk and covered his hand with mine.

He snatched his hand away. 'No, Emma. Another time maybe.'

Something inside me snapped. 'You made a commitment to mentor me, but it's – it's almost as though you're trying to wriggle out of it!' Before Saturday, the very suggestion would have been music to my ears; whereas now . . .

He got up, crossed to the window and stared out at whatever he'd found so absorbing when I arrived. 'I'm not. I just don't think taking you to Ashridge is a good idea at the moment.'

'On the contrary, from my point of view the timing's bloody perfect. The research would be very useful before I do the focus groups and, as I've already told you, on the mentoring front I need advice about Philip, urgently.'

He kept his back to me and his tone was cold and clipped. 'The answer's still no.'

'We'll see about that,' I muttered, under my breath.

And I left without another word.

MARK

There was no way I was spending time on my own with Emma in my present frame of mind. Especially at Ashridge, a former stately home in a beautiful wooded setting; a very romantic environment, which I'd been hoping would revitalise my feelings for Tamara. Although it was barely an hour's drive away if there were no hold-ups on the M25, I'd arranged for us to stay overnight . . .

Tamara emailed me early on Wednesday to say she'd been to my flat in Mumbai, cleared out her belongings and returned everything I'd left at her place. It looked as though she'd already moved on.

So had I, as she'd so bitterly pointed out on Monday night. But ever since then I'd been tormenting myself; not about what I'd left behind with Tamara, but about what I wanted to move to with Emma, however ridiculous that seemed in my more rational moments.

Her visit to my office was a wake-up call, however. When I realised that she'd come as a friend and not for any other reason, I knew I had to stop fantasising and get on with my life – which, in the short term, would consist of work and not much else. After a week or two, I was sure I'd be able to continue mentoring her. Just not at the moment.

I spent Wednesday morning preparing my presentation for the next day's Board meeting, thirty odd slides on Donwell Organics' progress towards achieving its strategic objectives. I was just eating a sandwich at my desk when the phone rang. As Cherry was at lunch, I answered it.

'Knightley.'

'Mark?'

'Henry, good to hear from you.' I knew better than to ask, 'How are you?'

'I've got a little favour to ask.' He hesitated. 'Emma says you've got a spare ticket for a dinner at Ashridge this Friday?'

So now Henry was angling for an invitation. I smiled to myself; taking him would be an entirely different challenge, but one I felt far better prepared for.

'Yes,' I said. 'It was going to be for Tamara—'

'Ah yes, sorry to hear about you two. I imagine the time of year had something to do with it, our English autumn must have been a terrible shock to her system. Do you know, I think she might have caught a chill on Saturday night? I'm sure you'll be able to resolve any little differences once you're back in India with her.'

I steered the conversation firmly away from Tamara and me. 'You were saying, about Ashridge?'

'Ashridge?'

'The dinner on Friday.'

'It's the speaker I'm particularly interested in. I believe it's Charles Durham talking about sustainable and ethical growth in the food and drink industry, a subject very dear to my heart.'

I wondered where he'd got his information from. I couldn't imagine him surfing the Ashridge website, given that he didn't even have a PC in his office. Not that it mattered; the main thing was that I would certainly have a much more relaxing evening than if I took Emma.

'It's dear to mine as well,' I said. 'And I've heard he's rather controversial, so I'm looking forward to a lively debate with you on the drive home.'

He chuckled. 'My dear boy, the spare ticket's not for *me*, you know I don't go out at night if I can help it. It's for Emma, of course. She tells me she's been fascinated by Charles Durham's work for a long time and it would be a dream come true to go and hear him speak.'

'Are you saying you want me to take *Emma* to Ashridge on Friday?' I said heavily.

'Yes, please. And since you're a bit behind with the mentoring, you can do some of that as well, can't you? As she says, you may be one of our oldest friends, but business is business all the same.'

EMMA

Harriet returned to work on Wednesday and I decided to tell her about Philip as soon as a suitable opportunity came along.

With this in mind, I took her out to lunch at Chez Pierre, a smart little restaurant in Crossingley. I had plenty of openings to discuss Philip; in fact, he was the main topic of conversation throughout our meal. Over the wild boar pâté, she wondered what he might be doing in Bristol. Next, the sole Véronique reminded her that he raved about the fish in beer batter at The Ploughman. Then, as we enjoyed a large bowl of profiteroles each, she confided that his behaviour towards me at the Board meeting was due to his star sign, which she believed was Virgo. When I asked her to explain, she told me that his horoscope for Monday had predicted 'a cosmic clash with a feisty female work colleague'.

By the time coffee was served, however, I felt I couldn't delay any longer.

I took a deep breath. 'Harriet, I've got something really awful to tell you.'

She clattered her elegant little bone china cup down on its saucer. 'Is it about Rob? Is he going out with someone else?'

'No, it's not about *him*, why on earth would you think—?' I broke off, took another deep breath and tried again. 'It's Philip. It seems we've been – mistaken about him.'

Her jaw dropped. 'He's gay, isn't he? Trace says these days most of the shaggable ones are.'

I thought of Saturday night and suppressed a shudder. 'He's certainly not gay.' I looked her straight in the eye. 'He doesn't fancy you. It's me he's been after, all along.'

She stared at me, a strange glassy stare, and her face turned a peculiar whitish green.

'If it's any consolation,' I added gently, 'I'm pretty sure he doesn't fancy me now.'

Then, to my dismay – and that of everyone else in the restaurant – she lurched to her feet and said in a loud voice, 'I think I'm going to be sick.'

I held my napkin to her mouth and bundled her into the Ladies, just in time. As I stood outside the cubicle listening to her throwing up the entire contents of her stomach, I decided it was as though she was cleansing herself of the excesses I'd been feeding her – Philip's supposed infatuation as much as Pierre's cooking.

Eventually, the retching stopped.

I tapped on the cubicle door. 'Would you like me to take you home?'

'Yes, please, but only so I can get changed.' Her voice wobbled. 'I'm coming back to work.'

'Oh, Harriet, there's no need, just take the afternoon off—'

'No, I'd rather be in the office with you than home alone.'

I wasn't sure that was meant as a compliment, but I didn't argue. While she washed her face, I went to pay the bill and fetch our things.

On the way to her house, she asked the question I was dreading. 'How did you find out about – about all this?'

I sighed and launched into edited highlights of my journey home with Philip. I left out his insulting remarks about her, of course, and my fears for my safety, and finished with an apology.

'I'm so sorry, I should have realised what was going on right from the start. And I can't forgive myself for misleading you and building your hopes up.'

'You didn't do it on purpose,' she said sadly. 'You were just being nice. No one else would have believed that someone like him could fancy someone like me.'

As I waited outside Harriet's house, I decided she was behaving very sensibly about the whole thing. If I ever wanted to acquire a sort of child-like simplicity, Harriet Smith would make a great role model. Then I remembered who I was. Like it or not, I would never get away with childlike simplicity; the name Emma Woodhouse was synonymous with sophisticated complexity.

But I could take some learnings from this experience, especially around self-awareness. I reached for my personal organiser and set myself three little goals: to take no one at face value ever again; to focus on completing the Harriet's Secret Recipes research project; and to stop match-making. Which would be a real shame because there was a new solicitor at Thrayles, our legal advisors, who might suit Harriet very nicely.

Back in the office, I had some final words of wisdom for Harriet. 'I think Philip's unprofessional behaviour at the Board meeting is just the beginning. My advice – not that you have to take it, of course – is to keep well out of his way.'

She shook her head. 'No need, I've just checked

his horoscope for the next month and he's entering a period of harmony and growth in his personal relationships.' She gave a trembling smile. 'You realise what that means, Emma? I've still got a chance with him after all!'

My heart sank. Getting Harriet to face reality was going to be harder than I'd thought. I could only hope that Philip would indirectly help me out – by being as obnoxious as possible.

MARK

I called at Hartfield on my way home after dinner with the Board – against my better judgement, but I needed to finalise arrangements for Ashridge with Emma. Although I could have phoned her, I decided to use this as a practice run for the next day.

When she opened the door and saw it was me, her face lit up in a mischievous grin. 'This is a great honour, are you sure you can spare the time out of your busy schedule? Or are you looking forward to our little outing so much that you've turned up half a day early?'

I smiled, in spite of myself, and stepped into the hall. 'Sorry to disappoint you, I just came to bring your tin back. You should be very proud of me, I managed to make that delicious cake last longer than a day.' I gave her the tin, making sure our fingers didn't touch.

This was the way to do it, keep everything at the level of brotherly banter.

'Thank you.' She put the tin down on a marble-topped telephone table nearby and picked up a folded white handkerchief. 'And I've been meaning to return this.'

Instead of handing it to me, she leaned forward and tucked it into my breast pocket. I closed my eyes; tried to shut out her nearness, even as I breathed in her perfume . . .

'Are you tired?' Her voice was soft – with sympathy, not seduction.

My eyes flew open. 'Yeah, sorry, it's been a long day.'

She drew back, thank God. 'I hope you get a good night's sleep, you've another long day tomorrow,' she said, her tone brisk again. 'What time are you picking me up?'

'I thought twelve thirty, from Highbury Foods.'

'Great, I'll make sure I have everything I need with me. I'm taking a change of clothes for the evening, they said the dress code was business wear but—'

'They?' I said, sharply.

She blushed. 'I phoned Ashridge.'

'Before or after Henry rang me?'

'Before.' She shot me a provocative look from under her eyelashes. 'I was curious when you said the speaker wasn't anyone I'd know.'

Curious? That was laughable. She'd phoned Ashridge because she was determined to out-manoeuvre me. She'd got the information she needed, fed Henry some crap about being

Charles Durham's biggest fan and left him to do the rest. Between them, they'd wrong-footed me completely.

Needless to say, I didn't sleep well that night. The practice run had not been a success and the prospect of our visit to Ashridge stretched out before me like a minefield.

One false step could be fatal.

CHAPTER 6

HOT CROSS BUNS

EMMA

On Friday morning, I was at my desk composing a letter to selected customers about the focus groups, when I heard someone come into the outer office.

Batty's voice wafted through the open door of my room. '. . . Mother's terribly sore chest, all the coughing you know, must get David Perry out to her as soon as . . . Now here's Harriet, she'll be your PA.'

I stopped typing immediately. Who was she talking to?

My worst fears were realised when she babbled on, 'This is Jane, Harriet. I know we didn't expect her *quite* so soon, but it's wonderful to have her *any* time, of course, and I've cleared it all with Henry just now. She's starting properly on Monday, today's a – what did you call it, dear?'

'An orientation day, to get my bearings.'

That voice. I'd never yet heard it raised in anger, or breathless with excitement, or anything other than bland, monotonous and intensely irritating.

Batty tittered. 'Such a clever girl, you can tell she doesn't take after me! Emma's through here, dear, I expect you'll be sharing her office, unless . . .'

Infuriating pause. Unless – what? In a bid to defend my territory, I almost sprinted across the room and came face to face with Saint Jane.

She was, as usual, a picture of restraint: not a dark hair out of place, eyes demurely downcast, expression so bloody *pious*. Dressed in a plain black suit and prim white shirt, she looked like a terrifyingly efficient female undertaker.

I smiled brightly and held out my hand. 'Jane. Great to see you.'

'Emma.' Her fingers brushed mine with all the impact of a limp lettuce leaf.

I turned to Batty who was fidgeting beside her. 'Pity you didn't tell me about this, Mary, I'm going out shortly and I won't be around for the rest of the day.'

'So sorry, Emma, it's all been a bit last-minute.' She lowered her voice to a furtive whisper. 'Jane couldn't bear to stay in Weymouth once Charlotte and Dan left. That's the Campbells' daughter and her husband, they've gone to live in Ireland, Jane's missing them already, aren't you, dear?'

Jane said nothing.

'They wanted her to go with them, Dan even offered to fix her up with something at his company in Dublin, he's in marketing, isn't he, Jane?'

I could have sworn Saint Jane blushed, and I began to wonder . . .

'The timing wasn't right,' she said, removing an imaginary speck of dirt from her sleeve.

Much to my annoyance, Batty changed the subject. 'Then a friend offered her a lift to Highbury, too good an opportunity to miss, dropped her off here barely an hour ago. Who was it, Jane?' – shrill giggle – 'I don't believe you told me, was it a *man*?'

'It's not important, Aunt Mary.'

I cut in with, 'Why don't we have a little chat, Jane? Come into my office' – delicate emphasis on the 'my' – 'but I can only spare half an hour, I'm afraid.'

'Marvellous, Emma, I'll leave you girls to it,' Batty simpered, while Jane followed me into my room.

We sat at opposite sides of the table and I leaned forward encouragingly. 'Tell me about your degree course, then I can see where you'd be most useful.'

She folded her hands neatly in her lap and studied her skirt. 'If you like, although I think it's all sorted. I've had a brief word with Henry and he thought I'd be ideal for the Harriet's Secret Recipes project. It also meets my course requirements perfectly – taking something from a sketchy concept and seeing it right through to its launch.'

Sketchy concept? Was that how Dad had described all the work I'd done to date? Somehow I doubted it; it was more the sort of thing dear

Jane would say as she prepared to step in and take all the credit.

'Really? How do you plan to do that?' I asked, through clenched teeth.

She proceeded to drone on about various marketing tools and how she would apply them to my project: Ansoff's Matrix, the AIDA model, the Marketing Mix and so on. I knew them all backwards, so I doodled on my notepad and waited for Mark to arrive. At last, I heard his deep voice in the outer office, followed by an inevitable giggling fit from Harriet.

I got to my feet. 'Very interesting, Jane, but we'll have to leave it there. You remember Mark Knightley? He's just arrived to take me to an important business engagement and we need to get away promptly.'

As I went towards the door to show her out, it opened abruptly and Mark cannoned into me.

He drew back instantly, without even looking at me. 'My fault, sorry.' Then, in a much more cordial tone, 'Jane, lovely to see you again. It's been so long, I hardly recognised you.' He seized her hand and shook it for several seconds.

She smiled, ever so briefly. 'Mark.'

He continued, his eyes fixed on her, 'I didn't realise you were in a meeting—'

'We've just finished,' I said coldly. 'See you on Monday, Jane. In the meantime, I'll have a think about where I can put your amazing expertise to good use.'

She murmured her thanks and slipped out of the room.

Mark shut the door behind her. Then he turned to me and said quietly, 'Have you seen Elton today?'

'No, thank God.'

'So you don't know that—'

Before he could finish, Batty burst in. 'So sorry to interrupt, but I thought you'd both want to hear the news as soon as possible.'

I covered my irritation with a thin smile. 'What news is that?'

'Philip's got a girlfriend! He met her in Bristol and she's coming to stay with him this weekend, he's only known her a few days, must be serious, mustn't it? Funny, I always thought he was after someone *much* nearer to home.' She shot me a coy glance.

I flushed and said nothing.

Mark cleared his throat. 'That's what I was about to tell you, Emma.'

Batty's face fell. 'And how did you find out?'

'From Elton himself. I was passing his office just now and he rushed out to ask if I could recommend somewhere for a romantic dinner. Before I could answer, he went off into a long explanation of his eyes meeting this woman's across a crowded room and hardly being apart from her since.'

'That's more or less what happened with *me*, except he wanted the name of a reliable cleaning lady,' – she lowered her voice until it was barely audible – 'because Gusty would be practically *living* with him from now on and she's highly allergic to household dust.'

I frowned. 'What did you call her? For a moment I thought you said Gusty—'

'That's right, odd sort of name, must be short for something, let me think . . .'

Mark raised his eyebrows. 'Well, Mary, I hope you helped him out with a cleaner. We wouldn't want Gusty to get dusty, would we?'

It was a lame joke, but we all burst out laughing anyway. I for one needed to relieve some tension; the effect of having Saint Jane around, no doubt.

Batty got her breath back first, of course. 'Oh dear, I couldn't help him, although I did wonder about Mrs Burn,' – knowing look at Mark – 'she might want the work if you're going back to India to, um, sort things out with . . . ?'

'I'm not going anywhere until my father's home, as planned,' he said smoothly. 'But I'll ask Mrs Burn if she can spare a few hours. And now Emma and I really must go. Otherwise, from what John's told me, we'll be spending the afternoon parked on the M25. Got everything, Emma? We can call in on Henry on our way out.'

I grabbed my Louis Vuitton dress carrier and briefcase and almost hustled Batty out of the room. Harriet was nowhere to be seen, so I scribbled her a note of the work she needed to do and followed Mark along to Dad's office.

177

Dad was at his desk, contemplating a dry cracker with the air of a martyr.

'Don't wait up,' I said, 'we'll probably be back quite late. But I'll phone you after dinner, just so you know I've survived Ashridge's haute cuisine.'

'Yes, do that, darling. And Mark – drive carefully, won't you?'

I cut in before Mark could answer. 'Come on, Dad, you know I couldn't be in safer hands.'

With a reassuring smile, I kissed my father goodbye and left him to the prospect of an even quieter evening than usual.

MARK

The journey to Ashridge went quickly, despite a build-up of traffic on the M25. A light rain was falling, nothing too troublesome. I'd brought a lunch of sandwiches and fruit, which we ate in the car.

At first we talked about family matters: John, Izzy and the children, my father's latest cruise report and her father's current health fad. Then, as the traffic started to flow more freely, I tackled her about Jane Fairfax.

'I'm pleased you decided to have Jane working in Marketing.'

She gave a scornful laugh. 'Actually I didn't, it was decided for me. Batty can be so bloody devious sometimes and Saint Jane's just as bad.'

I pretended she hadn't spoken. 'She'll be an

asset to your team. Highly intelligent, I seem to remember.'

She went straight on the defensive. 'Are you suggesting I'm not?'

'Not at all, but I have a few doubts about your emotional intelligence.'

'Meaning?'

'Meaning you have to learn to get on with the Jane Fairfaxes of this world. And you'll meet far worse, believe me.' I glanced at her; she was frowning, and the tip of her tongue was just visible between her lips. I kept my eyes firmly on the road ahead and continued, 'I can't understand what you've got against Jane. You really should be more friendly to her, she's had nothing like the advantages in life that you've had.'

'No obvious reason, then, for her to be so – so stuck up!'

'She's just shy.'

Another scornful laugh. 'I'd call her sly, not shy. And I'm suspicious about this Weymouth fiasco. I think she's had a fling with her friend's husband but he doesn't want to leave his wife, who's just moved to Ireland with him. He wanted Saint Jane to go too, so she must be playing hard to get by coming here . . . Not that I know anything for definite,' she said hurriedly. 'Just call it a woman's intuition.'

I refrained from pointing out that her woman's intuition had let her down big time where Elton was concerned. I merely said, 'You'd better keep your thoughts to yourself, you know how fast rumours spread in Highbury.'

She was highly indignant. 'I don't spread rumours, I wouldn't dream of lowering myself to gossip about people.' She added, without any apparent irony, 'By the way, Kate says Flynn Churchill's in London today, meeting the BBC about a TV contract worth mega bucks. He's spending the week in town, then coming to Highbury. Just think, we'll meet him at last!'

'I can't wait.'

'You're always rubbishing him when you don't even know him.'

I managed a grim smile. 'No, and I don't particularly want to, unlike the rest of Highbury. I don't approve of the way he treats Tom – and now Kate. Of course, if they'd been the ones with the money, you wouldn't have been able to keep him away.'

'You think it all boils down to money, don't you? You can't imagine he has genuine feelings for that old dragon Stella!' Her tone softened. 'I think he must be a very kind and considerate man, putting up with her all this time.'

My patience snapped. 'It just doesn't add up. If he's so kind and considerate, why isn't he like that with Tom?'

'Because Stella has no one else but Flynn.'

'Neither did Tom for years, until Kate came along.'

'Men don't need other people as much as women do.'

'Absolute bollocks.'

She didn't reply, or maybe her words were drowned by a sudden battering of rain against the windscreen.

I switched the wipers to top speed and said, 'I didn't mean to be rude, I just don't agree with you.'

'I understand.' A pause; then, 'You must be missing Tamara terribly.'

'Actually, I'm not. We've both moved on.'

'I don't believe you move on from a five-year relationship as easily as that.'

'True, but let's just say it had stopped working a while ago. In the end, when I couldn't promise her what she wanted, she wasn't prepared to settle for less.'

'Did she – did she want to marry you?'

'Yes. At least, that's what she implied. Asked me if I could see her living at Donwell Abbey. She knows I'll inherit the place. Dad wants to keep it in the family and John prefers to live well away from the office.'

Her eyes widened. 'I hadn't thought of you at Donwell Abbey with – with a wife! And I certainly couldn't imagine Tamara as a sort of lady of the manor.'

'Neither could I. So she left.'

'Do you think you'll ever get married?'

It was a straightforward question, no strings attached, driven by friendly curiosity. Yet my heart missed a beat at the thought of Emma as my wife, my own perfect lady of the manor. The rain had eased and I switched the wipers to intermittent. In the top right-hand corner of the windscreen I noticed a smudge of bright blue sky.

I took a deep breath. 'I'd like to, one day. How about you?' Shit, what if she thought that last bit had a double meaning?

But she seemed oblivious to any undercurrents. 'That's just how I feel, with the emphasis very much on "one day". I've got my career to think of. Maybe in ten years' time I'll think about marriage and children and all that.'

Ten years? My hands tightened round the steering wheel. God, in ten years' time I'd be forty-bloody-five years old! Stupid to think we could ever . . .

I cleared my throat. 'Steve said the other night that Forbury Manor's just re-opened after that fire back in February. Doesn't Henry usually have the Highbury Foods Christmas party there?'

'Yes – Batty made a provisional booking ages ago, but perhaps someone had better go and make sure it's still suitable. Where are you having the Donwell Organics Christmas do?'

The conversation moved to safer ground and I could concentrate on the last stage of our journey. We'd left the motorway and were skirting round the small town of Berkhamsted, when the clouds parted and the sun shone down on us like a blessing. The narrow road sliced through a forest of stately beech trees, their wet leaves gleaming like burnished copper, a sanctuary to the fallow deer that roamed the estate. As we slowed down for the speed ramps, the forest gave way to a large grassy common on the left and Ashridge Business School on the right.

Even though I'd been there many times, that first glimpse of the house always moved me. I loved the quiet elegance of its limestone façade, and the timeless simplicity of its large square towers and tall arched windows. In spite of my reluctance to bring Emma here, I felt my shoulders relax and my spirits lift.

I turned my head; our eyes met. God knows what mine betrayed, but hers were wide with wonder.

'Oh, Mark . . .' She sighed. 'So this is where you did your MBA.'

'You sound almost envious.'

'Who wouldn't be?'

I parked the car and got our bags and coats out of the boot. 'We've got to check in at Reception first. Then I thought we'd go to the Learning Resource Centre – that's their name for the library – and get the Mintel reports out of the way. We should still have time for a look at the grounds before dark.'

We walked towards the house; just before the entrance, I stopped.

'Look up there.' I pointed to a stone cross, clearly visible on the horizon through a cutting in the surrounding trees.

183

'What's it for?'

'It's a sad story. One of Ashridge's previous owners, Earl Brownlow, had it built in 1917 as a memorial to his wife, Adelaide. She was said to be a great beauty, very kind-hearted and a wonderful hostess – which brought people like Disraeli here, and Oscar Wilde, and the Shah of Persia. After she died, the Earl was heartbroken and walked to that cross every day.'

Emma let out a long breath. 'It's not a sad story, it's beautiful. That's what I call true love.'

'They were lucky, then,' I said. I hesitated for a moment, overcome by a strange feeling of melancholy, then squared my shoulders. 'This way.'

I swung open one of the two massive half-glazed doors and let her through. She took a few steps, then paused to gaze up at the richly decorated ceiling and sweeping stone staircase. I smiled to myself and went past her to the desk.

The receptionist gave me a cheeky grin. 'Hi there, stranger.'

'Hi, Steph. How are you?'

'Very well, thank you. Just sign in as usual, Mark, here's your name badge and a visitor's badge for your companion. The door code's 315 today and you're in room 210, that's Greenborough building in case you've forgotten. Here's the key.'

I stared at her. 'Didn't I cancel the room booking?'

'No – at least, there's nothing in our records. So

you booked a room originally, but now . . . ?' Her voice trailed off as she looked over at Emma.

I gave a nervous laugh. 'My, er, plans have changed. I'll pay for the room, of course, but we won't be needing it.'

Emma appeared at my side. 'Yes, we will,' she put in, smiling at a bemused Steph. 'Since Mark's paying for it anyway, we can use it to change for dinner.'

Being alone in a bedroom with Emma, even for a little while, was a daunting prospect. But I heard myself saying heartily, 'Yes, why not?'

EMMA

Ashridge just blew my mind.

The Learning Resource Centre was a revelation compared to your average library; some sort of barn conversion, a superb mix of modern technology and olde-worlde ambience. We did what we'd come to do – found a couple of relevant Mintel reports and printed off tables of statistics on dining out and gourmet food sales – but mostly I just wandered about, spellbound. Then Mark took the bags to our room while I sat in a large conservatory, looking out into the walled garden beyond. He wasn't gone for long, but I missed having him there to share my enthusiasm. Ten minutes later I was glad to see him striding towards me, relaxed and smiling, a different person from the last few days.

We meandered through the gardens, enjoying the sun's lingering warmth on our faces. Even at this time of year there was plenty of colour: red and gold Japanese maples, mauve Michaelmas daisies, yellow-green larch fronds. There were formal areas edged with regimented miniature box hedges, not a leaf out of place; and away from the house there was more of a wilderness, bushes spilling over grassy paths and vaults of trees arching across the darkening sky.

I went as near to the boundary fence as the undergrowth – and my new Gucci boots – allowed, and stared at the rolling fields and woods beyond, wondering if the view had changed much in the last thousand years.

I turned to find Mark looking at me.

'Penny for your thoughts?' I said gently.

He flushed. 'They're not even worth that.' Then, glancing at his watch, 'Time to go indoors, it'll be pitch black soon.'

I tucked my arm through his as we walked back in the direction of the house. 'I'm going to soak in a lovely hot bath – our room does have one, doesn't it? Or do you want to do some mentoring first?'

He cleared his throat. 'Not at the moment. Not here.'

I frowned; the break-up with Tamara was obviously having more impact than he cared to admit. 'OK, we can leave that for another day, it just needs to be soon. Philip's started messing me about, and on top of that I've now got Saint Jane to contend with.' I pulled a face. 'If you don't hurry up I'll be needing psychiatric treatment, not mentoring.'

His laugh sounded a little strained. 'I'll get Cherry to fix up a meeting for next week, if at all possible.'

'Thanks. Oh, is this the way to our room?' We'd left the main path and gone down a few steps to a modern two-storey building. I let go of his arm while he keyed in the door code, then followed him into a brightly carpeted entrance hall and along a corridor to the right. He unlocked room 210, switched on the light and stepped back.

I breezed past him and had a quick look round. 'Smallish, but it's got everything we need. Double bed if you want a power nap, TV if you don't. The bathroom's tiny, no room to swing a cat, but at least there's a bath as well as a shower. Do you mind if I go in there first?'

I didn't wait for his answer but took off my coat and hung it in the wardrobe. My dress carrier was already there, so I unzipped it and shook out my dress – a Wedgwood blue floaty thing I'd picked up in Selfridges. Since it was sleeveless, I'd brought a little silvery jacket for extra warmth.

'No, go ahead,' he said. 'I didn't get much sleep last night, so I think I'll have that power nap you mentioned.' He drew the curtains, then flung his coat and jacket over a chair.

I picked up my toilet bag and turned to him.

'You know, if you don't fancy driving home tonight, we could always stay here. I'm sure Dad won't mind when I explain how tired you are.'

He gave me a long, serious look. 'That's out of the question.'

'Why? It's not as if we've never spent the night together before.' I giggled. 'It was the last time we all went camping, remember? In Darnley Woods – you, John, Izzy and me. Izzy wanted to share a tent with John instead of me and I couldn't imagine why. Then you and John had a big row and we almost went home. But in the end you and I shared one tent, and they went in the other.'

'That was entirely different. You were twelve, if that, and we were in sleeping bags—'

'Yes, of course it was different, but that doesn't change the fact that we spent the night together!' I laughed and went on, 'I was really cross with Izzy, so you gave me a pep talk about her being old enough to know what she was doing and told me those awful ghost stories to distract me. I don't know which was worse, being cross or terrified.'

Silence; then he said, 'If I have a nap now, I'll be fine to drive home.' He kicked off his shoes, stretched out on top of the bed covers and stared up at the ceiling.

I shrugged. 'See how you feel later.' I went into the bathroom and started running my bath, wondering why he'd been so abrupt with me; defensive, almost. Then I twigged. Oh, shit! Did he think I was that desperate?

I poked my head round the door and said haughtily, 'You needn't worry, I might have said I hadn't kissed a man for over two months, but I'm not about to hit on *you*. If the thought of staying in the same room as me is so off-putting, you can bloody well forget it!'

When he turned his back on me without a word, I knew I was right.

Arrogant bastard!

MARK

I stared moodily at the plain cream wall, remembering that last camping trip. I'd been as angry with John as Emma had been with Izzy. At twenty-three, I hadn't exactly relished sharing a tent with a gawky twelve-year-old while my brother got his end away with her sister. The situation wasn't helped by a poor night's sleep; Emma had tossed and turned in her sleeping bag next to me, while I couldn't avoid overhearing occasional noises from the other tent.

Now, years later, the opportunity to spend the night with her aroused a very different reaction. The irony was that she believed I was worried about *her* hitting on *me*! Bloody good job she couldn't mind-read.

I sighed, rolled onto my front and closed my eyes. Maybe everything would seem better after a nap . . .

I must have dozed off; I don't know for how long.

I woke slowly, silently, to a scene more seductive than any dream. The sound of someone humming under their breath. A delicious fragrance, like a summer garden after rain. In the lamplight, a girl with her back to me, dark brown hair curling damply over bare shoulders, skin glowing honey-gold against the white of a towel that enveloped her body but did little to disguise her shape.

Emma; no longer a girl, but a woman.

The humming stopped. She turned her head; checking up on me, no doubt. Instantly, my eyes flicked shut.

A soft thud, as something hit the floor. Please God, let it be the towel.

Casting caution to the wind, I opened my eyes again.

Same view, only now with her full beauty revealed – and I drank in every detail. In my mind, I got up and crossed the room in a single stride; captured the narrow span of her waist between my hands, traced the smooth hollows of her back, reached down to cup the inviting curve of her hips. In my mind, she turned round with the sweetest of smiles, offering my urgent fingers other delights to explore, and raised heavy-lidded, lustrous eyes to mine before pressing herself against me. In my mind, we fell onto the bed, a hot fusion of mouths and limbs, and didn't give dinner another thought . . .

Pure fantasy. The real Emma pulled on a pair of white briefs, wriggled into something blue and all-concealing, and moved out of sight; but not, unfortunately, out of mind.

Then, from the foot of the bed, 'Mark.'

I feigned sleep. What else could I do? Although I must have looked unconscious, inside I was only too self-aware; voyeuristic lust battling it out with intense shame. After all, she'd told her father she couldn't be in safer hands . . .

'Mark, wake up.'

I gave what I hoped was a convincing start. 'Whassat?'

'Time to have your shower. We've got pre-dinner drinks in thirty-five minutes, according to the programme I saw at Reception.'

And time to face facts; in her eyes, I was simply part of the furniture. But then I'd done nothing so far to encourage her to see me any differently.

Maybe I should give her a taste of her own medicine.

EMMA

While Mark took a shower, I sat on the bed and gave myself a quick manicure. I'd just started on my last nail when something blocked my light.

I glanced up. Mark was standing in front of me, wearing nothing but an apology for a towel round his hips. I found my gaze fixed on his tanned, well-shaped thighs, each dark hair clearly visible at such close range.

'D'you think I need to shave?' he said. His voice was low, almost husky.

I swallowed. 'No. I think hairy legs can be very appealing – on a man.'

There was a pause. 'I meant my face.'

My gaze travelled upwards, passing hurriedly over the skimpy towel to the taut muscles of his stomach and the broad expanse of his chest, where the hair was still damp . . .

At last I looked at his face. His eyes widened in mock surprise and he gave a deep chuckle.

I felt myself go bright red. 'Just checking you over for signs of ageing. You're not in bad shape – for thirty-five.'

'It's been a while since anyone checked me over *that* thoroughly,' he said silkily.

I scowled at him. 'Yes, you do need to shave and you'd better get a move on. I want to use the mirror in the bathroom for my make-up.' I bent my head and continued with my manicure.

'Ah yes, you and your make-up.' He sounded amused, as if I was a little girl playing at being grown up. 'I'll try not to keep you waiting too long.'

As he went away, I thought of Tamara. He wouldn't have kept her waiting at all; she'd have been in the bathroom with him the whole time, and no prizes for guessing what they'd have been up to in the shower.

Five minutes later, the door opened and he emerged once more, dressed only in a pair of black boxers. I averted my eyes, darted past him into the bathroom and locked the door behind me. But it was full of *him* – his cologne, his shaving gear, his clothes. And there, draped over the side of the bath, was the towel he'd been wearing, still warm . . .

I stared at my reflection in the mirror. Without make-up I looked like an unsophisticated teenager, which was precisely how he'd thought of me for years. Well, I'd show him. I carefully applied lots of dark brown eye liner and lash-tripling mascara, followed by several layers of vamp-red lipstick.

By the time I'd finished, I felt I could take on the world – and any dodgy feelings for Mark Knightley. I lifted my chin and stalked out of the bathroom. He was sitting on the bed; fresh shirt, different suit, nice tie. I put everything away in my dress carrier and looked round for my jacket. Only then did I notice that he was holding it.

'Allow me,' he murmured.

He stood behind me, helped me slip it on and, on the pretext of straightening the sleeves, turned me slowly round to face him. His eyes met mine, briefly, then focused on my mouth. Seconds passed, God knows how many. For one wild, weird moment, I thought he was going to kiss me . . . He didn't; but my relief was short-lived as he looked down at my neckline, studying every inch of bare skin. All in silence; no need for words, when his eyes spoke volumes.

Then he said briskly, 'Fasten that jacket, you'll catch cold,' and turned away.

I pulled myself up short. Idiot! I'd imagined too much . . . I squared my shoulders, picked up my handbag and left the room. As I didn't know where to go next, I stopped at the main door and waited, taking deep calming breaths and trying not to feel like an even bigger fool.

At last he arrived, grinning broadly. 'It's not far to the house,' he said, as we went outside. 'Drinks are in Hoskins and dinner's in the Lady Marian Alford room. That'll make you fall in love with the place, if you haven't already.'

I gave a frosty smile and said nothing.

We entered the house from a small courtyard and went along a plush corridor, past watercolours and drawings of Ashridge through the centuries, from its origins as a medieval monastery to the stately building of today. We crossed the Reception area and walked into a room that took my breath away. It was decorated in the same blue as my dress, with magnificent white plasterwork on the ceiling. Around the walls were bookcases and portraits, including one of a sleeping, rosy-cheeked child.

Mark followed my gaze. 'That's a Joshua Reynolds, doesn't it remind you of Emily? We should take a photo for Izzy's collection.'

I laughed, and the tension between us eased. He handed me a glass of wine and introduced me to Judy Scott, the Alumni Association organiser. We hadn't been talking long when a fat man in a crumpled suit swayed up to us, already the worse for drink.

'Long time no see, Mark,' he brayed. 'Out in Africa, weren't you?'

Within half a minute, I knew that his name was Baz Lorimer, he'd been at Ashridge at the same time as Mark and he was Head of Customer Relations for DK Clothing, which I hoped had absolutely nothing to do with Donna Karan. I also discovered that, like most large, unfit men, he had a serious perspiration problem. Judy and I continued our conversation, but it was impossible not to hear what Lorimer was saying.

'High-class totty, the one in the blue.' He let out an appreciative belch.

I didn't catch Mark's reply.

Then Lorimer bellowed, 'Are you shagging her, or have I got a chance?'

Heads turned in our direction, while I blushed to the roots of my hair.

Judy gave me a sympathetic look. 'Would you excuse me, Emma? Charles Durham's just arrived with our Chief Exec and I need to check something.'

This time I heard every word Mark said, his voice deceptively even. 'Yes, you've got a chance, arsehole – a chance of getting your face smashed in, nothing else.'

'No need to be so touchy, you wanker.' Lorimer stumbled off, while Mark and I stared at each other in embarrassed silence.

Mark cleared his throat. 'Sorry about that.'

I shrugged. 'It's not your fault. And, believe me, I've been called worse than high-class totty.'

'And I've been called far worse than a wanker,' he said, with a rueful smile. 'Come on, let's go and talk to that guy in the pink shirt over there. I happen to know he's a market research expert, so you can pick his brains about your focus groups. And I guarantee he's not a bit like Lorimer.'

He guided me across the room, his hand in the small of my back under my jacket. Meaningless etiquette, nothing more; but I missed its warmth when he took it away.

It seemed no time at all until dinner was served. If I'd been impressed by the elegant restraint of Hoskins, I was dazzled by the gilded opulence of the Lady Marian Alford room: huge pillars of rose marble, ornate fireplaces, and the most fabulous painted ceiling showing gods and goddesses at play. Our table companions were entertaining, without being overpowering; the food was exquisitely cooked and presented; and Mark was on top form – charming, attentive, funny – as if he wasn't missing Tamara one bit. I knew better than to take him at face value, though; he was certainly putting on some sort of act.

I had my own problems, however. Although, as he'd predicted, I'd fallen in love with Ashridge, there was a most peculiar side effect. During the meal, I found myself looking at Mark and imagining us together in that cosy little room for the night. As there was nothing else to sleep on, we'd have to share the bed. Would we lie rigid at its edges, or snuggle up to each other to keep warm? Another scenario came to mind, but I dismissed it instantly. That was why I was so determined to go back to Highbury tonight – to prove that I had no designs on him whatsoever.

It was fortunate that I'd arranged to ring Dad, as it provided a temporary distraction; I couldn't resist describing the meal in mouthwatering detail.

He tut-tutted down the phone. 'Far too much saturated fat, especially at this time of night. Crème brûlée for dessert, did you say?'

'Yes, Mark says it's acquired a cult status among the Alumni. And it was absolutely delicious, the topping caramelised to perfection and the custard so thick and creamy.'

He gave a faint moan, presumably of disgust, then asked to speak to Mark. I guessed this was to make sure he sounded sober enough to drive me home and we laughed about it later, over coffee.

'All he supposedly wanted to know was whether there was a frost,' Mark said. 'I told him I hadn't really noticed, which immediately put the fear of God into him. But I think I managed to reassure him I wasn't paralytic, just unobservant.'

I sighed. 'He still thinks I need protecting.'

Mark raised one eyebrow. 'From me?'

'Hardly,' I said, trying not to blush. 'I wasn't thinking of anyone specific.'

'Of course.' That amused tone again. 'Look, I think Charles Durham's about to speak – do you want another coffee, or something from the bar?'

'Coffee, please. I have a feeling you're going to interrogate me afterwards, so I'll need all my wits about me.'

A teasing look. 'Am I really that bad?'

'You know you are – with me, at least.'

For once, it seemed, those steely blue eyes softened. 'I could change, if you wanted me to.'

I pulled a face. 'I'm not sure I could cope with a changed Mark Knightley.'

Before he could respond, a man I assumed was the Chief Executive got to his feet. 'Ladies and gentlemen, it gives me great pleasure to introduce our speaker. He's known to have extremely high principles and, more unusually, the integrity to live by them. Please welcome Charles Durham!'

During the polite applause that followed, I reflected that Ashridge seemed to have done Mark a power of good. He was more mellow, almost flirtatious; great company, provided you didn't take his attentions seriously.

In the end, I spent far too much time thinking about Mark, at the expense of listening to Charles.

MARK

'Good speech, wasn't it?' I said, as we walked back to the room. To pick up our bags, of course. Nothing more.

198

'Brilliant.'

'Was it what you expected?'

'Definitely.'

Why so cagey? I decided to draw her out. 'I thought you might object to his views on packaging.'

A pause; then, 'Which views exactly?'

I tried desperately to remember the details. I'd been too busy reliving that scene in the bedroom to pay much attention to the speech, whereas she'd seemed totally absorbed by it.

'The need for packaging at all,' I said, hesitantly. 'Didn't he suggest going back to the old days, where far less food was pre-wrapped? I just don't believe that's a viable solution any more.'

'Surely he didn't say that?'

'I must admit, after that huge meal I wasn't concentrating all the time, so I may have misheard him.'

We'd reached the room; the bags were in front of me, ready to go. It was just a matter of putting out my hand and –

'Are you sure you're OK to drive?' she said, and I drew back my hand instantly. 'I mean, if your concentration's not all it should be?'

'I'm fine now, thanks.' I cleared my throat. 'Although if you want to see more of Ashridge, we could always stay . . .'

My heart started to hammer so loudly that I barely caught her reply.

'No, we'd better not,' she said, with a frown. 'Dad's expecting me.'

'I thought you told him not to wait up?'

'I did, but he'll probably be lying awake imagining the worst until he knows I'm home safely.'

She threw on her coat and rushed out of the room as if it was possessed. I let out a long breath, picked up the bags and followed her into the corridor.

We walked back towards the house in silence; this time, we took the longer, more open route that led to the car park. Except for occasional snatches of laughter from the direction of the bar, the only sound was Emma's heels tapping on the frosted path. The moon glinted in the black velvet sky like a sliver of crystal. New moon, new hope . . .

I left her in the car with the heater on and went to Reception to drop off the room key and pay the bill. Steph wanted to chat, but I brought the conversation to an end as soon as I could and hurried outside. My eyes turned once more to the stone cross; or rather, to where I knew it stood in the darkness. A simple but lasting expression of one man's love for a woman.

Then it dawned on me. What I felt for Emma was much more than physical desire. I loved her, as I'd never loved anyone else. And I knew I'd been waiting my whole life for her; everyone else, even Tamara, had just been a distraction.

Tonight, whatever the consequences, I had to do something . . .

By the time I returned to the car, Emma was fast asleep. I sat watching her for a while, thinking things through. I'd taken a few risks in my life, but only when it didn't seem to matter. With the things that were important, I'd always played safe.

Until now.

I recalled the three kisses on her birthday card; we were two down, one to go. I reached out my hand and stroked her cheek; but she didn't stir.

Just as well. Be patient. Get her home first.

I turned the key in the ignition and set off for Hartfield.

EMMA

Drifting up through clouds of sleep, I found myself in a strange car and had a moment of panic. Then I saw Mark at the wheel. I remembered that he was taking me home from Ashridge in his father's Mercedes and, reassured, I closed my eyes again.

When I next woke, we were drawing to a halt outside my house, the engine purring too softly to disturb Dad, whose bedroom overlooked the driveway. I smiled to myself. That was Mark all over, considerate to the last.

Following his lead, I tiptoed to the front door and let myself in without a sound while he brought my bags. The hall was beautifully warm, so I slipped off my coat and jacket and hung them on the banister. Behind me, the door shut with a muffled click. I turned round. Mark was barely a foot away, closer than I'd expected.

'How about a coffee?' I kept my voice low. 'Or maybe a nightcap?'

He made no answer, just stared down at me.

I swallowed. 'So . . . do you want to discuss the mentoring? Although it's very late and I'm whacked.'

'I just want to thank you for a wonderful evening,' he said softly. 'Like this.'

He paused. My lips framed a question, but no words came. Then he reached out and cupped the back of my head, threading his fingers through my hair, spreading his hand wide so that the tip of his thumb brushed the corner of my mouth, over and over, building to a slow, hypnotic rhythm. I looked into his eyes, willing him to stop; but his gaze never wavered. At last, he rested his other hand on my waist, bent his head and kissed me.

I suppose I should have guessed what he was after . . . but I couldn't, wouldn't, believe it. The gentle circling of his thumb lulled first my mind into a false sense of security – and then my mouth into an unthinking response.

There was a time, long ago, when a kiss from Mark Knightley had been my life's ambition. But things happen for a reason. Back then, I could never have appreciated the erotic play of his tongue, the skilled caress of his hands, the unspoken invitation to give myself to him completely. Because a man who kissed like that had no intention of spending the night alone.

And, back then, I would probably have mistaken lust for love.

Now, thank God, I could see it all for what it was. A kiss that promised much, but meant little. A kiss that discovered my mouth, but remembered Tamara's.

And yet . . .

I was lost. Lost to all sense of time. Lost in the heat of his mouth, the scent of his skin, the feel of his body against mine. Each kiss lasted an eternity, but finished too soon. Each kiss left me satisfied, but kept me wanting more.

In a little while, I would end it. I would break away, laugh it off, dismiss it as an error of judgement on his part. An understandable error, perhaps, after a long day that he should have spent with *her*.

Upstairs, a floorboard creaked.

'Emma, is that you?' Dad, sounding anxious.

I would have ended it anyway. I know I would.

MARK

'Emma, is that you?'

At her father's voice, Emma twisted out of my grasp.

'I didn't realise I was a substitute for Tamara in *everything*!' she hissed, before calling out, 'Yes, Dad, it's me. And Mark, who's just leaving.'

203

I grabbed her arm. 'Tamara? What's she got to do with it?'

She glanced nervously at the stairs. 'Shhh! He's coming.'

'For God's sake, we need to talk.' I racked my brains for a convincing excuse. 'Tell him I'm mentoring you for the next hour or so.'

'Don't be so bloody ridiculous!' She wrenched herself away just before Henry appeared at the top of the stairs. He took his time coming down, stopping every so often to fasten his dressing gown more securely or turn up his collar against a non-existent draught. She ignored me and watched his irritatingly slow progress. I could see she was trembling, and I longed to hold her close . . .

'Had a nice evening, the pair of you?' Henry said, cautiously navigating the last stair as though it was a ten-foot drop.

I forced a smile. 'Lovely, and it isn't over yet. We're just going to have that long overdue mentoring meeting—'

She cut in with, 'Oh no, I'm exhausted – and I'm sure you are too. We wouldn't be able to do it justice, which would be a complete waste of Highbury Foods' money.' She gave a hollow laugh and hurried to a safe distance halfway up the stairs, her dress shimmering around her.

Henry nodded. 'Quite right. And I must say, Mark, you look stressed out. I'm not surprised, all that rich food and then driving at this ungodly hour.'

I looked past him, straight at her. 'Just a few minutes, Emma, please—'

'Not tonight,' she said stonily, avoiding my gaze. 'Come back in the morning, when you've got whatever it is out of your system.'

And then she was gone.

Henry's eyes gleamed. 'System? Have you got indigestion – or food poisoning perhaps? Let's go through to the kitchen, I'm sure I can find something to—'

'Thanks, but no thanks,' I said sharply, and his face fell. I pulled myself together with an effort. 'Sorry, Henry. You were right, I'm not feeling my best, but it's nothing to worry about. I'll be along in the morning to see Emma. Around nine, probably, if she'll be up by then on a Saturday?'

'Oh yes, Emma's an early riser these days, even at weekends.'

My mind was in turmoil as I said goodnight and let myself out. I drove the short distance home on autopilot, thinking only of her. She certainly hadn't pushed me away when I'd kissed her; no, she'd kissed me back, over and over again. God knows, if Henry hadn't interrupted us, we might easily have . . .

It was probably for the best. When we made love – and I knew now that it was a question of when, not if – I needed her to understand that I wasn't in this for a cheap thrill. I wanted to be with her for ever.

But how on earth could she think she was just

a substitute for Tamara? That would be the first thing I'd clear up when I saw her the next day. Except – why wait? I reached for my phone and tried her mobile.

It was switched off.

I let out a long uneven sigh. It looked as though I'd have to be patient for a little longer.

EMMA

Up in bed I tossed and turned, wondering how to deal with Mark.

I didn't dwell on why he'd kissed me. I knew it was because he missed Tamara, whatever he said about moving on. And I didn't dwell on why I'd kissed him back. He was a fantastic kisser, might as well enjoy it.

But what would happen now? Would we ever return to some sort of normality? We had to – I couldn't imagine him not being part of my life.

And then I started thinking . . . If Dad hadn't interrupted us, would we have got carried away and, well, slept together? Not at Hartfield, of course; Mark would have taken me to Donwell Abbey, where we'd be completely alone all night long . . .

A disturbing thought, and one that I returned to time and again. I even composed the little note I would have left for Dad:

Gone to Donwell with Mark – temporarily taking over Tamara's bedroom duties.

New packet of porridge is behind fennel tea in pantry.

Love, Emma.

P.S. Don't worry, have got Health & Safety covered. We're calling at Open All Hours – which means by the time you read this the whole of Highbury will know we've spent the night together.

All pointless bloody speculation. It hadn't happened, and I'd make sure it was never likely to.

CHAPTER 7

BOMBE SURPRISE

EMMA

After only a few hours' sleep I got up, anxious to prepare myself for Mark's visit. Because he would come to sort things out, I knew. In the kitchen I made bread and imagined how it would go. It was possible, of course, that he'd simply take me in his arms and tell me he loved me with a passion he'd never felt for Tamara or anyone else. Possible, but impossible.

I pummelled the dough as I rehearsed far more likely scenarios.

There was the contrite Mark: 'I shouldn't have taken advantage of you like that. Can you ever forgive me, dear sweet little Emma?'

The angry Mark: 'Why the hell didn't you stop me making such a complete fool of myself?'

The philosophical Mark: 'These things happen, even between friends. Remember that film, *When Harry Met Sally*? We're not like them, though. Let's just gloss over it and carry on as before.'

There was even a version that had him down on his knees, begging: 'Surely you understand a man's needs, especially after a woman like Tamara? If you're interested, why don't we come to a little arrangement while I'm over here? Sex without any strings, so to speak.' At this point, naturally, I would take great pleasure in slapping his face.

When the doorbell rang just after half past nine, I was ready to give him whichever piece of my mind suited his mood.

I certainly wasn't prepared for anything else; although you could say I'd spent years waiting for this very moment . . .

MARK

I slept well; so well, in fact, that I didn't hear the alarm go off at half past eight. I woke – cursing – just before eleven, got showered and dressed in seven minutes flat and rushed downstairs.

No time for breakfast; anyway, there was bound to be something on offer at Hartfield. I could see it now: Emma and I rustling up bacon and eggs under Henry's disapproving gaze – the first of many breakfasts together, I was sure.

I walked to the car with a spring in my step, pausing only to breathe in the crisp, apple-scented air. It was almost Hallowe'en. Maybe we'd go to John and Izzy's this morning and take the children shopping for scary masks and pumpkins; on the way home we'd stop for lunch, then go back to Donwell for the rest of the day, and all night . . .

Exactly five minutes later I was at Hartfield, smoothing my hair and ringing the bell. As I waited for what seemed like ages, I began to wonder if I was being overconfident. In all the years I'd known her, dealing with Emma had never been straightforward.

At last the door opened; but it was only Henry, smiling benignly. 'Good morning. Fully recovered, are we?'

'Yes, thank you. Look, I'm sorry if I was rude last night—'

'No need to apologise, Mark. I understand – more than most people – the trials and tribulations of the digestive system.' He gave a little morbid sigh.

'And I'm a bit later than I intended.' I hesitated. 'Is Emma still around?'

'Very much so,' he said, with a chuckle. 'We've got another visitor, you know, besides you. I was just making them more coffee – would you like a cup?'

'I'd love one.' Another visitor? I cursed myself again for sleeping in, and glanced right and left; the only cars on the drive were Emma's and mine.

'Just go through to the drawing room.' Henry shut the front door behind me and shuffled off towards the kitchen.

'Who else is here?' I called after him, but he didn't reply. I frowned; if it was Mary, I wouldn't get Emma on her own until lunch time.

Through the open drawing room door, I heard Emma give a throaty laugh of encouragement. This brought a smile to my face; the visitor definitely wasn't Mary Bates! Then – a man's voice, unfamiliar, his tone so low that I couldn't make out the words, and another laugh from Emma.

I took a couple of steps forward, my legs strangely heavy.

That voice again, the words audible now, the accent marked. New Zealand, wasn't it? Or maybe Australian . . . 'Emma Woodhouse, it feels like we've known each other for years.'

I walked into the room and stopped short.

They were on the sofa together, their knees almost touching; he was half turned towards her, his hand on her arm. Her cheeks were flushed and her eyes sparkled. I couldn't see all of his face, but I knew who he was, instantly.

Flynn Churchill.

Several seconds passed before Emma noticed me. 'Oh, there you are,' she said, dismissively, and looked straight back at him. 'Flynn, this is Mark Knightley, I'm sure Tom will have mentioned the name.'

He jumped to his feet and tried to win me over with the same engaging grin I'd seen in that photo-shrine on the Westons' sideboard. We shook hands – he wasn't as limp-wristed as I'd have liked – and I schooled my features into a mask of polite indifference; inside, I was wishing him miles away.

So he'd finally shown up in Highbury, after all those false boasts and empty promises. Putting the Westons to great inconvenience, no doubt; I vaguely remembered Emma saying he wasn't expected until the end of the week. And, with impeccable timing, he'd decided to visit Hartfield at a critical moment between Emma and me.

I took a seat opposite them and willed her to look at me. All in vain; it became increasingly obvious that I may as well not be in the room. He was centre stage, the focus of her attention.

I'd only just met him, yet I hated him – more than I'd ever hated anyone in my life.

EMMA

I was over the moon at seeing Flynn. For one thing, his arrival delayed that uncomfortable little chat with Mark. For another, the man himself was everything I'd dreamed he would be: gorgeous-looking, great fun – and here, in the flesh, at long last.

Mark, normally so socially adept, sat there in silence. Eventually, he got to his feet and announced that he had to go.

I glanced at the clock on the mantlepiece and did a double take. 'Twelve o'clock already? Would you like some lunch, Flynn? What about you, Mark?' I risked a quick look and saw that his face was like thunder. 'I've got home-made minestrone and freshly baked rolls,' I added, addressing Flynn again.

'I can never resist the offer of a roll,' he said, and we both giggled.

Out of the corner of my eye, I saw Mark's mouth twist into an unconvincing smile. 'Thanks, but I've got things to do. Are you around this afternoon, Emma?'

'Oh dear, I'm not, I'm seeing Harriet at two thirty.'

'This evening?'

I hesitated, searching frantically for a plausible excuse.

'That reminds me,' Flynn put in. 'Kate's organising a dinner tonight in my honour, seven for seven thirty, I'm cooking. You're both invited, and Henry of course.'

'I don't think—' Mark began stiffly.

'And it sounds as though you two are free, at least,' Flynn continued, with a sly wink at me. 'I've told Kate not to buy things in specially, I'll work with what she's got. It'll be Flynn's Cook-in comes to Highbury, without the TV cameras.'

I laughed. 'Can't wait.' Then my face fell. 'I'd better bring something for Dad, though. Don't take it personally, he's just very particular about what he eats.'

He wagged his finger at me. 'I won't hear of it, Em. I'll sort Henry out, I'm an expert at managing fussy old fogies. God knows, I've had to keep Stella sweet for years.'

I couldn't take offence, not with those mischievous green eyes looking into mine. In the distance, I heard Mark say something.

'What was that?' I tore my gaze away with an effort; when I looked round, he'd gone.

'He said he'd see himself out,' Flynn replied. 'Not much of a talker, is he?'

As if in response, the front door slammed.

I breathed a sigh of relief. If I could avoid any one-to-ones with Mark for the next few days, I was sure we'd both forget about last night and things would return to normal between us. Anyway, now that Flynn was on the scene, a kiss from Mark Knightley was bloody irrelevant. And utterly forgettable.

Flynn interrupted my thoughts. 'Shall I give you a hand with the lunch?'

'Yes, please. I'll try not to be intimidated by having a celebrity chef around.'

Not that I felt intimidated in the slightest; more as if all my Christmases had come at once. Until, as we crossed the hall, he came out with, 'What do you think of Jane Fairfax?'

I stopped dead and tried to keep my tone as neutral as possible. 'Jane Fairfax? How on earth do you know *her*?'

He stared past me and his eyes widened. 'Wow, what a great kitchen! The layout reminds me of Stella's, which I designed as it happens. It wasn't difficult, the old bird gave me a free hand – and a blank cheque.' He walked purposefully over to

214

the island unit and ran his hand over the gleaming granite worktop.

I followed him, frowning. 'But how do you know Saint Jane of Highbury?'

'Saint Jane of—?' He looked puzzled, then he laughed. 'Oh, that's a good one, I'll have to remember that.' He strolled across to the Aga and fidgeted with the tea towels on the rail.

I was beginning to wonder if he could even remember my question from two seconds ago; I made one last effort. 'You see, I've known Jane for years, but she's never mentioned you.'

He spun round and disarmed me with that wicked grin. 'How could she? We only met three weeks ago, when I was at The Mulberry Tree.'

'Ah yes, I remember Tom saying you'd been asked to cook there. I didn't realise it was in Weymouth, though.'

He shook his head. 'It's not, the restaurant's a good hour's drive away. But the family Jane was staying with are loaded, you know, and they eat there all the time. They came on my first night and that's how I met Jane . . . And the daughter and her husband as well, but they've moved to Ireland—'

I couldn't resist cutting in with, 'I know, and I have a little theory about why Jane suddenly decided to move to Highbury.'

He gave me an appraising look. 'Before you do your Sherlock Holmes impersonation, where's that soup? I'm starving.'

'It's here, it just needs heating up.' I turned on the hob under a large pan. 'Give it a stir while I set the table. There'll just be the two of us, Dad's having his dry crackers and hot water in the study.'

I put out two bowls and side plates, with soup spoons and small knives. The rolls and butter were next, then a jug of fruit juice and two glasses, and finally a dish of grated Parmesan to sprinkle on the minestrone.

When I'd finished, Flynn said, 'Soup's ready. So, what's this theory of yours?'

'Could you bring the pan here?' He carried it over and I ladled the soup carefully into the bowls. Then I went on, 'Man trouble. Even Saint Jane can't be a saint *all* the time, she was having a secret affair.'

Flynn almost sent the pan flying across the room – no mean feat with Le Creuset cast iron. He recovered himself quickly and put it back on the hob. 'Sorry, not used to these things, they weigh a ton. A secret affair, did you say? Interesting. Who with?'

'Charlotte's husband, of course,' I said.

'Strewth, you mean Dan Dixon?' He seemed genuinely stunned. 'I've obviously underestimated the bloke. This is a revelation, Em. Has Jane talked about him much?'

My lip curled. 'Does Jane talk about anything? Apart from her marketing expertise, that is. She's never been very forthcoming about her personal life.'

'I can understand that, I suppose,' he said, with a sigh. 'I'm the same – for quite different reasons, I imagine. It's one of the pitfalls of being a celebrity – every look, every comment is in the spotlight. It goes against the grain – I'm normally such a spontaneous sort of person, you know? And I'm being especially careful over here, with everything I've heard about the British press.'

I nodded sympathetically. 'It must be awful having no privacy.' Then I smiled. 'Although Highbury's probably the safest place in England, the old biddy mafia will sniff out any paparazzi long before you do, and run them out of town!'

He laughed. 'I think I'm going to enjoy Highbury.'

'I hope so. Anyway, let's have our soup before it gets cold.'

We sat at the table and ate in silence for a few minutes; but my mind was buzzing with this latest information. How weird – and annoying – that my bête noire had met Flynn Churchill before I had!

'You've probably guessed that Jane and I aren't exactly best friends,' I said. 'I've always found her very difficult to get close to, but perhaps she's different when she's away from Highbury. How well did you get to know her?'

He paused to swallow a large spoonful of mine-strone. 'This is delicious! You know, I've always wanted to go to Italy and sample the real thing, but there's no need, I can come here instead.

217

You're a fantastic cook – and aren't you half Italian?'

'My mother was from Florence.'

'That would account for your lovely colouring, of course.' He stared at me, and I felt myself blush. 'I'm fed up with pale skin,' he said. 'Makes me think of uncooked pastry.'

I giggled. 'That's a bit harsh. Some women with pale skin are considered very attractive. Jane, for example, everyone thinks she's so pretty . . . How much did you see of her in Weymouth?'

Another disarming grin. 'As much as I ever want to. The Campbells took a shine to me and invited me over whenever I was at a loose end, which was most days – until one of Stella's spies turned up.'

'Spies? Did she actually send someone to check up on you?'

'Yes. She kicked up a big fuss, told me I was over here to work, not socialise, and threatened to put an end to my TV career in Australia.'

I gasped. 'Can she really do that?'

'Oh yes, she's got her finger in lots of pies and, at the end of the day, money talks.' He scowled, then his mood changed abruptly. He leaned forward, eyes twinkling. 'D'you know what? I think there might be something in your little theory. Dan was very attentive to Jane, even when Charlotte was there, as though he couldn't help himself. And I bet I know how it all started – when he saved her from drowning.'

'Which would hardly be necessary since she walks on water,' I said, with a derisive laugh. 'But I'm intrigued – what happened?'

He leaned even further forward, until I could feel his warm breath on my cheek. 'Apparently – mind, I only heard this second hand – Dan and Jane were out in the Campbells' boat. On their own – Charlotte was off somewhere with her mother. Everything was fine until they got into some choppy water, and Dan had to hold onto Jane all the time, to stop her going overboard, even though she was wearing a safety jacket. I wouldn't be surprised if he gave her the kiss of life, just as a precaution . . . And the rest, as they say, is history.'

'Poor Charlotte! I wonder if she suspects anything?' I frowned as I refilled our glasses. 'Jane looks as though butter wouldn't melt in her mouth, but she's always been far too reserved for my liking. Ask her a simple question and she gives you some wishy-washy answer that means nothing. I don't think you'd even get her to say the Pope's Catholic.'

His face darkened. 'I know. Some people are so scared of committing themselves, they go for the safest option every time, complete silence. Well, it may be safe but it's a bloody pain and I—' He stopped and ran his fingers through his copper curls. I watched, fascinated, as they sprang back, but in a different direction. Everything about him was like that, new and shiny and exciting; even

219

now, when he was scowling. Then, 'Sorry, Em, didn't mean to go on like that. It's just I don't think I'm cut out for someone reserved, I'm such an open, in-your-face sort of person.'

I smiled. 'I know you are. But I suppose a certain amount of reserve can be very appealing, provided you get the odd glimpse behind the mask.' For some reason Mark came to mind; the relaxed Mark I'd seen at Ashridge, the totally uninhibited Mark who'd kissed me. Now it was my turn to frown. He was the last person I should be thinking about, especially with Flynn around.

I got abruptly to my feet. 'More soup?'

'Sure, and I'd love the recipe – if it's not a family secret.'

'Of course it is – but I know I can trust you, I'll write it down before you go. By the way, would you like a lift back to Randalls? I could drop you there at quarter past two, when I go to meet Harriet.'

He hesitated. 'Actually, could you drop me in Highbury? Kate thinks I should call on Jane and introduce myself to the dreaded aunt. Jane may not be one for conversation, but apparently Mary Bates more than makes up for it. No wonder her mother's gone deaf.'

I groaned. 'You don't need to tell me about Batty, I've known her all my life.'

'Batty? Great nickname, must remember not

to use it to her face.' He gave a deep sigh. 'Can't say I'm thrilled about seeing them, but I'd do anything for my lovely stepmother. And it fills in the time until Dad can take me to fetch my hire car – had a bit of an argument with a lamp post in London and the front headlight's had to be replaced.' He paused and looked me straight in the eye. 'You know, if these talks with the BBC go well, I could be staying in Highbury for some time. And believe me, there's nothing I'd like better.'

I took this as a very encouraging sign.

MARK

I wanted to call Kate as soon as I left Hartfield and give my apologies for tonight; but I didn't have the number for Randalls on my mobile, so it was a question of waiting until I got home and found Father's address book.

Just as I got in the door, Kate herself rang. I was about to launch into a half-baked excuse – an urgent business proposal or something – when she forestalled me.

'Flynn's sent me a text to say you can come to dinner tonight. I'm so glad, because I've got a little favour to ask.'

That bastard Churchill. He'd made sure I couldn't escape watching him move in on Emma.

'What sort of favour?' I said guardedly.

'Could you give Mary and Jane a lift? Mary's car wouldn't start this morning and it's had to be towed to the garage. I know she'll offer to get a taxi, but—'

'I'd be happy to.'

'Thanks, Mark, I'll tell her you'll call for them at seven.'

She hung up, leaving me with a sickening sense of déjà vu. Was it only a week since I'd given Mary and her mother a lift to Randalls? I'd spent the whole evening going through the motions of a relationship with Tamara, when I ached to be with Emma. Even when Tamara and I split up two days later, a future with Emma still seemed inconceivable.

Until last night . . .

Now Churchill had arrived – and I had an even tougher fight on my hands.

EMMA

As part of my secret campaign to rid Harriet of her infatuation with Philip, I'd suggested a get-together away from the office. She wanted to go to The Ploughman one evening, but I knocked that idea on the head immediately; we were sure to bump into Philip himself or, even worse, Robert Martin. So I invited her to meet me at Tilly's Tea Rooms in nearby Findlesham on Saturday afternoon. I hadn't spoken to her since I'd heard about Philip's whirlwind romance with the mysterious

Gusty, just before I left for Ashridge on Friday. In theory, this would make it easier to convince Harriet that she had no chance with him, but I couldn't be sure.

Although I'd made this arrangement before Flynn arrived, it turned out to be a far-sighted decision; I now felt like wearing something new to the Westons' – and Findlesham had a very select dress shop.

Tilly's was one of those quaint establishments that was, and had been since time immemorial, truly customer focused; the staff waited unobtrusively on your every need, brought any tea you fancied – Highbury Foods had supplied some of the more specialist blends for years – and made dainty sandwiches to individual order. Knowing that Harriet would drink something you could stand a spoon in, I ordered a pot of Earl Grey for one and settled down with the latest issue of *Fortune*.

Ten, fifteen, twenty minutes passed and still Harriet didn't appear, with no reply whenever I called her mobile. At last she hurtled through the door, almost half an hour late and breathless with agitation.

'You'll never guess what happened!' she said, her eyes suspiciously bright.

It was obvious she'd heard about Philip and Gusty. I took a sip of Earl Grey and prepared soothing phrases. She crashed down on the chair opposite and ordered 'a pot of really, really strong tea, nothing posh, and a ham and pickle sarnie'. This prompted the waitress to launch into a gentle interrogation. Did she want white bread, malted grain or wholemeal? Crusts on or off? Butter or a healthy alternative? Smoked ham – or plain Wiltshire, freshly cut off the bone? By the time we got to the choice of pickles, I'd almost lost the will to live.

The waitress turned to me. 'What would you like, Miss Woodhouse?'

'The same, and another pot of Earl Grey,' I said. 'As quickly as you can, please, I'm running late.'

When we were on our own, Harriet gave me an apologetic smile. 'Sorry, Emma, I was on time, honest, then I noticed I'd nearly run out of petrol. So I turned into Ford's—'

'Ford's?'

'Yeah, that garage in Little Bassington—'

'I know exactly where Ford's is,' I said, grimly. 'But what on earth were you doing *there*? Findlesham is the other side of Highbury and there's a perfectly good petrol station on the way.'

She looked down. 'Well, you see, I've been going past Philip's house at least once a day.'

'Oh Harriet, why?'

She shifted uneasily in her seat. 'Dunno, just a habit.' She took a deep breath and went on, 'Anyway, Ford's is a crap garage, more for repairs, innit? The man has to come and work the pump for you, but he wasn't around. And it was raining, so I just waited in the car. Then – guess what?'

'I have no idea.'

At this point, her pot of tea arrived. She gave it a thorough stir and poured out a cup of what looked like treacle. Half the jug of milk followed, which seemed to defeat the object of having such a strong brew in the first place. After a couple of gulps she lurched forward, as if the information she was about to share was highly confidential.

'*He* came,' she said, in a loud whisper.

'Philip?'

She looked at me as though I was an imbecile. 'No – Rob.'

'Robert Martin?'

'Yes, I knew it was him because his van has yellow furry dice hanging from the mirror thingy.'

I gave a delicate shudder. 'Not many of those round here.'

'He only got them because I said I liked them.' She took a paper napkin from the little silver holder and started fiddling with it. 'He was with his sister, but for one horrible moment I thought she might be a new girlfriend . . . Not that I care,' she added, shredding the napkin into dandruff-sized pieces on her plate.

'What happened exactly?'

'Alison – his sister, remember, the one that was going to Amsterdam—'

'Yes, yes,' I said impatiently. 'What did she do?'

'She got out of the van and came across to me,

so I wound down the window and – oh Emma, it was awful!' She dropped what remained of the napkin into the sugar bowl and covered her face with her hands, knocking over the milk jug in the process. A waitress appeared as if from nowhere and calmly cleaned everything up, while I took a fortifying drink of tea. There was another delay while our sandwiches arrived. Harriet peeped through her fingers at them but made no move to uncover her face.

'Harriet,' I said sternly, 'pull yourself together and tell me what Alison said.'

She lowered her hands at last. 'She said,' – her voice trembled – 'she said "Have you been waiting here long?" or something.'

My eyes widened. 'Is that all?'

The hands waved wildly about, narrowly missing the little vase of golden-bronze spray chrysanthemums. 'It was the shock of her even speaking to me, after – well, you know—'

'Yes, yes.'

She started dissecting another napkin. 'I told her I'd been sitting there at least five minutes. So she smiled and said she'd get Rob to go and find Dave to do the petrol. And I said I didn't want him to get wet and she laughed, but not in a nasty sort of way, and said he was big enough to look after himself. Then she went and the next thing I knew *he* was there, even closer to me than you are, and – and guess what he said?'

I sighed. 'I really can't imagine.'

'That Dave was on his way and I needed to wind the window up otherwise I'd get wet.'

'Gosh.'

'He must still like me . . . d'you think?'

I was silent. I had to admit – rather grudgingly and only to myself – that, if Mark Knightley had time for him, Robert Martin must be a decent man. And, in my view, a decent man didn't switch from one woman to another that easily. Whereas it appeared that Philip Elton had forgotten me as soon as Gusty batted her eyelids at him across a crowded room . . .

I took a deep breath. 'Harriet, please stop fiddling with that napkin and listen to me. I need to talk to you about Philip.'

She dropped the napkin, cocked her head on one side and said vacantly, 'Philip?'

'Yes, Philip.' Another deep breath. 'He seems to have acquired a girlfriend at that conference last week.'

'Yeah, that would be about right.' She took a sandwich and crammed it in her mouth.

I was completely taken aback by her reaction, or lack of it. 'What do you mean?'

She gave me a pitying look as she swallowed the sandwich. 'Don't you ever read horoscopes? I checked Philip's on Thursday and it was obvious he'd found someone in Bristol, it said "love blossoms from a chance meeting in foreign parts". That's when I knew there was no point fancying him any more.'

I frowned. 'But it didn't stop you going past his house today.'

'Told you, it's just a habit,' she said, with a shrug. 'And I'm interested in seeing who he's got off with, aren't you? He'll want to show her his lovely house, so I'm bound to see her some time soon.'

'Apparently she's staying with him this weekend,' I said. 'Or so Mary told me on Friday. You weren't in the office at the time, you must have been at lunch.'

She looked puzzled. 'I can't remember where I was, but I didn't have any lunch, I know that. Too much to do.'

'I didn't think I'd left you a lot of work. You must tell me if—'

'Oh, it wasn't *your* work,' she said airily. 'Well, it was in a way, since Jane reports to you. She thought it would be good if I got a whole lot of stuff ready for her to read on Monday. Took me ages, but I didn't mind. She's lovely, isn't she? Sort of looks like a Goth, only nicer. It meant I didn't quite finish that presentation you'd given me, but Jane told me not to worry.'

My lips tightened. 'In future, Harriet, *my* work takes priority over Jane's.'

'Sorry.' She took a quick slurp of tea. 'Did you get much research done with Mark?'

It was a question I'd been expecting, but it caught me off guard. Two vivid recollections invaded my thoughts: that look in his eyes as he reached for me, and the feel of his mouth, making love to mine . . .

My hand shook, ever so slightly, as I poured myself another cup of tea. 'Yes, I did. Quite enlightening at the time, but I don't need to do any more.'

She giggled. 'I wouldn't be thinking about work with him around, I'd be hoping for a storm so we'd have to stay the night at Ashridge.'

'I can assure you there was nothing further from my mind,' I said coolly.

She looked at me curiously. 'How long is it since your last shag?'

'Harriet!' I glanced round to see if anyone was listening, then leaned forward. 'The other big news is that Flynn Churchill's arrived in Highbury at long last – you know, Tom Weston's son, the celebrity chef from Australia.' I sat back and reached for my purse to pay the bill. 'Which reminds me, I need a new dress for tonight. Come to Estella's next door and help me choose something that Flynn won't be able to resist.'

I had no intention of being guided by her at all, of course. She sat in the dress shop working out how many tops she could buy at Primark for the price of one of Estella's silk camisoles, while I tried on five or six outfits. In the end, I bought a sexy black dress that fitted me to a T, and made sure she didn't see how much it cost.

Just as we were walking back along the high street, a horribly familiar blue sports car swung into the parking area and screeched to a halt next to my BMW. Philip leapt out from the far side, ran round, flung open the passenger door and hovered expectantly, like an eager puppy returning a carelessly thrown stick.

Harriet and I paused to watch the next part of the performance. First two sturdy legs emerged, encased in Evisu jeans and Ugg boots; then a pair of enormous breasts, jostling with each other to escape from a tight red scoop-necked jumper; and finally, the sort of swirling golden tresses you'd normally see in a L'Oréal advert. This apparition had hardly toppled out of the car when Philip grabbed her and started devouring her. We had an uninterrupted view of her hands slipping down the back of his trousers to fondle his buttocks.

'I think we've seen enough,' I said to Harriet in a disapproving tone. 'Let's go and sit in your car until they've gone.'

But I was too late. Philip swivelled round, detaching his mouth from the woman's in the nick of time. 'Emma, wait!'

They tottered across the car park towards us, welded together from shoulder to hip, Philip smirking in a 'Didn't take me long to find someone, did it?' kind of way.

'Let me introduce Gusty,' he said to me, ignoring Harriet. He added with a leer, 'We've only just

230

got up, so it's afternoon tea at Tilly's instead of breakfast.'

Gusty flicked her hair back from her face and bared her teeth in the semblance of a smile. She was pretty enough, though not a patch on Harriet, and immaculately made up.

'So this is the famous Emmurrr Woodhouse,' she drawled in a strong Bristol accent, holding out a gleaming set of nail extensions. 'I've heard so much about you and your little marrrketing efforts at Highburrry Foods.'

Remembering where her hand had just been, I said coldly, 'Do you mind if I don't shake hands? My father's immune system is very fragile at the moment and he's insisting that I take every precaution . . . This is Harriet, she's a great help to me in my little marketing efforts.'

Harriet mumbled something, but neither of them paid her the slightest bit of attention.

'Give this to Henry and tell him I'll be in touch,' Gusty said, handing me a little white card from her pocket.

I held it rather gingerly by the edges. It was of good quality and had 'Augusta Hawkins, ACA, Strategic Financial Consultant' across the middle, with a five-lobed leaf below, all in gold. I turned it over and read: 'The Maple Grove Consultancy, for businesses that can afford the best'. I was surprised, however, to see that the contact address began '3, Paradise View, Little Bassington'.

'So you're going to be based here?' I said.

'Until Pipkin tires of me.' She poked Philip playfully, but hard, in the ribs.

'That'll never happen, babe, and you know it.' 'Pipkin' leaned into her and started nibbling her ear.

I gave a brittle smile. 'Looks like you're hungry, mustn't keep you from your tea.' With that, I steered Harriet firmly over to her car. By the time she'd found her keys, dropped them in a puddle and fished them out again, the lovebirds were safely inside Tilly's.

Harriet frowned as she unlocked her car. 'That's a funny name – Gutsy.'

'Gusty. It's short for Augusta.'

'She's so-o-o cool.'

'I thought she was rather vulgar,' I said, with a sniff.

'He's crazy about her.'

'Looks like it, although I really can't understand what he sees in her, compared to you – or me.'

'They're obviously at it like rabbits.'

'Yes, we were getting that message loud and clear.'

'Lucky them. Go for it while you have the friggin' chance, that's what I say.' She let out a long noisy sigh and got into the car. 'Thanks for the tea, see you Monday.'

She turned the key in the ignition, revved up the engine, fumbled through various gears and drove off, narrowly missing my foot.

I stood in the middle of the car park, deep in

thought. 'Go for it while you have the frigging chance.' Such a simple philosophy.

Well, I felt sure I had a chance with Flynn. And I'd be going for it – come hell, high water or Mark Knightley.

CHAPTER 8

CAPERS

MARK

The evening at Randalls was just about tolerable, until Churchill started playing his little games.

The seating arrangements didn't help. He and I were directly opposite each other, which made him difficult to ignore. And I found it even harder to ignore Emma, who was next to him. Especially in that dress, or what there was of it.

I had to admit that the food was good, although I couldn't believe Churchill had made do with what Kate had in her kitchen. On the other hand, knowing Kate, she'd have an impressive range of ingredients permanently in the fridge and plenty more in the freezer, neatly labelled no doubt. Whatever the truth of the matter, he'd managed to produce smoked salmon pâté, orange-glazed roast lamb and a rum-soaked pineapple cake, all washed down with a few bottles of Château Margaux 1959 from Tom's antique wine cellar.

Henry, meanwhile, spooned his way through three courses of orangey-yellow mush. I suspected this was simply a purée of what we were eating, but Churchill gave him some bullshit about it being carrots and saffron specially blended with artichoke, which the Aborigines swore by for improving the digestion. Everyone greeted this pronouncement with oohs and ahs of wonder – except me. Anyway, Henry seemed happy enough; or maybe he was too distracted by Mary to notice what he was eating.

'Dave Ford's been so kind,' Mary said, as soon as there was a lull in the conversation. 'He wouldn't take any money today for towing my car, said he'd just add it on to my bill, which is very considerate of him when you remember his wife's . . . But unfortunately he thinks my big end's gone, or was it my cylinder head gasket?'

Out of the corner of my eye, I noticed Churchill whisper something in Emma's ear and send her off into a fit of the giggles.

Mary continued, 'Either way, he says it's going to be *very* expensive and he might have to keep the car for three weeks, with all the other work he's . . . If there was only me to think about, I'd just hop on my bike—'

'Your bike?' Henry leaned forward, his eyes wide with horror. 'You'd be mown down by a juggernaut in no time, especially with the nights drawing in.'

'No need to worry, Henry, I won't even consider it because dear Jane needs to get to work as well. Although I do believe we've still got that old bike

235

of hers . . .' She tittered. 'She was quite the demon racer at one time, left all the children round here way behind – don't you remember, Emma?'

Emma's face darkened and I couldn't resist saying in a loud aside to Kate beside me, 'Emma was always going to take her cycling proficiency test but she never put in the hours, did she, after her initial burst of enthusiasm?'

Henry frowned. 'I'd offer you both a lift with Emma and me, but I'm afraid our morning routine's rather unpredictable at the moment. Porridge for breakfast, you know,' he added, as if that explained everything.

Mary said hesitantly, 'I don't suppose there's a spare company car? Of course, I need an automatic, I never learned to drive a manual . . . Just a thought, Henry.'

'I'll have a word with Terry,' Henry said doubtfully, 'but I don't think we've got many automatics. Have you looked into hiring something?'

She coloured. 'Of course, but you see it's a lot of money and Mother's got a little problem with her . . . So she may need to have an operation privately, there's such a long waiting list with the National Health . . . Never mind,' she added, with a sigh, 'I'm sure Jack Thomas will do me a special price for a taxi there and back each day, and we always have *such* a nice chat.'

Once again, Churchill whispered something to make Emma laugh.

It was time to bring this particular subject to a

close. 'I'll give you and Jane a lift to work and back,' I said firmly, 'for as long as you need.'

She gave a squeal, half delight, half dismay. 'But it's too much out of your way and—'

'No "buts". I'll be outside your house at half past eight on Monday morning.'

Her relief was evident. 'Thank you, Mark. Always so kind, just like your father.'

It was over coffee that I really detected Churchill's Machiavellian tendencies at work. He presented each of us with what he called his 'special fortune cookie', a small biscuit wrapped in a piece of tissue-like paper, and instructed us not to open it until we were told.

'Dad and Kate first, I think,' he said. 'And read them out, please. There's a common theme and I've got a prize for the person who guesses what it is.'

Tom opened his little parcel, wolfed down the biscuit and chuckled to himself as he read the piece of paper. 'This is an old one, Flynn, I'm surprised you've heard of it. Listen, everyone: "Blue moon, you saw me standing alone, without a dream in my heart, without a love of my own." What's yours, Kate?'

Kate laughed. 'Same song, but a different line: "And then suddenly appeared before me, the only one my arms could ever hold." I can even quote the rest: "I heard somebody whisper, 'Please adore me', and when I looked the moon had turned to gold." One of my all-time favourites.' She smiled warmly at Flynn. 'You can't possibly have known that, though.'

Churchill grinned back. 'You're right, I didn't. I chose it because it reminded me of you two.'

'Lovely thought,' Kate said.

'Much appreciated, son,' Tom added.

I hadn't heard 'Blue Moon' for years and the lyrics brought me up short. I glanced at Emma, willing her to look in my direction, but she was gazing affectionately at Tom and Kate. Not at Churchill, thank God; at least, not yet.

'Jane, you're next.'

At Churchill's command, Jane started and went pink. 'Do I have to?'

For once, she seemed uncomfortable in the spotlight; I stared at her, wondered what was going on behind those dark expressionless eyes.

'I forgot to mention that there's a forfeit,' Churchill said briskly. 'Anyone who objects has to perform the song, not just say the words. So be warned.'

'Jane's got a wonderful voice,' Mary put in. 'People are always asking her to . . . Who was that man, Jane, who begged you to sing at his wedding? Oh, silly me! It was Charlotte's husband, wasn't it, Dan Thingummy-Bob.'

Emma leaned forward. 'What did you sing for Dan – and Charlotte, of course?' Her sudden interest made me suspicious; was she winding Jane up about something?

Jane went an even deeper shade of pink. 'It was "The Power of Love".'

Emma smirked. 'Ah yes, "'Cause I am your lady and you are my man, whenever you reach for me I'll do all that I can" – is that the one?'

'I believe so.'

'Come on,' Churchill said, 'read out your fortune cookie before I give you a forfeit.'

Jane hesitated, then slowly unfolded her piece of paper. 'It says "I'm hopelessly devoted to" followed by a question mark.' She added coldly, 'I've no idea what it means.'

'Haven't you?' Churchill countered. 'I'll move on to Emma, then.'

I watched Emma closely as she unwrapped her biscuit and read her words in silence. A slow, sweet smile spread across her face, and my heart sank. 'Mine says "You're the one that I want".' She looked at Churchill. 'I think I know what the common theme is now, but I'm not a hundred percent sure, so I'd better wait.' She giggled, then took a small bite out of her biscuit and closed her eyes. 'Mmmm, ratafia – absolutely delicious. Did you make these yourself?'

'Of course,' Churchill said smoothly. 'Your turn, Mary.'

'So exciting, let me just get my reading glasses, I wonder where I put my handbag? Oh, thank you, Tom . . . Good gracious, these are Mother's, I must have picked up the wrong ones when I . . . . Mark, would you? So kind.'

I took Mary's piece of paper and scanned it quickly; the words seemed harmless enough, and vaguely familiar. I handed the paper back to her. 'It says: "This car is automatic, it's systematic, it's hydromatic." Very topical.'

'Automatic . . . systematic . . . hydromatic . . . It does sound like my car, doesn't it? I don't *think* mine's a hydromatic, but it might be . . . Dave will know, I'll check with him when I . . . You said they were all songs, Flynn, but what's the common theme? Blue moon, hopelessly devoted, the one that I want and now a car – let's see yours, Mark, that might help.'

Churchill nodded at me. 'Go ahead.'

I opened up the paper, removed the biscuit in order to read the words – and felt the colour drain from my face.

How could the bastard know? How *could* he?

'Something the matter?' Mary said, anxiously.

With an effort, I brought myself under control. He couldn't know how I felt about Emma, because I hadn't told anyone, not even her. He must have chosen these words by accident . . .

I cleared my throat. 'Not at all, I'm just trying to place these lyrics: "Can't you see, I'm in misery. We made a start, now we're apart." Any ideas?'

In the silence that followed, Mary's stage whisper to Henry could be heard loud and clear. 'Poor man, he's missing Tamara terribly and this has obviously brought it all back to him. A *very* unfortunate choice of words . . .'

She was way off track, but she'd unwittingly put my mind at rest. I realised that Churchill wasn't

240

taunting me about Emma at all; he was referring to my break-up with Tamara. Someone would have told him about that during his first day in Highbury, I was sure.

Still a bastard, only not as clever as I'd thought.

EMMA

It was the look on Mark's face that got to me. I wanted to put my arms round him and kiss the sadness away. As a friend, nothing more . . .

But the next moment Flynn was murmuring in my ear, 'Oops, put my foot in it there, didn't I?'

I gave him a sympathetic smile and whispered back, 'You weren't to know.'

He raised his voice. 'So, Em, are you ready to have a guess at the answer?'

My smile broadened. 'Depends what the prize is.'

'Can't say, you'll just have to trust me when I say it's worth winning.'

I took a deep breath. 'OK then, I think what they all have in common is—'

'What about Henry?' Mark put in. 'He hasn't read his out yet, it may give more people a chance to win the prize.'

Flynn hesitated, then shrugged. 'Henry's probably gives the game away, but if you insist . . .'

Dad unwrapped his biscuit and stared at it longingly. 'I don't think I dare risk it—'

'The paper, Henry, read out what's on the paper,' Batty squeaked.

He looked down and blanched. 'Oh dear, I feel quite queasy. It says, "Grease is the word".'

'Songs from *Grease*,' Mark and I said, at exactly the same time.

'Correct, both of you.' Flynn paused. 'But you're the winner, Em, I heard you first.'

'Oh, what a shame, can't they share the prize?' Batty said, much to my annoyance.

He shook his head. 'I'm afraid it's not that sort of prize.'

'I'm not bothered in the slightest,' Mark said heavily, 'but you could at least tell me what I'm missing.'

Flynn grinned at him. 'Sure. I'll be taking Em out for a meal, no expense spared.'

My heart skipped a beat. I could picture it now – an intimate candlelit dinner, wine and conversation flowing, and a goodnight kiss . . . 'That sounds wonderful,' I said. 'We'd better arrange it soon, before everywhere's booked up for Christmas.'

Jane got to her feet. 'I've got a migraine coming on. If you don't mind, I'll call a taxi and go home.'

Batty gave a little shriek. 'Oh, poor Jane, wait until I've finished my coffee and I'll come with you—'

'You stay here, Mary,' Mark put in. 'I'm quite happy to take Jane home now and come back for you later.'

While everyone fussed over Jane, I went to the kitchen to make some camomile tea for Dad and me. I'd just put the kettle on and set out the cups and saucers on a tray, when Kate arrived.

'I'm glad I've got you on your own, Emma. I've been dying to ask – who does Jane remind you of?'

Several answers sprang to mind, none of them complimentary; I decided to play safe. 'No idea.'

'Who've we met recently with black hair and really white skin?'

Oh God, she was right; the physical similarity was striking. Why hadn't I seen it before?

'Tamara,' I said, slowly. My hand trembled as I poured the boiling water from the kettle into the teapot. Amazingly, I managed it without scalding myself, although I spilled some on the bench.

Kate was too busy topping up the coffee machine to notice. 'Exactly. There must be a certain type that appeals to Mark and now he's falling for Jane hook, line and sinker.'

Jane Fairfax at Donwell Abbey? Over my dead body!

'What gives you that impression?' I said, carefully mopping up the water.

'You can just tell,' she said vaguely. 'He's always made it obvious he likes her, but tonight he seems to have moved things up a gear, suggesting all those lifts to work when it's so far out of his way.' She took the empty coffee packet over to the bin. 'And he couldn't take his eyes off her when she read out, "Hopelessly devoted to" – oh!' She paused. 'Well I never, there's an empty ratafia box in here. Didn't Flynn say he'd made those biscuits himself?'

'I don't remember,' I said impatiently. 'But I think you're wrong about Mark and Jane. It's just his style, he's always helping people out.'

'You wait and see.' She closed the bin with a frown. 'I wouldn't be at all surprised if Jane takes over where Tamara left off. A man like Mark is never without a woman for long. And don't forget, Tom and I got together after he gave me a lift home from your dinner party. Maybe she's asking him in for a nightcap even as we speak—'

I slammed the teapot onto the tray. 'Never. He couldn't bear it – if he got into any sort of relationship with Saint Jane, he'd have Batty haunting Donwell day and night, and probably Old Mother Bates as well!'

She laughed. 'I imagine he'd put up with an awful lot for the right woman.'

'Huh, with her he'd bloody well have to.'

I marched into the hall with the tray and bumped straight into Flynn.

'Wondered where you were,' he said, putting his hands on my shoulders to steady me. 'Thought you might have gone home with a migraine too, but I bet *you* don't give up that easily . . . Did you like the fortune cookie I gave Jane?'

I smiled up at him. 'A lot more than she did, by the look of it. She knew you were getting at her and Dan, didn't she? And did you see how red she went when I asked her what she sang at his wedding?'

Before he could answer, Batty poked her head round the living room door. 'Ah, there you are, Emma.' She sidled up to us. 'Your father's asking for his tea and I wouldn't mind a cup as well, we're just moving from the table to some more comfortable seats.'

'Allow me.' Flynn took the tray and dodged past her into the living room.

I made to follow him, but the blasted woman clung to my arm like a limpet.

'It is camomile, isn't it, dear? You're father swears by it for getting to sleep and I could do with a decent night . . . So much to think about at the moment, what with—'

'Your car,' I said hurriedly, before she repeated the whole saga. 'Yes, it must be a terrible worry.'

She gave a noisy sigh. 'It's not just my own worries, I found poor Sandy Perry in tears when I called this morning with a tiny present for . . . You'll never guess what that son of hers has been up to, when I think of how he sang in the church choir for all those years, like a little angel . . . And apparently, if he does it once more he'll be expelled from King Edward's. David's furious and of course Sandy's torn between the two of them, *such* a shame, isn't it? Anyway, David wants it all hushed up, he is a doctor after all, you'd think he'd know if his son was up to *that* sort of thing . . . So don't breathe a word to anyone – mind, I was so upset that I had to tell Jane, but she's the soul of discretion.'

'I never gossip,' I said coolly, trying to shake her off my arm.

Just then Kate appeared with fresh coffee and I managed to give Batty the slip. For the rest of the evening, I kept well away from her relentless wittering and stayed as close as I could to Flynn. We spent most of the time in stitches at his stories about near disasters on Flynn's Cook-in.

At one point, Tom took a phone call from Mark. It seemed he was delayed, but we were not to worry; Jane was safely home and he'd taken the opportunity to deliver some paperwork to one of his directors, which would involve a cup of coffee and a chat. With Kate's prediction ringing in my ears, I didn't believe this pathetic explanation for a moment.

When at last I heard his voice in the hall, I glanced at my watch. It had taken him over an hour to drive to Batty's front door and back, a journey of less than a mile each way. Had Saint Jane invited him in? Had he kissed her the way he'd kissed me? Had Old Mother Bates heard them and come downstairs, just as Dad had done last night?

Then I remembered. Old Mother Bates was deaf and could hardly walk without help, let alone cope with the stairs. She couldn't have interrupted them if she'd tried.

Did I care what Mark Knightley got up to with Jane Fairfax?

Absolutely not.

MARK

Not surprisingly, after taking Jane home I was in no rush to go back to the Westons'. I drove straight on to Kingston and came back to Highbury by an extremely slow and circuitous route. Being in the car reminded me of last night, with Emma sleeping beside me.

It felt like a century ago.

When I walked into the living room at Randalls, the first thing I saw was Emma and Churchill in a corner together, laughing their heads off. I sat down beside Henry, refused his offer of cold camomile tea and gratefully accepted Kate's of freshly brewed coffee.

Churchill immediately broke off his conversation with Emma and grinned unpleasantly at me. 'We were wondering where you'd got to, Mark, until you rang and explained. Do you often dish out work on a Saturday night?'

I kept my tone as neutral as I could. 'Not usually, but it couldn't be helped.'

'And how was dear Jane?' Mary said.

'When I left her, she was about to take a painkiller and go to bed.'

'Did you see Mrs Bates?' This from Emma, the first time she'd spoken to me all evening.

Mary gave her a puzzled look. 'I wouldn't have thought so, dear. I put Mother to bed before I went out, with the TV on and the phone next to her, of course. And she can't get very far on her own, as you know.' She turned to me. 'I imagine she was asleep by the time you arrived.'

'I imagine she was,' I said, with a reassuring smile. 'She certainly didn't disturb us.'

Emma jumped up, scowling. 'Time to go, Dad. I'll get our coats.'

I sensed she wasn't at all happy with my answer, although I couldn't for the life of me see why.

EMMA

I vowed never to drink camomile tea again. What was the point of dosing yourself with something that tasted like stewed grass – which technically it was, I suppose – if it didn't do what it was meant to? Instead of dropping off to sleep instantly, I lay awake for the second night in a row, mulling over everything that had happened.

Most of the time I thought about Flynn, of course. But there was also Harriet's incomprehensible fixation with Robert Martin; then that distasteful encounter with Philip and Gusty; and finally, the possibility that Saint Jane would very soon be snugly – or should that be smugly? – installed at Donwell . . .

Kate phoned the next morning, with the news that Flynn was coming to see me. 'He's gone to

Mary's first, she left her mother's specs here last night and he offered to drop them off on his way to you.' She paused. 'Tom and I were just saying, you seem to have made a big impression on him already.'

I smirked at myself in the mirror above the telephone table, then did a double take. Shit! After that lousy sleep, I looked a complete wreck. 'When do you think he'll get here?' I said, anxiously.

She laughed. 'Who knows? He said last time he called at Mary's he was trapped there for three hours. We all know what she's like, don't we?'

I brought the conversation to an end as soon as I could, and raced upstairs to change my clothes and put on some make-up. Then I waited, and waited . . .

After an hour and a half, the phone rang; it was Flynn, full of apologies.

'Made the mistake of asking Mary if there was anything she wanted, as she's without a car,' he said. 'So here I am at Asda, in Kingston, with a list as long as my arm and Jane lecturing me about my expensive tastes.' He broke off and murmured something, presumably to Saint Jane. He went on, 'Apparently Mary's idea of a nice joint of beef is the opposite of mine – she means something you Poms call brisket, whereas I'd rather have a piece of rump any day. And I've bought her the biggest one I could find, just to show her the difference.'

I frowned. 'How thoughtful. Although I'm

surprised Batty asked you to go shopping for her, she's always been dead against Sunday trading.'

'Ah, but this is an exception, because she couldn't do any yesterday.' He sounded more amused than upset by my lack of sympathy. 'Anyway, Em, what if I come round this afternoon – say two o'clock?'

'I'm afraid not, Dad and I are going over to my sister's,' I said, trying to hide my disappointment; I added quickly, 'How about tonight?'

He hesitated. 'Sorry, Mary's invited me to dinner. You can imagine how it went – "It's the *least* I can do, *so* kind of you to take *dear* Jane shopping" and the rest. God knows I'd get out of it if I could—'

'Not to worry, let's have lunch tomorrow instead.'

'That would be great, I'll give you a ring at work in the morning.'

As I put the phone down, I realised how much I'd been looking forward to seeing him. Now I'd have to wait another twenty-four dreary hours.

It must be love, mustn't it?

MARK

On Monday, I drew up outside the Bateses' house at half past eight on the dot. Instantly, Jane appeared at the front door, walked sedately down the path to the car, opened the nearside rear door and settled herself in the back.

'Good morning,' she said quietly, 'and thank you for going to all this trouble.'

I was just reassuring her that it was no trouble at all, when a flustered Mary arrived, tried to get in at Jane's side, realised her mistake with a shrill squeal and scuttled round to the front passenger seat.

'Oh, Mark,' she gasped as she scrambled inside, 'I thought you'd have put Jane in the front, you don't want an old chatterbox like me distracting you—'

'Just shut the door, please, before that van takes it clean off,' I said, more brusquely than I intended.

She gave another squeal and yanked the door shut. Then, 'Oh dear, I seem to have got my coat caught in the . . . Just a minute and I'll . . . There, all set and ready to go. We're so grateful, Mark, really we are, I was saying to Mother only this morning . . .'

I tried to ignore her and concentrate on negotiating the traffic, but it was more of a challenge than I'd expected. Although we reached Highbury Foods in ten minutes, it felt like thirty, with Jane never saying a word and Mary hardly pausing for breath. Later, as I drew into my parking space at Donwell Organics, I calculated that three weeks – Dave Ford's estimate for repairing Mary's car – would mean twenty-nine more journeys like this morning's.

In the office, things went from bad to worse. I

found that one of my best employees in India had resigned and Cherry was off sick. Just as I was switching my phone through to Sue, the Finance Director's PA, it rang with an external call.

I answered it, in the absurd hope that it might be Emma. 'Knightley.'

'Is that *Marrrk* Knightley?' A woman's voice, but definitely not Emma's.

'Yes,' I said. 'Who is this?'

'Augusta Hawkins, strategic financial consultant at The Maple Grrrove Consultancy, for businesses that can afforrrd the best. Now, Marrrk, I've been reading up on the orrrganic food industry and I just know I can save your company lots of money. I need to come and tell you all about it, how about tomorrow at two thirrrty?'

'I've never heard of you or your company, Augusta, so—'

'Call me Gusty,' she purred.

Gusty? Ah yes . . . 'Are you Philip Elton's, er, friend?'

'I am, and he's putting in a good word for me at Highburrry Foods even as we speak, so you'd better get in quick, Marrrk, because my services will be in grrreat demand.' Her tone hardened. 'Tomorrow at two thirrrty, have you put it in your diary yet?'

'Hold on, I'm not putting anything in my diary,' I said, testily. 'It's very kind of you to offer to help out, Gusty, but I'm going to have to say no. Now I'm sure you've got lots of other phone calls to make, so I'll let you get on.'

'You have such a charrrming way of saying no that I'm even more determined to make you say yes.' She gave a husky laugh. 'But I can hold off until we get to know each other. Mind, I've heard a lot about *you* already from our mutual cleaning lady, Mrs Burrrn. And, once you've got to know me – we'll be moving in the same cirrrcles, of course, professionally *and* socially – you'll be begging to join my elite clientele, as we say at Maple Grrrove.'

I did my best to remain civil. 'We'll just have to wait and see, won't we? And now I'm due at a meeting. Goodbye.' I slammed the receiver down and switched my phone through to Sue without further delay. Gusty sounded like the sort of person I'd go to great lengths to avoid; I was sure she and Elton were made for each other.

There was no meeting to go to, but my flimsy excuse to get rid of Gusty prompted thoughts of another meeting – the one that I'd expected to have on Saturday morning and that now looked less and less likely to happen. On impulse, I decided to give it one last shot and dialled Emma's mobile. No answer, so I tried her direct line at Highbury Foods.

'Emma Woodhouse's phone, can-ay-yelp-yoo-oo.'

'Hello, Harriet, it's Mark Knightley.'

She gave a nervous giggle. 'Hiya, Mark.'

'Listen, I need to fix up my next mentoring meeting with Emma. I know it's short notice but

I wondered if she was free for lunch today?' A full and frank discussion, over a slap-up meal – somewhere classy, where she would think twice about storming off – and who knew what might happen?

'Seems OK, nothing in the diary – oh, hang on, she's looking cross and she's sort of waving at me.'

Trust Harriet to let that one out of the bag; I heard furtive whispers and steeled myself for rejection.

Harriet went on, as if reading from a script, 'Sorry, I forgot, Emma already has a lunch appointment today.'

'Oh? I thought you said there was nothing in her diary?'

This put her immediately on the defensive and ensured I got all the details. 'Well, you see, she's expecting it to happen but Flynn hasn't actually rung yet to confirm it. And she only fixed it up yesterday, but I couldn't put it in her diary then because the office is closed on Sundays, innit?'

Churchill – I might have known; my hand tightened round the receiver. 'Any other lunch times free this week?'

There was a scuffling sound and I guessed Harriet had put her hand over the mouthpiece; not very effectively as it turned out, because I could still hear her clearly. 'He says, have you got any other lunch times free this week?'

Although I didn't catch Emma's reply, I had no doubt that Harriet's next words to me repeated it parrot-fashion. 'Only Thursday, but she thinks that's when you usually have your Board meeting, so it looks as though this week's no good, which is *such* a shame.'

'Actually,' I said silkily, 'I may be able to get away on Thursday for an hour or so. I'll check the agenda for my Board meeting and let you know.'

In Cherry's absence, it took a little while to track down the agenda. As soon as I found it, I rang Harriet back.

'It's Mark again—'

She interrupted me with, 'That's so-o-o spooky, I was going to ask Emma if I should ring you. Guess what? Flynn's just phoned her and cancelled lunch, he's got to go into London. Some emergency grooming, Emma said.'

So he'd stood her up, the toe rag! 'Needs his chest waxing, does he?'

My sarcasm completely passed her by. 'Ooh, I don't know about that, she only mentioned a haircut.'

'All the way to London – for a haircut? . . . Bloody pansy,' I added, under my breath.

'Yeah, Emma tried to persuade him to go to Antonio's in Kingston, so they could still have lunch together. But he said he'd already made an appointment at this posh salon in the West End. Anyway, what time do you want to meet her today?'

'Unfortunately, since we last spoke I've been invited out to lunch myself.' A downright lie, but I needed to get down to some work. And I

certainly wasn't going to play second fiddle to the
toe rag. 'So it'll have to be Thursday after all, I'll
pick her up at Highbury Foods at one.'

'I'll tell her.' She giggled. 'I'm dying to see this
Flynn geezer, he sounds amazing, but Emma says
I'm not allowed to fancy him because she saw him
first. Life's a bitch, innit?'

I could only agree and hang up, before I said
something I really regretted.

EMMA

As I came into Harriet's room, I couldn't help
overhearing the last part of her phone conversation.

'Why on earth did you tell him about Flynn
going to London for a haircut?' I said sharply,
knowing that Mark would waste no time in
throwing that back in my face.

She flushed. 'I thought maybe you could see him
today after all.'

I let out an exasperated sigh. 'Please tell me you
haven't arranged anything.'

'I haven't, he can't do today any more. But he
says he can do Thursday and he'll pick you up
from here at one o'clock.'

Huh, I'd been so confident that my suggestion
to meet on Thursday would be a non-starter. I
screwed up the letter I was holding, a glossy invitation to learn 'intuitive influencing skills', and
hurled it at the waste paper basket. It missed.

'Shit.' I gave Harriet a tight-lipped smile. 'Sorry, must have got up on the wrong side of bed.'

It wasn't strictly true – I'd been fine until Flynn's phone call. This was the second time he'd let me down; not a very promising start, given that we'd only known each other for two days. When I told him as much, he just laughed and said there was another reason for going into London, but he wasn't at liberty to tell me. I immediately thought of his negotiations with the BBC and felt slightly less annoyed.

The morning dragged by; in desperation, I invited Saint Jane out to lunch. We went to Chez Pierre, where I hoped the haute cuisine and a large glass of Chablis would loosen her tongue on two subjects: everything she knew about Flynn from her time in Weymouth, and what had happened with Mark on Saturday night.

It didn't go to plan at all; instead, *she* subjected *me* to an hour-long interrogation on my marketing strategy. The only thing I learned about Flynn was that he claimed he'd increased The Mulberry Tree's revenue by an average of thirty per cent a week. More importantly, however, I got the impression that he didn't have a girlfriend – which was all I really wanted to know.

When it came to Saturday night, I tried the subtle approach.

'Mark's been behaving quite strangely since his split with Tamara,' I said. 'Didn't you notice, when we were at Kate and Tom's?'

She paused with a forkful of Caesar salad halfway to her mouth. 'What, exactly?'

Trust her to quibble. I racked my brains and came up with, 'He was staring at people.'

'Can't say I noticed.' She began to chew the salad, very slowly.

'What about when he took you home?' I leaned forward. 'Did he do anything there that was, um, out of the ordinary?'

I had an agonising wait while she finished chewing. At last she said, 'Not that I recall.'

So they hadn't even . . . I mean, surely the woman would recall a kiss that made you feel like . . . Oh shit, why did I have to remember it all so vividly?

Maybe she was lying; but somehow I knew she wasn't. As I'd thought, Kate was totally off track about her and Mark.

Back at Highbury Foods, we were walking to the lift when Jess, one of the receptionists, rushed over to us, grinning broadly.

'Your car's just been delivered, Jane, here are the keys.'

Jane stopped dead. 'My what?'

'Didn't you see it in the car park? An old Jaguar, an E-type, the man said. Go outside and look over to the left, it's a lovely bright red, you can't miss it.'

Jane was silent for a moment. Then, 'There must be some mistake.'

'So you weren't expecting it this soon?' Jess said. 'Chill out, it's not often things arrive early—'

'I wasn't expecting it at all,' Jane said abruptly. 'You must have got me mixed up with someone else.'

'No way, I saw your name on the papers – Jane Fairfax, Marketing Department, Highbury Foods. Here, see for yourself.' She held out a large brown envelope.

Jane made no move to take it, just looked down at the floor.

Jess giggled. 'If you don't know anything about it, you must have a very nice boyfriend.'

'Thank you, Jess, I'll have the envelope, and the keys,' I said. I took them from her, then steered Jane back through the main door and into the car park.

I spotted the Jag in one of the visitors' spaces, low and sleek, its immaculate red paintwork gleaming in the pale autumn sun. We came to a halt several yards away and simply gazed at it. I reckoned it must have cost several thousand pounds, maybe even five figures. Some car. Some present. Some boyfriend.

For the first time in my life, I heard a little moan of pleasure escape from Jane Fairfax's lips. 'Isn't it beautiful? I've always wanted one exactly like this.'

I said nothing; such an unexpected glimpse into her inner world threw me completely. Saint Jane, secretly hankering after a red E-type – whatever next?

Then she folded her arms and said, 'Now I'll have to send it back.'

I stared at her. 'Send it back? Why?'

'I can't possibly accept it.'

'Nonsense.' I paused. 'Do you know who sent it?'

She went crimson. 'Of course I don't.'

Of course she did.

'I'm sure the papers will tell you which garage it came from, but why send it back?' I said. 'It's obviously a very thoughtful gesture by someone, just when you need it, what with Mary's car being out of action.'

She gave a deep sigh. 'I might just sit in it for a few minutes, but that's all.' She took the keys from me, opened the door, ran her hand lovingly along the leather upholstery and settled herself behind the wheel. She didn't put the key in the ignition, however, and I really think she might have sent the car back – if Batty hadn't arrived on the scene.

'Jane, Jane, I came as soon as I heard,' she bleated. 'Oh my goodness, isn't this a splendid ... I feel so much better now that poor Mark doesn't have to ferry us round any more.'

Jane immediately got out of the car and locked it. 'I'm going to phone the garage that brought it here and get them to take it back.'

'Jane dear, think about—'

'I don't even know who it's from.'

Batty's face brightened. 'Oh, now don't you remember? You mentioned all the inconvenience we were having when you were on the phone yesterday to the Campbells. This is just the sort of thing they'd do, isn't it? I mean, money's no object to *them*. And I don't like to impose on Mark, when he's so . . .'

I left them to argue it out and went back to my office. I knew Batty was wrong about the Campbells; they'd merely passed on the message. It was obvious to me who'd given Jane the car: Dan Dixon.

Jane's argument with Batty must have lasted a long time; at any rate, she didn't return to the office until twenty minutes after me.

'Made your decision?' I said, as soon as she walked through the door.

'Yes, I'll keep the car for the moment,' she said primly. 'By the way, Flynn Churchill's waiting downstairs. Shall I get Reception to send him up?'

'Please.' While she was ringing Reception, I touched up my lipstick and wondered if anyone else would hear the thud of my heart.

A few minutes later, Flynn burst into the room. My gaze went automatically to his hair; it had been well cut and the shorter style really suited him. He came straight over, held out his hand palm upwards and looked soulfully at me.

'Please miss, I'm ready for my punishment.'

I couldn't help laughing as I waved his hand away. 'Your punishment is to have lunch with me tomorrow instead.' Out of the corner of my eye, I saw Jane get up and go through to Harriet's room. I added, in a low voice, 'Did you notice a red E-type Jag when you parked your car?'

He frowned. 'Don't think so. Whose is it?'

'It arrived this afternoon for Jane, from a secret admirer.'

'Or a not-so-secret admirer,' he said, with a knowing wink.

I giggled. 'You think it's from Dan, don't you? A token of his undying affection.'

'Well, it's certainly a token of *someone's* undying affection, more like passion if it's bright red. But I daren't speculate who—' He broke off as Jane came back, then went on, 'I have to go. Can't make tomorrow, Em, I'm going to a wine auction with Dad. Keep Thursday free instead.'

'You'd better not cancel,' I said, trying to sound severe and failing miserably.

He grinned and sauntered out of the room; I heard Harriet shriek with laughter at whatever he said to her in passing and smiled to myself. He couldn't help it, could he? He just had a knack for making people, especially women, feel good. I reluctantly turned my attention to a string of unread email messages.

Jane gave a discreet cough. 'Could I have Mark's number, please? I'd better tell him there's no need for any more lifts.'

'His direct line's 432501,' I said absently, staring at an email from Dad which seemed to make no sense whatsoever.

Then it hit me. What if the car was from Mark? After this morning's journey with Batty, no doubt he'd be willing to part with vast sums of money to avoid repeating the experience. But he could simply have paid for a hire car; a flamboyant gesture like this was so out of character.

Except – what if Kate was right and he was desperate for Jane to take Tamara's place? A chance remark from her about her dream car, maybe as he drove her home on Saturday night, then a few phone calls this morning – and there it was, all sorted.

Lucky Jane, being pursued with such determination.

Of course, it didn't matter to me at all, because I'd be getting up close and personal with Flynn, very soon. Very soon indeed.

And I couldn't wait.

CHAPTER 9

COQ AU VIN

MARK

By the time Thursday came, I was in a state of indecision about my meeting with Emma. Should I raise the subject of Friday night – or stay absolutely work focused and give advice on managing Elton? Bloody difficult, when I'd overstepped the same line.

And in that case, should I be mentoring her at all?

I arrived at Highbury Foods just before one o'clock, parked the car and rang her mobile.

'Hello, Emma Woodhouse speaking.'

Didn't she recognise my number – or was she just winding me up?

'I'm outside, I thought we'd go to—'

'You know, I don't think we need this meeting any more.' Her tone was cool and brisk. 'The matter I wanted to discuss seems to have resolved itself, and anyway I can't spare the time.'

I frowned. 'I'm glad the Elton situation's improved. But your excuse about being too busy won't wash – because that's what mentoring's about, helping you use your time more effectively.'

I paused, then went on, 'I don't think Henry would be very pleased if you cancelled. At this short notice, I can't really waive my fee.'

Silence, followed by the tap of high heels on stone steps.

'You're on your way down, then?' I said, with a complacent smile.

'No, Mark, I'm just finding somewhere more private to talk. You see, *I* don't think Dad would be very pleased if I told him what you did on Friday night.'

She really should have known better than to go down that route. 'You mean what *we* did on Friday night, I seem to remember that you gave as good as you got—'

'Don't play games with me, you acted un-professionally and you know it.' Her voice dropped to a hoarse whisper. 'The mentoring's over, can't you see that?'

'Maybe you're right.' I hesitated, then decided to go for it. 'But I'd still like to take you out for lunch. We need to discuss what happened – properly, where we won't be disturbed.'

'Some things are better not discussed.'

'Believe me, Emma, this isn't one of them.'

Silence again.

'It's not as if we can avoid each other,' I said softly. 'There's the Board meetings, your company Christmas do, then mine. And whenever John and Izzy bring the kids over, they like to see both of us. It'll look strange if we—'

'All right, all right,' she said, sounding flustered. 'Only not at the moment, I need some space.'

A result, of sorts; I didn't want to push my luck. 'Fair enough, just say the word when you're ready to talk. 'Bye for now.'

She said goodbye and hung up. Instead of returning to the office, I stayed where I was and made a couple of phone calls. Ten minutes later, I was just leaving the car park when I had to swerve to avoid a maniac in a black Alfa Romeo, apparently in a big hurry to get to Highbury Foods. The driver had red hair, rather shorter than when I'd last seen him.

So she needed space, did she? A Churchill-filled one, by the look of it.

My father's return couldn't come soon enough. Then I'd go straight back to India, giving Emma Woodhouse more space than she could possibly imagine.

EMMA

Immediately after cancelling my mentoring meeting with Mark, I rang Flynn to say I was ready for lunch whenever he was. I almost skipped up the stairs when he said he'd be straight over. It was all working out very well indeed.

There was a slight setback, however, as I went past the Finance office. Philip rushed out, ignored my protests about an urgent appointment and launched into a sales pitch about the tremendous value Gusty would add to Highbury Foods. As I'd told Mark, this particular problem seemed to be resolved; now that he had Gusty to go home to, Philip was being much more civil.

At last I reached my room. Flynn was already there, playing solitaire on my PC, while Jane was hunched over the table, engrossed in a report.

Flynn jumped up and said dramatically, 'I've come to take you away from this beastly place, my darling, let me carry you off to Forbury Manor.'

'Yes, please,' I said with a giggle. 'I've been meaning to check it out ever since it was refurbished. We're having our Christmas party there, as usual.'

'I know, Kate told me, so I thought it'd be the perfect place for the meal I promised you last Saturday.'

My face fell. 'I see.'

'Would you prefer to go somewhere else?'

How to tell him that I'd been hoping my prize would involve a long romantic evening rather than a brief lunch break?

'Not at all,' I said, as cheerfully as I could.

On the way to Forbury, Flynn fired off a constant stream of questions about the party. I couldn't answer most of them and suggested that he ask Kate instead, as she'd organised it for the past few years. All I knew was that we put on a dinner and a disco for all our employees and their partners, with overnight accommodation thrown in. Naturally,

Dad and Batty and a few others preferred to go home to their own beds, but we usually ended up taking over all the rooms in the hotel.

The Manor, a tastefully modernised Georgian pile, was impressive at the best of times; after its recent facelift, it looked positively amazing. The Corporate Events Manager gave us a quick tour; then we discussed the menu and other arrangements for the party, with Flynn contributing some useful ideas. Finally, we sat down to lunch at a table overlooking the gardens. The view was breathtaking: distant woods still ablaze with autumn colour, rolling green-velvet lawns and in front of us, fringed with weeping willows, an ornamental lake, where swans and ducks bickered over pieces of bread.

There was a perfectly adequate fixed-price menu, but Flynn insisted on going à la carte. 'I said there'd be no expense spared, remember?' He gave a wicked grin. 'It's also bribery – to make sure I get an invitation to this party.'

My heart started to thud. It looked like I'd get my romantic evening with him after all; with a couple of hundred other people around, unfortunately, but there'd be plenty of opportunity later for some privacy . . .

Then I remembered. 'I'm afraid Dad's being very strict on numbers this year – only current employees and their partners, if they've got them. He's made a special exception for Kate because she's only just left the company.'

Those dancing green eyes met mine. 'I'll go as your partner, then.'

I raised one eyebrow. 'What if I've already got one?'

He laughed. 'But you haven't. Kate told me.'

'She would,' I said, pleased that he'd bothered to find out. 'Trouble is, Dad knows I'm not dating anyone so he hasn't allowed for a partner in the numbers. Same goes for some of the others, like Harriet and Jane and Mark—'

'Mark?' His eyes narrowed. 'How come he's invited?'

'He's temporarily joined our Board as a non-exec, in place of his father. Not exactly an employee, I know, but in any case our families go way back.'

Another wicked grin. 'If anyone can wheedle something out of Henry, you can. Tell him I'll pay my own way—'

'It's not the money,' I put in. 'It's just Dad and his funny little rules.' Out of the corner of my eye I saw the waiter hovering. 'Look, I'll ask him as soon as I can find the right moment, but don't get your hopes up.'

'I can't help it.' He gave a deep sigh. 'You don't understand how awful my life's been in Australia since I became a celebrity. And it's only a matter of time before the press over here get onto me, especially if I do a deal with the BBC. But Kate says the local paper never bothers with the Highbury Foods Christmas party, so this is a chance for me to relax and enjoy myself. I love socialising, you see, just like my father.' He pulled a face. 'I suppose I'm just being selfish.'

'You're not being selfish at all,' I said indignantly. 'It's perfectly natural to want to party, especially at our age. Don't worry, I'll get you an invitation.'

'You're a star, Em. And there's something else . . . God, this whole situation is so difficult sometimes, I keep wanting to tell you all about it but—'

'Are you ready to order, sir?' It was the waiter, unable to contain himself any longer. I could have throttled him because, by the time he'd finished, Flynn seemed to have completely forgotten what he wanted to tell me. Instead, he started describing Tom's extension plans for Randalls in the style of a gay interior designer, until I was helpless with laughter.

Heads turned, but I couldn't have cared less.

MARK

I wasn't surprised to get a phone call from Henry about the mentoring. He'd paid a considerable amount of money up front, after all.

'How's it going?' he said.

I hesitated, wondering how best to break the news that it wasn't. 'Slowly. So far we've only had one proper meeting. I can't count Ashridge and we had to cancel the one scheduled for last Thursday.'

'And I've paid you for six sessions?'

'You have.'

'This isn't like you, Mark, you're normally so focused. There's a problem, isn't there?'

'Yes.' I braced myself for a showdown.

'And the problem, of course, is Jane. You feel she'd benefit from your expertise as much as Emma, if not more so.' He paused, and I decided not to correct him. He went on, 'I don't suppose you'd mentor them together for the same price?'

'That would never work,' I said firmly. 'It'll have to be just one of them for the remaining five sessions.'

'Hmmm. Naturally I'd prefer you to continue with Emma, but Jane might never have such a marvellous opportunity again, it would do wonders for her personal development. Hard to choose between them, isn't it?'

'Very,' I lied. 'But it'd better be Jane. As you say, it's a great opportunity and should make her even more effective while she's at Highbury Foods.'

'Excellent! I'm sure Emma will understand, when I get round to telling her. In the meantime you can start mentoring Jane – let me know how it goes.'

So, no more one-to-ones with Emma Woodhouse. No more treading that dangerous line between business and pleasure. No more fighting the temptation to take her in my arms and –

The relief was indescribable.

Over dinner a few days later, I found the right moment to ask Dad about an invitation to the Christmas party for Flynn. It was surprisingly easy to persuade him; almost as if he felt he owed me one, although I couldn't think why.

As soon as he'd settled down with a book in his usual corner of the dining room, I went upstairs, stretched out on my bed and reached for the phone. I smiled to myself as I dialled Flynn's mobile number.

He answered immediately, his voice warm and loving. 'Hello, gorgeous.'

I giggled. 'Hello gorgeous, yourself.'

A pause. Then, 'Is that you, Em?'

'Yes.' I added, somewhat confused, 'Didn't you recognise my number?'

'Of course.' Another pause. 'Just thought I'd check, better safe than sorry.'

'The reception's a bit dodgy. Where are you?'

'In the Lake District.' He laughed. 'Lots of sheep, just like back home.'

'The Lakes? But that's hundreds of miles away! What are you doing there?'

'It's a BBC thing, top secret,' he said. 'I meant to call and see you before I left, but I ran out of time. Made the mistake of going to say goodbye to the Bateses first and the aunt burbled on for hours.'

'More fool you for going,' I said drily. 'When will you be back?'

'Could be a couple of days, could be a few weeks. It depends.'

'A few *weeks*?' I let out a long ragged breath. 'It's just that I've got you an invitation for December 2nd.'

'What's on December 2nd?'

I tried to keep the exasperation out of my voice. 'The Highbury Foods Christmas party, remember?'

'Oh, fantastic! I promise I'll be there, wouldn't miss it for the world. Listen, Em, I know we've only just met but you must have realised that—'

There was a loud crackle and the line went dead. Shit! I slammed down the receiver and frowned at the ceiling. I knew what he'd been going to say, could hear the words as if he was in the room with me: 'You must have realised that I'm falling in love with you'. Very gratifying, but now everything would grind to a halt while he was in the Lake District.

Then I forced a smile. After years of waiting, what did a few more weeks matter?

As it turned out, I was right to be philosophical – Flynn was away until the day of the party. But he phoned me regularly at the office; I could always tell when he was on the line from Harriet's shrieks of laughter as she took the call.

Not that the time dragged; I had far too much work to do. Between us, Jane and I planned the research for Harriet's Secret Recipes with a view to completing everything by Christmas. It was a constant clash of wills. I took a pragmatic approach, where things didn't have to be perfect as long as they got done. Jane, however, was nothing short of meticulous. For example, she was taking ages to organise the focus groups, because she insisted on recruiting only those people who fitted our rather demanding profile to the letter.

One morning, I was about to remind her of the consequences of missing our deadline when, out of the blue, she asked if she could take the following week off. The reason that she gave, after much prompting, was 'a last-minute holiday with a close friend'.

I thought instantly of Dan and my lips tightened. 'You haven't worked here long enough to take five days off, so technically I should say no.'

She flushed. 'Please, Emma. I wouldn't ask if it wasn't important.'

I relented, motivated by the thought of a whole week in the office without her and having the focus groups organised by the time she came back. But I didn't ask her a single question about her holiday, either before or after. Nobody would be able to accuse *me* of conniving in her sordid little affair.

Batty also asked me to help her prepare for the Christmas party, in particular choosing a special menu for Dad and allocating rooms to those who were staying overnight. I took full advantage of my position and made sure Flynn's room was next to mine.

To my relief, I heard nothing more from Mark. But I had a new person to avoid: Gusty. She started pestering Dad to hire her for a strategic financial audit, whatever that was – something Mark had apparently already commissioned her to do for Donwell Organics. Dad kept stalling, which meant that Gusty pestered me instead, convinced that I would influence him on her behalf. When I stopped taking her phone calls, she swept into my office one day and confronted me; but I told her straight that I wasn't prepared to discuss the subject – with Dad, or her, or anyone else.

At this point, she switched her attentions to Jane. It was rather amusing to listen to her gushing compliments alternating with Jane's monosyllabic brush-offs. She even assured Jane that her talents were wasted at Highbury Foods and offered to get her a much better job through her Maple Grove contacts. The cheek of it, poaching a member of my staff right under my nose! I almost sent Gusty packing there and then.

But I didn't; because by now I was wishing Saint Jane miles away from Highbury. Working with her was a nightmare, thanks to our completely different styles; and I had another, more altruistic reason. Batty let slip that Mark had taken Jane out for a very long and expensive lunch the previous Saturday. Jane didn't mention it, of course, and I didn't ask her.

It shouldn't have mattered one jot what Mark

Knightley chose to do with Jane Fairfax. But somehow it did.

After all, even Mark didn't deserve to have Donwell Abbey infested by Battys.

MARK

Emma had asked me for space and that's exactly what she got. I even avoided Henry, just in case I bumped into her. After my first mentoring meeting with Jane, instead of giving him an update in person as I would have preferred, I made do with a phone call.

There wasn't much to tell. I'd found it difficult to establish rapport with her, although I'd chosen what I thought was a relaxed time and setting – lunch on a Saturday at the newly opened Box Hill Restaurant. Still, as I said to Henry, it was early days.

And, as I didn't say to Henry, it had been infinitely easier than dealing with his daughter.

But I wouldn't be able to avoid Emma at the Highbury Foods Christmas party. Or Churchill, who would no doubt be glued to her side. Or everyone's comments about how they made *such* a lovely couple.

As soon as I saw her that evening, the longing twisted inside me like a knife. She was standing beside the Christmas tree in Reception, talking animatedly on her mobile. Unnoticed, I took in every detail of her appearance. Stunning dress, white and strapless and hugging her body as though she'd been poured into it. Hair falling in glossy waves around her face. Eyes and lips provocatively defined, as if daring someone to accuse her of wearing too much make-up. And above the curve of her breasts a diamond pendant, its sparkle outshone by the golden lustre of her skin . . .

I turned and made for the nearest drink.

EMMA

My big night – or rather mine and Flynn's – had arrived at last.

He phoned me to say he was running late, but I couldn't be angry with him; the important thing was that he'd come back specially from the Lakes just to be here.

When a tall figure in black entered the room carrying two champagne flutes, my heart missed a beat. I soon realised my mistake, however; it was Mark, not Flynn. I gave him a tight little smile and received a curt nod in return. For a moment, I thought he was bringing one of the glasses to me, as a peace offering. But no, he headed for Jane, who was looking about as happy as a turkey on Christmas Eve.

Eventually Flynn appeared in the doorway, heart-stoppingly handsome in a white tux. He came straight over and kissed me lightly on the cheek. I'd been hoping for something rather more passionate, but I curbed my impatience.

'Sorry, Em, I'm even later than I expected. All in a good cause – I've been looking at the seating plan with Kate, to check I'm paired off with you.'

My heart missed another beat; I was sure that, like me, he was thinking of us pairing off for more than the dinner. I gave a little shrug. 'I know that each table's round and sits ten, but other than that I've kept out of it. I'd probably put the wrong people together – that's why I told Batty to get Kate to do it.'

He grinned. 'Kate's done it for years, hasn't she? She told me that this time she's tried a little experiment to get people to mix more. She's put couples on the same table but given them a different partner to sit with.'

'Sounds good,' I said, pleased that Philip and Gusty would have no opportunity to grope each other during the meal and put everyone else off their food. 'Who are we with?'

'Let's have some champagne while I try to remember.' He took several glasses from a passing waitress and knocked back a couple in succession. I did the same, keeping up with him for the first glass, but sipping my second more slowly. The last thing I wanted was to drink myself into oblivion. Not tonight.

Flynn clinked his third glass clumsily with mine. 'Cheers, Em. Now, where was I? Of course, how could I forget, Kate's put us with Philip Elton and his girlfriend Busty, very well endowed apparently.'

I burst out laughing. 'It's Gusty, not Busty!' Then

278

I gave a loud groan. 'But why's she inflicted them on me when—' I broke off as I remembered that Kate knew nothing about my little fiasco with Philip.

Flynn went on, 'Kate and Dad are on our table too, but I can't remember the other four.' He frowned in concentration. 'Oh yes, we've got Mark "I'm God's gift to Highbury" Knightley and Saint Jane. When I saw that Kate had them paired off, I made her give them other partners immediately – on the grounds of cruelty to dumb animals.'

Kate was certainly on a matchmaking mission; I forced a smile. 'Who's the dumb animal – Mark or Jane?'

He shrugged. 'Either. Both. Look at him talking to her over there.' His lip curled. 'He's probably holding forth about his exploits in India. You know the sort of thing – exciting late night negotiations to purchase biodegradable paper clips for the office, thrilling weekends spent sampling cups of tea for Donwell Organics' new line in Lapsong Souchong.'

'That's from China, you idiot,' I said, with a giggle.

'I'll take your word for it, my Darjeeling. But Mark Knightley seems to lead such a dreary life, doesn't he? Work, work, work – he must be the most boring man on the planet. What a waste of all those years in a place like India.'

I shook my head. 'Actually, from what I know

he had a very busy social life in India. But I agree, over here it seems to have been all work and no play.'

Especially since he split up with *her*, I added to myself.

Flynn stared across at Mark and Jane. 'Why do women bother with him?'

'Isn't it obvious?' I risked a quick glance myself, trying to see Mark through the eyes of a stranger. 'He's extremely good-looking. Very intelligent. Great company, believe it or not.'

And a sublime kisser.

I allowed my thoughts to wander, just for a moment . . .

Flynn's edgy laugh brought me back to earth. 'Strewth! Who'd settle for me when they can have all that?'

I reached up and put my finger to his lips. 'Be quiet, you know you're wonderful. Different from Mark, of course, but still wonderful.'

He pulled me to him. 'And you're very different from Saint Jane.'

I pressed my body against his, feeling curiously light-headed. His face was so close, I just knew he was going to kiss me. Here. Now. In front of everyone –

'Emma, your father wants you.' It was Mark, right beside us, his voice icy with disapproval. 'According to the agenda for the evening, you should have announced dinner three minutes ago.'

Flynn let go of me with a scowl. 'Three minutes, is that all? Keep your hair on, mate. Anyhow, looks like some of us have other agendas for this evening, doesn't it?'

'Speak for yourself,' Mark said, tersely.

Without a word, I lifted my chin and stalked off to make the announcement. Inside, I was seething. Trust him to interfere; Big Brother, always watching over me.

Well, he wouldn't be able to guard me all night, would he?

MARK

While I talked to Jane, I kept a close eye on Emma and Churchill; at least, as much as I could without seeming rude. Then Henry joined us, in a flap about timings and wanting Emma to call everyone through to dinner.

'I'll get her for you,' I said, suddenly aware that she was clinging to Churchill in a most suggestive manner. Needless to say, it was exactly how I'd have liked her to cling to me. So I interrupted them, then immediately regretted it; I must have sounded like a pompous old fart. And I wondered what Churchill meant about other agendas; could he sense that mine was to keep him away from her for as long as possible?

Emma's voice came across the public address system, clear and confident. 'Ladies and gentlemen, dinner's about to be served. If you haven't already done so, please look at the seating plan in the far corner and find out who your partner is. Then, in your pairs, form an orderly line by table number and we'll go through into the Marlborough Room. Thank you.'

As soon as she finished speaking, people surged to the back of the room, anxious to see the plan. I hung back, in no hurry to join the crush.

Elton sidled up to me. 'I don't need to look at the plan, someone said we were on your table. Gusty's gone to the Ladies, but she'll be back in a tick.'

Before I could answer, Kate arrived with Harriet in tow. 'Hello, you two,' she said brightly. 'Waiting for your partners?'

Harriet looked distinctly uncomfortable; I couldn't tell whether it was because of Elton, me, or the outfit she was wearing, which I could only describe as two black net curtains held together by large, vicious-looking gold safety pins.

'That's right,' Elton said. 'Gusty won't be long, she's—'

'Oh no, Philip,' Kate put in, with a peal of laughter. 'You're not allowed to sit together, I've deliberately split couples up so that they have to be sociable.'

Elton smirked. 'What a great idea, can't wait to see who you've got lined up for me. And Gusty won't mind a bit, she's always more than happy to network.'

At that moment Emma hurried up to us, her

face pale and set. 'Kate, I need a word about the seating plan. In private.'

Kate smiled at her. 'In a minute, Emma.' She turned to me with an apologetic look. 'Slight change to the original plan, you're partnering me now.'

'Delighted,' I said automatically, wondering what was bothering Emma; maybe Kate had slipped up and she'd not been paired with Churchill.

Kate turned to Elton. 'Philip, you're with Harriet. It's the first Highbury Foods party for both of you, I thought you could compare notes.'

The effect on Elton was instant; his features froze in an ugly mask. 'For fuck's sake, I can't possibly partner *her*.'

We all stared at him.

'Gusty knows no one here except me,' he went on, his voice rising to a petulant whine. 'It wouldn't be fair to split us up, I *insist* on us being together.'

Emma moved forward. I saw her hand start a swift upward swing and knew that in a couple of seconds she would slap Elton's face. Even though the wanker deserved it, I couldn't let her do it.

'Harriet,' I said, stepping quickly in front of Emma, 'I'd love you to be my partner – it's the first time here for me, too. Kate, would you mind?'

Kate let out a long breath. 'Not at all, I'll partner Terry. Which means you can partner your girl-friend,' she added, with a dismissive nod in Elton's direction.

283

I gave Harriet a reassuring smile. 'Shall we lead everyone in to dinner?'

As she came to stand at my side, blushing and giggling, something made me glance across at Emma.

She was looking straight at me, as if waiting for my cue . . . Her lips mouthed 'Thank you', then curved in a dazzling smile that made my heart pound like a drum. For a moment we were the only people in the room, sharing a secret, understanding each other perfectly, bound by old indestructible ties.

Perhaps the evening would be tolerable after all.

EMMA

Philip seemed unaffected by his outburst, devouring four courses with obvious relish.

Some of us weren't quite so relaxed. I merely picked at the meal I'd been looking forward to for weeks; Harriet was even clumsier than usual, dropping her cutlery with monotonous regularity and giggling every time Mark retrieved it; Kate barely spoke, as if she couldn't trust herself to be civil to anyone; and even Mark seemed to have lost his appetite. He made up for it in wine, though, and I couldn't blame him. We were on the Table From Hell.

With the normally talkative Terry hampered by a silent Saint Jane on one side and a glowering Kate on the other, it was left to Flynn, Gusty and

Tom to keep the conversation going. Gusty was more obnoxious than ever, boasting constantly about Maple Grove being 'something big in Bristol'.

I managed a wan smile when Flynn whispered to me, 'Doesn't she mean "Bristols"?', before returning to my thoughts.

Thoughts about Mark. Feelings of . . .

Gratitude, that was it; for my own sake as well as Harriet's. After all, he'd rescued both of us from a humiliating scene, although I suspected no one else had noticed my instinctive reaction to Philip's rudeness.

On one level, Mark had taken charge of the situation in his usual way – understated yet totally effective; on another level, his intervention had been nothing less than heroic. There was simply no other word for it.

I decided I would ask him for a dance, to thank him properly. So, when we'd finished the meal and the disco had started, I made my way towards him. But I had to grab the table to steady myself – probably the effect of too much wine and too little food. By the time I'd recovered, he was on the dance floor with Harriet; trust him to go the extra mile.

Dad beckoned to me from the next table and I went over, sympathy at the ready. 'How was your special menu?'

He grimaced. 'I'm not sure, there may be – repercussions. Kate and Tom are still taking me home, aren't they? I hope they don't stay too late.'

I made reassuring noises and moved away, on the pretext of checking that everyone was enjoying themselves. In reality, I was looking for Flynn. After such a promising start to the evening, I'd hardly exchanged two words with him. Now he was nowhere to be seen.

As I wandered round the room for the third time, I came to an abrupt halt. A few feet away, in a secluded corner, Mark was leaning back against a pillar; arms folded and eyes closed, the sadness on his face unmistakable.

He must really miss Tamara on a night like this . . .

I took a deep breath. 'Mark, would you like to dance?'

He opened one eye, then the other, and gave a sardonic laugh. 'With you? That's the last sodding thing I need.'

I clenched my fists and turned away, his rejection stirring dark memories. 'You're as bad as Philip. No, you're much, much worse!'

'Didn't mean it to come out like that, must be the drink,' I heard him mutter.

What sort of apology was that?

I whirled round and almost spat the words at him. 'Why did I bother even asking? I should've remembered – dancing with me won't do anything for your image, because I'm like your little sister. Funny, you didn't think of that when you kissed me. Not a very brotherly kiss, I seem to recall.'

'Emma, I—'

'Of course,' I went on, lowering my voice to a hiss of contempt, 'no one saw, so it didn't matter. Whereas dancing with me in front of all these people—'

He interrupted me with a quiet, 'You've got it all wrong.'

I waited for him to elaborate, but he just looked down at the floor.

In that case . . . Another deep breath. 'No, Mark, *you've* got it all wrong. I'm sick of you being Big Brother, always watching out for me and bossing me around. It may have worked in the past, but it's not working now!'

His head snapped up; his eyes met mine at last and his mouth twisted into a grim smile. 'You're right, it's not. Not in any way, shape or form.'

I hesitated, wrong-footed by his lack of resistance. Then, 'Does that mean you'll treat me like an adult from now on?'

'An adult?' He cleared his throat. 'What exactly do you have in mind?'

I said the first thing that came into my head. 'Pretend I'm Saint Jane. You know – beyond improvement, perfection on legs.'

'Perfection on legs? God, those legs . . . Got me into trouble with Tamara, that did . . .' His voice trailed away and I wondered what on earth he was rambling on about. He rubbed his temple as if soothing a nagging headache and went on, 'Have you seen Jane? I was dancing with her before, then she just rushed off. Seemed a bit upset – any idea why?'

'Ask her yourself. Ask her why she's been so moody since she came back from her little holiday. Ask her who she's having a secret affair with.' I gave him a pitying look. 'Funny, I'd have thought someone with your powers of perception could see through her, but you're as gullible as everyone else.'

His eyes narrowed. '*I'm* gullible? You can talk, falling for all Churchill's crap and wrapping yourself round him like cling film!'

How dare he!

For a few seconds we just glared at each other, provoked beyond words. Then I turned and fled to a place where I knew I'd be safe from him: the Ladies. As I burst through the door, I crashed into Batty and nearly sent her flying. When I mumbled an apology and tried to dodge past her, she grabbed my arm – almost, but unfortunately not quite, speechless with excitement.

'I've been looking all over for you, dear, fancy bumping into you here.' She gave a trill of laughter, then dropped her voice to a concerned whisper. 'Poor Harriet, I heard all about Philip's little . . . always knew there was a nasty streak in him, I remember that time when he . . . So Mark came to the rescue, did he? They made *such* a lovely couple on the dance floor, Sandy Perry and I almost wondered if there was something going on' – knowing look – 'but then he came over specially to ask Jane for the next one. And she agreed straightaway, even though she'd just refused to dance with . . . They made a lovely couple too, both so dark and tall and *striking*, as Sandy put it . . . Actually, I'm very worried about Jane, she's not been herself for weeks now. I wanted her to come home with me tonight but she insists on staying here as planned, although she did promise me she'd go up to her room nice and early. Which reminds me, dear, I've got a little bedtime treat for you . . . I expect you're like me and can never get to sleep in a strange place.'

She let go of my arm to rummage in her handbag, while I remembered the sort of treats she'd given me as a child – disgusting boiled sweets, hideous home-made clothes for my Barbie dolls – and steeled myself for the worst.

My eyes widened as she thrust a small bottle at me.

'Mother's sloe gin,' she twittered. 'We found her old recipe a few weeks ago and made some, she swears by it for a restful night. I've brought one for your father, and one for Mark, I expect he's not had a decent night since Tamara left . . . Goodnight, dear, I *do* hope it does the trick.'

And she was gone before I could thank her.

I stayed where I was, welcoming the silence, turning her gift over and over in my hands. With no Flynn around, a little drink in the privacy of my hotel bedroom seemed my best option. Clutching the bottle to me for safe keeping, I went to say goodnight to Dad.

'You'll be glad to know that Kate and Tom are taking me home any minute,' he said, stifling a yawn. 'And Mary's given me some sort of fruit tonic to stop me worrying about you, darling. I really don't like the thought of you spending the night here. Make sure you lock your bedroom door, you don't know who's on the prowl.'

I forced a smile. 'I'm hardly going to be molested by prowlers.'

Or anyone else by the look of it, I added to myself.

As I went upstairs to my room, I couldn't resist knocking on the door before mine, just in case Flynn was there; but I didn't get an answer.

Telling myself there'd be a next time, I opened the door of 107, kicked off my shoes, unscrewed the cap of my little bottle and took an experimental sip or two of its contents. Quite nice, like Ribena with attitude. I fetched a tumbler from the bathroom, carefully emptied the bottle into it and sank onto the bed, stroking the smooth glass with my fingers, dwelling on everything that had – and hadn't – happened during the evening.

After a few mouthfuls of sloe gin, I began to see the positive side. Far better to let my relationship with Flynn blossom – what a peculiar word! –

away from the public eye. Away from Mark Knightley's eye in particular . . . Mmmm, this drink was delicious; there weren't any obvious effects either, Old Mother Bates must have gone very easy on the gin . . . Another mouthful, and another, and . . . God, this was almost as good as sex! I laughed to myself, a throaty little laugh that came out as a hiccup. Weird. Soon – even sooner than I'd expected – I found myself staring at the bottom of the glass. All gone.

I gave a loud sigh as I took off my earrings and necklace. 'Time for bed. Time to see if Batty's silly magic potion works. Bet it doesn't.'

The thing was, I knew I had to do something first . . . Ah yes, get myself out of this dress. I stood up with barely a stagger and put the tumbler on the bedside table. Would you believe it – just as I did so, someone moved the table and the tumbler fell with a thud onto the carpet. I swore, reached round behind my back and fumbled with the fastening on my dress. Naturally, this sudden movement threw me off balance and I toppled onto the bed.

I lay there for a while, wondering what to do. There was only one thing for it; find someone to help. I knew Harriet's room was on the same corridor as mine, but could I remember the number? Never mind, it would come to me. I picked up my room key from the bedside table, which someone had moved again, and navigated my way out; always tricky in a strange hotel room, so many doors to choose from until you got to the right one – I mean, how many bathrooms and wardrobes did this room have, for God's sake?

At last I was in the corridor, shutting the door quietly behind me. Ouch, perhaps not as quietly as I'd thought. I walked past a few doors and read the numbers out loud, trying to jog my memory. I'd just got to the end of the corridor, when I heard a familiar high-pitched giggle.

Harriet. No doubt about it. Room 115.

The number didn't ring a bell, but at least I'd tracked her down. Did the giggle mean she had someone with her? A potentially embarrassing situation; although I couldn't imagine who it would be and, anyway, this was an emergency.

The door was slightly ajar. I pushed it open ever so gently, but it banged noisily against the wall behind and I had to put my hands out to stop it flying back in my face.

'Oops, must be stronger than I thought,' I said, with a nonchalant laugh. More of a hiccup again, actually; must do something about that . . .

Once I'd tackled the door and my eyes had adjusted to the low lighting, I took in the scene. Large double bed, undisturbed; desk; two chairs, with a jacket and shirt thrown across them; Harriet, only a couple of feet away from me; next to the bed, a man. The most gorgeous man, in fact. Naked from the waist up; such a beautiful body, all bronzed and nicely toned . . . I had the feeling I'd seen him somewhere before, quite recently, with even less on—

Mark Knightley. Here, in Harriet's bedroom. At least he wasn't in Saint Jane's.

But – *Harriet*?

I drew myself up to my full height and said haughtily, 'Sorry, am I interrupting something?'

Nervous giggles from Harriet. An appraising look from Mark.

'No, you're not interrupting anything,' he said, slowly and deliberately, as if speaking to an idiot. 'Harriet's just going – she only popped in for a quick word.'

'To say thank you for rescuing me,' Harriet put in excitedly. 'My knight in shining armour!'

Armour? What on earth was she talking about? I stared at Mark, trying to remember if he'd come to the party in fancy dress, then focused my gaze on Harriet. So this wasn't her room, it was Mark's. Mark – and *Harriet*?

Before I could stop her, Harriet edged past me and dashed out of the room. As the door slammed shut behind her, I frowned. Hadn't I been going to ask her something? Oh yes, to undo my dress.

I turned and caught Mark drinking something ruby-coloured from a tumbler, just like I'd done earlier. Fascinated, I watched the muscles of his throat contract as he drained the last drop. My gaze followed the tumbler as he cradled it in one hand and rubbed his forefinger along the rim, to and fro, to and fro . . .

Oh – my – God. All of a sudden, I knew exactly what I wanted.

But what if he rejected me? No, he wouldn't. Not this time.

'I need you to undo my dress.' I stumbled over to him – must have tripped on something on the floor – and flopped face down on the bed.

He cleared his throat. 'And I need you to go to your room. Now.'

'Can't undo it myself,' I went on, as if he hadn't spoken. 'Please, Mark.'

Silence. I closed my eyes and held my breath.

And then . . . warm fingers on the bare skin of my back, so gentle I could hardly feel them. Yet the very knowledge that he was touching me, in a way that he'd never done before, sent a quiver through my entire body.

'Sorry, did I hurt you?' he said, uncertainly.

'No.'

'There.' He took his hand away and his voice became brisk again. 'That's the little hook done, can you manage the zip yourself?'

I made a feeble attempt to reach behind me, then let my arms drop back onto the bed.

He gave a long, uneven sigh. 'Here, you can't do anything if you're hanging on to your room key for dear life, give it to me.' Our fingers touched briefly as he took the key; I heard the jangle as he placed it on the bedside table. 'OK, I'll unzip you,' he went on, 'then you're going back to your room.'

I felt the mattress dip slightly as he sat on the bed beside me, but it seemed like several minutes before his fingers touched my back again and started on the zip. Even then he took his time, unfastening it very, very carefully. As I listened to his soft, steady breathing, I wondered what it would take to make him lose control.

When he reached the most ticklish part of my back, I couldn't help giggling. I squirmed away from him, vaguely aware of my dress working loose.

'Don't, Mark, that tickles!'

I rolled over and stopped giggling instantly. He was staring down at me, at my naked breasts. And his face too was naked, stripped of its mask, revealing such hunger . . . Oh, I needn't have worried about rejection. From the look of him, I couldn't escape – even if I wanted to.

Our eyes locked. I reached up and traced his lips with my fingertip.

'Kiss me,' I whispered.

He pushed my hand away. 'No. Once I kiss you, I won't be able to stop.'

Didn't he realise? That was the whole bloody point. 'Kiss me, then.'

'For God's sake, Emma, you don't understand.'

He made a half-hearted attempt to get up, but I was having none of it. I put my arms round his neck and pulled him down towards me.

No going back now.

CHAPTER 10

PASSION FRUIT

MARK

I followed Emma upstairs, telling myself it was purely out of a Henry-like concern to see that she reached her room safely. But I couldn't help a sigh of relief when I saw her go through the door of 107 alone.

I continued along the corridor to my room, stripped off my jacket, shirt and bow tie and dropped them on the nearest chair. As I did so, something heavy clunked against the curved wooden back. I fumbled inside one of the jacket pockets and found the little bottle of sloe gin that Mary had given me earlier, with a coy assurance that it would help me forget all my troubles.

By this stage, I was ready to try anything. In some ways it had been a typical office party; too much drinking and people doing things they'd really regret the next day. In other ways, however, it had been a reality check – seeing Churchill's flirtatious behaviour towards Emma well and truly reciprocated.

I poured the vibrant pink liquid into a tumbler

from the bathroom, cursing when some spilled over my fingers and onto my bare chest. Too much hassle to wash it off now; it could wait until my shower in the morning. I turned down the lights, slumped in a chair, flicked through the TV channels and sipped my drink, enjoying its relaxing effects. While it didn't make me forget my troubles, it certainly made them a lot more bearable.

As I was contemplating whether to finish the last few mouthfuls now or later, there was a knock at the door. What if this was Emma? I would be polite but firm. Discussion at this time of night was pointless – and dangerous. I switched off the TV, put down the tumbler and went to the door.

'Polite but firm,' I muttered to myself, 'polite but – Harriet! What can I do for you?'

Without a word she rushed into the room, stopped and just stood there, staring at me. I deliberately left the door slightly open – you never knew with these highly strung types – and waited for her to speak.

After a minute or two, I said gently, 'Is something the matter?'

Still nothing; then the words came tumbling out. 'I've just read my horoscope again and it's all there, what happened tonight, spooky innit? It says, "You'll be eternally grateful to someone who saves you from embarrassment". That thing you did, asking me to be your partner, it was probably no big deal to you, but it was to me. And I just don't know how to show you I'm eternally grateful.' She gave a loud giggle and took a small but determined step towards me.

I backed quickly away, ending up nearer the bed than I'd have liked. 'No need, I only did what I thought was right. It's very good of you to take the trouble to come and thank me.' I did my best to conceal a yawn. 'Sorry, I'm whacked—'

At this point, Emma lurched through the door, almost hitting herself in the face with it. She weighed up the low lighting, my state of undress and Harriet's air of excitement and jumped to the obvious conclusion.

Except that the words came out in a drunken slur. 'Shorry, am I int'rupping shomething?'

At least, I think that's what she said. Thanks to the sloe gin, I was having difficulty making my brain function properly. On the one hand, this was the very situation I'd dreaded: Emma in my hotel bedroom, with me feeling at my most vulnerable. On the other hand, it was the stuff my fantasies were made of. Either way, it was best to encourage Harriet to leave. So I pulled myself together and explained to Emma that she wasn't interrupting anything and that Harriet was just going. I couldn't be sure whether Emma understood me, but at least Harriet took the hint and hurried out of the room.

We were alone. Totally alone.

I finished my drink and stood there thinking

about – possibilities. When she fell on the bed and begged me to unfasten her dress, it was as if she was telepathic. For a brief moment, I kidded myself that she wanted to make love; but of course it was only because she couldn't undo the dress herself.

After a feeble attempt to send her back to her room, I gave in. With self-preservation uppermost in my mind, I decided I'd undo just the hook and leave the zip to her.

That didn't work.

Then, although I couldn't avoid resting my fingers on her bare skin, I summoned every ounce of self-control to stop myself from enjoying it.

That worked, up to a point . . . until, with her dress unzipped, she turned over.

Such beautiful breasts, there for the touching. But I didn't touch, I simply stared.

'Kiss me,' she said.

'No.' I should have left it there, but I added, 'Once I kiss you, I won't be able to stop.'

She smiled up at me. 'Kiss me, then.'

It was as though she was throwing down a gauntlet, soft as velvet, strong as steel. And who could refuse those sultry eyes with their 'take me to bed' look, that provocative mouth, that slender but voluptuous body?

I tried one last time. 'For God's sake, Emma, you don't understand—'

Too late. Her tongue was in my mouth and my self-control was in shreds.

As we kissed, I touched her breasts at last. No, not touched, worshipped them . . . Caressed them, stored their contours to memory, felt the nipples harden and peak. Tore my mouth away from hers to trail urgent kisses down her neck and round the base of one breast in slow circles, up to the very tip. Teased it with my tongue until I could almost taste her arousal. Then started with her other breast. Caressed, kissed, teased all over again; this time knowing exactly how to draw out each murmur of response, each gasp of pleasure.

How long we lay like this, I don't know. I wanted to hold on to every second, delay the inevitable as long as possible, but it was driving me insane.

When I released her and made to stand up, she clung to me. 'Don't go!'

'Hey, take it easy. I'm not going anywhere.'

As I undressed, she lay back on the bed, her eyes never leaving me. When I'd taken everything off, even my watch, she held out her arms.

'I want you,' she said. 'So, so much.'

I let out a long, ragged breath. 'Not yet. Not until we get this posh frock off. And whatever you've got on underneath.'

As I spoke, I slid her dress and briefs down to reveal every inch of those perfect, perfect legs. For some time, I did nothing except look. And then looking became touching and touching became kissing . . .

Soft skin against my lips, the heat of her, the

taste. Just like in my dreams. No, better than in my dreams; this was real.

And then, finally, I was where I longed to be – inside her, to the hilt. We held our bodies completely still, except for small, secret movements. It all felt so right and yet, in a way, so wrong. Because I knew that, if we hadn't both been drinking, none of this would have happened.

She must have sensed my hesitation. 'Don't stop,' she said. 'Please, not now.'

'Are you absolutely sure?'

'Yes. Oh, yes.' A little sigh as she shifted under me, raised her hips, took me deeper. 'Oh, Mark.' Her eyes widened, then closed.

Hearing her call my name was all the confirmation I needed. I gazed down at her face, with its intimately familiar features, seeing them for the first time in the grip of physical desire. And in me awoke a long-forgotten joy in the power of my own body, an instinctive urge to create something that would last beyond these few precious moments, a burning need to make her remember this mad, unplanned act for ever.

What better way to show her how much I loved her?

So I took it slow, achingly slow at first; watched for her response; guided her gradually into a seamless, soaring rhythm that brought us to the edge. And we went over together, stifling each other's cries in one last, lingering kiss.

Afterwards I lay at her side, overwhelmed by a

301

sense of completeness. Always my friend, she was now my lover. I linked my fingers through hers, listening as our breathing steadied; anxious to talk, but unsure where to begin.

At last I said, with a catch in my voice, 'I love you, Emma. I think I always have. Since the day you were born.'

I turned towards her, ready to confess all my soul-searching of the last few months.

She was fast asleep.

EMMA

Somewhere, a clock chimed six, maybe seven times. I opened my eyes. The lights were on low; unusual for me – I liked to sleep in the dark. Given that I hadn't gone up to my room until nearly midnight, I mustn't have had my usual eight hours. But I felt good. And, for the first time in a long while, I hadn't spent the night alone.

I stretched a luxurious cat-like stretch, then curled round the warm body beside me. What bliss. I'd got the man of my dreams into bed after all, although the details were distinctly hazy. But it had been worth it, I knew that much. He could shag for England, as Harriet would say. Or should that be Australia?

Wait a minute – Harriet! I sat bolt upright, wincing as my head started to pound. Hadn't she been here, too? I looked wildly round in case there were three of us in a post-coital stupor. But instead of dark red curls on the pillow next to me, I saw a tousled head of black hair. What the—?

I knew, even before he rolled onto his back and greeted me with a sleepy smile. I knew it was Mark.

''Morning, beautiful,' he said, propping himself up on one elbow and reaching out to stroke my cheek with his other hand. Such a familiar hand, with its long tanned fingers and the signet ring that had belonged to his grandfather. But such an unfamiliar gesture, presuming intimacy. It stirred something within me, a vague memory of taking those fingers in my mouth, one by one, tasting sloe gin and . . .

I shrank away from him, grabbed the sheet and pulled it up to my chin. 'What are you doing in my bed?' I said, trying to keep my voice steady.

He grinned. 'Technically it's my bed, although you've spent just as much time in it.' He leaned over and traced my lips with a confident fore-finger; but I kept my mouth firmly closed, frowning as I absorbed what he'd just told me.

'Don't you remember, you hussy?' he said, his eyes dancing.

My heart started to pound as painfully as my head. 'Are you telling me that we . . . ?' I couldn't bring myself to say it.

'We certainly did, although I don't find it exactly flattering that you've forgotten so easily. Maybe you need an action replay.' He pulled down the sheet, bent his head and started nuzzling my breast.

'For God's sake!' I shook him off with such force that the sheet ended up in a useless tangle. Still, he must have already seen all I was showing – and more. I moved to the far edge of the bed and looked at him warily.

'Let me get this right. I came to your room and we . . . Oh, shit! I just can't understand how we could do such a thing.'

His eyes narrowed. 'Well, Emma, it's like this. I get hard and you get wet and we—'

I put my hands over my ears. 'No, no! I mean I can't understand *why* we would do it. With each other.'

Silence. Then he said, in a cold, clipped voice, 'Can't you?'

'Well, sort of, at a basic level. We both have needs, after all. But we're just friends, we're not into each other in that way.'

'Believe me, we were into each other in that way last night,' he said flatly. 'Correction, this morning. More than once, in fact.'

I looked at him in horror. 'You mean we – more than once?'

'Look, we'd both been drinking, but I'd have thought it was a bloody sight more memorable than you're making out!'

My mind went off at a tangent. 'Did you wear anything?'

'No.' He gave a scornful laugh. 'I seem to recall that you quite enjoyed watching me take everything off.'

I suppressed a shudder. 'I meant, did you wear a condom?'

He flushed. 'I didn't. I wasn't expecting—'

'Oh shit! What if—?' I made to get out of bed, but his hand closed round my arm like a vice.

'Where are you going? You can't tell if you're pregnant yet. And if you are, then you can't just run away and pretend it's nothing to do with me.'

Maybe that was true, but it wasn't what I wanted to hear. I lashed out at him, punching and kicking for all I was worth. It was futile, of course. With humiliating ease, he seized my wrists, pushed me back onto the bed and knelt astride me, completely in control. As we were both stark naked, it could have been, should have been, a sexually charged play fight. But that was the last thing on either of our minds.

His eyes bored into mine. 'We need to talk about what's happened.'

'Do I have any choice?'

'Not really,' he said grimly. 'So tell me – why did you come to my room?'

I focused on the picture hanging on the wall behind him, a run-of-the-mill still life – two oranges, a bunch of black grapes and a carafe of red wine. My head throbbed as I tried to recollect my actions. But a disturbing image intruded: my fingers raking his hair as his tongue teased my nipple in the most incredibly arousing way . . .

I took a deep breath and stared doggedly at the grapes. 'I needed Harriet to undo my dress, but

I couldn't remember which room she was in. When I heard her in here, I assumed that this was her room and came in. She went before I could ask her for help, so I asked you instead.'

'That's it? Nothing else?'

I looked him straight in the eye. 'No.'

'Then you certainly got more than you bargained for,' he said quietly.

I twisted my head to the side and studied another picture, a Constable print, all serenity and sunshine. 'Don't worry, I'm not about to accuse you of rape. I must have been willing, I suppose.'

'You *suppose*?' His voice was raw with some sort of emotion – injured pride, no doubt. 'God help me, Emma! You asked me to kiss you, even though I warned you what the consequences would be. You told me you wanted me, "so, so much". When I was inside you, you begged me not to stop!'

He was almost shouting now, and I flinched as each word hit home. I couldn't free my hands to put them over my ears, so I screwed my eyes shut. Tight shut. But still the accusations came, loud and clear.

'Oh yes,' he bit out, 'whatever state you were in, you knew exactly what you were doing. And who you were doing it with. You called my name over and over again. Screamed it, in fact, when I—'

I felt my face flame. 'That drink, Batty's sloe gin, it put me in the mood. And Flynn wasn't—' I broke off, opened my eyes and glared at him. 'Don't you understand? There was no one else around.'

'Give me strength,' he muttered, releasing my wrists and getting up from the bed. Then, in a bored tone, 'Forgive me if I can't get too ecstatic about being a stand-in for Flynn Fucking Churchill.'

At that, something inside me snapped. 'You've got one hell of a nerve, Mark Knightley! Wasn't I just a substitute for Tamara?'

My breath caught in my throat as he looked down at me, his mouth twisted into a mocking smile. 'Yes, you were.' A pause. 'Only not as good.' And he went into the bathroom without another word.

A few seconds later, I heard the hiss of the shower. I scrambled to my feet, pulled on my crumpled dress and held it up at the front to cover my breasts. Then I found my briefs and my room key, dashed to the door, opened it and peered round to make sure there was no one about.

Head held high, I walked along the corridor, willing the tears not to fall until I reached my room.

MARK

The shower acted like a balm, restoring most of my sanity and bringing with it intense remorse.

'Oh Emma,' I whispered, 'you must know I lied when I said you weren't as good as Tamara. Why did you make me want to hurt you like that? Why did you have to mention his name?'

I had to speak to her. Pausing only to turn off

307

the shower, I hurtled into the bedroom. But she'd gone. She'd taken her clothes, and her key, and gone.

I hardly noticed the water I was dripping onto the carpet; my eyes were drawn to the bed. For a few hours, it had been a cocoon from the real world, warm with passion and possibility. It was empty now, and cold.

Yet, when I'd reached for her during the night and we'd made love again, it was just like the first time, no holding back. Then, this morning, she was the first thing I saw – the woman I'd always loved. Briefly, foolishly, I'd allowed myself to imagine waking every morning to this, believing that she felt the same for me.

But she didn't. She was in some sort of denial, because of her infatuation with that bastard Churchill. And I knew her too well to try and make her change her mind right now; it was more likely to drive her into his arms. Ironic, wasn't it? Her maddening pig-headedness was one of the many things I loved about her.

So I'd play it cool. For a little while, at least. However hard that might be.

EMMA

I was fumbling to unlock the door of my room with one hand, when I heard someone approaching. A few yards down the corridor, the fire door swung open and Flynn breezed through.

Oh shit! Why did it have to be him?

When he saw me he did a double take, then recovered himself almost immediately and winked at me.

'Where've you been all night, you wicked girl?'

I held my dress up more firmly and forced a smile. 'I could ask you the same question.'

'Me? Oh, just been out for an early morning walk,' he said airily. 'Clear the cobwebs away, that sort of thing.'

'You must have been freezing.'

He was almost as underdressed as I was, his shirt unbuttoned, with no jacket. And weren't they the clothes he'd been wearing last night?

He grinned. 'Yeah, had to make it an early morning jog, actually. And now it's your turn to spill the beans. I'm intrigued – where did you spend the night?'

I blushed and blurted out the first thing that came into my head. 'In Harriet's room. We had quite a lot to drink and I just passed out on her bed.'

He raised one eyebrow. 'Harriet? Interesting. Didn't think you had leanings in that direction.'

'What on earth do you mean?' I said, with a nervous laugh.

'I can always tell when a woman's had a good time. And I'd say you certainly have.' His eyes flicked to the briefs I was holding. 'Never mind, your secret's safe with me. Strewth, and there's me thinking I'm a good judge of sexual orientation – hey, what's wrong?'

Tears were streaming down my cheeks. It was all such a horrible mess. I'd slept with a man I'd known all my life and destroyed our relationship for ever. And now the man I'd really wanted to sleep with thought I was a raving lesbian.

Flynn put his hands on my shoulders and gave them a comforting squeeze. 'Things are never as bad as they seem, Em. Why don't you get properly dressed and I'll make us a cup of tea and you can tell me all about it?'

I nodded and handed him my key. He made short work of the lock I'd been fiddling with for ages and pushed me gently into the room.

'You're cold, you'll feel better after a nice warm shower,' he said, busying himself with the kettle. 'Don't be too long, or I'll come and hurry you up!'

I thanked him with a wan smile, then stumbled through to the bathroom. And there, in the sound-proofed privacy of the shower, I washed away any traces of Mark Knightley – and sobbed my heart out.

But Flynn was right; I did feel better afterwards. In fact, I felt almost back to normal as I put on my jeans and a jumper and sat drinking tea with him. Except that 'normal' had changed. 'Normal' meant recalling random moments from the previous night when I was least prepared for them. 'Normal' meant my stomach churning at the very thought of seeing Mark again.

And as for Flynn . . . When he suggested that I told him everything, I couldn't. And at first I didn't understand why.

'So you went along to ask Harriet to undo your dress,' he prompted. 'Shame I wasn't around, I'd have undone it like a shot, then who knows how your night might have turned out?'

I glanced at him sitting on my bed with that naughty-boy look on his face and I realised that it was a charade, that he was all talk and no action, at least where I was concerned. It made me wonder how I'd ever thought of him as relationship material. Oh, he was good company and he made me laugh, but something about him didn't ring true. And this morning, for the first time, I didn't even fancy him. Those once-gorgeous green eyes had lost their magic.

'But you weren't around, were you?' I said coolly. 'You could have been, but you disappeared quite early on. What did you get up to for all that time?'

He smirked. 'I wish I could say it was something exciting, but I just went to my room and fell asleep. Anyway, we were talking about you, not me. What happened next?'

What happened next was that I crossed a boundary that should have been sacrosanct, had the best sex ever – and couldn't forgive myself for it.

Aloud I said, 'That's none of your business.' I softened my words with a smile and added, 'You've done me good, Flynn, and I'm grateful to you, but I think I'll go home now.'

'Well, you know where I am if you ever want to talk.' He got to his feet, came over to me and planted a kiss on my forehead. 'Just remember, you can't help your natural instincts. Don't fight them, go with the flow. These are enlightened times, even in a place like Highbury.' And he sauntered out, as if he hadn't a care in the world.

I took a deep breath. Time to move on.

MARK

As I walked through the car park, I looked for Emma's car. It was still there, which meant that I could call at Hartfield on my way home without any further confrontations.

Anxious not to disturb Henry, I left the car on the road and walked as quietly as I could up the drive. I was just about to slip an envelope through the letter box, when the door opened and there he stood in his dressing gown, beaming at me.

'Lovely morning, isn't it?' he said.

I glanced up at the overcast sky. 'If you say so.'

'Oh, I know the weather's nothing special, but I've had my best sleep in years. And it was all thanks to this.' He produced a little bottle and waved it in my face. 'I'm sure there's a business opportunity here, must look into it. Mary says her mother swears by this stuff for all sorts of things.'

'It's basically gin, Henry. It makes you forget all your inhibitions – or, in your case, your ailments. If you drink enough of it, you'll forget them permanently. But I wouldn't advise it. Drink never solved anyone's problems, did it?'

He looked horrified. 'You mean I've been in a – a drunken stupor all night? That's with Emma being at Forbury Manor, you know. If she'd been here, this would never have happened.'

'And neither would certain other things,' I muttered under my breath. In a louder voice, I said, 'Would you mind giving this to her?'

He gave me a quizzical look as I handed him the envelope.

'It's just some pointers from our mentoring discussions, as a sort of wrap-up now that I've switched to Jane,' I went on, knowing that he wouldn't open it and discover I was lying.

'Oh yes,' he said vaguely. 'Do you know, I don't think I've told Emma about that yet. I meant to, but I must have forgotten. I'll do it as soon as she gets here. She shouldn't be long, she's just rung to say she's on her way. Come in and I'll make you a coffee, then we can both tell her about the mentoring. Might be better that way, mightn't it?'

I shook my head. 'Sorry, Henry, must dash. And thank you for last night, it was a really good do.' I felt a right heel; it was like thanking him for the opportunity to sleep with his daughter. 'I'll be able to reciprocate in a week's time,'

I added, 'when you come to the Donwell Organics party.'

He smiled. 'It'll be a nice little family outing with Isabella and Emma there too.'

I managed to smile back, although I doubted that Emma would want to come; not now. 'That reminds me, I'd better book a babysitter. John and Izzy and the kids are all staying at Donwell Abbey that weekend.'

And with that I said goodbye and hurried off. There was no way I was going to risk bumping into Emma while my feelings were still so raw. I'd need all the time I could get to prepare for our next meeting.

EMMA

Dad dropped two bombshells almost as soon as I walked through the door.

'Lovely to see you back safely, darling. You've just missed Mark.'

Bombshell number one. I put down my overnight bag and said, as calmly as I could, 'What did he want?'

'To leave this for you.' He held out a crisp white envelope with the Forbury Manor logo in the top left-hand corner and my name scrawled across the middle. My fingers trembled as I took it.

'It's about the mentoring,' said Dad.

'Mentoring?'

'Yes, a sort of wrap-up, since he's going to be mentoring Jane in future.'

Bombshell number two. I knew he wouldn't be mentoring me any more, but . . .

Dad went on, 'He discussed it with me and, in the circumstances, we decided it was for the best.'

'What – what circumstances?' I felt myself go cold. Surely he wouldn't have told Dad about last night?

'Well, he's always been a great fan of hers, hasn't he?' Dad said cheerfully. 'And he seems to think she'll be more responsive than you, at the moment anyway. Benefit more from his expertise, that sort of thing.'

All at once I was back in the hotel bedroom shouting, 'Wasn't I just a substitute for Tamara?' And every word of his reply was branded on my memory: 'Yes, you were. Only not as good.'

Oh, I got the message all right. He may still be getting over Tamara but, when he did finally move on, it would be to Jane Fairfax. Such a deserving cause, so much more responsive than me to his bloody expertise! The mentoring would be a front for getting time alone together without raising too many eyebrows; no doubt he'd be just as un-professional with her as he'd been with me, as soon as he got the chance . . .

Dad was eyeing me anxiously. 'You do under-stand, don't you, darling? And Jane's only here for a short while, whereas you can have mentoring any time.'

I gave him a bright smile. 'Of course I understand. Let me just take my things up to my room, then I'll come and have breakfast with you. Put the kettle on, please, I'm gasping for a coffee.'

He went into the kitchen while I hurried upstairs. As soon as I reached my room, I sank onto the bed and ripped open the envelope.

The letter was very short and to the point.

> Emma,
> If you find out you're pregnant as a result of last night, please let me know as soon as possible. I would make every effort to discuss the situation sensibly with you and whoever else may have to be involved.

'Whoever else may have to be involved'. In other words, Jane.

> If you're not pregnant, then I suggest we forget what happened.
> Mark.

Forget what happened? Was it that easy to contract amnesia? Every time we met, I'd think of what he looked like naked. Every time we kissed at family gatherings, I'd be reminded of other kisses, far less platonic. Every time I saw his hands move, I'd remember exactly what they were capable of . . .

It was obvious that he thought of last night as a big mistake, just two sex-starved people who'd had too much to drink. But he was being his usual responsible self, ever mindful of the consequences of his actions.

If I was pregnant, I certainly wouldn't be going to him and Jane 'to discuss the situation sensibly'.

I'd handle it all by myself, whether he liked it or not.

MARK

On Monday I took Jane out for lunch and another mentoring meeting. It went quite well until we touched on more personal matters.

I'd been meaning to ask her about the Highbury Foods Christmas party and saw my chance when she made an apology for her poor appetite.

'You didn't eat much on Saturday night, either,' I said casually. 'And what happened to you later on? I didn't see you again after our dance.'

She lowered her gaze. 'I felt rather ill, so I went upstairs to lie down for a bit. I must have fallen asleep.'

'Ill? What was the matter?'

'Indigestion probably. And I was tired.'

'You seem to be generally off colour at the moment. Mary's quite worried about you.' I paused. 'I don't want to intrude, but I'm happy to listen if you've got a problem and you need to talk it through.'

She stiffened. 'That's kind of you, but really I'm fine.'

'The offer's always there if you need it.'

'Thank you, but there's absolutely nothing wrong. Now, did you want to look at my focus group results analysis and see if I've missed anything?'

I sighed and did as she suggested, reflecting that, if I ever needed to be mentored in stonewalling techniques, I'd know exactly who to turn to.

EMMA

By half past nine on Thursday morning, Harriet still hadn't turned up for work. Her mobile was switched off and I was just about to drive over to her house in case she'd overslept, when she burst into my room. She was a terrible sight: hair in disarray, mascara running, tights laddered, white fake leather coat stained and torn.

I jumped up from my desk. 'Whatever's wrong?'

'Friggin' Goths—' She glanced over at Jane. 'Sorry, no offence.'

Jane looked understandably baffled.

'Have a seat.' I took Harriet's arm and guided her to the nearest chair. 'Would you like a cup of tea?'

'Christ no, but I could friggin' kill for a bottle of Lambrini.'

Lambrini? I dreaded to think what sort of dubious plonk she wanted to pour down her throat. My lips tightened; it was as though she'd suddenly reverted to Late Neanderthal Chavette. The contrast with the image I wanted her to project for Harriet's Secret Recipes couldn't have been more marked.

'Calm down,' I said sternly, 'and tell me what happened.'

She perched on the edge of the chair and started shredding the leaves of the yucca next to her. 'I was on my way to work, along the high street, not through Little Bassington.' She gave me a meaningful look, then went on, 'I stopped at the lights and some Goths walked past. I mean, a bunch of Goths in broad daylight in the middle of Highbury! Where were the friggin' police?'

I sighed. 'Please don't keep using the word "frigging", it's not very nice. And stop tormenting that poor plant.' I hastily removed it from her clutches.

'Sorry, Emma, it's just I'm traumi – traumicised—'

'Traumatised? Why? What did the Goths do to you?'

'They tagged me.'

'They what?'

'Tagged me, they put a sticker saying "your car is shit" – sorry, "your car is poo" – on my windscreen.'

'Oh, that's horrible. But how did you get into such a mess? Did they turn on you after they'd, um, tagged you?'

She giggled. 'Actually, *I* went for *them*. I got really stuck into the biggest one, went for her piercings, you just grab and twist – like that!' She gave a demonstration that made me wince. 'Then Flynn Churchill turned up. Between us we could've hammered them, but he went all soft. Started apologising for me, told them I was under great pressure at work 'cos I was having a relationship with my lemo boss and—'

'Hang on,' I cut in, 'why did he call me a lemur?'

More giggles. 'Lemo, it's short for lesbian emo. You must know what a lesbian is, and emo's someone who's emotional, innit?'

Oh fantastic, hadn't he told me my 'secret' was safe with him?

'It's not true,' I said, indignantly. 'It was all a misunderstanding, and I wasn't that emotional – at least, not in front of him.'

Fortunately, Harriet wasn't the inquiring sort. 'I'm sure he didn't mean it, Emma, it was just something to say. And it worked, the friggin' Goths just walked off.'

I pulled myself together as I realised people wouldn't take Flynn's comment seriously. And a new thought was taking root in the fertile soil of my mind . . .

'But how romantic, Flynn riding to your rescue like that.' I gave a knowing little smile.

She looked at me blankly. 'He wasn't riding, he was walking.'

'Figure of speech, Harriet. Although I wonder

what he was doing in Highbury at that time of the morning? Kate says he's never usually up before ten.' I added with a laugh, 'Obviously looking for a damsel in distress.'

Just then, a stony-faced Jane scraped back her chair, gathered a few papers together and stalked out of the office, presumably to find somewhere less distracting. I didn't pay much attention; I was too busy visualising how appealing Harriet must have looked as she grappled with the Goths. Vulnerable yet feisty, a combination that would be irresistible to most men – and I had no reason to believe Flynn was an exception. Not that I'd make the same mistake again and put unsuitable ideas into Harriet's head; but there was no harm in pointing out the facts, was there?

'A man likes a woman with spirit,' I told her, 'but he also likes to come to her rescue once in a while. It does his ego no end of good.'

A dreamy look came into her eyes. 'I could get used to being rescued, by one geezer in particular.'

I was just congratulating myself on this new turn of events when I noticed the time. 'Right, we've got lots to do this morning. Why don't you go and tidy yourself up? Here's a new pair of tights, I always keep one in my drawer—'

That was as far as I got. Into my office swept Gusty, resplendent in a bright yellow jumpsuit which reminded me of rather lumpy custard.

Philip followed dutifully at her heels, his matching yellow shirt and tie providing a startling contrast with his usual sober suit.

The timing was most unfortunate. There we were, four of us crammed into one little room: Philip, the woman who was now dominating his life, the woman he'd wanted in his life and the woman who'd fantasised about it. No wonder he wore the expression of a man with a particularly friendly ferret negotiating his nether regions.

'Yes?' I said shortly. 'What can I do for you?'

Gusty gave a disparaging sniff. 'It's not what you can do for us, Emmurrr, it's what we can do for Jane. Isn't she here? Naughty girl, she knew we were coming to see her at ten o'clock. Never mind, she can't have gone far, I'll sit here and wait for her. Pipkin, get me a coffee.'

'Of course, babe.' Philip scuttled out of the office, obviously glad to escape.

I rounded on Gusty. 'You can't stay here, we're busy. You'll have to go and wait in Philip's room.'

She ignored me, sat down and glanced at some papers Jane had left on the table. 'Just as I thought,' she mused. 'This sort of stuff is child's play to someone like Jane. She doesn't know it yet, but I've got her a much better job. Actually, it was my sister who clinched it, she pulled a few strings at a client company, Sucklings of Bristol. You must have heard of them, big in organic meat products.'

'No, I haven't,' I said, with a scowl, 'and I'd like you to go—'

She cut in with, 'I've almost persuaded Marrrk to talk to them about a partnership. You know, *organic* meats and Donwell *Organics*, there must be huge business potential.'

I felt my voice rising in anger. 'I hardly think so, since Donwell are all about dried goods, with completely different storage and distribution requirements.'

She favoured me with a particularly nasty stare. 'Obviously, Emmurrr, you're just starting in the food business whereas Marrrk and I – well, all I can say is it's a true meeting of minds on the subject. On any subject, in fact. Gorrrgeous man, really gorrrgeous. If I wasn't already spoken for, I'd be appreciating *his* assets, I can tell you.'

Her words triggered memories that I fought to suppress: that first glimpse of Mark naked, the taste of his skin, the feel of him, slow and controlled – and then suddenly no control at all . . .

I found myself gripping the edge of the table so hard that I wondered why my fingernails hadn't gouged chunks out of it. 'For the last frigging time, I'm telling you to leave!'

Her eyes narrowed; she got to her feet, though, and drawled, 'I think I'll call in on Henrrry for a few minutes. But send Jane to Philip's office as soon as you see her, it's terribly urgent. Opportunities like this don't grow on trees.'

When she'd gone, I slammed the door shut, leaned back against it and let out a long shaky breath. 'Please God, keep me from wringing that woman's neck because I have no doubt she'd visit me in prison . . . Sorry, Harriet, did you want to get past?'

I managed a grim smile, however, as Harriet went off to the Ladies. Given the two previous men she'd fancied, who'd have thought she and I would ever be interested in the same person? Of course, that wasn't a problem now that I'd decided Flynn wasn't for me. Everything would work out beautifully, I was sure.

MARK

Izzy was not the sort of woman who took setbacks in her stride, especially if they involved her children. When I told her that her preferred babysitter wasn't available for the night of the Donwell Organics Christmas party, she became almost hysterical on the other end of the phone.

'What do you mean, Sarah Perry's sitting for another family? Why didn't you get in first? You've known the date for weeks!'

'Sorry, it slipped my mind, I've had a lot to think about recently.'

Such as your younger sister . . .

Izzy gave an exasperated sigh. 'I'll just have to miss the party and look after the children myself and John will be furious.'

'Sarah did say she'd ask round her friends—'

'Her friends? Good grief, Mark, you may as well just pluck someone off the streets! Or why don't you advertise – only drug addicts and paedophiles need apply?'

'Calm down, for God's sake.' I paused, then went on, 'Listen, why don't you just ask Emma?' I hadn't thought of it until now, but it seemed the ideal solution.

'Don't be ridiculous,' she spluttered. 'Emma won't want to stay behind and babysit. She's never been to your company do before, she'll want to make a big impression. I bet she's splashed out on some ludicrously expensive dress that'll make me look a complete frump.'

'Oh, you never know, you might be pleasantly surprised,' I said smoothly. 'I don't think she particularly enjoyed the Highbury Foods party, so she may be glad to give this one a miss.'

All I heard was a snort of derision before the line went dead.

The next day, however, John breezed into my office with a big grin on his face.

'Well done, Mark. Next time I need to find a win-win solution for something, I'll come to you for ideas. Suggesting Emma as a babysitter was a stroke of genius.' He laughed. 'Henry's a bit miffed that he'll only have one doting daughter at his side, but everyone else is delighted. The kids, because they love it when Emma babysits. Izzy, because she can relax all evening – plus it removes the biggest competition in the dress stakes. And Emma, for reasons known only to herself.'

I was delighted too, wasn't I? The next meeting avoided. No disturbing memories, no frustrated longing, no aching heart.

Except that it didn't work like that. I didn't need to see her in the flesh to feel the pain. It was my constant companion, whether she was there or not.

CHAPTER 11

SUMMER PUDDING

EMMA

Missing the Donwell Organics Christmas party to look after my nephews and nieces was a no-brainer. I'd already decided that I would back out at the last minute, pleading illness; Izzy's babysitting crisis merely gave me a more convincing excuse.

Even better, by the time Dad and I turned up at Donwell Abbey, Mark and John had already left; apparently Mark wanted to familiarise himself with the venue. As the party was at the exclusive golf club where his father had been a member for over twenty years and where the Knightleys held business functions with monotonous regularity, I saw this as a determined attempt to avoid me. Until I felt the tension ease from my body, however, I didn't realise how much I'd been on edge in case our paths crossed.

There was no danger of that now and I could focus on the little problem of getting Izzy out of the door. Emily had a slight sniffle, which meant that my sister was even more reluctant than usual to leave her children. Up in the bedroom, she rocked her youngest expertly and fired off a barrage of instructions, finishing with, 'She's had some Calpol, so don't you give her any – I'll do the next lot when I get back, if she's awake. Dad won't want to be late, I'll bring him at eleven then you can take him home. John and Mark will have to stay until the bitter end, of course. By the way, Mark managed to get someone to take your place – Jane Fairfax.'

What a surprise. Cinderella, you *shall* go to the ball.

I prised Emily from Izzy's arms. 'You'd better go, Dad'll be getting twitchy. And don't leave early on my account – you know I love babysitting the kids.'

She gave me a sharp look. 'Harry and James have to be in bed by nine at the latest, don't let them string you along.' She straightened Emily's sleepsuit, which I'd got slightly twisted, and went on, 'Make sure Bella brushes her teeth, she's playing up about it for some reason. And Mark still likes the Mog books at bedtime, so—'

'For goodness' sake, go! And try to enjoy yourself.'

I almost pushed her out of the room – no mean feat with a twenty-pound baby drowsing on my shoulder – then put Emily straight to bed. Bella was a great help, turning back the cot covers and showing me which toys went where. After we'd waited for Emily to settle, she led me along the landing and through a door at the end.

'Is this where you're sleeping . . .' My voice trailed off as I flicked on the light. We were in a big room with an enormous bed and a distinctly masculine feel. 'This isn't your bedroom, is it?'

'It used to be, but it's Uncle Mark's now. When he came home, he asked me specially if he could have it. He says the sun comes in and makes it nice and warm in the mornings, like it is in India.' She made a beeline for a large chest of drawers which held a group of rather faded photos in exquisitely carved frames: his mother and father, Izzy and John on their wedding day, me as a gawky bridesmaid, our nephews and nieces as babies.

'Look, here's his favourite smell.' She pointed to a small bottle next to one of the photos. 'He let me put some on him tonight and I put it on his nose and he laughed, but he smelled really nice. Why does everyone want a different smell? Why don't you and Mummy just use Uncle Mark's?'

Dismissing the rationale for the entire perfume industry with this innocent question, she dived onto the bed and started bouncing up and down. I stared unseeingly at her, wondering how it would feel to wake up in this bed with the sun shining . . .

'In the morning,' she gasped between bounces, 'Marky and I – are going to come – and jump on him – like this!' She landed squarely on one of the pillows, a fraction of an inch from the solid wooden headboard, and burst out laughing.

The near miss jolted me out of my reverie. 'Bella! Stop that at once before you have a nasty accident.'

'But you like bouncing on beds too, Aunty Emma, I know you do. Why don't you stay with me and Marky tonight, then you can help us wake Uncle Mark up?' All of a sudden, her face was very close to mine. 'You look sad, don't you want to stay here?'

I forced a smile. 'I'd love to, but I can't. Anyway, it's time for you and Mark to get ready for bed. Will you go and find a Mog book while I run the bath?'

After a long, noisy bath and several Mog books, Bella and Mark dropped off to sleep in seconds. That left Harry and James who, despite considering themselves very grown up, still liked a bedtime story.

'One of your made-up ones, please, Aunty Emma,' James said eagerly.

'As bloodthirsty as possible,' Harry added.

They hurled themselves onto the sofa in the TV room, while I settled myself more sedately between them and extracted all sorts of promises about going to bed at a sensible time and cleaning their teeth properly. Then I began my story.

'Once upon a time,' I said softly, 'in the Enchanted Kingdom of Highbury, Princess Harriet was on her way to see Queen Emma. Now Princess Harriet was very beautiful, with long golden hair and big blue—'

Harry interrupted me, his voice full of scorn. 'Is this a fairy tale?'

'Certainly not, just be patient.' And I continued for a little longer in the same lyrical vein, to set the scene. Then I picked up the pace and related the story of Harriet and the Goths, suitably tailored to my audience with transgalactic rocket-launchers, laser-phaser-blaster guns and a Flynn Churchill who was far more heroic than his real-life counterpart. Harry and James loved it and wanted to hear it over and over again – even the romantic bit, where Princess Harriet and Prince Flynn got married. I didn't mind; anticipating Harriet's and Flynn's happy ending made me forget my own troubles for a while.

Later, when the boys were fast asleep, I returned to Mark's room and tidied the bedclothes that Bella had disturbed. Then I picked up the bottle that she'd called his 'favourite smell'. Armani, Eau Pour Homme. I opened it and inhaled. Fatal. At once, I was back in that tiny bathroom at Ashridge, then kissing him in the hall at home and, finally, lying on his bed at Forbury Manor, doing more kissing, doing more than kissing . . .

I replaced the cap and set the bottle down, but the scent and the memories lingered. So I slipped off my shoes. Lay on top of his duvet. Rested my cheek on his pillow. Breathed in his essence. Part Armani, something I could buy anywhere. And part Mark. Unique. Unattainable. And still under Tamara's spell.

How long I lay there, I don't know. Long enough to make his pillow damp with tears. But at last I got up, put on my shoes, smoothed his duvet, turned off his light.

And went downstairs to get on with my life.

MARK

In the days leading up to Christmas, my workload eased and I decided it was time to contact Emma. We were certain to meet over the holiday period; why not clear the air in advance? If part of me hoped for a full and passionate reconciliation, then I didn't allow myself to dwell on it.

But I'd forgotten the disruption that an English winter could bring to the workplace. Donwell Organics was hit by a particularly virulent flu bug and most of our sales force – including Mitch, the Sales Director – went down with it. We were at a very delicate stage of negotiation with the new Parkinson contract and I had to drop everything to keep our chances of securing it alive.

So I worked all hours, right until the office closed on 24th December. I found the prospect of some time off strangely disconcerting. As I'd bought my presents well in advance, I didn't have any last-minute shopping to do and my thoughts turned inevitably to Emma; but I knew she wouldn't welcome a visit in the middle of her Christmas Eve preparations. It was the tradition for the Knightleys and Woodhouses, including John and family, to have Christmas lunch together. I'd missed out since going to India, preferring to visit England during warmer weather. This year, we were meeting at Hartfield and I knew I wouldn't be able to get out of it unless I feigned Bubonic Plague or something equally drastic.

I kept away for as long as possible, arriving shortly before the meal was due to be served. Henry answered the door and seemed to accept my excuse about waiting for a phone call from Father. He showed me into the drawing room, where I was immediately set upon by an army of wildly excited children – four, at any rate – demanding their presents.

'Emily gets hers first, she's better behaved than any of you lot,' I said, laughing and looking about for the youngest Knightley.

She was on her aunt's knee, surveying me gravely. In contrast, Emma avoided my gaze, pretending to be engrossed in something on the other side of the room.

I decided to treat them as a package. 'Merry Christmas, both of you.' I bent down and planted a light kiss on Emily's chubby cheek, then made a similar gesture in the vicinity of Emma, managing to avoid any actual physical contact. So far, so good.

The older children hovered impatiently while I rummaged in my carrier bags and took out two presents.

'This one's for Emily.' I helped her to unwrap

the cloth doll I'd bought her and she grabbed it with an appreciative gurgle.

'And for Emma,' I said heartily, holding the other present out towards her. She couldn't refuse to open it, surely?

It seemed she could. She flushed and mumbled something about having her hands full with Emily.

Bella came to her rescue. 'I'll help you, Aunty Emma.' In a second she'd taken the present from me and torn off the paper to reveal a book. She held it up to her face to read the title. 'It's about a shridge,' she said importantly.

Izzy frowned. 'A what, darling?'

'A shridge.'

I couldn't help smiling. 'You've got all the letters right, Bella, you just need to make it into one word. Ashridge. It's a special place I took Aunty Emma to, not long ago.' Not long ago? It seemed like a lifetime. I went on, 'The book's got some lovely pictures of the house and grounds, to remind her of our visit. And it tells you all about the people who used to live there, which is fascinating. I think so, anyway.'

Emma took the book from Bella as if it was a live cobra, put it straight down on the floor and studied the back of Emily's neck. 'Thanks, I'm sure I'll be duly fascinated.' She sounded anything but. 'Bella, can you bring Uncle Mark's present from under the tree?'

Bella was a willing go-between. As she gave me

the present, she beamed at me and whispered, 'It's your favourite smell.'

It was. Armani, Eau Pour Homme. With a tag that said simply 'To Mark, from Emma'; no love, no kisses, nothing. Was it that that made me see red, or was it the fact she'd been so lacking in imagination? I managed to mutter 'Thank you, very useful' and turned my attention to handing out my other presents.

Shortly afterwards, however, when she left the room, I followed her. I stood at the door of the kitchen, watching her pour the champagne and trying not to think what might have been. If Churchill didn't exist, I would have won her round after Forbury Manor, I was sure. And right now I would have taken her in my arms, laughed off her uninspired Christmas present and urged her to come back with me to Donwell Abbey for the evening, if not the night . . .

But Churchill did exist. And she wanted him, not me.

Still, things couldn't go on as they were. I took a deep breath. 'Emma.'

She whirled round, knocking a half-filled flute to the floor. Champagne and fragments of glass went everywhere. She looked as though she was going to burst into tears, then collected herself.

'That one was yours,' she said coldly, and went to fetch a floor mop and bucket from the nearby utility room. In a matter of seconds, she was sweeping the damp mop across the tiles with an air of vicious satisfaction.

I stayed out of her way, folding my arms and leaning against the door jamb to observe her with as much detachment as I could muster.

'Maybe I'd better not have anything alcoholic,' I said, in a casual tone. 'God knows, I should have learnt my lesson about the evils of drink by now.'

She looked up, her face pale with anger. 'Is that why you came in here? To taunt me about – about that?'

Incredible, it was as if she still couldn't bring herself to say that we'd slept together! I struggled to keep my temper in check. 'No, I came to tell you to make an effort, keep up the appearance that everything's normal in front of our family. It's Christmas, remember? At least let the children enjoy their day instead of involving them in whatever little games you're playing with me.'

She paused within a yard of me and gave a supercilious smile. 'Don't be ridiculous, I only asked Bella to give you your present.'

'She's a bright kid, they all are, they could tell there were – undercurrents.'

'How could they, when there weren't any? At least, not on my side.'

'Don't talk such crap, you wouldn't even look at me.'

Her eyes flashed. 'Oh, I forgot, I'm supposed to fall down on my knees and gaze at you adoringly, aren't I? I should be so grateful that Highbury's very own Sex God condescended to knock me off! Just a pity it wasn't more memorable. But, of course, I have that charming book to remind me of how it all started. You know, when you brought me home from Ashridge and behaved so unprofessionally. Such a thoughtful present from such a thoughtful man.'

I lost the struggle with my temper, but managed to keep my voice deceptively quiet. 'Ah well, it was a toss-up between that and a framed transcript of the proceedings at Forbury Manor, for you to hang on your bedroom wall. Shame you can't remember much about it, because your task focus was rather impressive for once – something you'd be well advised to transfer to the workplace. What did you say again? "I need you to undo my dress" and "Kiss me". Oh, and then there was "Don't stop, not now".'

I knew I was totally out of order, but it just didn't seem to matter any more. I went on, 'And let's see if I can recall the grand finale, when you actually begged me to—'

She slapped my face, hard. We glared at each other in silence while I rubbed my smarting cheek.

'I'm sorry.' It was out before I realised I'd said it. I didn't even know if I meant it. Part of me would never willingly cause her pain; but another part of me wanted to provoke her into some sort of physical retaliation, which was precisely what I'd got. So why didn't I feel good about it?

'Emma, I'm really sorry. I shouldn't have said

any of those things.' This time I meant it. And, God help me, I wanted her more than ever. I reached out and cupped her face with my hand, letting my thumb caress the corner of her mouth. It was exactly the wrong thing to do. She wrenched herself from my grasp and ran into the utility room, sending the mop flying.

I'd taken no more than a couple of steps after her when the doorbell rang. Cursing, I went to get rid of whoever it was, resolving to come straight back and sort things out with her. As soon as I opened the front door, however, I knew it wouldn't be that simple. It was Kate, laden with presents.

She greeted me with a kiss. 'Merry Christmas, Mark. Are you having lunch, or can we stop by for a while?'

'Of course you can,' I heard myself say, lamely.

I stood to one side while she came in, followed by her husband and, of course, her grinning stepson. I gritted my teeth and shook their hands – Tom's warmly, Churchill's as briefly as possible – then showed them into the drawing room, fully intending to leave them to it and slip back to the kitchen. But James was wearing the Doctor Who Cyberman mask I'd brought for him and clamouring to show me what a realistic noise it made. No sooner had I given him the horrified reaction he expected, than Harry wanted me to help him set up his Simpsons Game of Life. When I next looked around, Emma still hadn't returned and there was no sign of Churchill. My lip curled. They were probably locked in a passionate embrace in the kitchen. It was too much to hope that he'd impaled himself on the mop in the process.

I let out a long breath, pasted a smile on my face and played the role of doting uncle to perfection.

EMMA

I stared out of the utility room window; seeing nothing, trying to hold on to my fragile composure, remembering with intense shame the wave of longing that had flooded through me at his touch. I'd felt my eyes start to close, my lips part, my body sway towards him – all just moments after he'd humiliated me by repeating things I couldn't possibly have said.

No. Deep down, I knew I'd said those things.

And more . . .

Then, unbelievably, a few minutes later he was behind me, his arms round my waist, his breath ruffling my hair.

I dug him violently in the stomach with my elbow. 'Get off me, you bastard!'

He gave a loud groan and backed off. 'Em, what the hell was that for?'

Flynn! I spun round and blurted out, 'Sorry, I thought you were Mark.'

'Do you normally have to fight him off like that?' he said, with a frown.

I forced a laugh. 'Of course not, it's just because it's Christmas.'

'Thank God. And at least you weren't encouraging him, unlike some people I could mention. The man's insufferable enough as it is.'

'Oh, don't I know it – he treats me as though I'm still in nappies.'

He gave me an appraising look and raised one eyebrow. 'In that dress it's fairly obvious you're not wearing a nappy. In fact, Miss Woodhouse, it's debatable whether you're wearing any underwear at all – and Highbury is well and truly shocked!' He grinned. 'Anyway, there's me just wanting to wish you Merry Christmas and getting almost crippled for it. Shall we try again?'

He pulled me to him and kissed me on both cheeks. 'That's better.' He paused, then winked at me. 'And how are things with the lovely Harriet?'

'Look,' I said, with an exasperated sigh, 'there's absolutely nothing between me and Harriet.'

He winked again. 'That's exactly how I like to imagine the two of you. Quite a turn-on, believe me, on my lonely nights up in the Lake District for the past couple of weeks.'

'The lovely Harriet', 'quite a turn-on'? Was this empty talk, or an indication of something more serious? I stored these thoughts away in my mind until later, but decided I wasn't going to let him off the hook for now.

I placed my hands on my hips and scowled at him. 'You can stop your imagining, period, because it's simply not true. And why you had to call me a lemo in front of Harriet and those Goths, I'll never know. You told me you wouldn't say a word to anyone!'

He put on an injured expression. 'I was only trying to create a diversion. You'd better let me off, or else you won't get the really nice present I've got you.'

'I don't want a really nice present.' My lips tightened. 'And I need to see to the lunch, otherwise it'll be ruined. You can make yourself useful and take that tray of drinks into the drawing room. Presumably Kate and Tom are with you?'

'Yes. We meant to come earlier, but Kate wanted to call on the Bateses first.'

'I see. And how were they?'

'Oh God, same as usual. Except that Batty was still full of the Donwell Organics Christmas party, although she wasn't even there. "Dear Mark, so generous, *so* attentive to dear Jane, everything a girl could wish for . . . The most *wonderful* syllabub for dessert, with delicious little biscuits, almost like a . . . Then carriages at one, so not too much beauty sleep lost" – and so on, ad nauseam.'

I couldn't help smiling; he had Batty off to a T. 'You're a very wicked man, mocking her like that. Ask Kate and Tom what they'd like to drink – oh, and "dear Mark" too.' I bit my lip. 'If he doesn't want anything alcoholic, he can have either orange juice or lemonade, like the kids.'

Flynn did as he was told and returned a few

minutes later. 'Champagne for Tom – he says he's got lots to celebrate – and orange juice for Kate and God's Gift. Shall I see to it?'

'Please.' The less contact I had with Mark at the moment, the better.

I left Flynn in the kitchen and went into the drawing room to wish Kate and Tom a Merry Christmas. As I watched them give the children their presents, I noticed that they were unusually restless. Tom was shifting from one foot to the other and Kate kept glancing up at him; whenever their eyes met, they would both break into a smile.

I nudged Kate and said, with mock severity, 'You two should be behaving like an old married couple by now, but you seem even more excited than the children, if that's possible. What's your secret?'

She exchanged another look with Tom and he went dashing out of the room. Then she turned to me. 'Tom's gone to find Flynn because he's going to make an announcement. But I want to tell you our news myself.' She added, with a blush, 'I'm pregnant.'

My hand went instinctively to my stomach; then I hugged her and said brightly, 'That's wonderful. When did you find out?'

'A while ago, but I've just passed the three-month stage so we thought it safe to go public. We're going to tell the others once Tom's back.'

I did some rapid calculations in my head. Her baby would be born in early summer; whereas, if

I was pregnant, mine would be due very late August. Or even September, the time for an Indian summer. How appropriate, given who the father was . . . I corrected myself. There was, in effect, no such person. I would have to be both father and mother to my baby.

I squared my shoulders. 'I'm so happy for you. You'll be the perfect mother and Tom will have the chance to be a real father this time. Not like with Flynn.'

She sobered instantly. 'Yes, imagine fathering a child and not being able to see it grow up. Oh, I know it happens far too frequently these days, but that doesn't make it any easier for the man concerned. And the child, naturally.'

I felt my eyes fill with tears but, fortunately, Tom and Flynn came into the room with the remaining drinks and provided a distraction. Kate gave me a kiss and moved to Tom's side, while I found myself staring at Flynn. He hadn't turned out that badly, I supposed, but how did he feel about seeing so little of his father during his childhood? Of course, Tom had been in the Merchant Navy, unable to interfere even if Stella had allowed him to.

Mark would be entirely different. He was a more forceful character than Tom and, worse still, he was on my doorstep. But he was due to go back to India when George Knightley returned in February. With any luck he'd leave promptly, giving me the time and space to work out how to run my life – and Dad's – with a baby.

All of a sudden, it dawned on me. As my pregnancy started to show, I'd have to endure all the gossip. 'Fancy Emma Woodhouse making that sort of mistake! But then she always thought she was better than everyone else in Highbury. Now who could the father be?'

I wondered gloomily how Dad would react. I decided he'd either get permanently bloated, in the spirit of a sympathetic pregnancy, or become obsessed with the potential risks to my health.

Then there was Izzy; she'd probably accuse me of being immoral and irresponsible and forbid me to have anything more to do with her children. And what about John? What if, for once, he agreed with her?

I was sure Kate and Tom would be supportive; but naturally, when their own baby arrived, they'd have far less time for me and my problems.

As for Batty, she would be positively unbearable. She'd smother me with kindness and those endless pairs of pale yellow bootees she used to knit for Izzy. I could just hear her rabbiting on at me: 'You can't have too many of them, Baby's little feet can get quite chilly and . . . *Such* a lovely colour, it does for a boy or a . . . Still keeping us in the dark about its father, dear? Never mind, I'm sure we'll be able to tell who Baby looks like when it's born, so exciting, perhaps I'll organise a Guess the Daddy stall at the Autumn Fayre.'

Funny, until Kate told me her news, I hadn't thought any of this through. It was as though her pregnancy – so straightforward, so welcome, so *right* – made me realise what a mess mine would be.

But this much was clear: whatever the truth of the situation, I had to tell Mark I wasn't pregnant. I needed him safely back in India and out of my life.

MARK

I wondered what Emma and Kate were talking about. Whatever it was, it made Kate happy but left Emma quite upset. Once she was on her own, her face drained of its colour and, for a moment, I thought she was going to faint.

I frowned. Normally, I'd have gone over and probed a bit, or jollied her out of it. But there was no such thing as normality any more, only the appearance of it. And anyway, she didn't need me, she had Churchill. She certainly couldn't take her eyes off him, which filled me with a sense of foreboding. What if my playing it cool for the past few weeks had been completely the wrong tactic?

As a result, when Tom asked for silence so that he could make 'an important announcement', I broke out in a cold sweat – because I knew what was coming. Strange, though; I'd have expected Henry to do the honours, not Tom. Unless Henry didn't approve?

My mouth went dry as I glanced across at Emma. She looked strained rather than pleased, and there was no ring on her engagement finger. But, of course, she'd be concerned about her father's reaction; or perhaps Churchill wanted to put the ring on in front of everyone, like the flamboyant bastard he was.

Emily started to wail and Emma picked her up to comfort her; odd, when I'd have thought she'd need her hands free . . .

Just then, Tom cleared his throat. 'Thank you, everybody. I'm delighted to announce' – I closed my eyes to blot out the inevitable – 'that in June, all being well,' – oh, get on with it, for God's sake! – 'a new member of the Weston family will put in his or her appearance.'

I let out a long slow breath. In other words, Kate and Tom were expecting a baby. Why hadn't I guessed? It was the most natural thing in the world, even if they were both getting on a bit. I opened my eyes and grinned inanely at no one in particular.

Tom drew Kate's arm through his. 'Please join me in a toast to my lovely wife and the safe arrival of Baby Weston!'

As we raised our glasses and echoed his words, I took the opportunity to study the faces around me. Everyone seemed delighted, with two notable exceptions. Henry looked apprehensive, presumably speculating on what could go wrong with Kate's pregnancy. And, although I couldn't see Emma's expression properly for Emily's head, her eyes were suspiciously bright. They met mine, then flicked away.

I understood perfectly. Kate and Tom's news had been a timely reminder that she might be carrying my child.

And the contrast with Kate's happiness couldn't be more marked.

EMMA

After the toast, Flynn sauntered over to me, lifted a rather surprised Emily out of my arms and pressed a small, square, gift-wrapped box into my hand.

'Here's the really nice present I got you.' He gave Emily a wary look. 'Hope she doesn't throw up, this is my best shirt. Still, it looks as though I'll have to get used to having a baby around.'

I felt my face flush with embarrassment. 'But I haven't got you anything!'

'Just open it, woman.'

Inside the box was a pair of ornate sapphire and diamond earrings. Not to my taste at all and, judging by the name on the lid, horribly expensive. Grant's of Kingston was renowned for its showy jewellery and high prices; Tom had bought Kate's engagement ring there, against my recommendation.

With a pretence at regret, I said, 'A very generous gift, but I can't possibly accept it.'

'That's a real shame.' But he didn't sound at all disappointed; and he snatched the box back rather too quickly for my liking.

347

My eyes narrowed. 'Did you buy these for somebody else?'

He gave a nervous laugh. 'How did you guess?'

'Oh, it's my feminine intuition, it can be a real curse at times,' I said in a friendlier tone, thinking that these monstrosities were just the sort of thing Harriet would adore – provided she thought they were fake.

He hesitated, then said in a low voice, 'I was going to give them to a certain person we both know, but I was scared she'd hate them so I bottled out. And Kate and Dad assumed they were for you, so I decided I'd better play along. You see, I'm in their bad books because of all the time I'm spending away from Highbury.' He added, with a beguiling grin, 'Don't suppose you'd wear them, just while we're here? It'd do my credibility a power of good.'

Fortunately for him, this last revelation deprived me of the power of speech.

He went on, 'I'd need them back, of course, but there's no rush. How about it?'

I took a deep, steadying breath. 'I don't think so. If "a certain person" means so much to you, surely you'd want her to be the first to wear them. And remember, she works for me. I know she'll love them, she might just need some persuading to accept them. It's early days, after all.'

He laughed. 'You're right, I need to be patient, she's not used to being showered with expensive gifts. Em, you're a star!' He hugged me with such enthusiasm that Emily got almost crushed between us and started to cry.

I drew back with a tight little smile. 'See if you can calm Emily down, you obviously need the practice. Excuse me while I go and check on the lunch.'

It was a relief to escape to the kitchen and busy myself with undemanding tasks; I steamed the green vegetables, made the gravy and added the finishing touches to Dad's alternative Christmas meal, which this year was a daring combination of poached lemon sole followed by natural yogurt.

At half past two, when Kate, Tom and Flynn had left, the rest of us sat down to lunch. Dad and I were at opposite ends of the dining table and I put Mark next to Dad, as far away from me as possible. Only trouble was, every time I spoke to Dad, I found myself looking at *him*.

Needless to say, Izzy's sole topic of conversation was Kate's pregnancy. Over the turkey, she and Dad commiserated about all the possible complications Kate's age might cause. By the time I handed round the Christmas pudding and mince pies, she'd moved on to the subject of Randalls.

'They'll have far too much work to do on that house before June,' she said, disapprovingly. 'It's not at all suitable for a baby, you'd think they'd have sorted that first before she got pregnant.'

'Accidents can happen,' Mark said shortly.

At his words, my spoon clattered loudly against my plate.

Izzy gave him a frosty look. 'But they're old enough to know better—'

'Aren't we all?' he countered. 'Anyway, it's entirely their business. Henry, would you like me to pass you a mince pie to liven up that yogurt?'

Dad shuddered. 'No thank you, Mark, you've obviously forgotten what dried fruit does to me or you wouldn't even suggest it . . . But now I come to think about it, Emma, is there any of that nice stewed apple left from the other day?'

'I'm sure there is.' I stood up, glad to have an excuse to leave the table. As well as the conversation making me uncomfortable, I felt as though I'd eaten too much. Or maybe it was something else. As I crossed the hall, I stopped. I hadn't been mistaken; there it was again, a familiar dull ache in my stomach.

Instead of going to the kitchen, I made my way slowly upstairs to the bathroom.

MARK

When Churchill gave Emma a little jeweller's box, any relief I'd felt at Tom's announcement evaporated. I just knew it contained an engagement ring. Sick to my stomach, I watched her look at it in awe and presumably suggest they held off a while, so as not to steal Kate and Tom's thunder. And then the bastard took her in his arms, right there, in front of everyone. At that point, I became intensely interested in Bella's new Barbie doll.

Things improved after he left. Over lunch, Emma appeared to be heeding my words about making an effort in front of the family. But Izzy had to go and spoil it all, harping on about Kate's pregnancy. Naturally, she had no idea it was such a sensitive topic for some of us; she just saw it as the ideal opportunity to demonstrate her expertise in such matters. Eventually I changed the subject to Henry's diet, which could usually be guaranteed to dominate any conversation.

I sensed that Emma was as dismayed as I was by Izzy's comments. She certainly took a long time to fetch Henry's stewed apple and, when she returned, she looked pale and drawn. In fact, during our customary walk after lunch she barely said a word, even to the kids.

As soon as we got back to Hartfield, I decided I'd had enough. I said my goodbyes and fended off the kids' pleas to come back to Donwell Abbey, knowing that the only company I'd be fit for that evening was a bottle of whisky.

Emma had gone to the kitchen to make some tea. I popped my head round the door, intending to say thank you and goodbye as quickly as possible. But the words died on my lips. She was standing with her back to me, the tea tray all ready on the table next to her. At first glance, I thought she was just daydreaming; then I noticed she was hugging her stomach and her shoulders were shaking, as though she was crying. I paused in the doorway, paralysed by indecision. Should I go to her, or not?

At last I spoke, my voice hoarse with a cocktail of emotions – fear, frustration, yearning, love. 'Emma – what is it, what's wrong?'

She straightened up immediately, lifted the lid of the teapot and stirred the contents with a spoon. I couldn't see her face, but she sounded calm enough, matter-of-fact even.

'It's only stomach cramps, the ones I get every month. They can be quite painful until the ibuprofen takes effect.'

It took a few seconds for the message to sink in. 'So you're not pregnant,' I said, quietly. I stepped forward, arms outstretched, aching to offer comfort.

'No, I'm not . . . Thank God.' She spoke loudly and distinctly, her meaning unmistakable.

I stopped short and let my arms fall to my sides. What good was comfort if she felt only relief? 'You're right, perhaps it's for the best,' I heard myself say.

She didn't answer, just poured the tea carefully into the cups.

I cleared my throat. 'As I said in that letter, if you're not pregnant then maybe we should just forget what happened.'

A pause; then, 'Believe me, I already have.'

I didn't believe for one moment she had, but I certainly believed she wanted to.

Slowly, silently, I turned and walked to the front door.

He'd caught me unawares in the kitchen but I was pretty sure I'd put on a convincing act. I mean, he certainly hadn't hung around, hadn't even said goodbye. He must have been as relieved as I'd pretended to be.

Ironic, wasn't it? I'd only just decided I would tell him I wasn't pregnant, to get him out of the way. Then along came my period, right on cue, making the lie totally unnecessary. I should have been delighted that there would be no obvious consequences from that disastrous night. Life could return to normal once he went back to India. So why did I feel so empty? Why did I wish I was pregnant, if only – out of pure selfishness – to have a little part of him to myself? It was crazy, so crazy that I almost laughed out loud. Except – I couldn't; I felt more like crying.

I was about to take the tray through to the drawing room, when John came in.

'Thought you must have gone to China to pick the tea leaves,' he said. 'Presumably Mark delayed you.'

I gave a wan smile. 'Not really, he was only here a couple of minutes.'

'Oh?' He took the tray from me. 'What's going on between you two, anyway?'

'Going on?'

He rolled his eyes. 'For God's sake, your sister and father may be blind as bats but any normal person can see that something's up. And I can always tell when Mark's rattled.' He looked straight at me, waiting for an answer.

I took a deep breath and chose to be extremely economical with the truth. 'I guess his professional pride has taken a bit of a battering. Dad asked him to mentor me, but it hasn't worked out.'

John gave a loud guffaw. 'You mean Mark got Henry to pay for something he's been doing free of charge for years? Crafty devil. So why hasn't it worked out?'

'I've no idea. Why don't you ask him?'

'Oh, don't worry, I will.' And he strode out of the kitchen like a man on a mission.

CHAPTER 12

COLD TURKEY

MARK

Early on Boxing Day, the phone beside my bed rang and rang – until I answered it, purely in the hope that the caller would then leave me in peace.

A voice barked in my ear, 'We're coming home.' It was Father, sounding on the verge of an apoplectic fit.

'I know, in February,' I muttered, my brain fogged with sleep and whisky.

'No, we're coming home *now*. Well, as soon as we can. Once we've put into port, we're going to get off this bloody boat and stay on dry land until we find a flight. Might manage it before New Year if we're lucky.'

I sat bolt upright. 'You're not ill, are you?'

'Nothing like that, it's the lifestyle. Far too much food and no decent exercise, I'm longing to be back on the golf course. I've been complaining to Saffron for weeks but she wouldn't listen until today.' He lowered his voice. 'Got herself weighed this morning and went beserk. She'd put on three

355

pounds – only three bloody pounds! I feel as if I've put on thirty, I'm going to have to spend the next six months getting it off.'

I took a deep breath. 'Look, if you're—'

He ignored me and went on, 'She's driving me round the bend, it's no fun seeing so much of her, I can't—' He broke off, then said more calmly, 'Sorry, I interrupted you, what were you going to say?'

'Just – if you're coming home early, how do you feel about me going straight back to India rather than staying until February?'

He laughed. 'No problem, I'll be glad of the excuse to be in the office for hours on end. Missing Tamara, are you?'

I hesitated, debating whether to tell him about Tamara in case it made him even more stressed; I decided to get it over and done with.

'Actually, we broke up a couple of months ago.'

'Ah.' He didn't sound particularly surprised. 'Sorry to hear that, but it's best to find out now. I mean, I did wonder if you were planning to settle down—'

'Definitely not. Not with her or anyone else. Anyway,' I said in a brisker tone, 'let me have the flight details as soon as you know them. In the meantime, I'll get Mrs Burn to give the house an early spring clean.'

After the call I lay back, hands clasped behind my head, thinking about the implications of returning to India ahead of schedule. On the work front, it was unfortunate; there were a couple of initiatives I'd have liked to see through to completion, particularly the Parkinson contract. But this paled into insignificance beside the impact on my personal life; within one or two weeks I'd be thousands of miles away from the future Mrs Emma Churchill, in a place that could trigger no memories of her.

For the first time in a long while, I felt almost cheerful.

EMMA

Although our offices were closed for two weeks over Christmas and New Year, Harriet returned to Highbury after only a few days with her family. When she called me up to announce that she had something to show me, my thoughts went immediately to the earrings that Flynn had bought. He'd gone back to the Lake District until New Year, still refusing to tell me what he was up to with the BBC, but I wondered if he'd left them for her at her house.

I wasted no time in inviting her over. We sat next to each other on the sofa in the drawing room, warming ourselves in front of the fire and agreeing that, this year, we'd both have preferred to spend Christmas Day somewhere else. She explained that she'd have liked to stay in Highbury and looked wistful, no doubt imagining a romantic encounter with Flynn. But I didn't elaborate on my situation, the strain of seeing Mark and the repercussions – or lack of them – from that night at Forbury Manor. I merely said that I hadn't felt as relaxed as usual with my family.

Eventually she produced what she'd come to show me. It was a little jeweller's box. I tried to suppress a sense of déjà vu – even though I could see it wasn't the one Flynn had given me so half-heartedly. She prised it open and thrust it under my nose.

There was no need to act amazed; I would never have guessed what it contained, ever. 'Um, what exactly are these?'

She made a face. 'This is' – dramatic pause – 'my life.'

I was even more confused. 'I don't understand.'

'What I mean is, this *was* my life when I fancied Philip. Daft, innit? But now I've moved on, so I thought we could burn these, symbollocks like.'

'Symbolic,' I said automatically; then, 'No, symbollocks is far more appropriate where Philip's concerned. But you mustn't burn any of them until you've told me what they are.'

She settled herself more comfortably on the sofa, cocked her head on one side and studied the contents of the box.

'We'll start with this.' With an embarrassed smile, she showed me a little bottle of Tippex.

I stared at it blankly.

'Don't you remember?' she screeched. 'Philip was in our office and I'd spilt a bit of coffee on those mock-ups you'd spent ages over and my Tippex was all dried up so I couldn't use it. And you didn't have any so Philip brought some and said we could keep it. I put it in this box and I used to take it out and touch it, because *he'd* touched it.'

'I do remember it now.' I bit my lip. 'And I'm ashamed to say I had two bottles of Tippex in my drawer all along. But I pretended there wasn't any, so that he'd run round after you.'

She shrugged, replaced the Tippex in the box and picked up a folded piece of yellow paper. When she opened it out, I saw that there were a few words scribbled on it: 'milk', 'Rice Krispies', 'Anusol'.

'Philip's shopping list.' She frowned. 'What's Anusol?'

I couldn't help giggling. 'Dad's got some, it's for piles. Poor Philip, now he's got Gusty – which must be considerably worse. Where on earth did you get this?'

'At his house after the photo shoot, it was next to the computer. He mustn't have wanted us to see it 'cos he threw it in the waste paper basket, but I fished it out when I went back for your camera.'

There were some other 'relics': the stub of a

pencil, well chewed; a half-eaten chocolate bar; and a rather suggestive doodle on a scrap of file paper.

She gave a deep sigh. 'And now I'm going to chuck the whole lot on the fire.'

'Not the Tippex, it's flammable!' I snatched the bottle out of the box. 'Actually, there's quite a lot left in here, don't you want to keep it?'

A steely look came into her big blue eyes. 'No. It's all got to go.'

'Throw everything else on the fire, then, except the box. I don't think that'll burn easily, I'll put it in the dustbin later.' I paused. 'You know, I have a funny feeling you'll be getting another little box soon, but I'm not going to say any more.'

'You're so clever, 'cos I've just been thinking about starting one for—'

I held up my hand. 'Don't even breathe his name. If you don't tell me, then I can't interfere!' I added, with a laugh, 'But of course I know who you mean and I think it's lovely.'

'Do you? I thought you'd say he'd never want to go out with someone like me in a million years.'

'Oh Harriet, I wouldn't dream of saying anything like that. For a start, I don't know him that well—'

'Don't you?'

'Not well enough to discuss things like that, at any rate. Anyway, I'm not saying another word about it.'

She gazed dreamily into the fire. 'Bet he's a great shag. I couldn't take my eyes off him when he was dancing at the Christmas party, best butt there.'

'I've seen better,' I said tautly, suppressing a vivid recollection of Mark's back view.

'Have you? And there's me thinking you need to get out more! By the way, why don't you come to the pub on New Year's Eve? There's bound to be someone you fancy, specially when you've had a few Lambrinis.'

I forced a smile. 'Thanks, but I don't really feel like it. Dad and I've been invited to the Westons' and I don't really feel like that either, although for once Dad really wants to go.' I had a sneaking suspicion that he wanted to interrogate Kate about her pregnancy.

Harriet's eyes narrowed. 'Who else'll be there?'

'Mary Bates and Jane. David and Sandy Perry. Izzy and John, if Izzy can get Sarah Perry to babysit. Mark. And Flynn's driving down from—'

She cut in with, 'How about you come out with me for a few hours, then I go with you to the Westons'? That way, you'll keep both me and your Dad happy. We'll make sure we get to Randalls just before midnight.' She dug me in the ribs. 'I'm gagging for a New Year's kiss from you-know-who!'

I was silent. Under normal circumstances, given a choice between eating sand and drinking Lambrini with Harriet and her friends, I'd have opted for the sand, every time. But if it meant that she and Flynn got together, going to the pub with her was the least I could do.

At last, I said slowly, 'I'll check with Kate. If it's OK for us to come along later, then I'll go out with you first.'

I just hoped that my sacrifice would be worth it.

MARK

When I phoned John to tell him about Father and Saffron coming home early, he responded with a grunt and promptly changed the subject.

'Emma says you were mentoring her, but it didn't work out. Why's that?'

'Didn't she tell you?' I said, guardedly.

'She didn't know, or at least she claimed she didn't. Mind you, if your mentoring sessions were anything like what I saw on Christmas Day, no wonder they failed.'

'And what exactly did you see on Christmas Day?'

He paused, then said, 'Two people making each other unhappy.'

Ouch, how perceptive; I tried to fob him off. 'Really? Your imagination must be working overtime.'

'Well, give me a reason not to make my imagination work overtime. Tell me what's going on.'

'Nothing.'

'Cut the crap.'

'I mean it. No mentoring, no real communication, nothing. We're in limbo. Between the old relationship and the new, I suppose.'

'So what's caused this limbo?'

He was persistent, I'd give him that. I decided to start at Ashridge and hope I never reached Forbury Manor. 'I made a pass at her.'

'What – in the middle of a mentoring session?'

'Not exactly, but—'

'You idiot. You bloody idiot.' For a few moments, he was lost for words; then he went on, 'I just can't believe you'd do that. Does Henry know?'

'Do you think I'd have been at Hartfield on Christmas Day if he did?'

'True. And she told you where to go?'

'Yes.' Well, she had eventually, hadn't she?

He gave a snort. 'No wonder she can hardly bring herself to look at you. It must have felt almost incestuous.'

That really got under my skin. 'But we're *not* brother and—'

'I only said "felt", Mark. Calm down, for God's sake,' he said sharply. 'So when did you start fancying her?'

'Oh, I don't know. I suppose it was back in September, as soon as I saw her again . . . No, maybe it was long before that, maybe I've always fancied her, even though I didn't realise it at the time.' I paused and decided I may as well come out with it. 'Actually, it's much more than that. I love her, I want to spend the rest of my life with her. Except it's all gone pear-shaped.'

He wasn't listening; he was off down Memory Lane. 'That's just like me with Izzy. I woke up one day and suddenly it all fell into place, that she was the one, that she'd always been the one. Although she took some persuading at first, she wouldn't even—'

I tried again. 'John, there's something else. Emma and I – we got drunk at the Highbury Foods Christmas do. And – and somehow we ended up in bed together.'

That guaranteed his undivided attention.

'Jesus.' He let out a long noisy breath. 'A bit more than a pass, then.'

'Yes. We had a blazing row the next morning, about various things.' I swallowed. 'I was a substitute, you see, for – well, it doesn't matter who. And it's been – difficult – ever since.'

'You're telling me! So you still fancy her, but she fancies someone else.' He gave a short laugh. 'And really, how could she fancy you anyway?'

'Thanks a bunch.'

'Look, for years you've been that annoying old fart who lectures her at the slightest opportunity. More of an older brother, even a father figure at times, definitely not boyfriend material. You must see that, surely?'

'I think I get the picture,' I said, through gritted teeth.

'Sorry, it's just – I don't know, I suppose I just can't get my head round it, you with her. And yet I fell for Izzy, so why shouldn't you fall for her little sister?' He paused. 'I don't suppose you want me to tell her? Izzy, that is?'

'God, no. That would be even worse than telling Henry.'

'So what happens now? How are you both going to deal with this?'

I cleared my throat. 'It'll be fine once I go back to India. We won't meet for a while and when we do – well, we'll be different people, in different situations.'

'I hope you're right. It's a shame, though.'

'What – me going back to India?'

'I meant it's a shame about you and Emma not working out. Come to think about it, you've got a lot in common. You'd have made a great couple.'

For a split second, his words created a seductive image of what might have been; Emma and I, a great couple. Then reality hit home.

'But now we'll never know,' I said lightly. 'By the way, will you be at the Westons'?'

'Yes, the babysitter's sorted and Izzy's delirious at the prospect of seeing David Perry for a whole evening. Poor sod, I have a horrible feeling she'll treat him like a walking talking medical dictionary. What about you?'

'I'm going. I could have joined Steve and his mates for a piss-up round the villages but I can't be bothered. Maybe I'm getting old.'

I reflected on this as I got ready for the Westons' on New Year's Eve. Shit, I was so reluctant to leave my own fireside that it felt like I was turning into Henry. But I knew that tonight it was better for me to be with others – even if they included Emma.

The evening got off to a good start. The meal was delicious, the conversation entertaining and the company far from disturbing. It couldn't last, of course. At about half past eleven Emma arrived and my pulse quickened at the very sight of her: hair tousled, face aglow, tantalising glimpses of golden skin between her skimpy silver top and her hip-hugging jeans.

But it seemed that the only reason she'd come was to see in the New Year with Churchill – perfectly natural, I suppose. The first thing she did was ring him to find out where he was; and she couldn't hide her excitement when he turned up with less than ten minutes to go until midnight.

Churchill seemed even more hyper than usual and I wondered if he'd indulged in a few drinks already on his way back from the Lakes. He downed a large whisky almost as soon as he came through the door and his gaze darted nervously round the room, coming to rest on Emma, Jane and Harriet who were standing by the Christmas tree. Just as he was walking over to them, Tom grabbed his arm and introduced him to the Perrys.

Churchill frowned in concentration. 'Perry . . . Perry . . . Oh, aren't you the couple whose son got expelled from school for his extra-curricular activities?' He added, with a smug little smile, 'I did the same sort of thing myself and it hasn't done me any harm.'

The effect of his words was dramatic. David almost choked on his drink, while Sandy went white as a sheet and turned abruptly to Mary.

'I asked you to keep that to yourself,' she said, icily.

Mary coloured. 'I did. At least, I only told Jane, of course—'

'He wasn't expelled,' David put in, curtly. 'Only suspended.'

And then I saw Jane give Churchill a look of such intense reproach that I did a double take. It suggested an intimacy that I'd never suspected and I began to wonder . . .

Churchill sniggered. 'No one *told* me, I've obviously got psychic powers. Only suspended, was he? That's nothing these days, it suggests he's got a healthy disrespect for authority, something to be admired really.' He tried rather belatedly to turn on the charm. 'Lovely dress, by the way, Mandy.'

Sandy turned her back on him and walked to the other side of the room, David at her heels. Poor Tom was saved from further embarrassment by the chimes of Big Ben on the TV.

'Come on, everyone,' he said, with a hollow

attempt at his usual enthusiasm, 'let's join hands for "Auld Lang Syne".'

I found myself crossing arms with Jane on my left and Harriet on my right. Emma was directly opposite, wedged between Churchill and Henry. As we sang the familiar words, they seemed even more poignant than usual. I knew that this would be my last visit to Highbury for a long time, especially once Emma announced her engagement. And so, when the kissing started, I kept my eyes firmly on the next person in line, giving myself no chance of seeing her in a passionate clinch with *him*. I went from Jane, a brief and business-like brushing of the lips; to Harriet, wet, surprisingly persistent and interspersed with giggles; to Kate, firm and friendly; Sandy, prim and puckered; Izzy, smelling strongly of baby lotion; then Mary, leaving a dusty deposit of face powder on my cheek; and finally . . .

'Happy New Year, Emma.' I held her lightly by the waist and risked a glance at her face; if she'd been wearing lipstick, it had been well and truly kissed away . . .

Her arms hung defiantly at her sides and her gaze stayed fixed on my shirt buttons. 'And to you, Mark.'

Given the bitterness of our last few conversations, I knew this was the nearest we'd get to a truce. And yet, when her eyes flicked upwards and met mine, I wondered if she was asking me to kiss her. But I couldn't. Not while the memories were so raw: her mouth meeting mine on that lamplit bed, offering me everything I'd ever wanted. And, God, how I'd enjoyed taking it . . . Like a masochistic fool, I allowed my fingertips to brush the warm flesh of her back, before moving quickly away to shake hands with the men.

The Perrys left soon afterwards, with the excuse that their babysitter had to go at half past twelve. John and Izzy went too, with Henry, so that the Perrys could call at Hartfield on their way and take Sarah home with them.

For some reason, Tom decided the rest of us would play Scrabble. Maybe he wanted to show off the brand new set he'd got for Christmas, or maybe he was anxious to avoid more conversational faux pas by his son. I looked pointedly at my watch and muttered something about having lots to do the next day; but he insisted I stayed, for the first round at least.

Unfortunately, my mind wasn't on the game at all; it was back in Forbury Manor . . .

'Ooh Mark, is that the best you can do?'

Roused by Harriet's breathless voice next to me, I frowned at the word I'd unwittingly placed on the board: BED.

'You could make BEAD – no, you haven't got an A,' she went on, looking shamelessly over my shoulder. 'What about BREED? You'd get a double word score then.'

'Thank you,' I said heavily, adding an R and another E.

'I can use your B to make BABY!' She screamed with delight, selected a couple of tiles from her rack and threw them down on the board.

Tom started arranging them, then stopped. 'Harriet, have you got a B there?'

'No, I'm using Mark's B, from BREED.'

'There are two Bs in BABY,' he explained, with the patience of a saint.

'Ooh, silly me. I don't think I've got a B, can you check my letters, Mark, in case I've missed one?' She pushed her Scrabble rack in front of me and leaned in close.

'Not a B to be seen.' I smiled and gently moved the rack back to its place. 'But you could make—'

'Time's up, you'll have to just leave it at BAY,' Emma put in – rather sharply, I thought. 'That's eight points. Your turn, Flynn.'

Churchill immediately went to a different part of the board and laid down five tiles with a triumphant smirk. I noticed Jane glaring at him. Oh yes, definitely something going on there . . .

Harriet peered at the word he'd made. 'What's a COCKU? And why's it got a blank at the end?'

'It's meant to be a P,' Churchill said.

She squealed, right in my ear. 'COCK-UP, that's a bit rude, innit? I didn't know you could have things like that in Scrabble.'

'It's perfectly all right, Harriet, you'll find it in

any dictionary.' Churchill gave a wolfish grin. 'You know, meaning "blunder" or "mistake".'

Then Jane said tersely, 'But it has a hyphen, so it's not allowed.'

Churchill threw up his hands in mock horror. 'Oh, I declare, Miss Fairfax,' he said, with an affected Texan drawl, 'you're so cruel, can't you show some mercy for once?'

Tom had been leafing through the Oxford English Dictionary on the table beside him. Now he looked up and clicked his tongue in commiseration. 'Bad luck, Flynn, Jane's right.'

'Sod it, I'll just have to leave it at COCK. Does that satisfy you, Jane?'

Jane flushed. 'How I feel is irrelevant, you need to learn the rules of the game.'

'Bring on the cane, Jane, and I'll take my punishment like a man.' He nudged Emma, who was sitting next to him. 'Now it's your turn, my lovely.' He mouthed something in her ear and made her giggle, as usual.

'I know you like whispering sweet nothings to Emma,' Tom said good-humouredly, 'but I'm sure she doesn't need your help. She's a Scrabble expert, always beats me by miles.'

Churchill ignored his father and mumbled in Emma's ear again. She was almost helpless with laughter, but managed to gasp, 'I can't.'

He raised one eyebrow. 'Oh? I always thought you were the adventurous sort, like *Dan* Dare.'

She glanced furtively across at Jane. 'Shh,

you are awful. Anyway, proper names aren't allowed.'

He gave a petulant sigh. 'If you won't do it, I will.' With a flourish, he placed four of her tiles on the board in front of an N. 'There, triple word score, thirty-nine points.'

It was DIXON; the word meant nothing to me, but once again Jane went red.

This time, Kate intervened. 'Come along, Flynn, no proper names. And share the joke with everyone, please, not just Emma.'

'Sorry, Kate, the joke's strictly private and confidential,' he said breezily. 'Oh well, Em, you'll just have to think of an alternative. Can you manage as many as five letters, or will you be a safe, boring and unimaginative three?'

This was a not-so-subtle dig at my previous effort and I noticed Emma blush as she set out the word VIXEN. Not blind to *all* his faults, then. At least, not yet.

I resolved to go home as soon as this round was over; until then, I remained on my guard for any more clandestine interaction between Jane and Churchill. Their behaviour reminded me of Emma's and mine; so little said, so much left unspoken – like an iceberg, where only the tip is visible to the unwary traveller. No one else seemed to have noticed anything, however, especially Emma. God, she was so trusting! But I would keep my eyes and ears open until I returned to India; from then on, I'd ask John to do the same.

If I ever found out that Churchill was cheating on her, with Jane Fairfax or anyone else, I would kill him with my bare hands.

EMMA

I was relieved Mark hadn't given me a New Year's kiss. The touch of his fingers was disturbing enough . . . Yes, it was definitely relief I felt, not disappointment. I reserved that for Harriet, who didn't seem to be making much progress with Flynn. Their kiss at midnight was nothing more than a peck, but then it must be rather inhibiting trying to get off with each other in front of people like Dad and Batty. Afterwards, when we were playing Scrabble, no wonder the poor girl was all over Mark in a blatant attempt to make Flynn jealous – which only succeeded in making him flirt with me.

I couldn't help noticing that Mark got very little in the way of loving from Jane. Maybe she'd put her foot down about displays of passion in public. What a waste of the man's talents! He really needed someone to take him somewhere more private for a few minutes and welcome in the New Year with a complete lack of respectability . . .

With an effort, I dragged my thoughts back to Scrabble just in time to hear Harriet babbling something about making a baby with Mark. Shit, calling at Randalls was turning into a really, really bad idea. By the time it was my turn, I was thinking – how could a game of Scrabble be so surreal? We'd already had 'breed', 'baby' and 'cock'; goodness knows what would come out next, it was just as well Dad had gone home.

When Flynn whispered in my ear, 'Try DIXON, go on, see what she says', I couldn't stop myself from bursting into hysterical laughter. Even though I refused, he went ahead and put the letters down. I felt like shouting out, 'It's the name of Jane's married lover, she's not so perfect after all!' I didn't, of course, but I did wonder if Mark had any suspicions about her. In spite of everything, I didn't want him to get hurt.

As soon as we finished the first round of Scrabble, he got up to leave. Strange, there was no mention of Jane leaving with him, but then theirs was obviously not a straightforward relationship. When Tom went out of the room to fetch Mark's coat, I followed and waited outside by the porch. I wrapped my arms round myself and looked up at the sky. It was a crystal clear night, like that time at Ashridge; I shivered, and it wasn't just with the cold.

'Emma?' Mark's voice, warming me instantly; but then – 'Get inside, you little idiot, you'll freeze out here!'

Bloody typical, still treating me like a kid.

I turned towards him, half ready to pick a fight. But when I saw him in his dark overcoat, with the collar turned up, all I could think of was snuggling up to him and sharing a long, deep kiss.

'I need to speak to you,' was all I said, more curtly than I'd intended.

'Can't it wait?' He sounded impatient and I wondered if he had a secret assignation with Jane, something along the lines of 'I'll go first, then you leave five minutes later, drop Mary home and come on to Donwell'. Lucky old Jane, spending the night in Mark Knightley's arms. But, for the moment, lucky old Jane was nowhere to be seen; and this was my chance to warn him about her.

I took a deep breath. 'There's no time like the present. Especially as we don't seem to find it easy to talk these days.'

He frowned. 'OK, but get in the car where it's warm.'

And more private for what I had to say, I added to myself.

He led the way down the sparkling gravel path to the Mercedes. It was only a few steps, yet it felt as though I was jumping over an abyss. And then I was in the passenger seat next to him, just like on the way home from Ashridge, and I felt safe and – and cherished, somehow. He had the engine running and the interior light on and the heater was going full blast. I didn't look at his face; I just watched his fingers drumming on the leather-clad steering wheel and gave in to all sorts of wild, impetuous imaginings . . .

'Yes?' he prompted.

I started and glanced nervously across at him, twisting my hands together in my lap. 'It's just, um, I'm not sure if you know who Dixon is.'

'Dixon?' he said, blankly.

'The word Flynn made from my letters.'

He stiffened and looked away. 'Oh, that. I don't want to know, I'm not interested in little private jokes between the two of you.'

I swallowed. This was going to be even more difficult than I'd thought. 'It wasn't just something between Flynn and me, it involved Jane too. You see, we were referring to Dan Dixon. He's a friend of hers.'

'So?'

'More than a friend, if you know what I mean.'

'What's that to me?'

I gave an exasperated sigh. 'Surely you don't have to be so discreet all the bloody time? Everyone knows you're – well, Kate's been speculating for weeks that – oh, you know what I'm saying, that Jane and you . . .' I let my voice trail off, desperate for him to bail me out.

He stared at the windscreen, his face expressionless. 'That Jane and I – what?'

'Come off it, giving her the Jag, taking her out for expensive lunches, then asking her to partner you to the Donwell Organics do. Not forgetting how much you've always gone on and on about how marvellous she is.'

At last he looked straight at me. 'You mean you

– and Kate, and God knows who else in Highbury from the sound of it – think that I'm sleeping with Jane?'

Just saying it made it seem real, too real. I felt tears sting the back of my eyes, but I nodded and managed a nonchalant smile.

He ran his hand through his hair. 'Sometimes I hate this place – people adding two and two together and making at least eight!' He let out a long uneven breath, then went on, 'Look, I certainly didn't give her the Jag, I thought it was from her friends, the Campbells or whatever they're called, although now I'm not so sure . . . And the lunches were only for our mentoring sessions, I felt it would be more relaxing for her than my office. As for the Donwell Organics party – well, she was the obvious choice in the absence of – of anyone more suitable. Of course I think very highly of her and I don't mind who knows it, but that's as far as it goes.' He gave a grim laugh. 'I have absolutely no plans to get her into bed. She's not my type at all.'

I didn't buy that for one moment. 'But she's so like Tamara, all long black hair and white skin—'

'I don't mean her looks, I mean her personality. Too reserved, secretive almost. I may as well be mentoring a block of wood. I prefer a woman who's much more spontaneous and in your face and—' He stopped and cleared his throat. 'Just believe me when I say that I don't want to sleep

377

with Jane and I'm pretty sure the feeling's mutual. Oh, and please make sure the rest of Highbury gets the message.'

There was a pause while I digested this information. I should have felt ecstatic that he didn't fancy Saint Jane of Highbury, of all people. But my mind was off at a tangent. Did that mean he fancied someone else? If so, who? And if not, then maybe, just maybe . . . Oh, what was the point of even thinking about it! He'd told me in no uncertain terms that I wasn't as good in bed as Tamara. And yet . . . a little voice inside me begged for another chance.

Then, out of the blue, he said, 'How long has Jane known Churchill?'

'Why do you want to know?' I was genuinely puzzled; he'd just denied being interested in her, hadn't he?

He scowled. 'Just answer the question, please.'

His abrupt tone got under my skin. 'Work it out for yourself,' I said sullenly. 'They met in Weymouth shortly before she started at Highbury Foods.'

'Three months, say. And how *well* do you think they know each other?'

I shrugged. 'As Flynn said to me when I asked him that very same question, he knows her as well as he ever wants to.' I added, with a frosty smile, 'I think it's safe to assume that means hardly at all.'

'I think it's safe to assume nothing of the sort,'

he said, frowning. 'There was something funny about their behaviour tonight. With each other, I mean. Especially him, he was provoking her, making her upset.'

So that was it. Poor little Jane always managed to get the sympathy vote, didn't she? My lips tightened.

He went on, 'Somehow it made me think that they were—' he hesitated, as though searching for the right words '—more intimate than they've led any of us to believe.'

That sounded uncomfortably like him and me. I shifted in my seat and forced a laugh. 'Flynn and Saint Jane – intimate, as you so delicately put it? That's absolute bollocks.'

'How do you know?'

Funny, I could have sworn there was a catch in his voice. Typical Mark, he may not fancy the woman, but he was obviously concerned about her well-being. I looked him straight in the eye and smiled broadly, to give him all the reassurance I could.

'Because Flynn's in love with someone else. I can't say who just yet, for various reasons, but it's definitely not Jane Fairfax.'

He closed his eyes, as if in relief, and leaned back against the headrest. I took the opportunity to study his profile. How many times over the years had I looked at him without really seeing him? Except for that unfortunate teenage crush, I'd always taken his physical appeal completely for granted – the deep brow, the strong straight nose, the unbelievably sensual mouth and determined chin. With a strange sort of hunger, my gaze returned to his mouth. I watched his lips move, the words just audible above the noise of the heater.

'By the way, I'm going back to India.'

'I know, when your father gets home,' I said, absently. That would be some time in February, which gave me at least a month, perhaps six weeks, to see if we could . . .

He opened his eyes and I hurriedly averted my gaze. 'My father's coming home in two days. John and I told the others tonight, before you arrived. And my flight's on Sunday.'

I blinked rapidly at my reflection in the passenger window. 'Wh-what did you say?'

'I'm leaving on Sunday.'

'So soon?' I sounded amazingly calm, almost dismissive.

'There's nothing to keep me here,' he said, and there was an air of finality in his tone. Thank God I hadn't allowed myself to hope . . .

When his warm hand covered mine, I nearly jumped out of my skin; but I kept my face turned away.

'Emma, if there's ever anything troubling you, just call me.' His voice was low and grave. 'You know I've always been there for you, don't you? And that won't change, wherever you are, whoever you're with.'

It was as if the words had been in my head for years, but jumbled up. Now, at last, they made perfect sense: 'I want to be with you, wherever you are.'

I didn't say them, of course. I couldn't trust myself to speak. I had to get out of that car with some semblance of dignity before I gave everything away. So I took a deep breath, pulled my hand from under his and opened the door with as much composure as I could manage.

'Goodnight, Mark.'

And I ran from the car without a backward glance. As I reached the porch, I heard his tyres crunching down the frosty drive.

In a week he'd be gone. The dream was over before it had even begun.

MARK

Thank God the holiday period was over. I'd gone to the office most days in an attempt to distract my thoughts; not easy when the place was empty. But now, on the first working day of the new year, there was a welcome buzz of activity which I drew on to boost my own flagging energy levels. I'd also made progress on the personal front; even though I couldn't be happy myself, I'd decided that I could make someone else happy.

So I started to put my plans into action. At nine sharp, I called the Executive together and told them that my father would be home the next day and back at work by the end of the week. From then on, there would be no need for an acting MD and I would return to India.

Most of them had some experience of Saffron, so they fully understood the situation. 'Surprised George stuck it out this long,' one of them muttered as they left the room.

John stayed behind. To my relief, he didn't raise the subject of Emma; instead, he asked me if I wanted a hand with the arrangements for tomorrow.

'Tomorrow?' I said, preoccupied with opening an urgent email about the Parkinson contract.

He chuckled. 'That little informal surprise party Saffron's expecting, remember?'

'Oh, that.' I rolled my eyes. 'Between us, Mrs Burn and I seem to have it all under control. Everyone should have got their invitation this morning. As it's such short notice and the numbers are small, I didn't bother with RSVP. And I've said drinks and canapés, so that people feel they can drop in even if they're already booked to go somewhere else for the evening.'

'Poor Father, a party'll be the last thing he feels like.'

'Do you think he had any choice in the matter?'

Another chuckle. 'No, but we did.'

'Sorry, I couldn't be bothered to fight this particular battle,' I said, with a hollow laugh. 'I'd like my last few days in England to be relatively happy and healthy ones.'

'Point taken. Have you heard what time they're getting here?'

'Mid-afternoon, Saffron's stopping on the way for some emergency repair work. You know, hair, facelift, and so on. Oh, there is something you could do for me.'

'What's that?'

'On your way into work, can you collect Tao from the kennels and take him to Donwell? Mrs Burn will be there from half past eight.'

He grimaced. 'I get all the good jobs, don't I?'

Just after he'd left, Cherry called out, 'I've got someone on the phone for you. Wouldn't give me her name, just said something about Mrs Burn.'

Shit, all I needed was for Mrs Burn to fall ill or something. 'Better put her through, whoever she is.'

But as soon as I heard the voice, I knew I'd made a mistake.

'Marrrk?'

''Morning, Gusty,' I said coolly. 'What's this about Mrs Burn?'

'Sheila's come to do some extra cleaning for me and she says you're organising a little soirée to celebrate the return of your father and step-mother.'

Good God, it hadn't taken her long to extract that information out of poor Mrs Burn, it was barely twenty past nine.

I made an effort to remain civil. 'I can't see how

that concerns you. It just means she'll be working longer hours tomorrow, when she usually comes to Donwell anyway.'

'Actually, Marrrk, there are one or two things that *do* concern me,' she purred. 'Firstly, Philip and I don't seem to have received our invitation and Sheila assures me that they were all posted first class on Saturday. And secondly, I hate to be blunt, but it sounds like a rather low-key affair.'

She paused and I took the opportunity to deal with her first point. 'You and Philip haven't received your invitation because I haven't sent you one.'

'Oh, a little oversight, we can soon remedy that,' she said airily. 'But I have some very exciting ideas for livening up the party and there's no time to lose. As soon as you give me the nod, I'll get started. My sister once hired a very classy—'

I cut in before she could enlighten me further. 'There's only one woman I'd consult about this party.'

After a moment she snapped, 'Not Kate Weston, surely.'

'No.'

'Who then?'

'Mrs Knightley.'

'Mrs—? Oh, your stepmother. But she's thousands of miles away—'

'I don't mean her either, I mean Mrs Mark Knightley.'

'*Who?*'

'My wife. And since that person doesn't exist, I'll continue to organise everything myself. But thank you so much for offering. 'Bye.' I slammed down the receiver and yelled, 'Cherry!'

She came rushing into my room. 'What is it?'

'That woman who just rang, would you recognise her voice?'

'Oh yes, quite a strong West Country accent.' She pulled a face. 'And a terribly bossy manner.'

'Good. If she phones again, say I'm unavailable. Travelling to Mars, on my deathbed, anything.' I stared out of the window, feeling indescribably weary.

'You sound stressed out, why don't you take the rest of the day off?' she said, in a motherly tone. 'I've got plenty to get on with – and you don't seem to have had much time away from the office over the holidays.'

'Thanks, but I'm fine.' I gave her a reassuring smile. 'There's one other thing, I'd like you to organise my farewell lunch for Friday. I thought a buffet in the conference room would be best, then everyone can come and go as they please.'

'Is it just for staff, or are you inviting people from outside the company?'

'Just for staff, I'm taking my family and a few friends out for dinner on Saturday night. Could you book that, too? The Box Hill Restaurant, seven thirty, for about twenty people. I'll give you exact numbers nearer the time.'

She gaped at me. 'Box Hill, for twenty? You'd better take out a mortgage.'

I shrugged. 'I may as well go off in style. I won't be coming home for a long time.'

EMMA

After the New Year break, I went back to work and steeled myself to get through the week. As I scanned my personal organiser, I found the three goals I'd set after the Philip fiasco. Normally, I'd have congratulated myself on my progress; I was convinced I'd taken no one at face value, I'd completed the research stage of the Harriet's Secret Recipes project and I'd kept my matchmaking instincts well and truly under control.

But somehow I didn't feel like celebrating. Mark was leaving in only four days' time.

With everyone returning to work this morning, I was looking forward to some company, even Saint Jane's. But Batty announced that Jane was too ill to come in – 'pale as a ghost, hardly eating a thing, wasting away'. That left Harriet, who could normally be relied on to provide an endless stream of drivel to distract me. I heard her clattering about in the outer office and waited for her to bring in the post, which we normally went through together.

After a few moments, I called out, 'Hi, how are you?'

No answer. I popped my head round the door that divided our two rooms. She was at her desk, staring at a pile of unopened letters.

'Are you OK?' I said.

She looked up. 'Mmm?'

'What's the matter, are you pining for FC?'

'Who?'

'FC, the man of your dreams, you know I can't mention his name.'

'Yeah, but—' She paused, then cocked her head on one side. 'What does FC stand for?'

I knew her English was basic at times, but this was ridiculous. 'F for Flynn, C for Churchill,' I said, as patiently as I could.

She let out a squeal of disgust. '*Him*? Why would I want him when I can have Mark?'

'Mark? Mark who?'

'Mark Knightley, of course,' she said, looking at me as if I was mentally deficient.

I felt the colour drain from my face. 'Mark *Knightley*?'

'Yeah, and it's looking good.' She hugged herself like an excited child. 'Can't wait for tomorrow night.'

My stomach churned. 'What's happening tomorrow night?'

'Didn't you get your invitation this morning?'

'Invitation?'

'Here.' She rummaged in her pocket and handed me an ivory card, much creased as if she'd been fondling it ever since it arrived. I snatched it from

387

her, hardly registering the printed words about a party for George and Saffron. I was desperate to read what was scrawled across the bottom, in handwriting that was heartbreakingly familiar: 'Hope you can come – there's something I need to ask you. Mark.'

Harriet giggled. 'The food sounds crap, innit? Friggin' canopies, whatever they are. What are you wearing?'

'Nothing.' Was that a Freudian slip? God knows I'd have pranced round Donwell Abbey stark naked if I thought there was any chance of getting together with Mark . . . 'I mean, I don't know if I'm going.'

Her eyes widened. 'Haven't you had an invitation?'

'Of course I have. I just can't decide whether I can fit it in.' I glanced casually through the pile of letters, but there wasn't anything that looked like an invitation. 'Start opening those, I'll be back in a minute.'

I walked quickly round to Dad's office, my heart pounding. I didn't dwell on the revelation that Harriet fancied Mark instead of Flynn; I was more concerned about tracking down my invitation to Donwell. Harriet didn't even know George and Saffron, so why had Mark invited her? And what on earth could he want to ask her? I reassured myself that there'd be a similar message written on my invitation, if I could find it.

Dad was by the window, examining the pad of

his thumb in the watery sunlight. 'Just cut myself on some paper, would you believe,' he said, with a mournful sigh. 'I'm an accident waiting to happen.'

I went straight to the point. 'Did we have anything from Mark in this morning's post?'

'Look at it, do you think it's infected?'

I squinted at a tiny cut in his flesh and wrinkled my nose. 'How could it be? You smell like you've bathed in antiseptic. Listen, apparently there's a party tomorrow night, to welcome George and Saffron home. Does that ring any bells?'

'Party? Oh yes, we had an invitation but I don't think we should go.'

I let this pass for the moment. 'What did it say?'

'Let me see . . . Seven thirty for drinks and canapés. Those things never agree with me, far too exotic.'

I tried again. 'What I mean is, did Mark write anything on it?'

Dad gave a wry smile. 'Our names of course, darling.'

'Nothing else?'

'No. Anyway, as I said, I don't think we should go.'

'Why not?'

'There's snow forecast. Isabella's just phoned, she doesn't want to go either. She's really worried about leaving the children, but John doesn't understand—'

For once, my patience was exhausted. 'We're going, Dad, or at least I am. I'll book a taxi if you don't want me to drive.'

I left him apprehensively prodding his thumb and walked slowly back to my office. I'd been so blind, so absolutely stupid. Because I'd thought Harriet fancied Flynn, I'd persuaded her that she had as much chance as anyone else to get him. But all along she'd meant Mark; she'd wanted to go to the Westons' on New Year's Eve to see *him*. And her flirting with him over Scrabble had been genuine, not an attempt to make Flynn jealous. Later, when Mark had told me that there was nothing to keep him in England, he must have already been planning to take her back to India; far better to start their relationship away from the prying eyes of Highbury. Tomorrow night, at the party, he'd ask if she wanted to go with him. She'd say yes, yes, *yes*, and then . . .

I'd been so blind.

I found Harriet still gazing vacantly at the pile of letters, but at least she'd opened them. Not that it mattered. All of a sudden, I didn't give a shit about Highbury Foods. How was I going to get through the next four days? How was I going to get through tomorrow night, come to that?

But the show must go on, for as long as possible. 'Right, Harriet,' I said firmly, 'it's about time we got down to some work.'

MARK

Rob Martin and I met in The Hare and Hounds at six thirty. He'd seemed surprised but pleased when I rang to suggest a quick drink. He said he'd been about to do the same; there was something he had to tell me before I went back to India. This put me immediately on my guard – I'd only just set things in motion with Harriet and the last thing I needed was Rob throwing a spanner in the works.

We'd barely sat down with our pints when he said brusquely, 'I've decided to take a break from work and go travelling. God knows what Mum and Dad will say – they'll have to hold the fort at Abbey Mill – but I can't stay here any longer.' He added, with a rueful smile, 'It's Harriet. I'm finding it hard to get over her.'

I let out a long breath; it was just how I'd felt about Emma. And I was dealing with it in the same way – escaping to somewhere far removed from Highbury. But at least I was going to a life I knew, to activity and structure, things I believed Rob badly needed.

'Seems a bit drastic,' was all I said. 'When are you planning to leave?'

'Soon as I can stick a pin in a map of the world and book a flight.' He buried his face in his hands. It was an almost childish gesture, at odds with his large calloused fingers and deep voice. I could hardly make out his next words. 'I know it's irresponsible, but I'm desperate.'

I took a long drink of beer before I spoke. 'It's not irresponsible, but it'll never work.'

The hands dropped to the table with an ominous thud. 'And why the hell's that?'

I looked him straight in the eye. 'Rob, I've known you for years. I'd say you're even more of a routine merchant than I am. You'll go stark staring mad camel-trekking across the Sahara, or whatever you end up doing to fill in the time.'

He snorted. 'Routine merchant, am I? I'm too old to join the bloody army, if that's what you're suggesting.'

'I'm not. I just don't think you've found the right solution. And that's probably because you've misdiagnosed the problem.'

'Impossible. The problem's simple enough, Harriet's the woman I want to spend the rest of my life with, but she's not interested in me.'

'Look, Harriet's—' I stopped before I said too much; I hadn't even talked to Harriet yet. But his sudden wanderlust was playing right into my hands. I went on, 'I've got a better idea. Why don't you come and stay with me for a while in Mumbai? You could help me with some ideas I've got for our operation out there – and then go travelling, if you still want to. You don't have to decide now. Sleep on it and let me know in the morning.'

His face brightened. 'I don't need to sleep on it. Of course I'll come, I've always fancied India. Hang on, though – what about jabs and stuff ?'

'Leave it all to me. I'll book your ticket and let you know what you need to do. But don't tell anyone except your parents.'

'Why's that?'

I gave a faint smile. 'Trust me, I have my reasons.'

CHAPTER 13

CRUMBLE

EMMA

The next evening I dressed with care, selecting a deceptively simple black pencil skirt and turquoise shawl-neck top that showed off every curve. As I piled on the foundation to conceal the dark shadows under my eyes, I remembered that day last September when Mark had walked into the boardroom and criticised me for wearing too much make-up. Tears welled up and I had to blot them away before my mascara ran.

Dad was staying at home and I debated briefly whether to do the same. I knew only too well that this would be one of the last times I'd see Mark before he left; and I had a horrible feeling that it would be the first time I'd see him coming on to Harriet.

Harriet! I pulled myself together and grabbed my coat. I'd offered to drive her to the party and back, even though it meant a considerable detour. I told her it was because her car was unreliable in cold weather and she might get stranded if the snow came; the real reason was that I wanted to interrogate her about Mark on the way home.

As she teetered down her front path, I wondered what – in Mark's eyes, at least – she had that I hadn't. Rather ironic, given that for the past four months I'd been trying to make her more like me. Not that I'd succeeded; as they say, you can take the girl out of Essex, but you can't take Essex out of the girl.

I'd never have guessed she was Mark's type. He'd described her as 'pretty and compliant, but that's about all'; hardly a promising start. At the time, however, he'd been furious with me for advising her to ditch Robert Martin. And fancying someone wasn't exactly a lifelong commitment; people were always changing their minds – just look at me with Flynn.

But I remembered retaliating at Mark with something like, 'If you ever break up with Tamara, you could do a lot worse than Harriet'. Those words had certainly come back to haunt me now.

Unaware of my gloomy thoughts, Harriet chattered happily all the way to Donwell Abbey. She'd bought a new dress especially for the party, had a bikini wax – which she described to me in excruciating detail – and spent ages doing her face.

'Why splash out all that money on a bikini wax at this time of year?' I said curtly. 'You're not off on a secret holiday in the sun, are you?'

She giggled. 'No such luck. Call it a thong wax

then, I bought a new thong at Ann Summers, just in case.'

I was silent as I turned into the Knightleys' drive. When we were nearing the house, I said, 'Just in case what?'

'In case I get to shag Mark tonight.'

I nearly crashed into George's Mercedes. Somehow I hadn't envisaged things happening so quickly. On the other hand, Mark and I hadn't exactly held back at Forbury Manor; at least, I hadn't. *I need you to undo my dress . . . Kiss me . . . Don't stop . . . Not now . . .*

Harriet was clutching at her seat belt. 'Shit, Emma, did you forget where the brakes were?'

I reversed to a safe distance behind the Mercedes, yanked on the handbrake and said stiffly, 'I expect you'll tell me if you don't need a lift home.'

'Knowing my luck,' she said, with a snigger, 'there'll be loads of snow and *everyone*'ll be staying at Donwell for the night. What a friggin' thought!'

What a frigging thought indeed. Well, I wouldn't be hanging around while Harriet and Mark . . . No, I'd get home if it killed me.

'Let's go inside, it's freezing.' I slammed my car door shut and walked briskly to the house while she scrambled out of the passenger side to join me. I stood on the front step and rang the bell, my heart pounding as I waited for Mark to open the door. But it was Gusty who came, swathed in a garish orange sari, waving a clipboard and chanting, like some deranged Tibetan monk, 'George and *Saffron* . . . David and *Sandy* . . .'

'Excuse us.' I pushed past her into the warmth, dragging Harriet with me.

Gusty clicked her tongue and studied her clipboard. 'Emmurrr Woodhouse, yes, you're on my list.' The word 'unfortunately' hung unspoken in the air. 'No Henry tonight?'

''Fraid not,' I said, smiling at a harassed-looking Mrs Burn as she emerged from the kitchen. 'Hello, Mrs B, where shall I put our coats?'

Before Mrs Burn could answer, Gusty said officiously, 'Don't distract her, she'll tidy them away later.' She gave Harriet a withering glance. 'But I wouldn't take *yourrrs* off yet, I don't seem to have the name Smith on my list.'

I slipped off my coat and helped Harriet with hers. 'Your list's wrong, I've seen Harriet's invitation. Mark even added a personal message.'

Harriet blushed and her eyes sparkled. Suddenly, I could see how her simplicity and self-consciousness might appeal to Mark. Then I noticed her new dress: four skimpy panels of black patent leather with sugar-pink voile inserts, leaving very little to the imagination. All I could think was that she must have had to travel a long way from Highbury to find something so bizarre.

'Through here, Harriet.' I dropped our coats over the banister and hurried her into the drawing room before Gusty could put my thoughts into words.

The first person I saw was Mark, his elegant stone-coloured trousers and black polo-neck jumper fitting like a second skin. His eyes lingered on Harriet's dress, but his expression was inscrutable.

He walked over to us. 'Glad you could both make it.'

'We nearly didn't,' I said drily. 'Gusty makes a very good bouncer.'

'God, what have I done to deserve that woman?' He grimaced. 'She and Philip weren't even invited, they just turned up saying Mrs Burn asked them along to help. Not that Gusty's doing much. She seems to be using this as a networking opportunity and handing out her business cards to anything that moves.'

'Not quite anything, she didn't bother with us. Where's Philip?' I scanned the room anxiously. I couldn't face any embarrassing scenes between him and Harriet tonight. Especially if I had to watch Mark being a knight in shining armour again.

He gave an exasperated sigh. 'Would you believe he's setting up a cookery demonstration in the conservatory? It's Gusty's idea of an icebreaker. I've told her there's no need to break any ice, we've all known each other for years.' He grinned at Harriet. 'Actually, that's not quite true, you've never met my father and stepmother, have you? Let me introduce you.' He was about to lead her away when he added, as if it was an afterthought,

'They're looking forward to seeing you again, Emma.'

I fixed a bright smile on my face. 'You two go ahead, I need a quick word with Kate first.'

Kate and Tom were holding hands by the fireplace, in a world of their own. It was a pity to interrupt them, but I certainly didn't want to play gooseberry to Mark and Harriet.

'How are you?' I said, my eyes on Mark as he guided Harriet over to George and Saffron, his long tanned fingers in the small of her back.

'Fantastic.' Kate sounded excited. 'Guess what happened today?'

'What?' My response was automatic, my attention elsewhere. Across the room, Harriet seemed to be making an impression; Mark and George were laughing, while Saffron looked distinctly frosty – although that in itself was nothing unusual.

Kate was saying, 'I had an ultrasound scan. Oh Emma, we actually saw our baby!'

I roused myself with an effort. 'Oh yes, the scan, wonderful.' She'd mentioned the appointment to me on New Year's Eve; normally I'd have rung her this afternoon and asked all about it, but I'd completely forgotten.

'An amazing experience,' Tom added. 'Something I never had with Flynn. By the way, he'll be here soon. He's coming direct from the station, had to go up to London unexpectedly, a big meeting with the BBC.'

'It was very kind of Mark to invite him,' Kate put in, 'especially as he's never met George and Saffron.'

Just then Harriet came dashing over to us. 'This house freaks me out, it's so posh, innit? Except I'm sure those are Skir wine glasses from Ikea, two for a fiver, although Saffron says hers are from Harrods, she'd never be seen dead in Ikea. Is that her idea of a joke?'

So that was what Mark and George had found so funny; and of course Saffron had taken offence, big time.

'Saffron's fine once you get used to her,' I said. 'I'd better go and say hello.'

As I approached, I saw Saffron talking to the Perrys while Mark was deep in conversation with his father. I heard George say, 'And you think she'll agree?'

Mark nodded. 'I'm sure of it, otherwise I wouldn't even be asking—' He broke off when he noticed me.

George kissed me warmly on both cheeks. 'You look ravishing, my dear. Doesn't she, Mark?'

Mark didn't seem to be listening. 'I'll go and have that word with Harriet,' he muttered, and moved away.

'He's got a lot on his mind at the moment.' George smiled apologetically, then gave Saffron a discreet nudge. 'Here's Emma.'

'Darling!' Saffron went through her 'kiss and miss' routine, 'Mwah!' somewhere beside my left cheek and 'Mwah!' near my right. 'Lovely to see you.' She lowered her voice the merest fraction. 'This village is going to the dogs. That funny little girl in the hideous dress bleating on about Ikea and that frightful woman Mark asked to organise the party, what in God's name was he thinking? But you haven't changed, thank goodness. Just remind me to give you Felice's phone number, she'll show you how to do your hair and make-up properly, darling.'

George cut in hastily with, 'And how are things going at Highbury Foods? Mark tells me you're very talented at marketing.'

Really? He'd given no sign of being impressed so far. I was about to say something to that effect, when Gusty clapped her hands to draw our attention.

She surveyed us all with a condescending smirk. 'Ladies and gentlemen, I know it's the middle of winter but I thought I'd bring you a taste of summer with a little cookery demonstration. I'm making Fraises à la Neige, which means strawberries in snow for the uninitiated, so simple that even my better half Philip can do it. Everything's set up through here' – gesturing grandly at the conservatory – 'although it's impossible to get decent strawberries at this time of year. These ones were flown in from Spain or somewhere, but of course in the summer I'd pick them, fresh. Make a little outing of it, you know.'

Batty piped up, 'That's just what we do every

June at Bob Taylor's pick-your-own fruit farm on the Kingston road. Poor man, he's never been the same since he . . . We take a picnic and have a wonderful time, you'd be welcome to join us, dear.'

Gusty scowled. 'I'm going to be organising my own pick-your-own outing. Up to London, Fortnum & Mason in fact, very *select*.'

I caught Mark's eye and, for a split second, we shared one of our old knowing looks. Then he turned abruptly away.

As if in a dream, I watched Gusty bully everyone into the conservatory; at least, almost everyone. The sight of Mark leading Harriet off in another direction wasn't a dream – it was a short, sharp dose of reality. Behind me, I heard a loud curse as someone collided with the door.

I whirled round to find Flynn rubbing his elbow. 'Oh hi, Tom said you were on your way.'

He grimaced. 'I gave up dinner at the Ritz for this, hope it's bloody well worth it. Funny how people are too ill to see me but not too ill to come *here*.'

'What on earth are you talking about?' I said, giving him a bemused look.

He forced a smile. 'Sorry, it's been a long day. Don't suppose there's any decent whisky in this place?'

'I'll see what I can do.'

Just then, Gusty came marching up to us. 'Flynn, you gorrrgeous man, I want your *professional* opinion of my strawberries in snow.' She slipped her arm coquettishly through his. 'Come along, don't be shy.'

Flynn jerked his arm away. 'You can stick your strawberries up your—'

'We're not in the mood,' I put in quickly. 'Another time maybe.'

Gusty glared at me. 'I hardly think so. Do you realise how much time and effort this demonstration's taking? Not to mention the expense, although I told Sheila Burn to claim back every penny she's spent from Mark, it's nothing to do with me.' She spun on her heel and stalked off.

Flynn ran his hand through his hair. 'Any chance of that whisky?'

'Mrs B will track some down, she's probably in the kitchen. This way.'

'What would I do without you, my lovely?' he said, flinging his arm casually round my shoulder.

As we entered the hall, Mark and Harriet came out of the study opposite. At that moment, my worst fears were realised. He seemed rather pleased with himself; but she . . . she looked like she'd just won the National Lottery, a rollover jackpot on a £1 ticket.

'Remember, not a word to anyone,' Mark said. When he saw us, his expression darkened. 'Can I get you something?'

I dropped my gaze from Harriet's radiant face and stared at her high-heeled, open-toed shoes. They were black patent, like her dress, and through her black tights – or was she wearing

403

stockings, all set for seduction? – I could see that her toe nails were painted alternate black and pink. I wondered what Mark would think . . . But then, if he was besotted with her, he'd find everything about her irresistible, wouldn't he?

'Whisky,' I said, quietly. 'Flynn's had a long day and he'd like a whisky.'

Mark's voice was cold and clipped. 'Shall I bring it to you here or are you looking for somewhere more private?'

We weren't; but I felt a sudden need to get back at Mark, make him believe someone found me desirable, even for just one minute. So I leaned in closer to Flynn and pressed my lips to the pulse just below his ear. If he was surprised, he didn't show it; instead, his arm tightened round me.

I gazed up at Flynn but my words were for Mark. 'The drawing room's private enough, everyone's in the conservatory. Come on, Flynn, we've got a lot of catching up to do.'

As soon as we reached the drawing room, Flynn shut the door and pulled me gently round to face him.

'What is it, Em?' he said. 'I mean, I'm very flattered but I don't believe for one moment that you fancy me.'

I buried my face in his shirt in a useless attempt to shut out my despair. 'Just hold me,' I whispered. 'For a minute or two. Please.'

And he did. He held me so tight that all I could hear was the steady beat of his heart. It soothed me, kept the tears at bay. When at last I stepped away from him, I noticed that someone had placed a decanter of whisky on the little table just inside the door.

There were two glasses, not one. That was Mark, thoughtful to the last.

MARK

My conversation in the study went well. As I'd anticipated, Harriet needed very little convincing to come to India. In fact, I had the feeling she'd need very little convincing to jump off a cliff; which was why I always knew I'd have to get her away from Highbury, to give the relationship a chance – although maybe India was taking things a bit far. Not that she asked me anything about the place; all she wanted to know was what clothes she'd need and whether she could take emergency supplies of something called Lambrini, which apparently always got her 'in the mood'.

Her next question took me even more aback. 'What's that big white thing stuck in the middle of a pond, somewhere in India?'

I hazarded a guess. 'The Taj Mahal?'

'That's it, Mum's always wanted to sit on that bench where Princess Di sat. Now at least I can send her a photo of me doing it.'

I was about to explain that the Taj Mahal was over a thousand kilometres from Mumbai and I wasn't sure there'd be time to visit it, when she came out with the question I had been expecting. 'What shall I tell Emma?'

'As little as possible,' I said firmly. 'She'll only try to talk you out of the whole thing, that's why it's got to be a secret. Just tell her you've had the offer of a holiday out of the blue, all expenses paid, too good to miss and so on. It's the truth, isn't it? If she kicks up a fuss and says she needs you in the office, let me know immediately. But, as you're a temp, there shouldn't be a problem, the agency can always send someone else to do your job.'

She nodded eagerly. 'Oh Mark, you're brilliant, you think of friggin' everything.'

'I'll finalise the travel arrangements and phone you tomorrow,' I went on, opening the door into the hall. 'Remember, not a word to anyone.'

As soon as I saw Churchill standing there with Emma, I knew India wasn't too far away. When I took the whisky into the drawing room, they were already in each other's arms; nothing passionate, just being close. Over the top of her head, Churchill caught my eye and smirked, as if he could see right through my air of indifference.

Just three days to go. Then there'd be no more need to pretend.

EMMA

After Flynn had poured himself a large whisky, I suggested letting Kate and Tom know he'd arrived.

We found them in the conservatory, next to George and Harriet. Gusty was behind a table at one end of the room, stirring something in a pan over a little primus stove, with Philip hovering devotedly beside her. Mark was nowhere to be seen; neither was Saffron.

'I'm using white chocolate, but it needs to be *excellent* quality.' Gusty gave a supercilious smile. 'Philip thought the cheap stuff would do, he can be so half-witted at times. Pass me the platter, Philip – no, no, that's a bowl, I said the *platter*.'

'You know who she reminds me of?' Tom said, with a chuckle. 'Fanny Cradock, bossing Johnnie about in those old TV clips. Ah, watch out, I think she's looking round for her next victim.'

Fortunately, Gusty's beady gaze got no further than David Perry. '*Doctor* Perry, I'm sure you'll be an expert at this, it's quite a delicate *operation* and needs a steady hand!'

As David stepped forward apprehensively, Kate said under her breath, 'For heaven's sake, doesn't she know he's a GP, not a surgeon?'

'You take a strawberry and hold it by the stalk – so,' Gusty continued. 'Then you dip it into the melted chocolate, wave it about to cool and put it on the platter – like this. Strawberries in snow, you see?' She pretended not to notice the spattering of white chocolate across the pristine slate-grey Amtico tiles. 'You try this one, David. Anyone else like a turn?'

Batty darted to the table and picked up two

strawberries at once. She was about to dip them into the chocolate when she hiccupped and promptly dropped them. She then staggered into Philip, causing him to lurch sideways and squash the fruit to a gooey pulp with his heel.

Kate groaned. 'I think Mary's had too much to drink. Flynn, you're nearest, bring her over here before she gets hurt, that floor looks lethal.'

Flynn frowned. 'Isn't her niece looking after her?'

Kate shook her head. 'Jane went home about ten minutes ago. She felt ill, but she insisted she was OK to drive and we said we'd give Mary a lift later.'

As Flynn hesitated, Saffron and Mark arrived and swung into action. Saffron thrust a roll of kitchen towel at Philip and a mop and bucket at Gusty, while Mark led a flustered Batty to a chair. I saw Flynn fidget with his mobile and leave the room, presumably to make a call away from the general chaos.

Meanwhile, Saffron raised her delicately sculptured eyebrows in distaste and surveyed the scene in her once-immaculate conservatory. 'Now you two can start clearing up this mess.'

Gusty opened her mouth to object, but Saffron silenced her with one Medusa-like stare and went on, 'After that, there's plenty to do in the kitchen. I'll see you get the going rate for your work.' Her voice hardened. 'Provided it's up to my standards, of course. Through here, everyone.' And she swept majestically into the drawing room.

As we all trooped after her, I heard Mark say to Batty, 'I'll get your coat and take you home – that's if no one's blocked the Mercedes in.'

I turned to face him. 'I have, I'm afraid. I'll move my car right now.' I added irritably, 'I didn't expect you'd be going anywhere tonight.'

'Neither did I.' He gave an apologetic grin. 'Although if you're leaving soon, could *you* drop Mary off? That would help me out, I may need to calm things down here.'

This was my chance to find out if he and Harriet . . . I took a deep breath. 'I'm supposed to be taking Harriet home – unless you have other plans for her?'

He paused and there was no mistaking the flicker of guilt in his eyes. No mistaking at all. I blinked back the tears and schooled my expression into one of total disinterest.

Another grin, far more contrived than the previous one. 'Plans? Absolutely not.' I didn't believe him for one moment; he would simply be waiting for a less public opportunity to make his move. He continued, 'I'll let her know you're about to leave. And – Emma?'

'Yes?'

'Drive carefully, there's a heavy frost out there.'

Of course, he wouldn't want anything to happen to his precious Harriet, would he?

Within fifteen minutes, I was driving away from Donwell Abbey as fast as the frost would allow. Since Harriet's house was on the way to Batty's, it would have looked odd if I'd not dropped her off first – but that meant I couldn't find out what Mark had asked her. I reasoned that she probably wouldn't have told me anyway; there was a vacant, dreamy look about her that didn't bode well for getting any work done tomorrow.

After dropping Harriet off, I drove into Highbury and parked outside Batty's house. As I was helping her up the path, a red Jaguar appeared and screeched to a halt behind my car.

Batty twisted round and said in bewilderment, 'It's Jane, where's she been, I thought she was going straight home.' Then, as Jane got out, 'Are you all right, dear?'

Jane glanced over, her face clearly visible under the streetlight. 'I'm fine,' she muttered. But she was pinched and drawn and all the signs were that she'd been sobbing her heart out.

I steered Batty firmly towards her front door before she noticed that anything was wrong. 'Come inside and put the kettle on, I'm sure Jane would love a nice cup of tea.'

'So thoughtful,' she twittered. 'But let's get Jane inside first, it's very cold.'

I turned to Jane, racking my brains for a good reason to speak to her alone. 'By the way, I've got some project stuff in my car that I need your view on. I didn't like to bother you when you were ill, but as I'm here . . .'

'OK, I'll have a quick look,' she said. 'I'm sure it won't take more than five minutes.'

'Don't be any longer than that,' Batty put in.

'I'll make you a Horlicks, or maybe some of Mother's Complan, you need building up.'

When I returned to my car, Jane was huddled in the passenger seat. She eyed me suspiciously as I got in.

'I gather there is no project stuff – you just wanted a private chat?'

'Correct.' I hesitated. 'You don't have to tell me anything, but it's obvious you're upset and I wondered if I could help.' Silence; I tried again. 'You left Donwell Abbey rather suddenly – was it something there that upset you?'

That produced a response, rather too glib for my liking. 'It was Gusty, she's fixed up an interview for me in Bristol next Monday. If I've told her once, I've told her a hundred times – I'm not interested. But she doesn't take no for an answer.'

'Understatement of the year,' I said, giving her an appraising look. 'There's more to it than that, though, isn't there? I can imagine Gusty making you annoyed, but not upset. What – or who – has had you in tears?'

She pursed her lips. 'OK, let's just say I'm having relationship problems and leave it at that.'

So it was some furtive phone call with Dan Dixon that had made her cry. Unless . . . what if she actually meant Mark? Maybe he was wrong and she was hopelessly in love with him. Weird to think I might have that in common with her. And weird to think he could have had either of us, yet he'd chosen Harriet.

411

I let out a long breath. 'Join the club. I used to think I was an expert, but now . . . I've had two serious relationships and I managed each of them like a project. You know, see it through to completion in an organised way, evaluate the learnings and all that crap. Now I realise that was because I always engaged brain rather than heart.'

She gave a faint smile. 'You don't get your brain broken, do you? People talk about brain ache, which suggests some sort of minor discomfort that you recover from fairly quickly. But a heart *breaks* – much more catastrophic.'

Another silence, this time almost companionable.

'When do you think you'll be back at work?' I said, at last.

'Would you mind if I stayed off until Monday? It's not that I'm too ill to work, I've been doing some at home. It's just – well, Aunt Mary's a lovely person, but I'm a bit fragile at the moment, I need some space. If I come into the office, she'll fuss round me all day and I'll lose it with her, I really will.'

For once in my life, I felt I could come to respect Jane Fairfax. With time and a following wind, of course.

MARK

The rest of the week was full of meetings with Father and the other directors. In between, I made

412

all the remaining arrangements for India, passed on the relevant medical information to Harriet and Rob and started my packing.

And then it was Saturday, the day of my farewell dinner at the Box Hill Restaurant. I drove there alone an hour ahead of my guests. John was bringing the rest of the family along later and Father had offered to drive the Mercedes home at the end of the evening, so that I could indulge in a few celebratory drinks. Celebratory drinks? More like drowning my sorrows. All week I'd kept my despair at bay – but only just. Now I could feel it looming like a thundercloud.

I was determined nothing would ruin tonight, however; not even my own masochistic tendencies. And yet, as I arrived at Box Hill and was shown into the large lounge area, I couldn't help hoping that Emma would be impressed by its ambience. Rough-cast cream walls and exposed black beams blended surprisingly well with chunky chocolate-leather armchairs, ethnic rugs and modern artwork. The heavy burnt-orange curtains had been left open and the soft glow of the lights was reflected in the dark glass, so that the room seemed doubly warm and welcoming. I sat down beside the log fire, ordered a gin and tonic and willed myself to relax.

I hadn't seen or spoken to Emma since the party at Donwell. Within the hour, however, she'd be here and I'd feel the beat of my heart quicken at the very sight of her . . . Strange how you live for the next twist of the knife.

The waiter came to see if I wanted another drink and I took the opportunity to check tonight's bookings. It had just occurred to me that, by some awful coincidence or contrivance, Gusty might turn up. I heaved a sigh of relief when he announced there was nothing under the name of Elton or Hawkins.

Another gin and tonic later, I was still on my own and getting more and more dejected. What if my plans for Harriet and Rob didn't work out? I'd have raised their expectations and disrupted their lives for nothing. And what if things had changed on the business front in India, even in such a short time? I'd tried to protect our supply chain from four thousand miles away, and I had some good local contacts to help me; but people could be fickle, particularly in a developing market. Most of all, what if I couldn't handle seeing Emma tonight? Especially with *him*? I'd invited him because I'd been brought up to do the right thing, even when it hurt like hell.

I let out a long, ragged breath. Perhaps the only solution was to drink until I was incapable of causing GBH.

The arrival of Steve and my other good friend Ben, along with their wives, forced me to pull myself together. They were soon followed by the Perrys, who'd brought Mary and Jane; and John, with Izzy, Father, Saffron and my nephews Harry and James. I'd invited all the children, but Izzy didn't approve of the younger ones eating out, as their digestive systems were 'still so delicate'. I had to smile; John obviously hadn't told her about the Chicken McNuggets Bella wolfed down when he took her to see the latest Disney film over Christmas.

Despite all these distractions, I knew the moment Emma entered the room. I turned round and there she was, standing just inside the door, in the blue dress she'd worn at Ashridge – the night we'd first kissed, the night before Churchill came on the scene. The dress didn't fit quite as well as I remembered, as though she'd lost a bit of weight, and she looked tired. I hoped it wasn't sleepless nights over Churchill; the bastard wasn't worth it.

Talk of the devil. Just as our eyes met and held, he materialised at her side, took her arm and walked her jauntily towards me.

''Evening,' he said. 'The others won't be long, Dad's just parking the car, Henry's removing ninety layers of clothing and Kate's in the Ladies, where she seems to spend most of her time these days. Bet you're glad you're not pregnant, Em.'

I froze. How much had she told him about that night at Forbury Manor? Had she ever confided her fears that she might be pregnant with my child? She gave an almost imperceptible flinch and looked away, while he fixed his gaze on something

415

– or someone – behind me, apparently unconcerned. Somehow I knew that it was just one of his careless remarks and he was unaware of that particular tension between us.

'Right,' I said, forcing a smile, 'now that everyone's here, let's get started on the champagne.'

EMMA

'Now that everyone's here' . . .

Everyone except the new person in his life, Harriet.

Not that I minded in the least that she wasn't here tonight; I'd had enough of her in the office, smiling into space and singing love songs – oh, and suddenly announcing that she was taking the next two weeks off and hoping it wouldn't inconvenience me *too* much.

The morning after the party, I'd asked her outright what Mark had said; but she told me he'd sworn her to secrecy. I could piece it all together, though, from her scribbled reminders about suntan lotion and malaria tablets, and the India-related websites she surfed when she thought I wasn't looking. I'd guessed right; she'd be boarding that plane with him on Sunday so that they could get to know each other far away from the twitching net curtains of Highbury.

And yet, as I sat in the Box Hill Restaurant knocking back the champagne and staring blindly at the menu, it still didn't quite add up. Mark and *Harriet*? Should I confront him about it or accept that, in this particular case, the laws of attraction were beyond all understanding?

Eventually we went through to the dining area, a maze of interconnected rooms, all decorated in a similar style but with different layouts. Our room had a tank of tropical fish, which immediately fascinated the boys, and a large rectangular table. Whether deliberately or instinctively, we sat by age group: Dad, George, Saffron and Batty at one end, the Perrys and the Westons at the other, and the rest of us in the middle, with Mark and Jane opposite Flynn and me.

When more champagne arrived, George stood up and waited until he had our full attention. 'As you all know,' he said, 'four months ago Mark put his life on hold and came back to England to look after Donwell Organics. Leaving the company in such safe hands helped Saffron and me enjoy our cruise far more than was good for us, which is why we're back and he's giving this farewell dinner a few weeks earlier than planned.' He paused until the ripple of laughter died down. 'Seriously, I am so grateful. Mark never made me feel I was imposing on him, and the same goes for John who's been his right-hand man.' He looked around the table. 'Quite a few of you are parents, so you'll know what I mean when I say my children have taught me far more than I ever attempted to teach them.' Then, raising his glass, 'To Mark – don't stay away too long this time.'

'To Mark,' everyone chorused. My lips shaped the words, but no sound came. One day, I might be able to wish him well – and Harriet, if she was still with him – but not tonight.

I thought Mark might have responded with a little speech, but all he said was 'Thank you'. Maybe, like me, he wasn't enjoying the meal. My crab starter might as well have been fish paste; the Chablis Premier Cru, lemonade.

Shortly afterwards, as I toyed forlornly with my Dover sole, Flynn hissed in my ear, 'You look bored stiff. I'll liven things up a bit, just for you.' He rose from his seat and tapped his glass to get everyone's attention. 'Miss Emma Woodhouse and I,' he intoned, 'Highbury's answer to Posh and Becks, want to hear exactly what you're all thinking. No fibbing, mind, just give it to us straight.'

Mark gave a grim laugh. 'I'm not sure that's a good idea.'

'Why not? Have you got something to hide?' I said, with an insolent stare, and wasn't surprised to see him colour and look away.

Flynn sighed loudly. 'OK, since our dear host objects, let's make it easier. You all have to say something entertaining, but it needn't be the truth.'

Tom chuckled. 'Depends what you call entertaining. Some of us will find it easier to be truthful.'

'Fine, we'll give you a choice – quality or

quantity,' Flynn went on. 'You can say one extremely clever and entertaining thing, two quite interesting things, or three amazingly dull things. Who's going first?'

On the far side of Mark, Batty leaned forward. 'Oh, it'll be three dull things for me, as soon as I open my mouth I say dull things, no problem' – shrill titter – 'except I might not manage as many as three at once.' She blinked happily at us, secure in her self-humiliation.

A sudden shiver went through me. It was like seeing myself in thirty years' time . . . An object of ridicule – or pity, thinly disguised as kindness. Making up the numbers at Highbury's pathetic little social gatherings. Doting on my nephews and nieces, in the absence of any children of my own. Living alone with an elderly parent – because, given the wonders of modern medicine and a basically sound constitution, Dad could live well into his nineties, couldn't he?

No, it was impossible, I was nothing like Batty!

But what if she hadn't always been this way? What if she'd been completely different when she was younger? What if she'd lost the love of her life too, and never really got over it? Perhaps we were more alike than I could ever imagine. Oh God, what a horrible thought . . .

Next to me, Flynn murmured, 'Who's she trying to kid – "I might not manage as many as three"? We'll never shut her up.'

I started to giggle. 'You're so right.' I raised my

419

voice. 'Nonsense, Mary, you'll definitely manage three dull things. It's stopping at three that'll be your little challenge.'

She giggled too; then, as my words sank in, her smile faded and she shrank back behind Mark. I heard her say to him, 'Oh dear, I didn't realise I got on her nerves so much, I'll try not to in future. I mean, she wouldn't have said anything, would she, if she didn't think—'

Mark interrupted her, his voice thick with anger. 'Don't worry, Mary, it's nothing to do with you, she's just being a silly little teenager all over again.'

I couldn't bear it any longer. I got abruptly to my feet and walked out of the room.

MARK

As soon as I felt I could leave Mary, I went to find Emma. I guessed she'd taken refuge in the Ladies, so I paced up and down the corridor outside. Five minutes passed, then ten; I was just beginning to wonder if she was somewhere else, when the door swung open and out she came. The instant she saw me, her troubled expression switched to one of defiance.

I took a step forward, blocking her path, glaring down at her. 'How could you?'

Her eyes widened in mock surprise. 'How could I what?'

'Be so – fucking – rude to Mary.' In my fury, I almost choked on the words.

She laughed, she actually laughed in my face. 'You call that rude? It was only what everyone else was thinking. Anyway, she probably didn't understand what I meant.'

I grabbed her arm. Her golden skin was warm and soft, just as I remembered. Part of me ached to gather her close and kiss away her maddening, pig-headed indifference. But, in my present state of mind, such feelings didn't stand a chance.

Instead I ground out, 'She understood perfectly, and you know it!'

'Get off me.' She tried to wrench herself free but I tightened my grip, beyond caring whether my fingers bruised her flesh. 'Ow, you bastard, that hurts!'

'I couldn't give a toss, I hope I'm hurting you as much as you've hurt Mary. How could you say that to her? She's my guest, and my friend. And God knows she's always been a good friend to you.'

Her lip curled. 'Oh yeah, get the violins out.'

'What the hell's got into you?' As if I needed to ask; it was Churchill's influence, the useless piece of shit.

She looked up at me and swallowed, but her gaze never wavered. 'I just don't need you in my life, telling me what I should and shouldn't say. Get lost, Mark Knightley, you're history!'

I stared at her as each word stabbed into me. For a few seconds, all I could hear was my laboured breathing as I fought to bring myself under control.

At last I let go of her arm. 'Old habits die hard,' I said coldly. 'Can't help giving you a lecture when I think you need it. Still, after tonight you won't have to put up with me any more.'

And I walked away without another word.

CHAPTER 14

PURE HONEY

MARK

I didn't go straight back to my guests. Instead, I walked round the car park a few times and returned just as they were studying the dessert menus. I wondered if our orders reflected our individual states of mind. Mary, Jane and I had nothing; Churchill chose Devil's Food Cake, which he ate with relish; Emma went for Passion Fruit Fool and left it untouched. Everyone else had home-made ice cream; apart from Henry, who ordered crème brûlée – much to my surprise.

'Just a tiny portion, please, with none of that sugary stuff on top,' he told the waiter. 'I had it once, in 1995 I think, and I quite fancy some tonight, after all it is a special occasion. And Emma raved about it when she went to Ashridge, not just the crème brûlée, everything in fact.' He called across to her, 'Remember when Mark took you to Ashridge, darling?'

'Not really,' she said in a subdued voice, her eyes downcast.

'That's odd.' Henry turned to me. 'She seemed very impressed at the time, couldn't stop talking about the place for days afterwards.'

'She's always had a convenient memory,' I said heavily. With a savage sort of pleasure, I watched her go red and knew she was thinking about our bitter confrontation in the bedroom at Forbury Manor, just as I'd intended.

While we were moving through to the lounge area for coffee, Churchill's mobile went off. He immediately left the room and came back a few minutes later, face flushed, eyes glittering.

'That was Stella, she's just landed at Gatwick. Sorry, must dash, my taxi's due any moment. Thanks for the meal, all the best.' He gave a dismissive nod in my direction and turned towards the door.

Tom put his hand none too gently on his son's shoulder. 'Hang on, what's Stella doing in England? The woman's never been over here for thirty years. I think you owe us more of an explanation than that!'

Churchill edged away from him. 'OK, but it'll have to be quick, she's not the most patient of people.'

I saw Kate's lips tighten and suspected she was running short of patience herself. I wondered briefly why Churchill hadn't mentioned Stella's visit earlier and glanced across at Emma to gauge her reaction; but she was looking down at the floor, so it was impossible to tell.

A petulant note crept into Churchill's voice. 'I was going to tell you anyway, it's just that Stella's got the final say-so, it's her money after all.' He paused and his eyes flicked across at Emma – or was it Jane? 'Here goes, then. Most of you know I've been in the Lake District for the past couple of months. What you don't know is that I've been getting my own restaurant up and running, the Brook Inn, near Kendal. Once Stella's happy with how I've spent her money, I'll be ready to start filming my new show for the BBC, Flynn's Cook-in at the Brook Inn.' He gave one of his flashiest grins. 'Hope to see you all up there on opening night.'

We all made appropriate congratulatory noises – with varying degrees of sincerity, I was sure.

Tom brightened visibly. 'That's great news, Flynn, I'm looking forward to hearing all about it when you've got more time. Where's Stella staying? Have you booked her in anywhere?'

'It depends on – various things,' Churchill said evasively. 'Look, my taxi must be waiting, I'll phone you later.'

And with that he was gone, leaving Tom with just enough information to be able to speculate long and loud about his son's brilliant career prospects.

EMMA

I was barely aware of Flynn dashing off; I simply wanted the evening to end. Only then would the ordeal of saying goodbye to Mark be over.

Before, I'd been terrified of breaking down and making a fool of myself. Now, after that scene outside the Ladies, I couldn't wait for him to be gone. When the time came, we played our parts well and kept up the pretence of normality in front of the others; a brief, clumsy hug and some glib lies about staying in touch.

And yet, back at Hartfield, I felt duty bound to wish Harriet well, whatever my feelings. I rang her from my bedroom and she answered immediately, dashing my hopes of just leaving a message.

'Yeah?' I could tell from the wariness in her voice that she recognised my number.

'I wanted to say . . .' I took a deep, painful breath. 'I know you're going there, to India, and I hope you'll be – very happy, with *him*.'The words came out stilted and wrong, but it was a miracle I'd said them at all.

'Shit, so you know, did Mark tell you?'

'Oh Harriet, it wasn't that hard to figure out.'

Brief pause; then she said, sounding relieved, 'I wanted to tell you, but I couldn't, Mark said you might try and talk me out of it.'

I felt a surge of anger at being judged so unfairly. 'If you really want something, no one should be able to talk you out of it—' I broke off, remembering how easily I'd persuaded her to drop Robert Martin for Philip Elton. Maybe Mark had a point, maybe he already knew Harriet better than I did. 'I need to go, it's late and I'm sure you've still got packing to do. Have a good trip and I'll see you in a couple of weeks.'

'If I come back at all,' she said cheerfully and hung up.

I threw the phone on the floor and cried myself to sleep.

The next morning, I woke up with a pounding headache. Dad made me his favourite hangover remedy, uncooked porridge oats in barley water, but after a couple of mouthfuls I couldn't face any more. There was something weighing on my mind, something I needed to do as soon as possible. I found an unopened bottle of vintage port in the cellar, grabbed my car keys and poked my head round the door of the dining room, where Dad was tut-tutting over the Sunday papers.

'Just popping into Highbury to give this port to Mary's mother, I promised it to her ages ago.'

'Fine, darling, best to call now before they go to church.'

Kings Row looked congested, so I parked on the high street and dashed across the grass verge that separated it from Batty's house. I rang the door-bell and waited as patiently as I could.

When Batty eventually came to the door, she seemed even weirder than usual. 'Oh, it's you, have you heard already, did Kate tell you?'

I decided to ignore her ramblings and get my

apology over and done with. 'I brought this for you and your mother, I know how much you both like port.' I paused. 'And I've come to say sorry for last night, I don't know what got into me.'

She took the port with a distracted smile. 'That's very kind of you, of course I thought nothing of it really, after . . . Do come in, dear, we're all at sixes and sevens this morning but I'm just about to make another cuppa.'

As I hesitated, she added in a stage whisper, 'Jane's gone off to live in sin with Flynn Churchill, Mother would have kittens if she knew! I've had to say she's in Ireland visiting Charlotte Dixon.'

I stood stock still for a moment, absorbing what I'd just heard. Then I closed the door behind me with a firm click and almost pushed her into the tiny kitchen. I switched on the kettle and stood between her and the tea things, in an attempt to keep her focused on the task in hand.

'Right, Mary,' I said with an encouraging smile, 'I'll make the tea and you can tell me all about Jane.'

MARK

As far as I knew, this morning would be Rob and Harriet's first meeting for several months. I'd told each of them that they could back out of the arrangement at any time, but neither of them

428

showed any signs of doing so. Still, until they saw each other again, I was on tenterhooks.

Rob lived outside the village, on the road we'd be taking to Gatwick Airport, so I planned to pick him up last. At eight o'clock sharp, Jack Thomas collected me from Donwell in his taxi and we went from there to Harriet's house. I could see in a split second that she had too much luggage, but it took far longer to persuade her to ditch any of it. At last, she agreed to leave all the fake leather behind; January might be Mumbai's coolest month, but temperatures could still reach twenty-eight degrees and the humidity was always high.

It was just after nine o'clock, well behind schedule, when we turned into the high street on the way to Rob's. In the distance, I saw a familiar figure in red trousers come out of Mary's cottage and walk slowly down the path.

I spoke without thinking, my voice taut with regret. 'Oh God, there she is, there's Emma.'

I needn't have worried; Harriet caught only the name, not the undercurrent of emotion. She loosened her seat belt, leaned across me and banged on the window.

'Oi, Emma!'

Emma didn't seem to hear. The traffic lights were on red and the taxi rumbled to a halt right opposite her as she opened her car door. Harriet banged on the window time and again, shouting her name and waving frantically, but Emma had her head down, as if in a little world of her own. Then the lights changed. The taxi lurched forward, Harriet fell on top of me and Emma glanced in our direction at last.

I was hardly aware of Harriet straightening herself up with an embarrassed giggle; all I could see was the look of utter anguish in Emma's eyes. And I had to find out what, or who, had put it there.

'Pull over,' I said to Jack.

As soon as he stopped the taxi, I jumped out and ran back down the street. Too late – Emma had driven off in the opposite direction. In three strides I was at Mary's front door, almost hammering it down.

She did a double take when she saw me. 'Mark, dear, aren't you meant to be—'

'Going to the airport, yes, and I'm in a hurry. But I've just seen Emma and she looked very upset. And I had to know – is everything all right?'

'She wasn't upset when she left here, more shocked than anything.' She gave a nervous titter. 'I don't suppose you've heard our news.'

I smiled grimly. 'It wouldn't be to do with Jane and Flynn Churchill, would it?'

Her hand flew to her mouth. 'How did you guess? Jane left me a note, she's with him and Stella in the Lakes, must have gone late last night, I didn't hear a . . . Poor girl, she says she's been in a terrible state ever since they met at Weymouth, not knowing whether he was The One, or whether

430

Stella had her spies watching, she threatened to cut off Flynn's . . . But they're hoping Stella will come round when she sees the Brook Inn and meets dear Jane.'

'And you told Emma all this?'

'Oh yes, we had quite a long chat, she came to apologise for last night, which I'd quite forgotten about, what with all the excitement this morning.' Another nervous titter. 'Like me, she never suspected anything . . . Mind you, I always wondered how Flynn knew about the Perrys' son nearly being expelled, because I only mentioned it to Jane and Emma. And Emma says she certainly didn't tell him.'

I checked my watch. 'I've got to go. Goodbye, Mary, don't worry about Jane, I'm sure she knows what she's doing by now.'

I gave her a swift kiss on the cheek and dashed back to the taxi. Harriet didn't seem inclined to talk, so I had time to think. I decided my priority was to get Rob and Harriet on the plane to Mumbai. Then I would come straight back to Highbury and offer Emma a shoulder to cry on. Judging by that glimpse I'd had of her face, the shock had already worn off and the heartache had started. And who else was there to comfort her? Her father and sister were about as much use as a chocolate teapot; and Kate, the obvious choice, just happened to be Churchill's stepmother.

We arrived at Rob's house with Harriet chewing

her lip and me feeling almost as apprehensive. Rob answered the door, his face white and set. I wasted no time in taking his bags and ordering him into the taxi. As Jack and I re-arranged the luggage so that we could get everything in the boot, I glanced into the back of the car. To my relief, Rob and Harriet were in each other's arms. I got into the front seat beside Jack and spent the rest of the journey learning more than I ever wanted to know about his recent hernia operation. I decided it was preferable to being too close to the heavy breathing in the back.

When we reached Gatwick, I took Rob, Harriet and their luggage to the Emirates Air check-in. It was there that I announced that something urgent had cropped up and I was postponing my trip. I told them my friend Anil would meet them at Mumbai airport and take them to my flat; he lived in the same complex and would be on hand to show them around. I wished them well and reminded them to contact me on my mobile if they needed to. I doubted whether they took in more than one word in ten; they spent the whole time grinning inanely at each other.

As soon as they disappeared through passport control, I returned to the taxi rank where Jack was waiting. I couldn't face any more of his medical history, so I pretended I needed a power nap and sat in the back. Soon we were on the M25 again, this time travelling clockwise. It was now raining steadily and the windscreen wipers kept up a mind-numbing rhythm that stopped me from thinking too far ahead.

By the time Jack dropped me and my luggage at Hartfield, it was nearly one o'clock. As I watched the taxi trundle down the drive, I realised that this was it, there was no going back. I rang the bell and waited, hands clasped behind me, one forefinger tracing the links of my watch.

When Henry answered the door, his jaw dropped. 'Mark? What are you doing here?' He stood back as I piled my bags into the hall.

'No time to explain, I need to see Emma.'

'She's not here, she went out about fifteen minutes ago. Didn't want any lunch, told me she was going for a walk to clear her head. She's not answering her mobile and I'm very worried about her.'

'I know, is – is she terribly upset?' I said, cursing the catch in my voice.

He raised his eyebrows. 'Upset? I don't know about that, but she went out without her coat. She'll catch her death, and then where will we all be?'

I bit back an impatient retort. 'I'll find her, don't worry. See you later.'

As I made to leave, he pulled me back. 'You're leaving those bags here?'

'Just for a little while – are they in your way?'

'No, no, I'm sure I won't trip over them.'

I sighed, shut the front door before he could

complain about the draught, and quickly stowed the bags under the stairs. I'd just yanked the door open again, when he gave a little moan.

I turned and glared at him. 'Yes?'

'Look at that rain, poor Emma's got no coat and that jacket of yours looks very flimsy, at least let me fetch an umbrella—'

I ignored him and slammed the door behind me so hard that the house shook. The rain whipped into me, but I barely noticed. From Hartfield, there was only one obvious walk – down the bridle path to Donwell. I started to jog, heedless of the mud spattering my light grey trousers, my eyes trained on the path stretching emptily out in front. Emma had a good head start, quarter of an hour according to Henry, and visibility was poor in the rain. As the minutes passed and I still couldn't see her, I wondered if I'd got it wrong. Perhaps she'd gone to Randalls to pour her heart out to Kate after all.

Suddenly, through the mist, no more than a hundred yards ahead, I saw red trousers bright as a robin's breast. I didn't call her name, just quickened my pace.

EMMA

I heard the footsteps behind me and whirled round. A tall, well-made man was running towards me, jacket flapping.

'The idiot,' I thought, 'he'll get drenched, like me. But I *want* to be cold and miserable.'

Then I saw who it was and my heart missed a beat. I hurriedly wiped the tears from my eyes with the back of my hand and fixed a defiant look on my face.

'Why aren't you at the airport?' I flung the words at him, like stones, as he approached.

He skidded to a halt within two feet of me, his breath coming in gasps, great shuddering gasps. 'I heard – the news – and I had to come.' When he'd steadied himself, he went on, 'I can see how upset you are about Churchill—'

'Churchill?'

'I mean Flynn,' he said quietly, 'and Jane. Come here.'

He gathered me to him, held me tight. I was soaked to the skin and my teeth were chattering, but I could have stayed there for ever, my face pressed against his chest, breathing his scent, listening to the thud-thud of his heart.

But I couldn't stay there for ever, because he didn't belong to me. For the first time in my life, I, Emma Woodhouse, wanted to be somebody else: Harriet Smith, chav. I blinked back more tears.

Then I heard him muttering to himself. 'The wanker doesn't know when he's well off . . . and to let you find out like that . . . I've a good mind to go to the Lakes and beat him to pulp . . .'

'Mark?' It came out as little more than a croak.

'Yes?' He held me away from him, his eyes bleak as they searched my tear-streaked face.

'What are you on about? Who are you going to beat to pulp?' I shivered, partly from the cold, partly from his words.

He folded me in his arms again. 'That bastard Churchill, who else?'

I laid my damp cheek against his damp shirt, now totally confused. He was meant to be on his way to India with Harriet; yet here he was behaving as if he was insanely jealous of Flynn – after denying any feelings at all for Saint Jane of Highbury!

'For God's sake, if Flynn wants Jane, good luck to him,' I said, in a choked voice.

My cheek rose and fell as he let out a long sigh. Several times he seemed about to speak, but stopped himself. I said nothing; it was enough to be this close for a few minutes more.

Then, at last, he broke the silence and it was his turn to sound choked. 'You're too generous, he doesn't deserve you, my darling. He'll never deserve you, ever.'

Hang on, Flynn deserving *me*? My *darling*?

I stifled a hysterical giggle. 'Mark, have you been taking too many of those malaria tablets?'

His arms tightened round me. 'This isn't a joke, just tell me what you want me to do to him and I'll do it.'

'But I don't want you to do anything to him.'

He held me away from him, his eyes wide with disbelief. 'You can't possibly want to go through with the engagement after *this*!'

I stared up at him. 'What engagement?'

'He wanted to give you the ring on Christmas Day, I saw the little box.'

I frowned, trying to remember . . . 'Oh that, it wasn't a ring, it was some very expensive earrings that he pretended he'd bought for me, just to impress Kate and Tom. But I wouldn't accept them, even before he told me they were really for someone else. He must have meant Jane, although at the time I thought they were for—' I stopped myself just in time from saying Harriet's name. But it reminded me that Mark had a new person in his life. I twisted out of his arms and turned away.

He seized me by the shoulders, forcing me to look at him. 'Engagement or no engagement, there was something going on between you,' he said hoarsely. 'Whenever I saw you together, he couldn't keep his hands off you.'

I gave a weary laugh. 'Don't you see? That was all a game, to fool people – especially Stella, if she sent her spies round. And to make Jane so jealous that, in the end, she'd make up her mind about him for once and for all. God knows he's the sort that would flirt with a block of wood, I was just a more convincing alternative. And I'm ashamed to say I never suspected a thing, I even played along, most of the time—'

'I'll say you played along, you were in his arms just the other night, at Donwell!'

'I needed a hug, that's all,' I said indignantly,

looking straight at him. 'Look, I admit I fancied him to begin with, I've been dying to meet him for years, but I soon realised that he wasn't the man of my dreams. Quite the opposite. He's good fun but, like you said, he's a wanker.' I stared down at my soaked trainers. 'So you certainly don't have to beat him to pulp for my sake, but I can see that you might want to for Jane's.' Then I remembered the agony of seeing Harriet wrapped round Mark in the taxi. But my agony couldn't compare to hers if she ever discovered that he was secretly in love with Jane. Poor, trusting Harriet . . .

I added bitterly, 'Although that wouldn't be very fair to Harriet, would it?'

He tilted my face gently upwards, his fingers warm on my ice-cold skin. 'What on earth are you getting at? Wait a minute, you don't honestly think—'

I wrenched myself from his grasp. 'I'll never understand what you see in her, you'd have been better off with Jane. At least *she* wouldn't have plastered herself all over you in a taxi, in the middle of Highbury high street! Still, whatever gives you your kicks, I suppose.'

And then he laughed; the bastard threw back his head and laughed, while I stood there in the pouring rain, feeling cold and wet and utterly alone.

'So glad I can still make you laugh,' I said miserably.

He gripped my shoulders, gripped them so tight it hurt; but I didn't want him to let go.

'Yes, Emma, you make me laugh . . . and you make me cry.' His eyes were fixed on mine and they weren't bleak any more, they were clear and bright. 'You make me cry, because . . .' He cleared his throat. 'Because I love you. I think I always have, since the day you were born.'

I felt more tears well up, tears of anger and disappointment. 'Yes, like a little sister, why don't you say it, you dickhead!' I aimed a kick at his shin, missed and burst into loud sobs.

His voice was low and tender. 'If you still think *that*, after all that's happened between us, then you're the dickhead, my love. Ever since I saw you again last September, I've had the most unbrotherly thoughts about you.'

I stopped crying at once. *Un*brotherly?

He went on, 'No wonder I couldn't resist you at Forbury Manor, it was like all my fantasies coming true. Don't you know how much—'

He got no further. I flung my arms round his neck and pulled him towards me. Our mouths met, hard with hunger, soft with longing. It was the kiss I'd been waiting for all my life, the kiss from the man of my dreams. When at last we drew apart, it felt as though we were already inseparable.

'I love you, Mark,' I whispered, 'you're the only one I want.'

He gave me a long, lingering smile, then his face

clouded. 'To think I might never have heard you say that! I only came back because I found out about Churchill and assumed you'd be devastated. Otherwise I'd be on the way to Mumbai by now, with Harriet and—'

'Harriet! What are we going to do about her?' With a groan, I twisted away from him.

'Absolutely nothing.' He stroked the corner of my mouth with his thumb. 'God, how I love kissing you.'

I closed my eyes, but I could still see Harriet's face, full of reproach. 'Mark, you'll have to tell her and you'll have to go to India to do it. Poor thing, stuck out there all on her own.'

He sighed. 'I've got a confession to make. She's not on her own, she's with Rob.'

I jerked my head round. 'Rob? Rob who?'

'Rob Martin, I thought they could make a go of things if they just had a bit of space. And they both seem very happy. Whatever you thought was going on in that taxi between me and Harriet couldn't be further from the truth.'

Relief flooded through me, relief mingled with unrestrained delight. Now wasn't the time for *me* to criticise *him* about interfering in other people's relationships, although I didn't intend to let the opportunity slip by! Now was the time to show him just how much I loved him. I slipped my hands inside his jacket and held him tight. The main thing was that he was here with me, and Harriet was none the worse for it; in fact, it looked as though she'd transferred her affections remarkably quickly back to Robert.

'Sorry, I interrupted you just then,' I said, with a slow smile. 'You were telling me how much you loved kissing me. And, as my mentor, I'm sure you told me that it's actions – not words – that count, didn't you?'

He laughed. 'As your mentor, I tried very hard *not* to think about kissing you at all. But I'm not your mentor any more, am I?'

And then his mouth sought mine and his hands moved urgently over my body, moulding me to him, stirring buried memories. Even through my wet clothes, his touch was electric; when he ran his fingers across the bare skin beneath my jumper, I was close to meltdown. Overwhelmed by need, we broke apart and simply stared at each other. Around us, raindrops pattered from overhanging branches, a counterpoint to our ragged breathing.

'Emma, I know Forbury Manor was a mistake—'

'Was it?'

'Wasn't it?'

I shrugged. 'I don't know. Maybe it was meant to happen.'

'I lied to you, about Tamara. I couldn't even start to compare her with you, you're—'

I put my finger to his lips. 'Then don't, my love. And I lied to you. After the initial shock had worn off, I remembered a lot more than I said I did.'

'Do you want to . . .' – he hesitated – 'refresh your memory?'

'Yes, more than anything in the world.' I smiled up at him as I slipped my hand into his.

'Where shall we go?'

I looked along the bridle path, towards Hartfield. 'We can go this way, I suppose, to my place—'

'Where Henry will insist on making you a custard poultice for your chest,' he put in.

I giggled. 'A mustard poultice, you idiot.'

'Far too spicy, darling, it has to be custard.' He turned towards Donwell. 'Or we can go that way, to my place, where I'm sure I can think of something equally therapeutic to put on your chest.'

I shot him a provocative look from under my eyelashes. 'That sounds promising, but what about George and Saffron?'

'They're out, not due back until early evening.'

I shivered, this time with pure pleasure. 'Your place it is, then, but I'll need to phone Dad. What if he goes on about me catching cold and insists on coming to fetch me?'

'Leave Henry to me,' Mark said briskly.

We shared one more lingering kiss, then broke into a run.

MARK

We reached Donwell Abbey in five minutes flat, half running, half walking, laughing all the way like a pair of kids. There was no sign of Father's car, thank God; so far, so good. We stood on the doorstep and held each other close. I tilted her face towards me, aching to feel her lips on mine again.

Instead, I found myself saying, 'Emma, are you sure about this? If you want more time—'

'I'm absolutely sure, don't waste your breath asking me unnecessary questions, you idiot.'

I grinned and felt automatically in my jacket pocket. Nothing. 'Shit, I gave my key back to Father this morning, didn't think I'd be needing it again.'

Her face fell. 'We'll have to go to Hartfield, then.'

'No, wait, there's still a chance I can get in. Stay here.'

I hurried round the back of the house. I'd just remembered that Father and Saffron were in the middle of a battle about the dog being relegated to the utility room whenever they went out. Saffron would tolerate this cruelty only if the window was shut, in case Tao caught pneumonia; Father wanted the window left open, to clear the smell of incontinent dog. Whether I could get into the house now depended on which one of them had been in the utility room last . . .

It must have been Father; the small upper window was wide open. With a whoop, I stretched up, reached inside, opened the big lower window, hauled myself onto the ledge and squeezed through the gap, nearly landing on top of poor Tao. He growled reproachfully as I dashed through the kitchen and into the hall to turn off the burglar alarm, before opening the front door for Emma. Then she was in my arms again; but this time we were somewhere warm and dry and totally private, and the possibilities were endless.

'You're wet through, you need to get your clothes off as soon as possible,' I said, letting go of her reluctantly.

She bent down to remove her trainers. 'That's the best offer I've had in a while.'

I felt myself harden just looking at her. 'Come upstairs. Now.'

There was a teasing glint in her eye. 'Not until you ring Dad.'

I almost sprinted across the hall and phoned Hartfield. 'Henry? . . . Yes, I've found her, safe and sound – but too far from home, so we came to Donwell instead . . . Yes, I'm going to warm her up as fast as I can . . . What was that? Get her to swallow a chopped garlic clove with a spoonful of honey? Fascinating. Actually, I've got another little remedy in mind . . . No, nothing to do with onions, although it could make her eyes water . . . Yes, I'll bring her home later.' I replaced the receiver and turned to Emma with a broad grin. 'There, that's Henry sorted. He's very interested in my little remedy, wants you to give him all the details so that he can add it to his collection.'

'You're shameless,' she said, peeling off her jumper and hurling it at me.

I swallowed as I gazed at her breasts, barely contained by a wispy black lace bra. 'Takes one to know one.'

She undid the belt of her trousers. 'Are you going to stand there all day?'

'I can think of worse things.'

The trousers came off and landed in my arms. I swallowed again. She was wearing a pair of microscopic black lace briefs, cut high at the sides, making her legs look even longer . . .

'You'll have to show me how the shower works,' she said, climbing the stairs two at a time.

And from the back, she looked incredible . . . In a matter of seconds, I was barely a step behind her. 'I think you already know exactly how to handle my equipment, Emma Woodhouse.'

By the time we reached my bathroom, we'd stripped off completely. I dropped our clothes in a sodden heap on the floor, got into the shower to turn on the water, checked there was plenty of soap and gel, and got out again. I fetched fresh towels out of the airing cupboard and arranged them on the heated rail.

'Go in, the water's just right.'

She hesitated. 'Aren't you coming in with me?'

'Not yet,' I said, with a smile. 'I want to enjoy the view.'

She blushed and stepped into the shower. The doors were made of transparent glass and Mrs

Burn kept them beautifully clean, bless her. As Emma twisted this way and that, revelling in the feel of hot water on her body, I leaned against the wall and studied her, every curve, every plane. I thought back to Ashridge, how I'd watched her get dressed while I pretended to be asleep. I'd so wanted to do then what I was about to do now. And yes, we'd made love at Forbury Manor, but my recollections of that night were hazy, thanks to the sloe gin, and scarred by the events of the following morning. This afternoon, I would treasure every moment.

This afternoon was now. Why wait any longer? I opened the door of the shower and got in. Instantly, her mouth met mine and it was like kissing in the rain all over again. Only this time it wasn't just lips on lips, it was skin on skin, silk against steel. As we kissed she touched me, her hands slow and skilled and slick with gel, stretching my self-control to the very limit. And I almost took her there and then . . .

'Come to bed.' My voice was thick with desire, warm with love.

We moved as one, stepping out of the shower and wrapping each other in the towels. It took three kisses to get dried, two to reach the bed and one to slide deep inside her. I held myself still as stone, watching her, wanting her, but waiting . . . And then I drove forward with strong rapid strokes, as she arched under me and cried out my name.

My name.
Over and over and over again.

EMMA

I wondered if it was all a dream. Here I was, in
Mark's bedroom at Donwell, lying naked in his
vast bed. In the fading light of a winter's afternoon, I recognised the large chest of drawers with
the framed photos. The little bottle of Eau Pour
Homme was missing, no doubt packed away in
his luggage. But the scent of Armani lingered, on
the pillows under my head and on the skin of the
man who had just taken me back to the most
unbelievable place.

Time crept by, cloaking the room in darkness,
stealing all sense of substance, except for the
sound of his breathing and the touch of his hand
in mine.

'Mark.'

'Mmm?'

'Is this real?'

I heard him ease himself up and my lips parted
in anticipation of his kiss. I wasn't disappointed.

His voice caressed my ear. 'Was that real?' He
trailed the tip of his tongue down my neck to
my breast, took my nipple between his lips,
tugged it gently, then released it. 'And that?' He
nudged my thighs apart with his knee
and guided himself into me, right up to the hilt.
'And this?'

I laughed softly. 'You want to do it *again*?'

'Yes, Emma. Just to prove it's real.'

MARK

I missed it. I missed that first moment when I'd stir from the depths of sleep in my own bed and know that these were *her* limbs entwined with mine; the moment when I'd take her in my arms and kiss her awake; the moment when I'd whisper, 'I love you, Emma'.

Instead, I was roused by the sudden glare of the bedroom lights and my father's voice, sharp with surprise.

'Mark! What the—?' He retreated onto the landing and called down the stairs, 'Saffron, no need to phone the police, it's only Mark.' He marched back into my room. 'We found the alarm off and the utility window open and thought we'd been burgled! Why didn't you let us know you'd come back? What happened – didn't you get to the airport on time? What about—' He stopped in mid-sentence as he saw Emma snuggled up against me. 'Is that who I think it is?'

I couldn't help a complacent grin. 'Yes.'

'You mean you've . . .' – he winced – 'with *Emma*?'

I nodded. 'Get real, Father, we're consenting adults.'

He turned away. 'Come down to the study, I need to talk to you on your own.'

I waited until he'd gone, then shook Emma gently by the shoulder. 'Wake up, beautiful.'

She opened her eyes, blinked, then closed them again. 'Too bright,' she said sleepily.

'I know. Believe me, this isn't the way I'd have preferred to wake you up. Listen, Father and Saffron are back, I'm just going downstairs for a quick word.' I leaned over and cupped her breast, teasing her nipple with my thumb.

Her lips curved in a smile. 'Keep doing that and you won't make it out of this room, sunshine.'

I laughed. 'Is that a promise?'

She opened her eyes and gazed into mine. 'When are you going back to India?'

'You haven't answered my question.'

'That's because you need to answer mine first. If you're going to India soon,' – she reached up and kissed me full on the mouth – 'I want to make every minute count. If not, we've got all the time in the world.'

I let out a long breath. 'I don't know, I need to talk to Father.'

It took no more than a few minutes to pull on some clothes and go to the study. Father was pacing the floor, taking long gulps from a glass of whisky. He may not have been the archetypal headmaster, but I certainly felt like a naughty schoolboy.

'Shut the door,' he said tersely. As soon as I'd done so, he came up to me and wagged his finger in my face. 'For Christ's sake, I hope you know

449

what you're doing. She's barely more than a child.'

'She's twenty-three, she's a grown woman by most people's standards.'

'But you're thirty-five, it's – it's indecent.'

I crossed to the drinks cabinet and poured myself a whisky. 'I'd have agreed with you when she was a teenager. But now she's in her twenties it's not at all indecent – in my mind, at least. And it certainly doesn't seem to bother her.' I sipped the amber liquid thoughtfully. 'Remind me, Saffron's how many years younger than you? Ten, is it? Or eleven?'

He clicked his tongue. 'That's different, we're both much older and it's a marriage, we've made a commitment to each other. For all I know, you've had your bit of fun at Emma's expense and you're off to India on the first plane tomorrow.'

I raised my eyebrows. 'Is that your only objection, that I'm not serious about her?'

He walked over to his desk and fiddled with an engraved gold paperweight, my mother's last gift to him. After a moment, he turned to me with a rueful smile. 'Your mother and I had it all planned out, years ago. Age-wise, we paired you off with Izzy—'

'God forbid.'

'And John with Emma. Not that we expected any of it to happen, it was just a nice little "what if ?" scenario.' He gave a wistful sigh. 'As time went on, and John married Izzy, I realised age wasn't the key factor at all. You and Emma were a far better match for each other, same sense of humour, same intellectual ability and so on. But it was still a pipe dream, I never thought for one moment—' He stopped and frowned. 'I've watched Emma grow up, she's like my own daughter. I don't want to see her get hurt.'

'What makes you think she's going to get hurt?' I said abruptly.

'You're going back to India, aren't you?'

Suddenly, it was all crystal clear. 'Not without her, I'm not going anywhere without her.'

'But she can't just leave Henry like that, or her job at Highbury Foods.'

'No, she can't. At least, not for long.' I hesitated. 'I want to make a go of things with her, spend lots of time together over the next few weeks, and then – who knows? So, if I sort out my replacement in India, how would you feel about me coming back here?'

His face brightened. 'Bloody brilliant! I wasn't going to tell you just yet, but Henry wants to discuss a possible merger between Highbury Foods and Donwell Organics.'

My eyes narrowed. 'A merger? But we're like chalk and cheese.'

'I know, but needs must, it's a cut-throat world out there. It'll mean a lot of work, but it's manageable if you're here as opposed to in India. And if you're thinking of settling down,' he added, with a meaningful look, 'I couldn't wish for a better daughter-in-law than Emma.'

EMMA

I'd just had a shower and was drying myself in the bathroom, when Mark came back. He stood in the doorway, folded his arms and tried to look grumpy.

'I see you've not waited for me this time – had enough of me already?'

'Mark Knightley,' I said sternly, 'don't push your luck.' Then I paused. 'So when are you going back to Mumbai?'

'As soon as you can tear yourself away from Highbury to come with me.' He gave me a long serious look. 'It won't be a long trip, I just need to sort a few things out before I come back here for good.'

I smiled, a long slow smile of relief. 'Actually, I wondered if you wanted to come over to my place this evening. We could tell Dad about, um, everything, and then you could maybe, um, stay the night.'

'Stay the night? I dread to think what Henry will say about that. I mean, are people allowed to have sex at Hartfield? I'm pretty sure John isn't.'

I let the towel drop to the floor and watched with amusement as his gaze switched immediately from my face to my breasts. 'You're so presumptuous, who said anything about sex? I'll be surprised if Dad allows you to sleep in the house, especially when there's a perfectly good shed outside.'

He slipped his hands under my hips, pulled me to him and kissed me long and hard. Then he let me go and gave a wicked grin. 'He'll soon change his mind, I'll tell him dreadful stories about the Highbury Humper preying on innocent young women in their own homes.'

'Ah-ha, that rules me out, I'm not exactly innocent.'

'But Henry thinks you are, so it may be worth a try.' He reached out and tucked a strand of hair behind my ear. 'Look, if you want to see your father at all, you'd better get dressed at once. Otherwise I'll have to take you back to bed and we'll end up spending the night here instead.'

I glanced at the pile of wet clothes still lying in the corner. 'Hang on, what am I going to wear?'

He frowned. 'I suppose I could ask Saffron if she's got anything.'

'Don't you dare, she'd take great delight in pointing out she's at least three sizes smaller than me.'

'What about something of mine? Remember when you took a fancy to that Aran sweater I got one Christmas? It came down to your knees and you wore it as a dress for a while, I've still got it in my wardrobe somewhere.'

'I was only about ten at the time,' I said, laughing. 'Somehow I think it'll come a lot higher than my knees now.'

He pretended to look hurt. 'I wasn't suggesting you wore it on its own, I've got some old tracksuit bottoms for you as well.'

He was as good as his word; which meant that going downstairs to see George and Saffron was a double ordeal. I had to face not only the embarrassment of them knowing I'd just slept with Mark, but also Saffron's undisguised horror at my outfit.

'Ah, here she is, here's the reason Mark's not in India,' George said heartily, when we found them in the kitchen. 'I should be cross with you both, but I can't be.'

'Can I have the car keys?' Mark said. 'I need to take Emma home.'

Saffron stared at me. 'Surely you're not going outside dressed like that, darling?'

'It's dark and we're in the middle of the country, no one will see,' I said breezily. 'My own clothes are still wet.'

'I'd lend you something, but I'm afraid I'm about three sizes smaller than you.' She gave a pitying little laugh.

George winked at me. 'I think you look very fetching, Emma. Here you are, Mark.'

Mark took the keys. 'Thanks. I'll be back first thing in the morning, before you set off for work.'

George and Saffron exchanged glances, then George said, 'So you're planning to spend the night there? Let's hope Henry's happy about you two, otherwise—'

'I know, I know.' Mark's voice was uncharacteristically edgy and my heart sank. Tonight, more than ever, I was relying on him to be as he'd always been with my father, kind yet firm. Anything else would spell disaster, I was sure.

We drove to Hartfield in silence, my hand resting lightly on his knee. His warm fingers caressed mine, except when he needed both hands for driving. I spent the whole time wondering how Dad would react and panicking more and more with every minute that passed.

Dad must have been listening for the car, because he came to the door as soon as we parked.

'Inside quickly, the pair of you, before you catch a chill,' he said anxiously. 'I've got the fire going in the dining room and there's whisky if you'd like it, Mark. You know Emma and I don't care for it, we only keep some for medicinal purposes and, of course, good friends like you.'

Poor Dad. If he'd known what his good friend had been up to, he'd have left him outside to freeze.

Needless to say, in Mark's Aran sweater I found the heat in the dining room unbearable. I dashed upstairs to change into a T-shirt as quickly as I could; when I returned, Mark had a tumbler of whisky in his hand and Dad was holding forth about Flynn.

'Poor Jane! I don't see how it'll last, she barely knows him, they only met last October.'

Mark cleared his throat. 'So, for a relationship between a man and a woman to be successful, you think they need to have known each other a long time.'

I gave a strained laugh as I sat down between them. 'Like Izzy and John, or even Mark and I—' But I got no further.

'Poor Isabella,' Dad said, with a sigh. 'She must have known what she was letting herself in for – no offence, Mark, but your brother is rather difficult – and still she went ahead.' He paused. 'Anyway, on to other things. Emma doesn't seem to have suffered any ill effects from her walk in the rain, I'm looking forward to hearing how you did it, Mark.'

Mark nearly choked on his whisky. 'Ah, Henry, I'm afraid my lips are sealed. It's a secret remedy that's been in the Knightley family for years. But back to relationships between men and women, Emma and I—'

'Secret family remedies?' Dad frowned. 'I didn't know you had any.'

'That's because they're secret,' Mark said patiently. 'As I was saying, Emma and I have known each other for years. Now – well, we've discovered we love each other. Very very much.' He smiled across at me and I smiled back.

Dad raised his eyebrows. 'Of course you do, you've always said Emma's like your little sister.'

Mark flushed and bit his lip. 'Just forget what I've said in the past. Believe me, that's not how I feel about her now.'

'We want to be with each other all the time,' I put in. 'Every hour of every day – and night.'

'Good gracious, I don't see any need for that nonsense,' Dad said. 'Far better to go on as you were. As Woodrow Wilson once said, if you want to make enemies, try to change something.'

Mark and I looked at each other in despair. Then Mark leaned forward and said in a grave voice, 'I was hoping I wouldn't have to worry you with this, Henry, but there've been some disturbing rumours recently. Do you remember Emma's little joke about the Highbury Humper? Well, it seems that he actually exists and he may be on the prowl this very minute . . .'

MARK

It was early spring before I could arrange a day at Ashridge for Emma and me. Until then, I'd been too busy progressing the merger between our companies and adjusting to life at Hartfield, which was enough to try the patience of a saint. And I certainly wasn't that.

I'd also taken Emma to India, as promised. I could have done at the Taj Mahal what I wanted to do at Ashridge; but we'd gone there with Rob and Harriet, which wasn't ideal. In any case, our time in India was rushed because I had to focus on getting Rob up to speed as my replacement. He and Harriet had fallen in love with the place and he'd been delighted to accept my offer of a job there. His parents had been less than delighted, but I'd managed to placate them by finding someone with the necessary experience to take over at Abbey Mill Haulage.

Now, as we approached Ashridge, the sun broke through the clouds and filtered between the green-tipped trees. It reminded me of our visit last autumn, except that this time I was filled with anticipation of a much more pleasurable kind. We parked the car and strolled hand in hand to the front entrance. Just before we reached it, I stopped.

'Fancy a walk up there?' I said, pointing to the wide cutting in the trees on our left.

She looked along the grassy path and saw, on the horizon, a pale slender column tapering to a small cross. She smiled at me. 'Why not?'

And so we retraced the steps of Earl Brownlow on his daily pilgrimage to his beloved wife's memorial. I let Emma do the talking, all about the synergy benefits she anticipated from merging Highbury Foods' marketing activities with Donwell's. The path ended at a road and we waited there for a couple of cars to pass. Directly opposite us was the cross, standing perhaps twenty feet tall on Little Gaddesden's village green. A few minutes later, we were climbing the steps up to it and reading the simple inscription: 'In remembrance of Adelaide. Mercy and truth have met together. Righteousness and peace have kissed each other.'

Emma turned to me, her eyes sparkling with unshed tears. 'When you first told me this story, I remember saying something like "That's true love". But at the time I didn't know what true love was.' Her voice faltered. 'I do now.'

I reached for her hand, took a deep breath. 'I can't make long flowery speeches, Emma. If I loved you less, I could talk about it more, but with me what you see is what you get.' I laid her hand against my cheek, covered it with mine. 'Only you would have put up with me like you've done over the years, all that lecturing and criticising – even though it had absolutely no effect! Not that I'd want it any other way, you know I love you just as you are. There's only one thing I want to change about you, and that is – I'd like you to become my wife.'

With my other hand, I brought the little box out of my pocket and flipped it open with my thumb. Her eyes widened as she saw the ring, diamonds encircling a large emerald. A tear spilled onto her cheek and I wiped it tenderly away.

'This belonged to my mother, but if you don't like it—'

'Oh Mark, it's perfect.'

I took the ring out of its box and slipped it onto her finger; a man giving a woman a token of his love, beside a memorial to another love, from another time.

DIGESTIF

Hartfield, the following Christmas

EMMA

While Mark carved the turkey beside me, I studied the faces around the dining table. They were the same as last year, with the addition of George and Saffron. But in other respects this Christmas Day was completely different from the previous one.

So many changes in such a short time. My name: Mrs Emma Knightley. My shape: I was five months pregnant. My relationship with Mark: the only tension between us today was whether I should risk a small glass of wine with my meal – although I gave up on that one as soon as Dad and Izzy weighed in with their expert advice. And among our presents to each other were another bottle of Eau Pour Homme and another souvenir of Ashridge; only now we understood – and valued – their significance.

And the changes didn't stop there.

Kate and Tom had called earlier with baby Anna,

461

now six months old. But this year they came without Flynn. It looked as though the only attraction Highbury had ever held for him was the girl whose skin he'd once compared to uncooked pastry. He hadn't set foot in our village since the previous January, apart from a fleeting visit with Jane to collect their belongings. They were apparently working all hours to make Flynn's Cook-in at the Brook Inn a success. I'd only watched the TV programme once; I switched off in disgust when Flynn broadcast his secret recipe for minestrone soup, which was uncannily like the one I'd entrusted to him the first day we met.

At least Jane seemed to spare us the occasional thought. She ordered several of my new Highbury Foods luxury hampers, to be delivered to Randalls and Kings Row; and further afield, to the Campbells in Weymouth and the Dixons in Ireland. Tom, the eternal optimist, was even hopeful that she could persuade Flynn to come to Anna's christening in a month's time.

I thought Mark showed admirable restraint. All he said was, 'I've always had a very high opinion of Jane Fairfax, but even she has her limitations.'

And I was actually warming to Robert Martin. He and Harriet were over from India for a couple of weeks and we'd been out with them several times. I began to think that they were quite well suited after all, in a Beauty and the Beast sort of way.

On the business front, there were three major

developments. First, the merger between Highbury Foods and Donwell Organics was going to plan and would be completed within six weeks. Second, following some promising research results, I'd launched Harriet's Secret Recipes; only a limited range of products to begin with, but sales were going extremely well. Finally, Philip had handed in his resignation; this was no great loss and even less of a surprise. Ever since Dad had announced the merger with Donwell Organics, Philip had been thoroughly disgruntled. He assumed, quite rightly, that John would be Finance Director of the new company and started job hunting almost immediately.

As Gusty had never found the work she believed was waiting for her in Surrey, she was more than happy to leave Little Bassington behind. When I bumped into her in the high street on Christmas Eve, she informed me that people round here hadn't a clue how to run a proper business, so she and Philip were off to Bristol, where their talents would be appreciated. And, by the way, her sister knew a man who'd had to share a house with his in-laws and the marriage had only lasted six months; how was dear Marrrk finding it?

I glanced at dear Marrrk now. He didn't look at all the worse for wear after living with Dad for almost a year. In fact, he looked positively irresistible . . .

When we'd finished lunch, I got to my feet with a long-suffering smile. 'Would you excuse me? I feel very nauseous, I'd better go upstairs and lie down for an hour or so.'

Izzy pursed her lips. 'That nausea's going on far too long, you really should see Doctor Perry about it. Or speak to one of my NCT contacts—'

'No need for that,' I said calmly. 'Mark will soon sort me out with one of his little remedies. I believe it's something to do with reiki, he has the most wonderful touch. Coming, Mark?'

'You bet.' He lifted a sleepy Emily off his knee and carefully handed her to John.

As we left the room, I heard Dad say, 'Mark certainly seems to be very gifted in that department, Emma says he's thinking of writing a book, *The Joy of Reiki.*'

John gave a snort of laughter. 'I think she's pulling your leg, sounds very like *The Joy of Sex.*'

'I beg your pardon?' Dad sounded aghast.

'Haven't you heard of it? Came out in the early seventies, been a bestseller ever since.'

Mark shut the door behind us and grinned. 'Trust John to spoil our fun. Do you think Henry'll believe him?'

'Dad will believe exactly what he wants to,' I said, tucking my arm through his. 'I'm sure he still thinks we only share a room so that you can protect me from the Highbury Humper.'

By the time we reached the top of the stairs, the noise from the dining room was no more than a distant murmur; at the far end of the house, our bedroom was swathed in silence. We stood there for a few moments, just looking at each other.

Then the man of my dreams took me in his arms and kissed me, long and hard.

I closed my eyes and gave myself up to the joy of 'reiki'.

AUTHOR'S NOTE

This book was inspired by Jane Austen's *Emma*, in particular this extract from Volume III Chapter II:

(Emma)
You have shown that you can dance, and you know we are not really so much brother and sister as to make it at all improper.

(Mr Knightley)
Brother and sister? no, indeed!